DESPERATE
PATHS

OTHER TITLES BY E. C. DISKIN

DESPERATE
PATHS

E.C. DISKIN

Published by Thomas & Mercer, Seattle

www.apub.com

Amazon, the Amazon logo, and Thomas & Mercer are trademarks of Amazon.com, Inc., or its affiliates.

ISBN-13: 9781542040334
ISBN-10: 1542040337

Cover design by Kristen Haff

Printed in the United States of America

For my parents—my biggest and best influences.
I'm grateful to be yours.

Three may keep a secret, if two of them are dead.

—*Benjamin Franklin,* Poor Richard's Almanack

CHAPTER ONE

DAY SEVEN
7:30 p.m.
BOLINE COUNTY JAIL

BROOKLYN STEPPED INSIDE THE CELL, cinder block on three sides, and inhaled the humid, stagnant air. High on the exterior wall, a one-foot-square window provided the only reminder of the outside world. The lock clicked into the wall of bars behind her, and she turned to see the door already closed, the guard leaving. His footfalls echoed down the long corridor while keys jangled from his belt loop. Another door in the distance opened, then closed. Finally, silence rolled toward her from the end of the hall like a tidal wave.

She hadn't cried yet, or yelled, or begged for a phone call. At the house, she hadn't focused on the police despite the constant shuffle of feet going up and down the front porch steps. Even the sight of the ambulance, driving away with the body, was a blur. Everyone around her had merged into a muffled background track while her mind looped through the previous hours, her thoughts stuck in a ditch. She'd already exhausted every emotion, and all she could hear was the sound of her own voice, yelling, screaming. She'd called him a monster.

The crows, squawking in the sugar maple by the driveway, had been the only voices to cut through the loop. She'd wondered how many were up in those branches, and if they knew what happened—if they smelled death in the air.

A young officer's words had come at her incoherently and in no order: *Go. You. Need. Station.* His hand on her back felt harmless, an attempt at kindness, as he directed her toward the squad car. Official things had to happen. "Watch your head," he'd said. She'd followed his instructions without question. He was going to help. Maybe she'd convinced herself it was a dream or a scene she was running—a lead role as the bad seed.

But the cell door had slammed shut like an alarm. Her father was dead, and she hadn't been able to explain why she was found wiping down the gun, why the room showed signs of struggle. Why his blood was on her hands. She looked down at them now, washed clean, but not.

Formal arrest and a mug shot would be next. Her blank expression would be interpreted as an admission of guilt. There would be national coverage of the small-town scandal. Everyone she'd ever known would see her photo on the evening news. They would all wonder if they'd ever really known her at all. Her sadistic former Eden High School gym teacher would probably be watching, nodding smugly at the news. He'd never liked her, and once she had realized there was no way to change his mind about the low grade he'd given her senior year, she'd told him that, someday, he'd see her on TV and realize that cutting gym class meant nothing in the scheme of things.

Instead, he would see her mug shot. Rumors would swirl. Those church ladies would whisper about her entire family. People would believe what they wanted to believe.

She sat on the bare mattress, leaning back against the wall, while rusty springs squeaked beneath her. Eyes closed, she silently pleaded for guidance. *Mom.* She struggled with what to say next. Her mom couldn't help. Maybe no one could. Brooklyn could not tell the police what happened. It was an impossible situation.

Her diaphragm froze into a solid mass as reality set in. Panicking, she tried for a breath but couldn't get enough air into her lungs. She kept inhaling as heat rushed up the back of her neck. Her hands began to tingle. Black spots appeared in her field of vision, the edges closing in. Jumping up from the bed, she pushed herself against the back wall of the cell, as if she needed to stop it from collapsing on top of her.

In seven days, she'd gone from strolling through New York's Central Park to being locked inside a jail cell in Boline County, Illinois. Seven days. Her mom used to say that if an entire world could be created in seven days, there was no better number.

But it was just another of Mom's lies.

She was tapping on her chest when a noise barreled toward her from the end of the hall. That giant steel door was opening, its hinges squeaking. She squeezed her eyes shut, pushed through the exhale. A single ray of light shining through the small window cast a tiny spotlight on the floor in the corridor—to a penny just beyond her reach. *Is help coming?* she silently asked the penny.

The guard's keys jangled on his belt with every step. There were too many footfalls. Someone else was with him. She moved toward the door and crouched, squinting at the coin. The keys and shoes were getting louder, closer.

Finally, she saw the Lincoln Memorial embossed in the copper. Tails.

She stood and backed away from the bars, bracing herself as voices bounced off the concrete and steel. She had her answer.

Help had not arrived.

CHAPTER TWO

DAY ONE
Monday, May 13

IT WAS JUST AFTER 4:00 a.m. when the bliss of unconsciousness ended and a piercing pain behind Brooklyn's eyes demanded attention. Her dehydrated brain was begging for mercy. As usual, the late-night tryst had done its job—distracting her and lulling her to sleep—but reality always returned too early.

Tony's arm was draped across her naked body. He slept like the dead. Lifting his limb to escape, she glanced at the activity tracker on his wrist, another reminder of how little they had in common. Brooklyn never sought out exercise or drank enough water, though she did walk a lot. Probably five miles yesterday. Maybe six. There was the walk from the East Village to the restaurant in the theater district, the constant hustle between kitchen and dining room during her seven-hour shift, and finally, around midnight, after several tequila shots, she and Tony had walked another seven blocks to Sixty-Fourth and Fifth, to his gorgeous one-bedroom that overlooked Central Park.

Her mom would be horrified. She used to joke about trying to be more modern but had always encouraged Brooklyn to avoid alcohol until marriage because it would lessen her resolve against "untoward advances and sinful desires."

After searching Tony's bathroom for Advil, Brooklyn lay on the couch, scrolling through Instagram on her phone. Her roommates had posted pictures from some bar in Hoboken last night. She wondered whether they'd fessed up to the stalking or played it cool. Cindy had come home a few days earlier gushing over a guy she'd met at an audition, and her online research had uncovered his bartending job across the Hudson in Hoboken.

Finally, the sun came up and it was safe to leave. Brooklyn bound her unruly hair up in a loose ponytail and pulled her jeggings, sweatshirt, and Birkenstocks from the cinch sack she'd dropped by the front door. The first morning after sleeping at Tony's, she'd put her stained white button-down dress shirt, black pants, and grease-bottomed sneakers back on and stepped into an elevator full of middle-aged power suits and yoga pants, exposing herself, like a girl in a cocktail dress, as the casual hookup she'd become. Now, whenever Tony texted to see if she was working that night, she brought a change of clothes. Her roommates had begged to meet the mystery man, but that would make him a boyfriend, and she didn't know what he was. All she knew was that nights were long and painful unless she slept at Tony's. He was the ultimate distraction.

She scanned the bed for anything she might have left behind. The bright morning sun filtered through the windows, spotlighting the prematurely thinning hair on the crown of Tony's head. He never mentioned it, but he was always rubbing that area, as if his hand were a yarmulke that would prevent her from noticing. He was probably obsessing about it. He was unlike anyone she'd ever known—his only religious dedication seemed to be to his daily two-hour prework workouts, and he moved through the world with supreme confidence. Her dad would be horrified by this exotic, Armani-wearing animal who waxed his back and got manicures and facials. He'd probably use the information as a segue to another sermon about how New York was full of weirdos—that, in fact, the whole country was being taken over by "gender-bending whack-a-doos."

Brooklyn grabbed her bag, scurried to the door, and, moving in slow motion, unlocked it with one soft click, turned the handle silently, and escaped without detection.

Outside, the park's thirty-seven acres of lush trees, shrubs, ponds, and wildlife reminded her of Eden, her hometown of six thousand in Boline County, Illinois. Brooklyn had run as far and as fast as she could from Eden, but after growing up in the country, she would always relish open spaces.

The sea lions in the zoo were barking loudly as she entered the park, flooding her mind with memories of her mother's first and only visit last August. Her mom didn't care about museums or shows, Ellis Island, or the Statue of Liberty, but she'd insisted that Brooklyn find them a church—probably hoping it would remind her daughter to join one—and asked to see the zoo. She had read about the zoo's exhibit of California sea lions, supposedly the most vocal mammals in the world. But that day, not one uttered a sound. In a failed attempt to get them to talk, her mom had shouted and danced around, sending both mother and daughter into hysterical fits of laughter. But now, a full chorus echoed through the early-morning air.

She made her way through Midtown and farther south, grabbing a coffee and later a cup of fruit from Benji, the vendor on the corner a few blocks from her place on Second Avenue near Fifth Street. Despite being in a city of eight and a half million, her neighborhood had a small-town vibe. The shop owners and vendors had become daily sources of smiles and waves. Dad couldn't have been more wrong about New York—or "that cold haven for godless souls," as he liked to say. There was nothing cold about it. And the best part, what he couldn't understand and she never said aloud, was that she finally fit in. No one was an outsider in New York City—everyone belonged, no matter where they came from, what they believed, or how they looked.

A shiny penny on the sidewalk in front of her building drew Brooklyn's attention to the ground. *Will I get good news today?* she silently asked. With three auditions in the last week, she hoped at least one would lead to something. But when she bent down to grab the penny, it was tails up. The answer was no. She looked around for more coins, refusing to accept the omen, but found none.

The apartment was quiet, the only noise coming from the beeping trash truck below their windows. Jess and Nina's bedroom door was slightly ajar: both were asleep. Nina was still wearing last night's clothes, and Jess's feet were hanging off the bottom of her bed. Brooklyn's room was empty—which probably meant that the trip to Hoboken had worked out nicely for Cindy.

Collapsing onto her twin-size bed, she dropped the penny into the mason jar half-filled with more of the same, emptied her bag onto the quilt, and recounted last night's cash. Fifty went to her purse and the rest to the cigar-box headshot fund. The photograph she was currently using, graciously gifted by her mom last summer, wouldn't do if she was serious about acting—it looked like it came from a Walmart photo booth back home.

She took a hot shower, chugging a cold-water bottle along with some charcoal tablets—her regular inside-out detox—and wrapped herself in a towel. The phone pinged from its perch on the toilet lid, and the screen lit up. It was a text from Ginny: Dad's in the hospital. You should come home. Burns Memorial.

Brooklyn stared at the words on the screen, dread rolling up her spine. She hit the "Call" button and sat on the toilet. She would forever associate that hospital with death.

Ginny's voice mail picked up.

"It's me. Just got your text." Brooklyn strained to keep her voice down. "Couldn't you at least call me? Please, Ginny, call me back." She hadn't spoken to her sister since December, days after Ginny had sent a nearly identical message.

Thirty seconds later, a trio of dots began dancing on the small screen until Ginny's response appeared: Can't talk right now. Working. Assumed you'd get that message later. He broke hip. Surgery today.

It should have been a relief that it wasn't something worse, but surgery at Dad's age felt like a big deal. And even if he came out of it okay, his recovery might be daunting. He was all alone in that big house. And he might even need her help at the store. He and Ginny barely spoke. That text was like an earthquake tremor, threatening to destroy her new life.

She went back to her room, threw on some clothes, and pulled up flight options on her phone.

A text from Tony popped onto the screen: Why do you always leave before I wake? Starting to think you're a vampire.

A smile emerged. He was far sweeter than she assumed he'd be the night he hosted ten other brokers in her section at the restaurant. They'd been obnoxious, growing louder with each bottle of wine. He'd left her a thousand-dollar tip and asked for her number. She'd pegged him for an ass, only relenting when he returned the next night, undeterred. But she always left his apartment early because their stark differences were too glaring in daylight. She was sure that her allure would be gone in the morning, and maybe his too. She was painfully aware that her attraction was connected to the way he made her feel and her desperation to escape reality, if just for the night.

My dad's in the hospital, she replied. I gotta get home. Be back in couple wks.

Three little dots appeared before she could exit out of the app. Sorry to hear it. Where's home?

BFE. Southern IL. Locals called southern Illinois "Little Egypt," a century-old nickname that had something to do with the Mississippi and Ohio Rivers converging along its southern borders like the Nile, so she and her childhood friends joked that whoever had first coined "BFE," a.k.a. "Bum Fuck Egypt," had obviously lived there too.

??? Why did I think Caribbean? Tony wrote.

She knew why. That first night together, he'd marveled that she was so different from the women he'd been with. She and Tony had lain in bed, naked, and he acted as if she were some sort of goddess. "Where do they make beauties like this?" he'd asked, examining her forearm as if she were a mannequin. "Dominican Republic," she'd drunkenly offered. He'd said her lips were like Angelina Jolie's, praised the wild black hair she'd spent her entire life trying to tame, compared her caramel skin to J Lo's, and said that her green eyes sparkled even in the darkened room. Every feature he praised had made her an outcast among her classmates as a child.

Her mother had constantly reassured her during those painful bouts of insecurity that she was a watercolor in a sea of charcoal sketches. "And everyone loves a watercolor." It always made her smile, but nothing her mom said had helped quite as much as that moment in the dark when Tony asserted with his over-the-top confidence that everything about her was magnificent.

Born there, she texted. Raised in IL. Adopted.

Ah. Hope your dad is okay. TTYL

She replied with a smile emoji and her own "talk to you later" and put the phone away. It was nice. Weird. They barely knew each other.

She packed a bag, found a cheap ticket online, and calculated the daylong journey ahead—the flight to Lambert in Saint Louis, the train to Carbondale, and, finally, the car ride home to Eden. Despite her best efforts, she couldn't seem to stay away. It felt as if the last year had been a cosmic joke.

Only nine months earlier, her mom had taken Brooklyn and her roommates out for a celebratory meal in their new, funky East Village neighborhood. Dad was furious that she was dropping out of school in Boston to live in New York, but Mom had volunteered to fly out and help her get settled. They'd sat at an outdoor table in a wildly decorated courtyard, sharing sangria and Italian bread, exhausted by the multiple trips up to the tiny sixth-floor walk-up.

"Life is full of unexpected twists and turns, girls, no matter how much you plan or try to play it safe," her mom said that day. "You might as well go for it."

"Oh my God, I love that accent," Cindy had remarked. Nina and Jess agreed. Her new friends were all from the East Coast and had never associated Illinois with anything other than Chicago. They couldn't believe that Brooklyn had never even been there. But Eden, five and a half hours south and close to the Kentucky border, was in coal country, more mid-South than Midwest, as most locals could trace their roots to the Carolinas, Tennessee, and Kentucky.

"Where's your accent?" Jess had pressed Brooklyn.

"Yeah, where is it?" her mom had teased.

"Actually, not everyone in Eden sounds like Mom," she'd said. It was true, but Brooklyn had worked hard to drop any hint of it and even used YouTube to learn different accents. She'd understood long ago that she didn't belong in Eden. And despite the beautiful scenery, she had no interest in reminding people of her connection to a place with little more claim to fame than being home of yet another racially charged police-misconduct case.

Her mom had looked fantastic that night at the restaurant, having dropped twenty pounds since the previous Christmas. "A low-carb diet," she'd said. Four months later, she was dead. Everyone had known she was sick. Everyone except Brooklyn.

And now, just five months later, her dad . . . Her heart began to race as the word *orphan* came to mind—she'd be all alone in the world, and before her twenty-first birthday. It was premature to panic—*don't spin out*. It was only his hip, assuming Ginny had shared the full story. And then she remembered that painful text from December when Ginny had said only that Mom was "sick." The understatement of the century.

She wrote a quick note to her roommates, grabbed her bag, and headed home.

CHAPTER THREE

BROOKLYN'S DAD WAS ASLEEP IN a bed surrounded by machines and a web of tubes and drips. A large bandage covered most of his forehead. Lifting his hand, marred by seventy years of spots and scars, Brooklyn was relieved to feel its warmth as she stroked the translucent, paper-thin skin. This was too familiar, too soon. The last time she was here, she'd arrived too late. Mom had already slipped into a coma. Four days later, she was gone.

A nurse walked in. Her bouffant-styled, platinum-blonde hair reminded Brooklyn of her mom, and she smiled, a silent hello, but the woman's face hardened. "Sorry, dear. It's after regular visiting hours. Family only."

Brooklyn blinked hard to contain her irritation before responding. "I'm his daughter."

"Oh," the nurse said in a tone laced with judgment before she turned and left. It was a quick jab, just enough to remind Brooklyn of why she'd been so glad to leave this place.

She sat in the chair beside the bed, watching her dad sleep. She'd always been aware that he was older than the other kids' dads, but at six five, with his blond hair still cropped like a marine, he'd never seemed old before. He'd always been the biggest, most intense man she knew—her personal protector, like a righteous version of the

Godfather, sitting in that big chair in his study whenever he wasn't at the store.

It was the first day of middle school when she first watched him yield that power. Tommy Waters had knocked her camouflage backpack to the ground, joking to all the kids around them that her curly hair looked as if she'd been electrocuted. She was quietly picking up her bag when she spotted her dad approaching. With that eyebrow raised like an inquisitor, his deep voice aimed at Tommy, he said, "You're not messing with my daughter, are you?" Tommy began walking away with his head down, but Dad just walked beside him, asking for his name. After Tommy answered, Dad said, "I know that name. I know everyone in this town. Well, almost. And when I don't, I just call on my good buddy Sheriff Wilson."

"Yes, sir."

"Hey, I know how it is," he said, placing his giant hand on Tommy's shoulder, softening his tone. Brooklyn crept closer to hear the conversation better. "First day in a new school. Time to make yourself known. Well, you did it. Now I know you. And you need to know that Brooklyn is *my* girl. So maybe you can spread the word for me. I don't take it well when anyone messes with my family. And people who mess with us, well, they tend to regret it."

"Yes, sir."

"Good," he said, removing his hand. "Pleasure to meet you, Tommy."

The intimidation hadn't worked—Tommy had teased her relentlessly for most of middle school—but she loved that Dad had tried. People in Eden called him a hero. His medals from the war hung in frames behind the counter at the store. He was fierce. Unstoppable. Loud. Well, except in church.

Brooklyn checked the wall clock and stepped over to the window, surveying the parking lot below. It was after six. Ginny should have been here by now. A few more television trucks had arrived, and several camera crews and commentators were hanging out by the hospital's main doors. Someone famous must have been admitted. Maybe a politician.

"Well, hello."

Brooklyn turned toward the voice. It was another nurse. Dozens of long, beaded black braids rattled like maracas as she entered with a laptop in hand.

"I'm Wanda. I hear this is your dad. I'll be taking care of him throughout the night."

Brooklyn returned to his bedside and held his hand. "Yes, I'm Brooklyn. How's he doing?"

"Just fine, hon, all things considered." Wanda examined all the machines and tubes.

"Did he need stitches on his head?"

"Let me see here." She opened the laptop and pulled up his chart. "Twelve stitches. Not too bad. Looks like he suffered a mild TBI too."

"What's that?"

"Concussion. But he regained consciousness in the ambulance, and his CT looked good."

"So it's no big deal?"

"As long as we don't let him get another one anytime soon, I think he'll be just fine," she said with a wink. "Sometimes it takes a little time. The doctor will tell you what to look out for."

Brooklyn turned her attention back to her dad, wondering whether it was normal for him to look so . . . *frail*. His face had thinned since she'd last seen him; he even looked smaller . . . She stopped herself. She was panicking again.

"Has my sister been here today?" she asked.

"Wouldn't know, hon. My shift just started."

She needed Ginny. Ginny was a nurse—she knew what had happened and could tell her exactly what would be involved in their father's recovery.

She alternated between holding her dad's hand and pacing the room. This time, when she reached the doorway, she spotted Ginny in the hallway, her unmistakable platinum-blonde hair twisted into a knot and secured with a pencil. She was talking to the attendant at the nurses' station. From behind, she looked like a scrawny thirteen-year-old girl. She wasn't wearing scrubs—just leggings, an oversize shirt that seemed to swallow her five-four frame, and flip-flops.

"Hey," Brooklyn said.

Ginny turned. Brooklyn was struck by the dark circles under Ginny's icy blue eyes, the caked makeup failing to hide them. She worked with a couple of women Ginny's age—*lifers*, as the other wait-staff liked to call them—who'd morphed from dreamers to realists, but none of them looked as haggard as Ginny did right now. She was only thirty-seven. Had she looked this bad at their mom's funeral? Brooklyn couldn't remember. That entire week was nothing more than a haze of casseroles and an endless parade of her parents' fellow parishioners at the house.

Ginny reached out and hugged her awkwardly. The pencil in her hair nearly poked Brooklyn in the face. "You made good time," Ginny said, pulling away. "You have the car?"

"Yeah." Brooklyn had taken an Uber after Ginny ignored her request for a ride from the train station in Carbondale, so she'd had to go to the house and grab her dad's car before heading on to the hospital, adding an extra thirty minutes to the journey.

"Sorry I didn't see your text. Crazy day." Ginny's gaze shifted from Brooklyn's face. She was a terrible liar. Ginny never went out of her way for Brooklyn.

"Whatever," Brooklyn said, walking back toward her dad's room. She'd spent a lifetime trying to get Ginny to like her, to accept that adopting her didn't mean their parents were replacing Ginny, but now that she'd moved away, she was done trying. "What happened, anyway?"

Ginny brushed past and went inside. "No idea. He was unconscious when I got to the house."

"What were you doing there?" Ginny rarely went to their parents' house. She barely spoke to their dad. Brooklyn had assumed that once their mom died, Ginny would never go home, except maybe on holidays, when she tried to fake family harmony.

"He called and asked me to come over," she said.

"Where did you find him? How'd he hurt his head?"

Ginny walked to the windows and turned around, resting against the air conditioner. "Probably hit it on the floor. I don't know. He was just lying there when I got there."

"Where?"

"In his study. Enough questions," she said. "Listen, he's not going home."

Brooklyn moved to the opposite side of Dad's bed. "What do you mean? It's a broken hip and a concussion. The nurse said he'll be fine."

"It's not just that," Ginny said. "He's disoriented a lot. We think it's dementia."

"That's crazy. I was just here a few months ago." Brooklyn put her hand on her dad's. "He's fine."

"You had to notice when you were home."

No, she started to say, but had she? He'd lashed out a couple of times, and he didn't always seem like he was there, sometimes staring blankly for long stretches, but wasn't that normal? "He was sad. Mom just died. Of course he wasn't himself." He'd worshipped Bonnie. She may have been half his size, but she was his center. And she'd always taken care of him.

"He doesn't always recognize me." Ginny came closer, bracing her hands on the rails at the end of the bed. "He gets dizzy. He falls. It's not safe for him to be alone in that house. I'm thirty minutes away. You're in New York. We can't leave him there."

"What are you suggesting?"

"He's going to need physical therapy for the hip. The doctor said that after he gets discharged, he should move into a rehab facility for a few weeks. And then a nursing home."

Brooklyn shook her head. "He'll need something to look forward to." She lowered her voice. She didn't want him hearing this nonsense. "What about the store?"

Ginny's gaze answered her.

Brooklyn dropped her dad's hand. "Sell the store? Jeez, Ginny, just kill him now." He was only seventy. They couldn't take him out of the town he'd lived in for almost fifty years, take him from his business, church, and home, and put him in a box for the rest of his life.

Ginny looked at her. "I've thought about it a lot . . ." It seemed like she had more to say, but she stopped.

Brooklyn glanced at their dad. "I haven't seen any signs of dementia. I talk to him every week." At least . . . she used to talk to him every week, back when her mom was alive and reminded her that her dad missed her, even if he didn't show it. Brooklyn would call home on Sunday nights, and the three of them would all be on the line. Her mother was like a great dinner host, instigating conversation topics. But since she had died, Brooklyn missed a week here and there, and when she did call, it was always the same. He'd ask if she'd gone to church, if she'd become an actress, if she needed money. She'd lie about church, stretch the truth about auditions, and always say she needed nothing. They weren't frequent talks, but he certainly knew who she was.

"He's just sad!" Brooklyn continued, her voice now raised enough to wake someone, though her dad didn't even stir. "He fell down. Can't we just help him get better?"

Ginny shook her head, and once again, her eyes suggested there was something more she wasn't saying. "You'll see." She turned toward the giant wall clock behind them, then headed for the door. "Anyway, the staff will try to get him moving in the morning. I just wanted to check in on him and see that you got here okay, but I gotta get home to Simon and the kids."

"So go."

Ginny turned at the doorway. "I'm not trying to be cruel. I just have to do what's best."

"So that's it? You're in charge?"

Ginny didn't answer. They both knew she was. It didn't matter that Brooklyn could count on both hands Ginny's visits home over the last twenty years. Suddenly, age—and blood—trumped the rest. Another reminder that, in Ginny's eyes, Brooklyn wasn't really family.

Brooklyn didn't know what else to say. She grabbed the nearest chair and pulled it close to the bed. Arms crossed, she fixed her gaze on her dad, willing him to wake. All he needed to do was raise that brow, say hello to her with that big smile, look at Ginny the way he always did—as the wayward child he'd lost twenty years ago—and Brooklyn would know he was going to be fine.

"He's not well, Brooklyn. I'm sorry, but it's true."

Brooklyn didn't even look at her sister. "Maybe I should be the judge of that."

Ginny sighed. "I've got to get home. We'll talk tomorrow."

Brooklyn took her dad's hand again after Ginny left. There was no way he would want Ginny making decisions for him. She might look like their mother, but it didn't mean she could step in and take charge the way Mom always did.

Her dad began to mumble.

Brooklyn squeezed his hand. "I'm here, Dad. It's okay. You're gonna be okay. Can you open your eyes?"

He lifted his lids slowly, shut them a few times, as if wiping the windows. He turned toward Brooklyn and smiled.

She dabbed at her tears. "Hey, Daddy-o," she whispered.

"What are you doing here?" The sound barely escaped his mouth, but he was fine, just sleepy.

"Ginny called me. I heard you broke your hip."

"I'm pretty brittle these days."

"You're gonna be fine."

"I don't know. I think I'm ready to go. How do you like it there?"

"New York?" Brooklyn asked, confused by the sudden topic change.

He blinked and smirked, a slow-motion reaction. He winced as if the tiny gestures hurt his whole body. "If New York is heaven, then we're in real trouble, B."

Brooklyn froze. *B* was what he'd always called her mom, Bonnie.

"No, Dad, it's Brooklyn. I'm home. I wanted to see how you're doing."

His brow rose as he stared at her, getting a better look. He closed his eyes again. "Brooklyn," he mumbled. "My little actress."

"That's right." He'd been calling her that since years before she found the stage in high school. It started one day when she went to the store after school and said she'd had a good day, while her eyes were still puffy from tears. He had been quiet for a moment, and then he patted her head. "My little actress." He nodded knowingly. "You're a tough kid, Brooklyn. It'll serve you well." Tough kids didn't spend lunchtime hiding out in bathroom stalls, but maybe she was tough if she pretended she was okay when she wasn't.

"You feeling all right?" she asked.

"Just sleepy. I'm fine."

He didn't say anything else, and his eyes remained closed. She let her head collapse onto the bed, resting on her folded arms, as the exhaustion of the full day of travel, the late night, and early morning all started catching up to her. It was hard to believe that twenty-four hours earlier, she'd been a few blocks from Times Square, balancing drinks and dishes, running around a dining room full of hundreds, capping off the night with her mind-numbing tequila-and-Tony routine while her dad had been in a hospital, in pain, needing her.

She felt a hand patting the top of her head, almost bouncing atop her curls. "That's my girl," he said. "My baby girl."

Brooklyn lifted her head.

His eyes were open again. "You came back to me. I knew you'd come back someday."

"Of course."

"I wanna tell you something."

"Okay," Brooklyn said.

"I forgive you."

Steely armor rose up inside her, despite the bridge-building words. She didn't want to defend her decision to drop out of college again, and she didn't really want or need his forgiveness. She just wanted his support.

"Dad . . ."

"Ginny, don't . . ."

Brooklyn's heart sank again. Something was definitely wrong. There was nothing about Brooklyn that could remind her dad of Ginny or her mom. But he was looking through her. Brooklyn's eyes filled with tears. She couldn't lose him too. "Dad . . ."

"I forgive you, Ginny. Okay? And I'll never tell. I always protect my family. You're my daughter, no matter what."

CHAPTER FOUR

NURSE WANDA STEPPED INSIDE THE room, asking if everything was okay. Dad had closed his eyes again, and now Brooklyn couldn't revive him.

"He was talking to me a second ago," she said, "and now he's sound asleep again. He seems really confused."

"All normal stuff," Wanda said. "Now I gotta change some dressings. You should get some coffee. Two floors down, family waiting room." Wanda's gruff, no-nonsense attitude was surprisingly comforting.

Brooklyn took her advice and left, but she couldn't shake Dad's comments. She knew that Ginny had been a difficult child, but her dad just said he forgave her, that he'd never tell—as if there was a secret between them. He'd said he'd protect her. From what? Brooklyn couldn't imagine—whether it was something Ginny had done recently, or even years ago.

Exiting the elevator, Brooklyn faced the backside of a tall, slim man in black and a shorter, plump one in a beige uniform. Both men simultaneously turned toward the open doors. At five nine, Brooklyn rarely felt petite, but the tall man towered several inches above her. He smiled politely as they made eye contact. When she gazed at the short, old man, his surprised expression matched her own.

"Sheriff!"

"Brooky!" Sheriff Wilson added *Y*s to everyone's name. It was a ridiculous nickname, but every time he said it, she smiled. He pulled her in for a hug while the other man stretched his long arm toward the elevator door to hold it open.

"Nice beard," Brooklyn said, pulling back from their embrace. "Looks like Christmas came early!" The sheriff always played Santa, and his new white beard, along with his already large belly, was perfect for the role.

"It's my new look of leisure. Donny here is about to be the new sheriff in town. As of next weekend, you'll need to stop calling me Sheriff."

The man beside the sheriff nodded and offered his free hand. "Don Goodwin." His red hair was buzzed short, like her dad's, and it highlighted large ears that protruded like a curious dog's. The idea that he was either blissfully unaware of or embraced his imperfections made her like him immediately.

"Brooklyn Anderson," she said, shaking his hand.

"Daughter of one of my oldest and dearest friends, John Anderson," the sheriff added. "Except when he's robbing me blind on poker night. Brooky here is gonna be a famous actress. Her dad says she's taking New York by storm."

She smiled, amazed that her dad would boast about a move he had so strongly discouraged. "I'm trying, anyway."

"What in the world are you doing here?" the sheriff asked.

"I'm here for my dad," she said. "You didn't know?"

"I'm here on a case. What happened to your dad?" he asked, his expression falling.

"Ginny called me early this morning. He fell, broke his hip, knocked himself unconscious. He's upstairs. Already had surgery."

"My Lord. At the store?"

"Home. But I don't know any details."

"Well, thank goodness he's okay."

As if on cue, the elevator bell began to ring, determined to close its doors.

"Donny and I have to get back to the office," Sheriff Wilson said, getting in, "but I'll be back tomorrow to see your dad."

"Sounds good," she said as the doors closed.

Sheriff Wilson, retiring. Her dad had once said no one ran against him in Boline County because there was no point. It was hard to imagine someone else in charge. But maybe his retirement meant more time for friends. And Brooklyn's dad needed his friends now more than ever.

The sheriff had spent at least a dozen evenings each year at the Andersons' Sunday dinner table. She'd once asked her mom why he came over so often, and her mom said it was the Christian thing to do, that he deserved more than frozen dinners.

Brooklyn liked it. Sunday dinners were like church—never to be missed, but always the same routine, and usually dull. Her parents seemed to enjoy silence—with Dad often reading and Mom working on her needlepoint—one of them always telling Brooklyn to turn off the music or shut off the TV, as if they found all noise exhausting. She figured that Ginny had long ago worn them out. But when the sheriff was over, they'd talk politics and share the latest Eden gossip. Her dad would pull out the whiskey, and they'd laugh and argue like brothers.

Brooklyn found the coffee vending machine in the family waiting room and collapsed into a chair, suddenly too tired to lift the foam cup to her lips.

An older black man was sitting in a chair across from her in the otherwise empty space, his arms crossed, one knee bouncing up and down, and eyes fixed on the carpet in front of him. She recognized the anxiousness of that knee. She remembered finding her dad in a chair outside her mom's room five months earlier, his knee doing the same thing.

"Coffee?" she asked.

E. C. DISKIN

The man looked up with glassy eyes, deep lines embedded in his forehead.

Brooklyn walked across the blue industrial carpet and extended her cup toward him. "I just got it from the vending machine," she said. "Haven't touched it yet. I'm sure it's not great, but it's hot."

"Aren't you a sweet girl," he said, accepting the cup. "Thank you."

"No problem," she said, taking the chair beside him. "If you'd like me to leave you alone, just say the word. I'm giving my dad a little privacy while the nurse does a few things. I'm Brooklyn."

"Martin," the man said, offering his hand. "I'm here for my son." Brooklyn shook his hand. "I hope he'll be okay."

Martin's lips curled slightly toward a smile, just enough so she knew he was glad for the company. "I hope so too. He's in surgery. Again."

Brooklyn nodded and said nothing more. Follow-up seemed invasive. Anyone dealing with a second surgery had serious issues. She wondered if it was cancer. If so, she'd have nothing helpful to say, anyway.

A doctor wearing scrubs walked into the room, and Martin stood.

"Good luck," Brooklyn said. "I'll pray for you both." He turned back and smiled before joining the doctor. Brooklyn wasn't one to pray, but good news or bad, nothing ever happened in Eden without the community offering those words to each other.

After Martin left, she got another coffee, sat, and checked her phone messages. Her manager had responded to the text she'd sent on the way to the airport. He'd arrange for someone to cover her shifts. Her roommates had texted their love and support. There were no texts or emails about last week's auditions, which probably meant she hadn't made the cut. She turned off the phone and thought of her oblivious stroll through Central Park that morning and the penny that had been more of an omen than she'd realized.

24

The TV hanging in the corner was muted. Brooklyn found the remote and turned up the volume. *E! News* was on. Growing up, she'd never been allowed to watch celebrity news shows. Dad would walk in to the family room, overhear some bit about a pregnancy or a Kardashian breakup, grab the remote, and shut it off. "Gossip is the devil's radio, baby. Don't be his DJ," he'd say. She wanted to point out that listening wasn't really being a DJ but never dared. Instead, she'd say, "Yes, sir." She never talked back. Her parents deserved one easy kid.

But she and her roommates watched all the time—it was news of her industry, after all.

The glamorous host reported on the biggest-grossing movies of the weekend and then switched stories, her expression becoming more serious, while a picture of the actor Darius Woods appeared in the upper right corner of the screen. "Darius Woods remains in critical condition at a hospital in southern Illinois today," she reported. Brooklyn's spine straightened like a rod. The image on the screen switched to a picture of the hospital. It was this hospital. Here. Darius Woods was here. She looked around the empty room as if to say, "Do you hear this?" to whomever she could find.

"The actor was visiting his father at the time of the shooting," the host continued. "No other details have been released at this point. The Boline County Sheriff's Office is investigating."

As the show moved to another topic, Brooklyn remained fixated on the screen, stunned. So that's why there were all those media trucks in the parking lot. Everyone in Eden knew the name Darius Woods. In the summer before Brooklyn's junior year, *Unbound* came out, a sleeper hit with Woods in a main role. Suddenly, his face was on magazine covers, and photos from his roles in Eden High School drama productions were on permanent display in the school. College graduates and success stories were rare enough, but a true celebrity from Eden was unheard-of. Then in January, he got an Oscar nomination for his latest role, and reviewers, in typically superficial style, started calling him the next Denzel. He made the dream seem possible. It didn't matter that Eden was Small Town, USA, or that Brooklyn had no contacts, agent, or experience beyond high school: Darius Woods had proved that miracles happened.

She couldn't imagine who would shoot him. He hadn't even lived there in twenty years. She wondered if this was what fame did, or if some old enemy begrudged his success. Vendettas were the stuff of local legend. Her history teacher used to tell them all sorts of crazy stories. And of course, she'd heard about violence in the county from her parents and the sheriff—the robberies and bar fights that turned deadly, drug-fueled crimes in neighboring towns. It never sounded all that surprising with more gun shops than grocery stores—but she'd always thought Eden was relatively safe.

Of course, Boline County did have its share of racists. She'd certainly seen plenty during high school football games, when her school would play against a more racially diverse team, or when she'd eavesdrop on whispered conversations in her all-white church that sounded a little too like the 1950s. There was no denying the undercurrent, the invisible lines, whether in the lunch room or on the bleachers. Eden was probably ninety-seven percent white, two percent black, and a few "others." Everyone stayed with their own—except Brooklyn, who didn't quite fit anywhere.

Mom had never really understood why Brooklyn struggled to make friends and fit in. She was an Anderson, and they were good Christians, respected and liked by everyone in town. But by age ten or so, Brooklyn understood that to some kids, it didn't matter who her parents were. She was a foreigner. Some of the kids even joked that she probably wasn't legal.

As she got into the elevator to go back to her dad's room, she thought about her conversation with the sheriff. He'd been on this floor, too—and the man she'd just met in the waiting room,

Martin—he was here for his son. Had she just shaken the hand of Darius Woods's father?

She said a real prayer this time, begging the universe to watch over her idol. The idea that Darius could die, that someone in Eden might have wanted to kill him, made her physically sick. *Let it be an accident,* she thought, *or a crazed fan.* Any reason would be tragic, but she couldn't bear to imagine that what happened to Darius was another race-based crime.

CHAPTER FIVE

SHERIFF WILSON LED DON GOODWIN past the media trucks and reporters in the hospital parking lot as the sun set, refusing to answer any more questions, repeating his mantra several times as he got into the driver's side of the squad car: "It's an active investigation . . . we're pursuing all leads . . . we'll share more information as soon as we're able."

Donny spoke up as they drove off. "Doesn't that freak you out?"

"What?"

"All that media. You handled those people like this happens every day. I recognized two of those reporters from TV!"

"Then you watch too much TV," Wilson quipped. "This is like every other case."

It was a lie, of course, but Wilson was not about to let this neophyte see him rattled. The shooting of a black man, and a celebrity no less, was the last thing Eden needed right now. Things were finally settling back down after that awful trial of his friend and former deputy, Tom Delaney.

"Every investigation involves questions," Wilson continued, "whether they're from the *Town Gazette* or the victim's parents. You get used to avoiding people till you're able to talk. Didn't you have to deal with reporters up in Chicago?"

"Well, my bosses did."

Exactly. It was still hard to swallow how this guy, an independent and an outsider, who hadn't policed in ten years, who'd never been in charge, anywhere, was able to swoop in and win the election in a county where new faces were never trusted. Especially new faces from up north.

"Well, here's the rule. Say nothing unless you need to," Wilson said. "They're looking for stories, not justice."

Donny chuckled. "Got it."

"And don't watch coverage of a case you're working on. I'm telling you, someday people will look back at our fossils and realize it was the internet that ended us . . . like the meteors to the dinosaurs."

"I take it you're not on Facebook?" Donny joked.

Wilson rolled his eyes.

"Actually," Donny said, "we're trying to limit all that too. Except for movies. But Rosa and I moved here for the land. Can't spend all our time inside."

"Exactly. You do any fishing this spring?"

"No, no. Not my thing. Hunting either."

This guy might as well have said he worshipped the devil. "What do you do then?" Wilson asked with a chuckle.

"We're building a big garden. We're both vegans and—"

"Vegans?" Wilson said. "I don't think I ever met one of those."

Donny smiled. "We're real. Anyway, I get out on the bike when I can too."

"You've probably joined the Little Egypt Off-Road Club then."

"I've passed the club grounds, but no."

"You've got to do it. Nine hundred acres. ATVs, four-wheelers, motocross . . . Kids love it."

Donny shook his head. "You misunderstand. I've got a road bike."

"A what?"

29

"You know, a bicycle. Like a ten-speed. But like twenty-one gears. We used to ride along Lake Michigan, but these open roads and hills are fantastic."

"You are an odd one," Wilson said. He could not think of the last time he saw someone biking down a road, anywhere. "How in the world did you end up down here?"

"Rosa's parents are in Kentucky, and we hiked the Shawnee Forest a few times. I couldn't get over it. The real estate is so cheap. I guess I had fantasies of owning land. Probably in my blood. Parents came from Ireland."

"Mm-hmm," Wilson replied. This guy had no idea what he was in for. He probably thought a sheriff's gig in a county of twelve thousand, with police chiefs under him handling all but the unincorporated Eden, would be an easy job.

"This area has *so* much potential," Donny said, gazing out at farmland.

"Screw you" came to mind as a reply, but Wilson shook it off. He was a good Christian, even in the face of a condescending know-it-all with only seven years as a Chicago cop and ten as a correctional officer up in Pontiac. It was ridiculous. Swooping in here outta nowhere two weeks before the election with his "Goodwin for Good" nonsense, winning by just seven hundred votes simply because some folks had confused him with the Goodwin clan that had spent more than seventy years quietly farming soybeans a few towns over.

Wilson suddenly wondered if he might wanna start taking bets on how long this guy would last. Tom Delaney should have had this job. But after Tom's acquittal, someone burned down his barn. The country was going crazy. He couldn't blame Tom for grabbing his family and getting out of town.

Wilson tapped his fingers against the steering wheel. No matter his personal feelings, he was a professional, and if this guy was taking over at the end of the week, it was better to help him learn. If Wilson couldn't get this case buttoned up before retiring, he'd at least be able to guide Donny in the right direction. A sheriff couldn't investigate people he didn't know or understand.

They grabbed some dinner and headed back to the station. Sitting on the old blue couch under the window, Wilson ate his burger and watched Donny ignore his pathetic carrot sticks while rapidly thumb typing into his phone. To the wife, no doubt, probably moaning about the long hours before he'd even taken the oath.

Wilson was in no hurry to call it a night and go home to Eddie. He never knew who he'd find. Saturday night, Eddie'd been high as a kite on God knows what and then disappeared all day Sunday. It wasn't until Wilson was leaving to deal with the Woods shooting when Eddie finally walked in, soaked to the bone, blabbering on about catchin' a big fish, even though it was dark, and raining, and lightning. And he was empty-handed. Wilson had wondered if the whole adventure was some hallucination. But Eddie looked okay, and he was home safe, and that was all Wilson ever hoped for these days.

He polished off his burger and returned to his desk. One of his officers had left a note: *Nothing in the woods.*

"What's that?" Donny asked, finally looking up from his phone.

"Whole lotta nothin'. Shootin' someone in the dark, during a downpour—I'd say that's a pretty good way to wash away evidence."

"Any chance this could be an accident or misfire? You said hunting's big around here. Some pretty good woods behind that house, don't you think?"

Donny had a lot to learn. "Hunting season is over."

"Well, there were only two holes in the glass at that house and two bullets pulled from the vic. Since the neighbor confirmed that she didn't see anyone in the yard, the shooter had to be way back in the woods, right? So whoever did it was a pretty good shot. Maybe that narrows the field."

"Ha," Wilson said. "We're only talking thirty or so feet to the tree line. Everyone round here knows how to fire a weapon."

Donny lowered his chin. "Everyone?"

"You think I'm jokin'? I had my kids hunting with me at eight, on the range by twelve."

The only other officer still in the building, Roger, came to the door. "Hey, y'all get anything from the hospital?"

"Got the bullets," Wilson said. "We'll send them up to Belleville tomorrow morning. At least then we'll know what kind of gun we're looking for. But my guess—a .38 Special or .357 Magnum. We'll see."

"You didn't get to talk to Woods, though?" Roger asked.

"No," Wilson answered. "He's in bad shape. Bullets entered from the back. Just missed his heart, according to the doctor. Lung collapsed."

Donny turned to Roger. "What did you learn about him?"

"Not much. Famous actor. No juvenile record while he was a kid here. Average student at the high school. According to his dad, he returns once a year for Christmas and flies his dad out to visit him in California. Sounds like a decent guy."

"What about his mom? Yesterday was Mother's Day, after all," Donny said.

"No mom. Died when Woods was a kid in Chicago before he and his dad moved to Eden. He gonna make it?" Roger asked Wilson.

"Jury's out on that one," Wilson answered.

"Maybe someone is jealous of his success," Donny chimed in.

"I'll ask around," Roger said. "But so far, no one other than his dad knew he was here. You find out why he was in town?"

"His dad said he's prepping for a movie," Wilson said. "Something he wrote, set in Eden."

"Well, that's kind of cool," Roger said.

"Maybe. Depends what kinda story he wrote."

"Guess we should get our hands on that screenplay," Donny said.

"Agreed. Rog, what'd you find out about the dad?" Wilson continued.

"You think Mr. Woods could have done it?" Donny asked, incredulous.

"Just coverin' the bases. I mean, Woods is some hotshot actor now, and his dad is still living in that crappy old house. What's that all about? What happened to takin' care of your own?"

"Mr. Woods didn't seem like someone who had problems with his kid," Donny answered. "He seems like a terrified parent, afraid his son's gonna die."

"Maybe he's terrified of the kid waking up and tellin' his story," Roger added from the door, like it was a fun conspiracy theory to consider.

"Come on," Donny said skeptically. "He was there when it happened. Called 911. If he was outside in the rain, taking a shot at his own kid through the window, then called it in . . . well, for one, he'd be soaked to the bone, and two, that sounds nuts."

"Well, he says he was there," Wilson said. "Coulda been him. He could have changed clothes and then called it in. And even if he didn't do it, that don't mean he had nothing to do with it. Not yet." He looked at Roger then. "You find out much about the dad's private life? Maybe Mr. Woods is dealing drugs. You said he was from Chicago."

"My God," Donny chimed in, chuckling. "Are we gonna jump to drug dealing because the man is black and from Chicago? He's like seventy years old."

"I'm not jumping to anything," Wilson said. "I'm just asking questions. That's the job. I don't assume someone's good or bad, I just ask questions."

"Well, I checked, Sheriff," Roger answered, "and he's a plumbing parts supplier, nearing retirement, from what I hear. No record, regular church attendee over at First Baptist on Wyland in Hobart. No sketchy connections."

"Financial issues?" Wilson asked. "I'm guessing he'd get some money if his son kicks it."

"House is paid for," Roger continued. "He donates to church every month. Drives a fancy new BMW convertible. Gift from his son."

Donny smirked at Wilson, as if the car proved the father had no motive to hurt his child.

"Well, that, right there, might be someone's motive," Wilson said. "People don't like that stuff. Driving fancy cars, acting all better than."

Donny shook his head like he didn't believe it.

"You never hear of resentment or bitterness up north?"

The edge of a smile emerged on Donny's face. "No, I guess that's universal."

Roger crossed his arms. "People round here been killed for less. Can't tell you how many bar fights over darts have ended with gunfire."

Wilson leaned back and propped his feet up on the desk, resting his hands behind his head. "I guess there's a chance that trouble followed Woods from Hollywood. Maybe he crossed someone. I don't know how it works out there. Could be corrupt as all get-out."

"I'll check out his social media," Donny said, raising the phone still glued to his hand.

"Good. And Roger, you see if he's got an assistant or agent or someone who can tell us more about his life and that movie he's doin'."

"Got it," Roger said. "And I'll dig a little more into who he knew when he was living here."

"Sounds good," Wilson said. "I want to know everything there is to know about Darius Woods."

Roger started to leave the office but stopped, turning back. "Oh, Sheriff, did you hear about John Anderson?"

"Yep," he replied, shaking his head. "I saw his girl Brooklyn at the hospital."

"Such a shame," Roger continued. "I'll have Bets send somethin' to the house."

"You do that. I'm gonna check on him tomorrow. He's not gonna like being cooped up in that hospital room. I was just with him yesterday after brunch at Mary's with my daughter."

"Mary?" Donny asked.

"Mary's Diner. Town staple. Probably a third of my congregation heads there after church. Try the pancakes."

"Got it," Donny said, smiling.

"No Eddie?" Roger asked.

"Eddie's my son," Wilson clarified for Donny. "He hit the Saturday Mass." Roger knew about Eddie's divorce and that he was living with Wilson, but that was all. It was bad enough that Eddie was broke and rarely got out of bed before noon. Wilson didn't need Roger or Donny or anyone else knowing that Eddie didn't even go to church anymore.

"Anyway," Wilson continued, "I popped over to John's store yesterday. He was fine. It's just hard to believe how things can happen in a flash."

"I guess Ginny called for the ambulance," Roger added. "Good thing she was there. I mean, what mighta happened otherwise?"

The thought of his friend, broken and unconscious on the floor, no neighbors in sight, made Wilson's belly flip a little. It *was* a good thing Ginny was there. A miracle even, given the tension between them. But maybe Mother's Day had brought out Ginny's kinder, gentler side. Wilson had watched Ginny scoop up her kids and leave after Bonnie's funeral without even saying goodbye to her dad.

It had been a rare and heartbreaking admission when John turned to Wilson that day, saying that Brooklyn was all he had left, that he'd lost Ginny a long time ago. Wilson knew the feeling. Eddie was still under his roof, but he and John had both lost their kids after high school, and Wilson had never really understood why.

CHAPTER SIX

BROOKLYN LEFT THE HOSPITAL AROUND eleven that night, driving along Route 60 and exiting onto Main Street. She continued through the center of town in darkness, the same route she'd traveled day after day during her mom's last week of life, never wanting to leave her side but always wanting to return home to be sure Dad was okay. He had barely spoken during that last week, refusing to stay at the hospital for more than an hour. He said the place smelled funny, complained of hunger, or talked about getting to the store, but each night Brooklyn had returned to the house to find him sitting in his living room chair, staring vacantly out the front bay window, as if he was waiting for his wife to come home, as if she wasn't really dying.

After turning onto another long country road, she could see the house, still nearly a mile away, looking lonely under the dark star-smeared sky, the only structure for miles around.

The car's headlights scanned the porch as she turned into the gravel drive. No flower baskets were hanging. Her mother had always planted annuals and hung the baskets on Mother's Day weekend.

Mother's Day. Yesterday. Brooklyn hadn't thought to call her dad. She'd been so consumed by her own grief, so determined to keep herself busy with work, she hadn't even thought to call. And here he'd been, alone, missing his wife of forty-plus years.

She passed her dad's shoes, covered in mud and soaking wet, on the porch beside the front door, as she hit the lights and walked inside. Everything about the house looked as it always had: well-worn, outdated, filled with love. The entry hall was still covered in that awful floral-print wallpaper from the 1970s—her mom's first and most controversial decorating decision. Her dad had refused to remove it, insisting that "we don't learn from mistakes if we don't have to live with them." Rather than resenting his stubbornness, her mom had smiled when she shared the story with Brooklyn, whispering that she thought he was just being lazy. Every other wall and doorframe in the house was white. Pictures lined the stairwell, and her mom's needlepoint pillows, covered in Bible quotes and proverbs, still sat along the window seat in the living room.

Brooklyn peered into the study off the front hall. The only change was a newer off-white carpet, shag style, that filled the space between his big desk by the front window and the La-Z-Boy in the corner. She tried to remember if the rug had been there back in December. She couldn't recall, but it looked cozy and soft, maybe her mom's most recent attempt to update a little. The previous carpet, one of those circular rope varieties, probably fifty years old, had never been comfortable, certainly never encouraged one to sit on the floor—though maybe that was the point. It was hard to imagine her dad lying in that room, unconscious. Even for Ginny, it had to have been terrifying to find him like that.

But where exactly had it happened, she wondered, stepping inside, looking for what might have caused a stumble. She thought of her dad's bandage. Twelve stitches. He must have hit his head when he fell, but on what? There was no blood on the carpet. Though maybe he'd hit the corner of his desk.

The squeaking floorboards and stair treads echoed though the empty house as she went upstairs. Standing in the doorway of the bedroom she and Ginny had both occupied, nearly two decades apart, she surveyed the room she'd tried so hard to escape. The teal desk she and her mom had painted together, a hand-me-down from Ginny (and formerly bloodred-horrible), was still covered by Brooklyn's old books and the jewelry she'd made during senior year when she began dressing like an island beach bum. The first time she left for school with her hair braided, wearing that jewelry, a flowy tie-dyed skirt, and flip-flops, her dad had peered over his newspaper with brow raised, but said nothing. Mom had smiled, remarking how beautiful she looked. She got teased at school, but by then, she'd stopped caring. If she was going to be treated like she didn't belong, she figured she might as well look like it too. Someday, she figured, those kids would see her on TV or in a movie and regret how cruel they'd been.

Atop the desk was a mason jar filled with pennies, and above it, a bulletin board overlaid with high school pictures—stage shots, mostly, along with a few participation ribbons from her short-lived attempt at track during freshman year. And in the corner, the photo taken during her parents' mission trip in 1999, which changed all their lives. She'd snapped a digital shot of it with her phone before moving away, so she'd always have it with her: her parents, smiling for the camera, their arms around a young, pregnant Dominican girl they knew from their annual church trips to the town. Her name was Eimy. It was just a week after the picture was taken when the Andersons learned that Eimy had died during childbirth. Ginny was about to leave for college, her mom's heart and home suddenly felt empty, and they couldn't bear the thought of Eimy's baby ending up like so many other orphans. And so they returned to the Dominican Republic—"moved heaven and earth," as Mom told it—and brought Brooklyn home.

Brooklyn spent years looking at Eimy's face, wondering what her biological family had been like, wondering what might have happened if Eimy, only fifteen at the time, hadn't died. It would have been difficult. Dad had once shared that many kids over there were forced to work in the coffee, rice, and sugarcane fields, that poverty was the norm. It was hard for Brooklyn to feel sorry for herself after learning that.

She didn't quite think of Eimy as her mom, but when she looked at the kindness of Eimy's smile, she imagined how close they might have been, how Brooklyn might have talked to her about boys or sex or every other topic she knew better than to discuss in her house, where her parents found answers to every question in the Bible. As a child, Brooklyn decided that every abandoned penny she found was a sign from Eimy, and soon she began asking the pennies questions, believing Eimy provided the answers. Even now, she couldn't pass a penny without asking it a question, despite the fact that she'd long ago lost confidence in the source of those answers.

She collapsed onto the bed, the weight of her exhaustion pulling her toward sleep, but her mind was swirling from the jarring reality of Dad's condition and being back in this town. Things were changing too fast. She'd felt untethered when Mom died, unsure how she'd manage without the phone calls and encouraging notes that had come every week after she left for college. Her mom had been her anchor. And suddenly Brooklyn was facing the potential loss of *both parents*, of losing *home* too. If Dad really was losing his mind, if Ginny put him in a nursing home, he wouldn't last long. Ginny had never seen Brooklyn as more than some unwelcome intrusion or replacement. She'd have no one.

He needed to be okay. And come home.

None of that could happen if Ginny didn't help. Brooklyn thought of what Dad had said about forgiving Ginny and holding her secret. She needed to tell Ginny about it. Maybe it would help. Maybe Ginny would explain what that was all about. Perhaps opening up about whatever that meant would bring the sisters closer together.

~ • ~

Ginny sat in a car while raindrops rattled against the glass like gunfire. Suddenly she felt someone pushing her. It was Simon, jostling her arm back and forth, rousing her from a dream. She opened her eyes. His lips were moving, but it took a second to hear him whispering her name again and again. The television and the nearby lamp were now off, the room lit only by the hall sconces. She had no idea how long she'd been out. "Okay, okay, I'm up," she said, slowly sitting up on the couch.

Simon backed away, and she tried to focus. Even in the darkened room, his disheveled hair and sloping shoulders punctuated the exhaustion on his face. He was holding the empty bottle she'd carefully hidden under cardboard boxes in the recycling bin. She looked at his eyes. It wasn't just exhaustion, she saw, it was disgust. He was a man without vices—disciplined and unsympathetic to weakness. When they'd met all those years ago, their first date had been to an ice cream parlor. He didn't drink, which at the time made him seem like some sort of divine savior, sent from heaven to ensure she maintained her still-new sobriety.

Simon wouldn't understand what led her to the bottle again. There was too much he didn't know. Tonight it had been Mikey. She'd been standing in the doorway of her son's darkened room a couple of hours ago, watching him sleep, his belly on the mattress, knees tucked up under him like a peaceful yogi, while hundreds of glow-in-the-dark stars and planets shone down from the fourteen-foot ceiling. And she knew her son would never know such peace again if the truth about what she'd done came out.

She'd grabbed her tools of avoidance—a bottle of Chardonnay, a glass, and a basket of laundry—and plopped herself in front of the TV in the family room. But after folding the clothes and disposing of the empty bottle, she'd melted into the sofa back while staring at the screen, unable to focus on the show in front of her. The wheels were in motion, the police investigation into Darius's shooting was national news, John might even start rambling. The truth was coming. This beautiful home, this family—it was all her kids had ever known, and it was about to disappear. Like a strobe light of torture, she was hit with images from the night before: blood, rain, EMTs loading bodies into ambulances.

Her world was spinning out of control, and she didn't know how to stop it.

She looked up at Simon, at his disappointment, the weariness in his expression, and braced herself for the yelling, thankful the kids were sound sleepers.

But he didn't yell. He sat on the coffee table in front of her, eyes pleading. "What am I supposed to do?" he asked. "I can't let my kids be cared for by a drunk."

"I'm not a drunk," she said, though even she could hear the slur in her words. "It's just been a difficult couple of days. Tomorrow will be better." It was the mantra her mother had always provided in the face of Ginny's distress. It didn't matter how bad things were, tomorrow would be better.

"And what if Lyla had found you like this?" Simon asked.

"You're being melodramatic." Lyla, her eight-year-old, had a habit of waking in the night from bad dreams and crawling into bed with her mom. Simon always found the invasions irritating, but Ginny never minded. Lyla would be curled into a tight ball like a roly-poly, and Ginny would wrap around her like a blanket. They fit together like two puzzle pieces.

"I don't appreciate that tone," he said, the same way he'd scold Mikey for talking back. "You need help."

She couldn't look at him. "You're overreacting, Simon. I'm a good mother. Look," she said, waving toward the basket. "Laundry is done. Kitchen's clean. Kids asleep."

He shook his head, stood, and walked away.

"Stop acting like I'm such a mess," she yelled. He gave her credit for none of her success. She'd gone thirteen years without a drop.

He turned back. "You were drunk when you finally came home last night. It was Mother's Day, for Christ's sake."

She closed her eyes, pushing the heels of her hands into the sockets, as if doing so could stop his judgment. "My mother is dead," she yelled. "And now my father's in the hospital. Excuse me for struggling."

As he stepped forward, his voice softened. "When's the last time you went to a meeting?"

"Saturday night, actually." She didn't mention that she got drunk before showing up.

"I think you should start seeing Pastor Gary again," he said.

Simon was a fool. But then, so was she.

He walked out and flipped the hall light switch before heading upstairs, leaving her in darkness.

"I'll go tomorrow," she whispered, oozing back into the seat cushion. And she would. She needed to tell the pastor what had happened. What was going to happen.

CHAPTER SEVEN

DAY SEVEN
7:40 p.m.
BOLINE COUNTY JAIL

As the footfalls came closer, Brooklyn backed up, breath held. But the guard stopped before reaching her cell and unlocked a door on the other side of the cinder-block wall. Footsteps followed, and a moment later, the bars closed, a lock clicked, and a cot squeaked under the weight of a body.

"So what's the plan here?" a man asked.

"No idea," the guard replied.

"You know what this is? It's false imprisonment," the man said casually.

The guard began walking away without a response, and her neighbor yelled after him. "It's been two days! This is bullshit. Tell my dad he better get me the hell out of here." The door at the end of the hall slammed shut.

Brooklyn's panic began to return at the thought of a whole night in here, let alone two days.

She stepped back to the cot and collapsed onto the mattress, the springs squeaking beneath her.

"Hey," her neighbor said. "I didn't realize I had company. What are you in for?"

She couldn't let her mind go back over what had led to this moment. She said nothing.

"Come on," the neighbor said. "I'm going batty in here. The only person I've seen in two days is that guard who escorts me to the bathroom and brings me crappy food."

Brooklyn didn't know what to say. She didn't know what was worse—the silence, fear, and isolation, or a constant dialogue with a criminal.

"Come on, man. What they get you for? Tell you what I'm here for: Nada. Nothin'. It's BS. Locked up, thanks to my own father."

Brooklyn stared at the wall between them—they were both locked up because of their dads.

"Well, whatever you did, I hope you've got a lawyer," the man said. "These douchebags are corrupt as hell. I mean, that frickin' deputy killed a man. You musta heard about that."

Brooklyn had followed the case, of course. The deputy had shot an unarmed black man after a traffic stop, and the case made national headlines. The man was headed to church at the time and had warned the deputy of a gun in his glove box. Sheriff Wilson had said it was more complicated than the media suggested. And the deputy had been acquitted.

"You know Sheriff Wilson?" he asked.

She leaned forward, waiting for what he'd say next. She was counting on the sheriff's help. He'd sat with her on the front porch steps as they waited for the EMTs and police to come deal with her dad's body, his arm around her. He believed her. At least she thought he did. He told her not to worry, even as she was put in the back of the squad car.

"He's the worst. Probably wants me to die in here. No phone calls, no judge, nothing."

Brooklyn leaned back against the wall. She hadn't been offered a phone call yet. Sheriff Wilson had said he'd call Ginny. He was her dad's best friend. He couldn't be corrupt, could he?

Just hold on, she silently told herself. Ginny would be there soon. She had to be. There was no one else.

CHAPTER EIGHT

DAY TWO
Tuesday, May 14

BROOKLYN WOKE EARLY, TOOK A quick shower, and pulled out the clothes she'd packed—jeans, leggings, and T-shirts. *My hospital uniform,* she thought. She hadn't even packed makeup or jewelry. There was no point. Another reason why she and Tony would never be more than a casual hookup. He always looked photo-ready.

Simon answered the phone when she called Ginny's house. Brooklyn attempted small talk, but Simon had never been much more than polite when the family gathered on holidays. He'd had no more interest than Ginny did in getting to know her. After a painful pause on the line, she asked for her sister.

"Sorry," he said, "she can't get to the phone right now." He sounded exhausted.

"Is everything okay?"

A short chuckle. "No. Can't say it is. Listen, I'm sorry, but I need to get the kids off to school. And I've got a surgery in an hour." Simon, a doctor, was probably the best thing that ever happened to Ginny—at least that's what Mom used to say.

"Is she sick? Can I help?"

"Thanks, but I've got it. Ginny's just hungover," he said. "Too ill to wake up and be a mother today."

Ginny's past struggles with alcohol had never been discussed with her, but when she was still in elementary school, she overheard her mom talking to a few friends in the kitchen while they worked on one of their church fund-raising projects. She'd looked up the term *alcoholic* online after overhearing their gossip. But she'd thought those issues ended before Ginny's kids came along.

"Honestly, I don't know how long this has been going on," Simon continued, "but she's a mess." He seemed relieved to tell someone.

"I'm so sorry." What else could she say?

"I think Bonnie's death has hit her hard, and now with John as he is . . . Well, it's a lot. I know you two aren't close, but maybe you can help. Just talk to her."

If Ginny was struggling over losing their parents, they did have some common ground. But Ginny had long ago made it clear she had no use for Brooklyn. She'd never accepted Brooklyn's offers to babysit, never came to one of her plays at school, never even celebrated her birthday. Brooklyn overheard a conversation once—she must have been about seven at the time—when Ginny chastised their mom for suggesting, years earlier, that Brooklyn be a flower girl in Ginny's wedding. Brooklyn didn't even remember Ginny's wedding, but pictures hung along the stairs. Clearly, she hadn't been in it. Ginny obviously preferred being an only child or couldn't handle the fact that Brooklyn and their parents had a good relationship, or maybe she was like all the classmates who simply thought Brooklyn didn't belong.

"I'm so sorry things are bad," she said. "I'm just not sure what I can do. She doesn't even like me, and now she's trying to get our dad shipped off to some nursing home like she doesn't care what happens to him. It kind of pits us against one another."

"I understand." He didn't assure Brooklyn that she was wrong about Ginny's feelings. Even now, it stung. "But I do think she cares about your dad. I mean, she insisted on visiting him both nights this weekend. She seemed worried about him being alone on Mother's Day in particular, his first without Bonnie. And how lucky, right? I can't imagine what might have happened if she hadn't been with him when he fell. Almost felt divine, given how little she's visited over the years."

Ginny had told Brooklyn she found their dad unconscious when she arrived on Sunday, but Simon had just said she was with him when it happened. "Did she tell you about those visits over the weekend? Did she say how my dad fell?"

"She called me from the hospital on Sunday night. She said they talked about their day, she told him about all the nice things the kids had done for her on Mother's Day, and then she made him some dinner. She said he made a remark about Bonnie that concerned her, like he'd forgotten she was gone, and after he left the kitchen, she heard him fall in the living room."

It was an entirely different story than what Ginny had told Brooklyn. Why would she lie about whether she was at the house with him when he fell? She'd even told Brooklyn she found him in the study but told Simon he fell in the living room. It made no sense.

"Anyway," Simon continued, "I've really got to finish making the kids' lunches and get going."

"Of course, I'll catch up with her later. Oh, one more thing, do you know if she'd going to see our dad today or does she have to work?"

"What do you mean?"

"What do you mean, what do I mean?"

"Brooklyn, Ginny isn't working."

"She stopped nursing? How did I not know that?" But the answer was obvious. They'd shared no more than brief, stilted family visits maybe twice a year. They were strangers.

"We thought the strain was too much," Simon continued. "She had such trouble holding her pregnancies to term. She left nursing before Mikey was born."

Mikey was now twelve. Ginny hadn't had a job in twelve years. Brooklyn thought back to Ginny's text yesterday morning and repeated its essence to Simon—that she couldn't talk because she was at work.

"Maybe she was referring to work around the house. I don't know," Simon answered curtly. His patience was ending.

Hers too. Her father's words, meant for Ginny, echoed back to her: "I forgive you." She needed some straight answers.

~ • ~

When Brooklyn arrived at the hospital, Sheriff Wilson was seated in the chair beside the bed, and Dad was awake.

"Wow! Look who's up!" she exclaimed, entering the room. The color was back in his cheeks. He was still looking too fragile, but at least he was awake and talking to his friend.

The sheriff stood, always the country gentleman. "Mornin', Brooky."

Her dad's face dropped when he saw her. "What are you doing here?"

"I had to come, Dad. Don't you remember? I was here last night too."

"I don't remember a thing," he said. "I don't know what the heck I'm doing here." He attempted to prop himself up and immediately winced.

Brooklyn quickly stepped forward. "Dad, you probably shouldn't try to move yet. You broke your hip and hit your head."

"Hmm," he said stoically, raising his hand to his forehead, as if he needed proof that he'd been hurt. "Well," he continued, "you're both making me feel like I'm on death's door, hovering over me like this. Wilson, please don't tell me you made a special trip. Brooklyn, did you call him?"

"She didn't," the sheriff assured him. "I've got official business in the hospital, actually."

"Is it Darius Woods?" Brooklyn asked curiously, dropping her purse on the table. "I heard about the shooting on TV last night."

"Another fan, eh? Yup. Looks like Eden's giving me one last case before retirement."

"How's he doing?" she asked. "The news last night said it was critical."

"Say some prayers. Last I checked it didn't sound too good."

The thought that he might die tugged on her heart. It shouldn't have mattered as much as it did. Darius Woods was a stranger. That was the thing about celebrities. Everyone felt like they knew them.

"John, let's talk about you," the sheriff continued. "How'd this happen?"

Brooklyn pulled the other chair closer to the bed to join them while her dad considered the question. "Was Ginny with you when you fell?" she added.

"Ginny . . . The garden flooded, and B . . ." Dad paused as if he were trying to remember.

Brooklyn looked at the sheriff, who appeared equally confused. She didn't know if her father suddenly thought he was talking to Ginny about her mom, or if he was talking about Ginny to her mom. Either way, he wasn't making sense.

"What do you remember, John?" Sheriff Wilson asked.

Her dad stared down at the white sheets covering his legs and said nothing. He looked up, opened his mouth to speak, but suddenly his focus moved to the doorway.

Brooklyn and the sheriff followed his gaze.

"What's going on here?" Ginny asked from the door.

The sheriff stood to greet her, but Ginny remained where she was, like she wanted a quick escape.

Simon's words swirled in Brooklyn's mind. Ginny was drinking again. She'd told Simon she was with her dad *when* he fell, not that she'd found him after. And now her cheeks were flushed. Was it the aftereffects of a binge, or had she been listening just now, nervous about whatever their dad might say about how his injuries had happened?

"We were just trying to find out what happened on Sunday night," Brooklyn answered.

"I don't think he knows," Ginny said, finally taking a step inside. "Isn't that right, John?"

When Brooklyn had been old enough to wonder why Ginny called their dad John, her mom explained that Ginny was a grown-up now, so she liked calling him by his first name. "Does she call you Bonnie?" Brooklyn had asked. But Mom laughed, mumbling, "Only when she's angry."

Everyone's focus returned to Dad, but he simply turned away, gazing absently out the window.

"Why are you here?" Ginny asked the sheriff, her tone unmistakably rude.

"Sheriff's here about the Darius Woods shooting," Brooklyn said. "Did you hear about it?"

Ginny opened her mouth to reply, but another officer arrived behind her. "Excuse me, folks," he said. Ginny visibly jumped. "Sheriff, you have a minute?" he asked.

"Sure, I better get going. Johnny boy, you take it easy," Sheriff Wilson said, walking toward the door. "Get up and pace these halls. That's the fastest way out. I'll be back. Girls, as always, great to see you both."

"You too," Brooklyn said. Ginny said nothing as she stepped aside while the sheriff passed.

"Neighbor saw someone at Woods's house," the officer said as they walked away.

Ginny watched them leave, as if nothing in Dad's room was more important. When she finally turned her attention back to Dad, Brooklyn turned to him and put her hand on his. "Can we finish this conversation? I want to understand what happened on Sunday night."

"I told you," Ginny said, coming closer. "He fell."

"I'd like to hear what Dad has to say," Brooklyn said curtly.

Slowly, Dad's gaze moved from the window to his girls. "Enough questions," he said, irritated.

Brooklyn looked to Ginny for answers, but she was silent.

"You girls better get going," he said, closing his eyes. "My family will be here soon."

"We are your family," Ginny said. "It's Ginny and Brooklyn."

He opened his eyes quickly and looked at Ginny. "It's going to be okay. Don't worry." He closed his eyes again and began muttering incoherently.

Brooklyn paced to the window, agitation threatening to send her shooting out of her skin. She was on the outside of whatever was happening here, whatever had happened. Either something was going on between these two or her dad really was confused. She looked down on the parking lot, the media trucks below. She had no idea what to do. If Ginny was right about Dad's dementia, there would be no way to avoid selling the house and the store. He couldn't live alone and run a business by himself.

Ginny stood beside her. "I told you," she said in a lowered voice.

"Why did he just tell you not to worry?"

"There's no making sense of this, Brooklyn. That could have been about anything."

"Well, this could be the anesthesia," Brooklyn insisted. She'd googled memory issues last night, and the drugs could do a number on cognitive function, particularly for older patients. One website suggested the effects could last for months.

"It's not," Ginny said.

Brooklyn looked back at Dad. His eyes were closed. His mouth had fallen open like he was already sound asleep. "We should have him evaluated by a doctor," she said softly.

"Brooklyn, this is real. I'm sorry. It's been going on for a while. Mom didn't want you to worry."

It felt like a slap. More secrets. She didn't think she could handle learning her mom had kept this from her too. "When did all this begin? I've only been away eighteen months."

"I don't know. Last summer when Mom went to New York to help you, she asked me to check on him while she was away."

Brooklyn and her mom had talked all the time. There had been dozens of phone calls in the months before she died. Each of them haunted her as she recalled Mom's cheerful disposition and interest in Brooklyn's life, while offering only generalizations and superficial stories about Eden. She'd said nothing about the cancer, nothing about Dad's memory problems. Her mom had always preached honesty, grounding Brooklyn for any white lie that crossed the threshold of their home. "Lies will destroy your soul," she always said. And yet, her omissions were far worse than any tall tale Brooklyn had spun as a kid.

She'd taken away Brooklyn's chance to be there, to help, to cherish those final days. And now the same thing was happening with her father. Did they really believe she was too fragile to handle it? If anyone was fragile, it was her alcoholic sister.

Brooklyn's back stiffened, and she bit on her lip, working the chapped skin in her teeth. The idea that Ginny knew more about their parents than she did was infuriating.

She turned to Ginny. "You look terrible."

"Well, thanks," Ginny said sarcastically.

Brooklyn immediately regretted the comment and thought of Simon's plea for help. "I just mean you look like you haven't been sleeping. I wish you wouldn't act as if you need to handle this alone. I'm here. I can help. I want to be involved in these decisions."

Ginny nodded and turned around, resting against the AC as she answered. "I know you do."

It was an irritating response. What she meant was Brooklyn wanted to help but couldn't because she either wasn't really family or wasn't really an adult. Brooklyn's olive branch was getting heavy.

"Who's taking care of the store right now?" Brooklyn asked.

"I put a sign in the window yesterday saying it was closed until further notice. People will understand."

The calls would probably start coming to the house. Locals would worry. It was that kind of town. Her dad had opened Anderson's General Store in the early seventies, right after returning from the war. In the nearly fifty years since, Anderson's had become as central to Eden as a town square. The store carried food, hardware, a little liquor, essential drugstore items, hunting equipment, and some popular guns and ammo—all the basics.

"I'll go over there and see if there are any bills that need handling or deliveries to deal with."

"Suit yourself," Ginny said.

Brooklyn had practically grown up in that store. She knew how to review inventory and track vendors. Perhaps it would make her dad feel better to know she'd put everything in order.

She leaned against the AC beside Ginny, watching her dad. "Is it normal for him to be out so much? I mean, I've been here most of the time since dinner last night, and he's been up for like two minutes."

"Yeah, that's normal."

Starting a conversation with Ginny was like pulling teeth. She needed to throw a grenade. "Simon says you're drinking again."

Ginny straightened. "He said that?"

Brooklyn waited for more.

"I'm not," Ginny said, facing her. "You don't know him, Brooklyn."

That was true. She didn't know either of them. The only thing she knew about Simon was that he was devout, a practitioner of "biblical family values"—code for families that shunned birth control and often ended up with eight or more kids—and Mom thought he was the best thing that had ever happened to Ginny.

"Maybe we could get some lunch together today," Brooklyn said, softening her tone. "I mean, you called me home because of all these issues with Dad. We need to talk. You could tell me more about where you think he should go if he can't go home." There were no nursing homes in town, so she planned to reject whatever Ginny had to say, but she would listen, anyway. Talking would be a start.

Ginny nodded. "We do need to talk," she said. She glanced around, as if what to say next could be found in the corners of the room, but then she shook her head and grabbed her purse. "I've got to get home to make the kids' lunch. Let's talk later." She was practically out the door before Brooklyn could respond.

"Wait," Brooklyn begged. "It's Tuesday. Aren't the kids at school already?" Simon had said he was taking them hours ago.

Ginny shifted uncomfortably in the doorway. "Yes. I just . . . Simon said I need to drop off their lunches."

Why was she lying?

"What did you do?" Brooklyn blurted.

Ginny froze. Slowly, her brows furrowed, but she said nothing.

"Last night, Dad thought I was you," Brooklyn said. "He said he forgave you. He said he'd always protect you. What was that about?"

Ginny ignored the question and looked at their dad. It was slight, but she shook her head, rejecting the comment.

"What is going on here?" Brooklyn demanded.

Ginny wouldn't look her in the eyes. "You can't pay attention to what John's saying these days. It's mostly nonsense. Like I told you, he's not himself." She turned again and walked out.

Brooklyn considered challenging her story about Dad's fall but reconsidered. It seemed like Dad had been about to say what he remembered and stopped when Ginny arrived. Something didn't add up, and blurting out accusations would do no good. She needed facts. She needed to talk to her dad without Ginny around, get his side if he could remember, and figure out if there was any reason her sister would lie.

Ginny suddenly walked back inside the room and dropped her purse on the table against the wall. "I'm sorry," she said. "You're right. We do need to talk." She blew out some air. "I'm not thinking straight. I need some coffee." She attempted a smile.

Finally. Brooklyn stood. "I'll get it. Just stay with Dad, okay? Be right back."

Ginny took a breath and collapsed into the chair. "Thanks." She began gnawing on a nail. As Brooklyn passed her to fetch the coffee, she noticed Ginny's other fingertips, red and swollen, each nail bitten back to the nub.

CHAPTER NINE

BROOKLYN TOOK THE ELEVATOR DOWN to the family waiting room and spotted the man she'd met there last night. Martin. She thought of Darius Woods, wondering again if this was his dad. Martin's eyes were set farther apart than Darius's, and they were brown, unlike the actor's green, but he was tall, too, and that voice—there was a similarity. Would it be rude to ask? With all those reporters hovering outside, maybe he wanted his privacy.

He stood, joining her at the coffee vending machine. "I was just thinking of you," he said. "You were just like an angel last night, bringing me coffee like that."

Brooklyn smiled. "It was nothing."

"I'm telling you, I often look for signs. My wife passed years ago. And you, those beautiful eyes of yours, I thought, that girl mighta been an angel. How's your daddy doin', sweetheart?" he asked.

"He's sleeping," Brooklyn answered. "He broke his hip. He's seventy."

Martin chuckled. "You say that like he's old. Heck, I'm seventy-two. I bet he'll be just fine."

The comment made the corner of her lips turn up, a hint of a smile, like he'd shown her the night before. "Thanks." It was hard to believe Martin was that old. With just a little gray around his temples, he still moved and stood like a much younger man. Only his forehead, grooved with decades of stress, showed some age. But his tone had lightened since last night. His son had obviously pulled through the surgery okay.

Brooklyn fed her bills into the machine. "Coffee?"

"Oh no, you go ahead. I just finished some."

"So is your son doing okay?" She doctored her coffee and left Ginny's black, throwing a few sweeteners in her purse.

Martin leaned on the counter, seemingly content to stay and chat. "He is, thanks for asking. He's now stable. It was a long night, but it looks like he's gonna be okay."

Brooklyn nodded. It was nosy, maybe presumptuous, but she couldn't stop herself. "I'm sorry if this is intrusive. I just saw something on TV last night . . ."

Martin's wide grin provided a quick answer. "That's my boy."

"Darius Woods is your son?" Her voice rose as she spoke. There was no way she could play it cool.

"So you've heard of him?" He chuckled again, his parental pride on full display.

"Are you kidding? I went to Eden High. Everyone in the drama department knows who he is. I imagine everyone in town does. I'm a huge fan."

Martin gestured toward two nearby chairs, and they sat. Ginny was waiting for her coffee, but this was Darius Woods's dad. She'd stay for just a second.

"I'm an actress," Brooklyn said, "well, aspiring actress is more accurate. I haven't actually done much yet. But I live in New York now, auditioning, waiting tables, hoping for something."

"That's how my boy started too. Everyone gotta start somewhere."

She'd thought about Darius several times last night and even pulled up his pre-Oscar interview on YouTube after she'd gone to bed. She'd been trying hard not to think about her dad anymore. Darius had seemed relaxed in the interview, kind of like Martin, she now realized, as if he was excited by the buzz but otherwise unfazed. He had this loud, almost goofy laugh, and his posture was so good. Her mom had always bugged Brooklyn about that. But he was comfortable in his own skin. She was still working on it.

"I hope it's not rude to ask this, but how did it happen? The shooting . . . was it an accident?"

"I don't think so. Two shots right through the kitchen window on Sunday night. We were just standing there, talking. I was looking in the fridge, and he'd just gotten up from the table. The bullets didn't even really make a sound when they came through the glass. He just fell to the ground. I didn't understand until I looked up and saw the holes. It's . . ." Martin said nothing for a second, and Brooklyn couldn't fill the silence. "It's hard to think about it," he finally added. "Thank God I was there."

She couldn't imagine seeing your own child like that. "That's terrifying. What do the police say?"

"They're not saying much. Just asking lots of questions right now. Not a lot of answers."

She thought about that officer who came to her dad's doorway earlier, pulling the sheriff out of the room. He'd said a neighbor saw someone at the scene. Maybe it was a lead. "Do you think it could be a crazed fan? It's so easy to find celebrities with social media . . ."

Martin sat back, crossed his arms, and sighed. "I have no idea. He'd only been home twenty-four hours, and the sheriff just told me a neighbor saw a white woman in a car watching him being put in the ambulance. I guess that's all they got so far. I just can't imagine anyone, a man or a woman, shooting someone like prey."

Brooklyn didn't know what to say. She'd automatically assumed that if someone had intentionally hurt Darius, it had been a man. *Unconscious bias,* she thought. Buzzwords of the year. She couldn't help but wonder if Darius's fame was the cause—someone either loving him or hating him for it. She'd heard enough gossip in the store and church over the years to know that judgment of others' successes was often as mean-spirited as that of failures. Maybe the shooter had been someone who used to know him, who'd struggled since their high school days and couldn't stand to see him rise above. Dad had always said desperate people were the most dangerous. It was why he'd installed that security system at the store.

"Damn guns," Martin continued. "I left Chicago because of all the damn guns."

"Well, I'm so relieved he's going to be okay. Does he visit often?"

"Usually just at Christmas, but he came for work. Supposed to make a movie in Eden later this summer. Wrote it himself."

Brooklyn sat up taller and worked to keep her face interested without showing the level of excitement building at the thought of Darius Woods doing a movie in Eden. "That's amazing. What's it about?"

"His life. He hasn't let me read it yet, but he promised I'll look good."

Brooklyn smiled. "Well, that's good. That's incredible, actually. You must be so proud."

"I am. Gotta admit, though, when he got interested in acting, I used to say, 'Why you wanna spend your life pretending to be someone else?'"

Brooklyn laughed. Her dad had said the same thing. He'd never understood that it was about more than pretending. It was a way to live a bigger life than what she saw around her. She wanted to understand the world and the reasons people did what they did. Even the mean kids in school—she always wondered what had happened that made them do or say things. Acting required getting inside other heads and trying to see the world with a new lens.

"I pushed hard for him to play sports. I figured it was the best way to get a scholarship to college and a good job. Every Christmas I tried a new tactic—a basketball hoop one year, a bat and glove another, a football . . . I was sure he just needed to find his sport."

"My dad too. Wanted me to run track." No one in town had more social standing than the high school star athletes.

"I figured the acting dream was as pie-in-the-sky as saying he wanted to be an astronaut." He smiled then. "But I learned my lesson. Only dreamers achieve greatness. Isn't that right?"

Brooklyn smiled. "I'd like some greatness." She leaned back into the chair and put the coffees on the table beside her. "Was he always a writer too?"

"Actually, I was pretty shocked by this whole writing thing. He'd never said a thing about it. But he's more excited about this movie than anything that's happened so far. I guess he wrote the story years ago when he was still in New York, hoping he could make his own big break, like that *Good Will Hunting* movie. No one ever gave a hoot about it until he got the Oscar nomination in January. Suddenly, the studio said it was gold." Martin chuckled. "He's even supposed to direct."

"That's incredible." Brooklyn's mind raced. A huge star was planning to make a movie in her hometown. She opened her mouth to ask more but stopped herself. It was crass. His son had just been shot. "My dad lives on Portner Road," she said instead. "What about you?"

"Ninth Street."

The other side of the tracks, literally. It was that kind of town.

"So I'm not assuming we'll get much justice," he added.

Brooklyn quickly shook her head. "Sheriff Wilson's a real good friend of my family. I don't think he's racist."

"*Mm-hmm,*" Martin said. "Never thought Deputy Delaney was, either, until he shot Jaden White on his way to my church."

"You knew that man?" she asked.

"Yep. Good, law-abiding family man. Ain't no way I'm gonna believe that deputy feared for his life."

Brooklyn didn't know what to say.

"Anyway, let's not think of such ugliness. Darius is gonna be okay. That's all that matters to me right now. Besides, I gotta watch the stress. Got a bad ticker. And I learned a long time ago that you can't fret about things you can't control. It'll kill ya. Besides, all this national coverage can only help keep the police focused. Now, tell me about your daddy. How long they keeping him?"

Brooklyn took a deep breath and let it spill. "I don't know. My sister is sure he needs to be put in a nursing home. She says he has dementia, and it feels like I don't get a say because she's so much older, and it's like I'm not really family, at least in her eyes, because I'm adopted. But she's the one who's barely family. She practically ignored our parents for twenty years. Our mom died a few months ago. And it seems like something hap—" She stopped herself, looked at Martin, embarrassed, and pursed her lips against the runaway train of chatter. "I'm sorry. Too much information?"

"That's okay. It sounds like it's a good thing you're home. Sorry to hear about your mama, by the way."

"Thanks."

"Any other family?"

Brooklyn shook her head. "Nope."

"Maybe now's the time to get to know your sister. Family's important."

"That's what my dad always said."

"Smart man. Can you stay in town for a while, help him out?"

"Yeah, I can. Thanks, Martin."

Martin left to check on Darius, and Brooklyn grabbed the coffees to head back upstairs, suddenly nervous that she'd left her sister for too long. She needed Ginny to finally tell her what was going on. It didn't seem possible to figure out how to help Dad until Brooklyn understood whether she could trust Ginny. She had to know what secret lingered between them.

CHAPTER TEN

WHEN BROOKLYN RETURNED TO HER dad's room, he was still asleep. Ginny was sitting in the chair, scrolling through her phone and biting her fingernails—what was left of them. Brooklyn handed her the coffee and sat at the edge of the bed.

"Guess who I just met?" Brooklyn asked, her tone intentionally friendly and light. Mom always said, "Kill 'em with kindness."

Ginny took a sip and waved her hand, as if to silently say, "Just tell me."

"Darius Woods's father. Sounds just like him too. Deep baritone voice. You know who that is, right?"

Ginny's expression turned more serious. She must have heard about the shooting. "Darius Woods? Sure."

"He was in your grade, right?"

Ginny nodded.

"Did you know him?"

She nodded again. "I was on stage crew my senior year." She sipped her coffee, her focus fixed on Dad.

"Isn't it so cool that he's like this huge movie star now? Did you ever talk? Would he remember you?"

Ginny opened her mouth to answer, but Brooklyn continued. "He's going to do a movie here." It was impossible not to get excited. Almost a year in New York, trying to break into the business, having made it into just a few callbacks and one day-player part on that indie movie in Queens, and she'd still never even seen anyone famous, and now, back in Eden, Illinois, one of her idols was here.

Ginny finally stopped sipping her coffee and looked at Brooklyn, her face pinched. "What are you talking about?"

"His dad told me—he's going to be okay and he's here because he wrote a movie about his life in Eden."

Ginny seemed to consider this. "Did his dad say what happened?"

"Just that he was shot through the window at home. Police are looking for some woman who was spotted on the street."

"What else?"

"I don't know. It didn't seem right to pry."

Ginny looked at their dad again, and Brooklyn followed her gaze. His mouth was open, and he was breathing heavily, a throaty grumble escaping with each breath. "We're not doing any good here," Ginny said. "I gotta get home and make those lunches."

"I thought we were going to talk about Dad," Brooklyn said.

"We will. Later. But you'll be here a few days, right?"

"I'm not just going to leave," Brooklyn said. "You still haven't even told me what happened."

"What do you mean?" Ginny sounded irritated again. "There's nothing to tell. He fell. I got him here."

"But you told Simon that you went there because you were worried about him being alone and that you made him dinner. You told me he called you and when you arrived, he was already unconscious on the floor."

Ginny stood immediately and went to her purse. "You sound like you're trying to create some big deception. He asked me to come over, okay? I agreed because it was Mother's Day. So I didn't lie to either of you. I made him dinner. I guess I forgot to mention that. But he was in the other room when he fell. I didn't see it happen." Before Brooklyn could press her about where in the house he fell or what

Dad had meant when he said he forgave her and that he'd protect her, Ginny said, "I gotta go." She left without another word.

~ • ~

Ginny walked outside to a herd of reporters and camera crew loitering by the hospital entrance. Slivers of light cracked through the gray sky, then thunder boomed in the distance. She ran to the car and jumped in just as the rain began. Driving on Route 13 toward Harrisburg, the windshield wipers battled the downpour, and she tried not to panic. Every new day was a continuation of Sunday's nightmare. She never should have called Brooklyn home. She'd still been drunk when she'd sent that text. She'd been sure Darius would die. But he was alive. His story would be told. She had no idea how she would ever unravel the mess she'd made so long ago.

And Brooklyn, oblivious, had asked if Ginny knew Darius, if he'd remember her. There was no chance either of them would ever forget the other. It was the spring of junior year. Her church youth group showed up at the high school's drama rehearsal to recruit volunteers to act in their social justice play. He was impossible to miss, the only black kid rehearsing on the stage, at least six feet tall, hair cropped close to his head, and built like an athlete but dressed more like one of those grunge kids with ripped jeans and an open flannel. She was sure he hadn't even seen her, but days later, he walked into Pastor Gary's office at the church without knocking. He definitely saw her then. He saw them both.

It had been more than twenty years since that day, but she could remember every detail like it was yesterday—the skirt she'd been wearing, the smell of pine in the pastor's office, the swirl of emotions she'd felt when Pastor Gary had taken her hand and led her to the couch to talk about the play. He always grabbed her by the hand and pulled her along like a best friend, a little sister, or a prized pupil. She loved it. The other girls were jealous. Sometimes he even spoke to the group while standing behind Ginny, massaging her shoulders. She was his favorite, and because she was the youth group leader, they were a team. With blue eyes, that swoop of dirty-blond hair, dimples when he smiled, he was like an older version of Leonardo DiCaprio's character in *Titanic*. And he had that same boyish charm.

But on that day, he'd sat beside her and asked if she'd ever had alcohol. "Of course not." She giggled nervously. The rules were clear, and she was not a rule breaker. Kids who drank were the kind who went to parties, and her social circle never grew past the two girls who'd befriended her in elementary school. He had to be joking. "Well, don't tell anyone," he said, leaving her at the couch and pulling a bottle out of his desk drawer. "It's Sambuca. A parishioner just gave it to me as a gift with a note that said it might even help ward off the flu because it's made with elderberries."

"Is that true?" she asked.

"No idea. Sounds like an old wives' tale, but it tastes like licorice. Try it."

She didn't say a word or accept the glass. Or move.

He smiled. "If you prefer, I'll keep this just between us."

Ginny's shoulders relaxed, and she smiled. He made everything about being youth leader more fun.

It tasted almost hot going down, but it was oddly sweet, with a black licorice aftertaste. "Not bad," she said. Her face squirmed from the burn.

Pastor Gary chuckled. "Right? Well, let's get on with it. Cast list first."

She pulled out the paperwork and began going through her notebook. Pastor Gary made some notations in the margins, and they laughed and worked for another thirty minutes while he finished his drink.

Finally, after they were done reading through the play together, he sat back and put his hand on her neck, twirling her long hair in his fingers. "Ginny, have you ever been sexually active?"

She felt the immediate rush of heat to her cheeks, even though it seemed like a reasonable question at the time. The play they'd written was a pro-life story for teens, about teens, that would help them understand the righteous path in the face of difficult circumstances. She'd looked down, smiled, and said, "Of course not." It had to be a test. The church prohibited premarital sex, and everyone in youth group had taken chastity pledges.

"Good," he said. "But . . . you should understand what temptation feels like."

His words lingered around her. She gripped her notebook in both hands, frozen, as she felt him slowly sweeping her hair to one shoulder. He was waiting for a response.

"Okay." Her focus never left the pages in front of her. She didn't know what she'd see if she looked at his face.

"Do you trust me?"

"Yes." It was barely a whisper. She sensed she was agreeing to something she didn't understand, that hand pushing her toward darkness.

He said he wanted to kiss her, to touch her, just so she'd know, she'd understand why, even when her body began to respond, it was important to resist.

She didn't know what to say.

His hand slid to her lower back. He said it would help her stay strong in the face of future temptation. He told her she didn't need to say or do anything.

She sat like a statue as he kissed the skin behind her ear, sending a shiver up her spine. He then kissed her shoulder and maneuvered himself in front of her, kissing her neck and moving toward her chest. "Do you feel anything?" he asked.

She said nothing, uncertain of the right answer. Was she passing the test? Her heart was pounding. She was sure he could hear it, sure her skin had turned red. She always got these giant red patches on her cheeks and chest whenever she had to speak in front of a class.

He pulled back and looked at her, but she couldn't look at his face. She focused only on the white collar, surrounded by black. He slowly moved his hand to her leg, sliding it up her thigh until his touch, like a cattle prod, shocked her, and she inhaled. It must have been the wrong reaction, because suddenly he was on top of her.

The door flew open.

It was hard to remember now if it was seconds later, or minutes. The whole thing was a blur. But she knew she'd failed when they both turned toward the open door.

Darius stood there in a Nirvana T-shirt and a huge Mr. Rogers–style cardigan, his mouth open. "Uh, excuse me," he said, turning away. He began to shut the door, but then he stopped and pushed the door all the way open. His faded jeans were ripped at the knees. He was no rule follower.

Pastor Gary jumped to standing and babbled nervously about how inappropriate they must have looked while he quickly moved to his desk, explaining that they were just working out the logistics of a scene. Ginny sat upright, pulling her skirt down, and crossed her legs.

Without missing a beat, Pastor Gary asked Darius if he'd read the play. Darius said yes and looked at Ginny. She couldn't meet his eyes.

"Listen," Darius said, turning back to Pastor Gary, "I thought this play was about social justice, like racism or equality or something. I just came here to let you know I'm not comfortable performing in this."

"You must agree that protecting unborn children is a matter of social justice," Pastor Gary said, nonplussed.

Darius opened his mouth, closed it, then said, "Actually, I'm not interested in this debate. I'm just here to tell you that this play is offensive."

"How so?"

"You suggest that no matter how a child is conceived, even by rape, abortion is never okay."

"That's what we believe."

"And you are casting me, the black guy, as the one who attacks a girl at a party after she's had too much to drink . . . like a black rapist is your worst-case scenario. It's racist, and the entire thing is . . . I don't like it. I'm out."

"Well, I'm sorry you're taking it that way, Darius. It's not what we intended. We wanted you for the role because you're known in the drama department as being a really good actor. Isn't that right, Ginny?"

Tears welled, and she wiped them aside as she whispered, "Yeah."

Darius stepped toward her. "You're Ginny Anderson, right?"

She looked at him. "Yes."

"We have history together."

They did not.

"I was really hoping to get those notes from you for tomorrow's test. Can I give you a ride back to school?"

"Actually, Darius," Pastor Gary said, "Ginny and I still have a lot of work to do."

"It's really important. I'm sure you'd agree that school comes first, right?" And then before the pastor could say anything else, Darius looked at her again. "Come on. I'll give you a lift."

Ginny stood, gathered up her notebooks, and walked to the door.

"Okay then," Pastor Gary said. "Ginny, we'll catch up tomorrow."

Darius led her to his car. Neither spoke the entire way to school. He parked; she said thanks without looking at him, and got out.

And he'd written about life in Eden, about his life and things he knew—and things he didn't know.

Ginny was sitting at a stoplight on Main Street, the rain still slapping her windshield, before she thought about where she was. It was as if she'd been on autopilot while her mind went swimming in the past. She scanned the empty storefronts across the street, that bagel and coffee shop that never had a chance and the gun shop up on the right, one of the few businesses in town that would always thrive.

She'd had such big dreams back in high school. Even after those dreams died, she was sure that Simon's proposal and his big white house would provide the escape she'd needed. But she couldn't run from her memories.

She drove another mile, took two more lefts, and pulled into the parking lot of the Church of Good Samaritans. She turned off the car, closed her eyes, and listened to the rain rattle against the roof. *God, grant me the serenity to accept the things I cannot change, the courage to change the things I can, and—*

A knock on the window startled her before she could finish. It was Pastor Gary, standing at the driver's side door, holding an umbrella. He leaned down and raised his voice to speak through the glass. "You here to see me?"

She focused on his dimples when he smiled, the thing that had first attracted her to him all those years ago, when she was just a girl and he was perfect. He hadn't aged well—between the weight gain and ruddy cheeks, that resemblance to DiCaprio had vanished. But his smile still caused a physical reaction. It wasn't butterflies anymore. Those flew away the day Darius found her in the pastor's office. Now it was the pain of their secrets, buried deep inside.

She needed to tell him what had happened to Darius and to her father. She had to tell him what she'd done. What she needed to do.

CHAPTER ELEVEN

WILSON WAS STILL ON THE phone when Donny appeared at the door to his office, a big book tucked under his arm. He waved Donny inside, directing him to sit.

"Okay, well, that would be great. I appreciate it," Wilson said into the phone. "Perfect, I'll look out for that. Sure . . . yep. All right. I'll be in touch." He hung up and leaned back.

"Who was that?" Donny asked.

"Woods's agent. Hold on," he said before yelling toward the open door. "Roger, get in here."

"Take a seat," Wilson said, motioning toward the chair next to Donny when Roger appeared at the door. "First off, I heard from Belleville. Those bullets came from a .38 Special. So that's our gun. Let everyone know. Now Donny, whatcha got there?"

Donny looked down and raised the thick, hardback book. "Eden High yearbook, 1999."

Wilson reached out for Donny to hand it over. "Oh, sure, that was Eddie's year."

"I found only a couple other current Eden residents who were classmates," Donny said. "Sarah Burrows, though she was Sarah Kellerson then . . ."

"I remember little Sarah Kellerson. Good kid. Her family went to our church."

"And Dave Marquette," Donny continued.

"Davey Marquette," Wilson said fondly. "Big football star back in the day. His picture would be in the paper after nearly every home game."

"Well, according to their statements, neither knew Woods. Mr. Marquette said Woods wasn't on the team, so he didn't remember him. Mrs. Burrows said she'd heard of Woods and even saw him on the Oscars. Said she was sorry now that she'd never done the theater productions in high school. Anyway, she offered up her yearbook."

"Have you asked Eddie about Woods?" Roger asked.

Wilson swatted away the question. "My son wouldn't have known him either. What about the social media stuff?"

"That's gonna be tough to do much with," Donny said. "Looks like he's got a couple of Facebook profiles. The regular one has about five hundred friends connected to it, but he hasn't posted in two years. I haven't seen yet whether any of the names are local connections, but it looks like he doesn't do much with that. Then there's a fan page. I'm guessing it's run by someone who works for him. About thirty thousand followers, and everything posted is that typical movie promo-type stuff, behind-the-scenes pictures, stuff like that. His Instagram is the same. Tons of followers, mostly nonsense."

"Hmm," Wilson said, leafing through the pages. "Hey, Roger, see if Mr. Woods has his son's old yearbooks."

"Sure, why?"

"See all these signatures, front and back and in the margins?" He lifted an open page toward Donny and Roger. "Maybe it'll give us a clue about his friends, maybe even his enemies."

"Good idea," Roger said.

Wilson continued turning the pages and found the seniors. There were nearly three hundred names and faces. He stopped briefly on Eddie's wide grin and smiled. That adolescent acne was probably the reason he struggled with girls back then, but it seemed like such a small problem compared to his current issues. Wilson had never known if depression led to addiction or the other way around, but it seemed like Eddie stopped smiling altogether after his mother died during his senior year.

The sheriff moved on to the clubs and classroom shots toward the back of the book. When he got to the theater page, to the spring musical, *Grease*, with Woods in the lead role of Danny Zuko, he scanned across the group shot of the cast and crew for any familiar faces. There was one face he knew well. She didn't live in Eden anymore, but the sight of her set off an internal alarm. He slammed the book closed, handed it back to Donny, and shook his head, as if to rid her name from his mind.

"Anyway," Wilson said. "I wanted to let you both know that I've talked to Woods's agent. Pretty nice lady. Didn't expect that. But here's the deal. Woods has a stalker. Had to take out a restraining order on a young girl that broke into his house. She seemed obsessed, sure they'd be together someday. Left naked pictures and love letters all over the place."

"Jeez," Donny said.

"Yep. Agent said he hadn't heard from her in more than six months, though. They both assumed it was over."

"You get a name?" Roger asked.

"I did," he said, handing over his notes to Roger. "Tomorrow I want you to track her down. Let's see if she's got an alibi. And check Woods's social media again while you're at it. See if people would have known he was heading to Eden."

"Got it."

"Good. I've gotta take care of something in the morning, so Donny, feel free to take my desk here, get a feel for the future." They both grinned.

"Everything okay?" Donny asked.

"Absolutely." Wilson didn't need Donny or Roger, or anyone else, knowing that Eddie had become unbearable. Last night felt like the last straw, watching him swing from high to low, rage to despair, and early this morning he'd finally convinced his son to go back to the treatment center in Fairfield. All the willpower in the world didn't seem to have a chance against his addiction.

"And what about the screenplay?" Donny asked.

"Agent is gonna send me a link via email. I'll leave my computer on, so you can look out for it. She said they assumed it might make some waves in his hometown when the movie came out, but she didn't think he'd shared it with anyone."

"Did she say what it's about?" Roger asked.

"Yeah. And it's exactly what this place doesn't need."

"What do you mean?" Donny said.

"She said it's essentially a coming-of-age, racism-in-a-small-town kind of thing."

"Great," Roger said sarcastically.

"What?" Donny asked.

Wilson answered. "You must realize that after Tom's acquittal and all that brouhaha, a movie calling Eden racist isn't exactly what this town needs. And frankly, I been sheriff for thirty-five years. I've dealt with some violent crimes, but Eden is the bright spot. You haven't lived around here long enough to judge. We got the lowest crime stats in the county, and I don't take too kindly to someone smearing my home."

"Well, low crime stats don't exactly mean no racism," Donny said, sitting taller. "Even my wife has felt it. Just the other day, this checker at the grocery over in Davisville asked her how long she'd been here—just because she has olive skin and dark hair, the checker clearly thought Rosa was a foreigner."

The sheriff stood and grabbed his jacket from the back of his chair. "First off, maybe the checker was just asking how long your wife had been in the area. It's called being friendly. It's not that big a place, and maybe she just thought your wife was a new face in town."

"It's been almost a year, actually, but no. The implication was clear, as was her expression, according to my wife. Rosa had just ended a phone call with her mother, speaking Spanish."

"See, that's the problem. Everyone's so frickin' sensitive. You and your wife took a harmless comment and made it some kind of racial profiling. And I don't appreciate it when someone's stereotyping my town as a racist hellhole because some bullies mighta called Woods a few names during his childhood. That stuff is universal. Kids pick on kids, for whatever they can think of."

Donny shook his head. "O-kay, well . . . I guess we should read that screenplay and see what he's referring to."

"Damn straight," Wilson said. "Rog, get goin'." Roger quickly exited without a word. Wilson could feel his heart pounding. Just the talk of racism got him riled up. The world was too frickin' PC. Just because people stuck to their own didn't mean anything.

Another officer appeared in his doorway. "Hey, Sheriff, can I interrupt?"

Wilson stopped. "Sure, what's up?"

"That neighbor who saw the woman watching the ambulance—she remembered a few digits of the woman's plate."

"In the dark and rain?" Wilson asked.

"I know. Not the strongest ID, but I got plate registrations within a fifty-mile radius that could be a match."

"And?"

"There are less than ten," he said, walking the paper to Wilson's desk.

"Neighbor said the woman was white, a blonde, right?" Donny asked. "Do we know what the stalker looked like?"

"Not yet," Wilson said as he took the sheet of paper. One name stood out. And that cast and crew picture he'd just seen in the yearbook confirmed a connection between Woods and this person. His stomach twisted at the thought of repeating history.

He looked at Roger and Donny but held his tongue. He'd have to handle this alone.

~ • ~

By three o'clock, Brooklyn began feeling restless at the hospital and headed over to her dad's store. After unlocking the front door and turning off the security system, she stepped inside and cursed Ginny's name. The lights were all on, the register drawer wasn't even locked, and in the back room, the computer was still on, as was the coffeemaker. An open box of half-eaten pastry was now being enjoyed by a family of tiny ants. If felt like another reminder that Ginny couldn't be trusted.

But the mess didn't make sense anyway. Her dad, a military man, was all for order. She'd been chastised more times than she could count for leaving things out of place in the back room, and yet newspapers were stacked up on the table—several weeks' worth—empty soda cans were on the counter, even boxes of inventory were left open. Something was wrong. He wasn't disorganized or forgetful, but this room looked like he'd become both. He couldn't run a store like this.

It wasn't even safe. A box of guns sat open under the table, an open box of ammunition beside it. Brooklyn checked the computer for recent sales. Her dad had sold a .38 two weeks earlier. She couldn't believe he'd forget to put the box back on the shelf, that he'd leave unregistered guns out in the open for two weeks. Brooklyn closed the box, put it back on the bottom shelf where it belonged, and returned the ammunition to the second shelf, hidden in back where he kept all the bullets. She took the garbage out to the bins in the alley, locked the back door, and powered down the computer before heading home.

The microwave zapped the casserole she'd found in the freezer while Brooklyn listened to the messages on her parents' answering machine. Three messages in a row, all from women, all wondering if her dad was okay, having seen the sign on the store window that it was closed indefinitely. They might have been doing "the Christian thing," as Mom used to say, or they might have been swooping in to make a play now that Dad was a widower. She'd seen both types over the years. "I'm prayin' for you, John," one woman said. "I'm sure you'll be just fine, John," another said, adding, "God protects the righteous!"

Brooklyn rolled her eyes as she grabbed the hot plate of food. She'd calculated it once—she'd probably sat in a pew nearly a thousand times during her life—and yet she still didn't know what she believed. It had always bothered her that everyone else seemed so certain about who was running the show, who was right and wrong, and who was going to hell. The only thing Brooklyn knew was that the universe was a mystery and anyone who acted like they had all the answers was suspect.

And these women had no idea if John would be okay. No one did. Nurse Wanda had told them it was important that he begin to move as soon as possible, but when she tried to help him swing his legs off the bed and put some weight on them, Brooklyn noticed again how thin he'd gotten. He looked at least twenty pounds lighter than he had been at the funeral. He winced, collapsed back onto the mattress, and began cursing and accusing Wanda of incompetence.

Brooklyn had never seen him so angry, and he'd looked at her without a hint of recognition in his expression. "I'm not some sideshow. Get out!"

He'd never yelled at Brooklyn before. Not once. If she ever got in trouble as a kid, his silence indicated anger. If he was merely polite, without asking her about her day, something was up. But if he remained quiet at dinner, she had to get the topic on the table. And she always did. She'd apologize, promise to do better . . . whether it was grades or missing curfew or forgetting to lock up the store properly. That's all it took.

He and Mom never held on to their anger. If Dad got riled up about something at the store or some news story, he did what most men in town did. He took off for the gun range. But today, he was mean. He was rude to the nurses, particularly Wanda, and even made some comment about her getting her "nasty braids" out of his face when she leaned over to adjust the machine behind the bed. Brooklyn had followed Wanda out of the room, apologizing on his behalf, and explained how concerned she was by his behavior. But Wanda said that between the reports of dementia she'd heard about when he came in and the residual effects of the anesthesia and the painkillers, she wasn't too surprised.

Brooklyn had gone back into his room after he'd rested. His face relaxed as he looked at her. "Hey, baby girl," he'd said, as if nothing had happened. "I don't want you worrying about me. You need to get back to school." She didn't have the heart to remind him that no, she didn't.

Standing at the kitchen sink now, Brooklyn ate her food in silence. She looked around the room, terrified of what was happening. What if her dad really had dementia? Could she arrange for help? Could they build a ramp so he could stay in his home? She could move his bedroom to the main floor. Maybe she could fly home every six weeks to check in.

She looked at the remaining food on her plate, the creamy chicken on her fork. It was making her sick. She dumped it into the sink, exhausted by the hurdles, the absurdity of thinking she could do it all. She was a waitress, a starving artist, living in a dump with three friends in the East Village. She was in no position to fly back and forth every month or two. If her dad needed her, she was not going to be able to stay in New York. As she braced the counter, her stomach began to turn. She'd barely begun living her dream.

And what about the store? Was she supposed to run the store, determine her dad's care, take care of the house and everything he needed? And for how long?

She began pushing the air out, gasping as if she could get rid of the anxiety building inside.

Suddenly, the floor was tilting. Spots filled her vision, and she felt nauseous. She lowered herself to the floor as a cramp in her chest wall began squeezing her insides. She'd never been able to prevent these attacks, even after learning years ago that they were not a heart condition, as she feared, but anxiety-induced. She sat on the kitchen floor as her body temperature soared and finally lowered herself to lie flat. Closing her eyes, she fought through the feeling of being trapped, of suffocating inside a burning building she couldn't escape. She tapped on her chest, guiding her breath back to normal. After a few minutes, she opened her eyes and took a few deep breaths. It had been a quick one.

Brooklyn sat up slowly, looking around at the crumbs on the floor and dust bunnies in the corner. Dad needed help. The evidence was all over his store and this house. Her mother had been gone five months now. Ginny had obviously been useless.

So why had Ginny been at the house on Mother's Day?

Brooklyn left the kitchen, wandering back toward the front hall and the study. Ginny was still holding back something about the night Dad fell. There was no way he had called her, no way he'd let her cook him dinner. Even if he was sad on Mother's Day, he was far too proud to show a child, particularly Ginny, that he needed help.

She stood in the hall, looking first right, into the study, then left into the living room. Both were carpeted. She stepped into the study and examined the rug more closely. Finding nothing, she did the same in the living room. Nothing. Her dad cut his head open. He was supposedly unconscious on the floor and needed twelve stitches. How was there no blood?

She returned to the hall, her gaze wandering as she considered it. And that's when she noticed the tiny red dots toward the bottom of the white doorframe that led to the study. Brooklyn got on her knees and wiped a finger over the spots. They didn't budge. Was it old paint? She licked her finger and wiped the spots again. This time, they came off.

Blood.

Had her dad been standing here, in the front hall, when he fell? Why not say that? She looked down, noticing more dark spots on the wood floor. And then she noticed the cast iron fleur-de-lis doorstop, neatly tucked against the wall by the front door. And on its tip, more blood. If he'd fallen and hit his head on this, why not say so? Why was it so difficult to get a straight answer? Why had Ginny finally seemed ready to talk and then suddenly left when Brooklyn returned with their coffees? It had been as if Ginny couldn't escape fast enough. It almost felt like the mention of Darius Woods had caused her to run.

Still kneeling on the hall floor, Brooklyn stared absently into Dad's sanctuary. He wasn't going to provide any answers if he remained confused. And if he was protecting some secret, he'd probably never tell Brooklyn. Her mom's cancer had already proven that he had no problem hiding the truth from her.

She looked around the room—at the books on the shelves, the file cabinets next to the desk. She'd have to find her own answers.

CHAPTER TWELVE

GINNY SAT ON A GIANT boulder and looked out at the vast, open wilderness. Her mom had always said there were two places to feel close to God. Being with the pastor at church hadn't done it. So she'd driven twenty-five minutes and hiked the observation trail to look out over the Garden of the Gods in the middle of the Shawnee Forest. The Garden was a favorite spot for locals, tourists, and the burnouts who ditched high school, but fortunately, the rain had kept others away, and she had the place to herself.

Just a smear of clouds remained, and the fading sun had turned the distant horizon pink. She took a long swig from the small vodka bottle she'd bought on the way and inhaled the spring air, gazing out over the 280,000 acres of perfection that could change her perspective like a kaleidoscope.

Growing up, Ginny had gone with her parents every fall to take in the blanket of changing leaves on the treetops below—a completely unspoiled, panoramic view of God's work. The rock formations jutting out above the trees, like stacked river-rock sculptures, had been millions of years in the making—320 million years, actually. She'd created a science fair exhibit in elementary school called "Beautiful Erosion" to demonstrate how the prehistoric rock, twenty thousand feet thick and four miles deep, with its millions of sandstone layers, was all thanks to the giant sea that had once covered parts of what was now Illinois, Kentucky, and Indiana. She'd learned, too, that Colorado had a more famous Garden of the Gods—but unlike its giant red spike-shaped rocks that few dared to climb, her garden's rocks were like perches designed for taking in the view. Standing atop the massive structures corrected a person's perspective: the world was grand. People were small.

Whenever life overwhelmed her, Ginny hiked up here to feel some peace and hope and try to remember that her problems were a speck of dust and her life nothing more than one layer of sand in the story of planet Earth. She'd sat on these rocks when everything fell apart the summer after high school, even fantasizing about the fast and easy end that might come with a simple slip or jump. She'd returned following every miscarriage, begging the universe for a respite from the pain.

The last time Ginny had brought the kids here, Mikey had said the rocks were like Jurassic versions of the drip castles he made with wet sand at the beach. Lyla had said the treetops looked like a forest of broccoli. That had been a great day. They'd shared their adventure with Simon later that night, and she'd expected praise for the educational outing, a day free of technology, but he'd chastised her for taking them to the Garden. A woman had died a couple of years earlier after falling off one of the rocks, and a couple of years before that, a boy Mikey's age had died as well.

"It's a magical place, Simon," she'd pleaded. "We can't protect them so much that they miss out on adventures. And we were careful."

"We were, Dad," Mikey insisted. "It was awesome."

Simon's silent stare told her the discussion needed to end. His job was to lead, her job was to follow, and conflict in front of the kids was forbidden. "Next time just check with me first."

The first time Simon had used that word—*forbidden*—she'd called her mom to vent. But Bonnie had backed Simon. "Kids need a united front," she'd said, "and you can't battle for power. The key to a good marriage is for your husband to believe he has the power." And then she'd giggled. "It's a dance."

So Ginny didn't argue with Simon about going to the Garden. She'd simply kept it a secret next time she took the kids there. She'd given up nursing to please him, she'd learned to hold her tongue, to submit on demand, but she couldn't stop going there.

The vodka softened the edges, and she leaned back on her arms, conjuring another visit, some twenty years earlier. It was late April of senior year. She'd been so excited to leave Eden by then. She was going to get as far from this town as possible. It had been a perfect night, at least until Eddie Wilson and his friends showed up, high on pills and acting like rabid dogs, taking the peace of that moment and violently ripping it away.

She never told anyone what Eddie did that night. The sheriff was her dad's best friend. Eddie was his son. And Eddie knew her secrets. That was the beginning of the end, she realized, as one terrifying moment had been followed by another, and another, like dominoes toppling, until her dreams of escaping her town had ended forever.

Ginny raised the flask to her mouth, stopping to examine her raw and swollen fingernails, a habit started back in high school. It had been a point of contention with her mom, who used to grab her hands and frown. "Ginny, no one wants to kiss the hand of a wild animal." *If only Mom had been right,* she thought. Pastor Gary always kissed her hand when she went to his office. It was part of the ritual. First, he'd place a drink in her grip, and once the glass was empty, he'd take it from her, kiss her hand, and move on from there.

And Simon thought seeing Pastor Gary would help her stop drinking. What a joke. The whiskey on the pastor's breath was the first thing she noticed when she got under his umbrella earlier today. After going to his office, she'd explained what happened on Mother's Day and he'd told her not to worry, saying she'd done the right thing. He said she didn't need to feel guilty, that everything would be okay and that God worked in mysterious ways. The poison allowed her to believe it.

But nothing would be okay, ever again. She'd heard "the truth will set you free" a million times in church, but it wasn't true. The truth would destroy them all. She imagined the day Darius's movie would premiere at the only theater in the area, fifteen miles away. The whole town would probably go. She imagined the whispers, the stories, the gossip that would spread from everyone who saw it. She sat up and crawled toward the ledge. The vodka made her feel wobbly, and she collapsed onto her stomach, inching herself forward until only her head dangled over the cliff. She couldn't see past the treetops below. Would they stop a body, catching it like some rough nest, or would someone simply crack branches and break bones the whole way down? She took her bottle, half-empty now, and opened her grasp, watching it fall, waiting, listening.

Death would be painful, she realized, but swift.

~ • ~

Brooklyn sat at her father's orderly and sparse desk, opening drawers. The top drawer revealed neatly stacked blank paper, unused pencils bound in one rubber band, and ballpoint pens bound in another, each pen cap facing the same direction. Finally, a sign of the military man she knew and loved. She opened a side drawer and found more neatly stacked papers, Post-its, paper clips. She wasn't even sure what she was looking for.

She sat back, her focus on that La-Z-Boy in the corner. Her whole life, Brooklyn had never headed to bed without finding her dad at this desk or sitting in that chair. The study door was always open. "Open doors, open hearts," her parents would say. Of course, by high school, the open-door policy simply felt like a refusal to give Brooklyn any privacy. And for a house of open doors, why did it feel like she was suddenly drowning in secrets?

She swiveled her chair toward the metal file cabinet. The drawer revealed alphabetically organized files: bank statements, car, church, health insurance, homeowner's insurance, kids, life insurance, mortgage, utilities. She had to laugh as she pulled out the file labeled "Kids." Seemed a bit vague.

Inside, the top sheet of paper was Brooklyn's acceptance to college. Her heart sank. It meant so much to her dad. She'd gone to school to act, and the theater department in Boston was fine, but once she'd experienced New York City, it was hard to return.

But then again, Dad had never gone to college. Mom either.

Behind the letter was a stack of Brooklyn's report cards. Not exactly worth saving. Behind those was Ginny's college acceptance letter—to Columbia University's nursing school. But Ginny had never gone to Columbia. She'd attended a community college at some point, but as far as Brooklyn knew, Ginny had never ventured beyond the borders of Illinois.

Behind Ginny's college acceptance letter were her report cards— A's, across the board. Every year. And a certificate indicating that she was a National Merit Scholar.

It was so strange. The passing comments about Ginny "finally getting her act together" over the years suddenly seemed at odds with the evidence in the file. She hadn't just been a good student, she had been at the top of her class and had gotten into a really good school. Why hadn't she attended? Brooklyn lifted the certificate and found another. This one was from their church, a certificate of achievement: youth group leader. The youth group was the pride of First Hope. They organized food and clothing drives and met on Wednesday nights for Bible study. The girls in the group had to pledge chastity in some awkward ceremony that involved their fathers.

Brooklyn had been sure her parents would make her join the teen group. First Hope was the center of their life. But Brooklyn didn't belong there. She'd known it for a long time. People looked at her as an oddity, an outsider despite having grown up in the church.

She was about nine or ten the first time she noticed the looks. She overheard some women a few rows behind them say something about how "those Andersons are saints." It seemed like a nice thing to say, and her ears perked up. But then one of the women whispered, "But you know Bonnie was so desperate for another child." She didn't see their faces, but something about the comment told Brooklyn she should feel lucky.

For years, she and the other kids were shooed off to Sunday school during the most boring parts of the service. She no longer remembered much about those hours, but she always remembered the Sunday before Christmas when she was eleven, sitting on the floor in a circle of kids, discussing the night Baby Jesus was born. The teacher was asking each of them to help provide details of Mary and Joseph's journey and struggles, what it was like in the stable, and who visited the couple and their new baby that night. Everyone was shouting out details, and someone said it sounded like a barn, with its dirt floor. That's when one girl said, "Just like Brooklyn." Everyone, including Brooklyn, turned to the girl, who looked at the teacher, suddenly embarrassed. "I heard she was born in a barn with a dirt floor." No one said anything else, and the girl looked at Brooklyn for confirmation. "Right?"

Brooklyn said nothing.

"At the orphanage . . . ," the girl continued. "My mom said . . ."

"Ew," a boy chimed in. "You're like a farm animal!"

Several of the others snickered, and the teacher said, "That's enough. Let's not get sidetracked."

The next week, when the kids were dismissed for Sunday school, Brooklyn stayed in the pew. "Go on," her mom nudged.

"I'd like to hear the sermon," Brooklyn whispered. "Sunday school is for little kids."

Mom smiled and took her hand. "My baby's growing up."

So when Brooklyn turned thirteen and Pastor Neil suggested she join the teen group, she'd expected a dinner discussion that evening. But after he walked away, her mom had leaned over and said, "You don't have to do it, baby." It almost seemed like Mom understood what Brooklyn could never say. "Pastor Gary," her mom continued, "used to be in charge. He left when you were about seven. Now, he was great, and the kids loved him. And so handsome," she added with a wink. "Dimples, dirty-blond. Just a cutie."

Brooklyn smiled and nodded, relieved that there would be no further discussion. Pastor Neil was a creep, always putting his hands on Brooklyn's shoulders when he talked to her mom about how important it was to stay on the righteous path and avoid the devil's temptations. It didn't help that his hair receded in a way that gave him a Dracula-like widow's peak.

Her salvation wasn't going to be that church. The best escape for her had turned out to be acting—spending hours every day pretending to be someone or somewhere else.

But Ginny had been one of those girls—a leader, even. And yet she'd never gone to church with Brooklyn and their parents when she visited for Easter and Christmas. She'd never said a negative word about the church, but by the time Brooklyn was twelve, she'd noticed Ginny's rejection of it.

And now, to see that she'd once been so involved, such an achiever—it was impossible not to think something had happened that threw her life off course.

Brooklyn thought about Dad's comment that first night at the hospital. He forgave Ginny. And he'd never tell. What did she do? And if it was something that happened years ago, why would it be on his mind? Was it possible that he *had* called Ginny home on Sunday, like she said, that they'd been talking about the past when he fell? Was that why she was lying?

None of it made sense.

The swirl of questions was exhausting. Brooklyn switched off the desk lamp and started for the door. The dark room was now bathed in light from the stairwell in the hall, and something glimmered at the end of the shelf by the wall, drawing her attention. Dad's gun safe. The little steel-plated door was half-open. She stepped toward it, like a little kid drawn to an opened treasure chest. She'd never seen it open. She pulled back on the open door. It was empty.

CHAPTER THIRTEEN

DAY SEVEN
8:20 p.m.
BOLINE COUNTY JAIL

BROOKLYN LAY ON HER MATTRESS, examining the outlines of water spots on the ceiling, fighting back her mind's masochistic desire to replay her day in painful detail. If she let herself go there, she'd start to scream and never stop. Getting out of here was the only thing she could focus on. Only the descending darkness outside that tiny window let her know that about an hour had passed. And no one had come for her.

The door at the end of the hall opened again, echoing down the otherwise silent corridor. It was the only sound that gave Brooklyn some hope that this nightmare might soon end. But the man in the cell beside her, who'd briefly given up on trying to make conversation, spoke up quickly.

"Dinnertime," he said.

He was right. After the guard delivered the trays and left, Brooklyn stared down at the shriveled peas alongside a mysterious meat patty covered in a beige sauce.

"I know what you're thinkin'," her neighbor said, "but I've actually seen worse."

Brooklyn put the tray on the ground and returned to her bed.

"Come on, man," he said. "Gotta talk over dinner at least, right?"

Brooklyn remained silent.

"How 'bout a little gossip? You know Darius Woods, the actor?"

Brooklyn looked at the wall between them.

"Still not talkin', huh? You must know who that is, right? He got an Oscar nomination in January? Went to Eden High? He's over at Burns Memorial right now. Shot in the back. National news. You must have heard."

She opened her mouth, unsure if she should say anything.

"I just wondered if you knew how he was doing. He's the reason I'm in here."

"What do you mean?"

"Holy crap. Sorry, I just assumed you were a man. What's your name?"

"Why did you say that about Darius Woods?" Brooklyn asked, ignoring his question.

"Why, you know him?"

"No."

"Well, it's all BS. They can't pin anything on me. Not that I don't wish him dead. That crap nugget almost killed me once. It's been twenty years, but every time it rains, I get shoulder pain that reminds me of that guy. Amazing how Hollywood celebrities are all assumed to be great people. They don't know Darius Woods."

Brooklyn sat up and gripped the edge of the mattress beneath her. Shoulder pain. Twenty years ago. She knew who was in the cell beside her. She was glad for the thick wall between them.

"So what did you do, anyway?" the man asked.

"Nothing," she said barely above a whisper.

The man laughed. "Exactly. I'll rephrase. What do they think you did?"

"They think I killed my father." The word *they* caught in her throat. What if everyone believed it? She needed a story. A way to explain what happened.

CHAPTER FOURTEEN

DAY THREE
Wednesday, May 15

ON WEDNESDAY MORNING, GINNY WOKE at eight, struck by a torturous headache. She rolled over to the empty space beside her in the bed, vaguely recalling a text from Simon the night before. Something about needing to get to the hospital early for surgery, which meant she needed to drive the kids to school, a task he usually handled on his way to work. School started at eight. She sat up abruptly, wincing from the sudden movement, threw the covers back, and raced down the hall to wake the kids. They usually pounced on top of her if she slept through the alarm. They must have both overslept as well. She didn't need Simon hearing about how the kids were late because of her.

Mikey's room was empty. She raced down the hall. Lyla's bed was piled high with stuffed animals. They were gone. She called their names. Nothing. She ran down the stairs to the kitchen. Remnants of breakfast—half-empty cereal bowls, banana peels, and a smattering of Cheerios—sat atop the kitchen table along with a note: *Couldn't wake you. I got kids off to school and had to cancel a surgery. Thanks. Simon.*

She collapsed into the chair. Another failure. She didn't think she'd had that much to drink, but the evening felt hazy. She remembered putting them to bed. She'd read Lyla a story. She must have fallen asleep before Simon got home.

Ginny slowly went back upstairs, got dressed, and made all the beds. She propped Lyla's favorite bunny on her pillow and scooped up Mikey's Legos into a bin, inspecting both rooms before heading downstairs, determined to clean up her life. Again. She'd turned to alcohol for four straight days. Thirteen years of sobriety out the window. But it wasn't helping. It was making everything worse.

She rinsed the cereal bowls, wiped the kitchen table, and made coffee.

The doorbell rang.

Peering out the living room window at a police car in the driveway, the pain in her head instantly spread down into her neck and shoulders. Her stomach began to burn from anxiety. When she opened the front door, Sherriff Wilson was there.

"Hey, Sheriff," she said, attempting nonchalance, despite knowing he'd driven thirty miles from Eden to see her. "What brings you out here?" She needed to appear oblivious.

"Can I come in, Ginny?"

"Of course. You want some coffee?"

"That would be great."

The kitchen fell silent while she poured him a cup and filled her own mug before joining him at the table. He seemed entirely too comfortable with the silence. "So how are your kids?" she finally asked.

"Maggie and Rick are busy with their families. They're doing great. Eddie is struggling a bit. He's living with me now."

"I'm sorry. He was always a nice kid." She didn't know what else to say. The sheriff had no idea what had happened between them that night at the Garden. She'd never spoken to Eddie again. "Please tell him I say hello."

"I'll do that, Ginny. He's always had such a crush on you. I'm sure that'll make his day." The sheriff took another sip.

Ginny couldn't handle the suspense. "I'm worried about my dad," she blurted.

"He's a tough old bird. I'm sure he'll be fine. Unfortunately, he's not the first friend to break a hip."

"It's not that," she continued. "He gets confused a lot. I think he has dementia."

The lines between his eyebrows deepened as he considered it. "I was with him on Sunday at the store. Had coffee together. Seemed fine to me."

She sipped her coffee. The sheriff saw her dad far more than she did. How could she convince him that his mind was going?

Finally, Sheriff Wilson put down his mug and sat back. "There's been a development, and I thought it better if you and I discuss it here."

Here we go. "Okay," she said softly, before taking a sip of her coffee.

"Ginny, I've known you since you were just a little girl, and even though I'm an officer of the law, I want you to know that, if I can, I will help you any way possible, okay?"

She said nothing.

"You remember Darius Woods?"

"The actor? Sure, he went to high school with us." And then, before she could stop herself, she added, "But I barely knew him." She took another sip, instantly regretting the comment . . . it was a lie too easy to unravel. Even her Facebook account would confirm their connection.

"But you were on crew in the drama department, weren't you?"

"Yeah."

"So you knew him," he said, nodding his head as if he already knew the rest.

She kept her eyes on the coffee. "Sure, I mean, obviously we're acquaintances."

"Do you know where he lived back in high school?"

"I mean, generally, probably. I don't know if I could point out his house or anything."

"Do you know why Woods is in town?"

She hesitated, but the secret was out. "Brooklyn met his dad at the hospital yesterday. He said Darius is going to make a movie set in Eden."

"That's right," the sheriff said. "Have you read the screenplay?"

She took a sip before answering, wondering if it was possible that he knew she'd gotten a copy. But he couldn't, could he? Unless . . . She shook her head before any words came out. She couldn't do it. "Of course not," she said. "Why would I?"

"Just curious," the sheriff said. "A copy of that screenplay is coming my way. I thought you might want to talk to me before this goes too far."

Darius had changed names in the script, but there was no doubt that the sheriff would figure it out once he read the story. Ginny's thoughts turned to the .38 hidden upstairs in her closet.

"Ginny, someone saw a woman outside Woods's house the other night."

Her gaze moved from the coffee to the sheriff. "What are you talking about?"

"The night he was shot . . ."

"I wasn't—"

"Just stop for a second. Before you say anything, let me tell you what we know, okay? Woods was shot with a .38. The neighbor didn't have a full license plate, but the last four digits match yours. She was pretty sure the person in the car was female—a blonde. We know you were in Eden that night because you were the one who got your dad to the hospital, right?"

"What in the world are you suggesting?"

"Your husband has a registration for a .38 Special, and I can vividly recall your blue ribbon at the fair twenty-odd years ago . . . the first girl to win that gun-range contest, with her dad's .38."

"You think I shot him?"

"I'm not saying anything yet, but this feels a little familiar, doesn't it?"

Ginny didn't say a word, trying to take in the stacking innuendo, the reference to events of two decades ago that had nearly destroyed her. The sheriff remained quiet as well, as if the weight of silence between them would break her.

"I can't believe you're doing this," she finally said. "I was never even charged with a crime."

"Thanks to that pastor," Sheriff Wilson said. "A little tough for the FBI to build a case against a teen when the entire church leadership is willing to testify about her being at church at the time. But you and I both know you were there. Maybe Woods knew that too."

Ginny said nothing.

"Your dad is one of my closest friends, Ginny. I don't want to build a case against his child. But suddenly there's reason to believe you were at the scene. I don't have much else to work with, and if Woods dies, this will be a homicide investigation and I'm only going to be the sheriff for a few more days. You need to tell me what's going on."

Ginny held her cup in both hands, watching to be sure they remained steady as she sipped her coffee and replayed the details of her drive to Darius's house in the downpour, trying to calculate, for the thirtieth time, how the chips would fall when the truth came out.

"Have you even asked Darius what happened?" she asked. "Did he see anything?"

"Don't know yet. If he pulls through, you can bet I'll ask him."

She couldn't speak. Someone seeing her on Darius's street couldn't be determinative, could it? It's not like someone saw her holding a gun. There were other reasons she might have been there—though in that moment, she couldn't imagine a single explanation that would help the situation.

She set her mug on the table. "I didn't do anything."

Before the sheriff could reply, she stood and walked to the hall closet and grabbed the lockbox on the high shelf. "Here," she said, returning and setting the box on the table. "Simon's .38. Take it, test it, whatever. I can't imagine why you'd think I would want to hurt Darius Woods, but you're wrong. I have never touched this gun. I went to check on my dad on Sunday night. It was Mother's Day. I was worried about him. When I got there, he was unconscious, and I got him to the hospital. That's it."

"I'm sure your dad would say the same."

"Then what are you doing here?"

"We both know your dad would do anything for his kids."

"That's true of all parents, don't you think?" Ginny had done vile things, but her children had always been at the root of every rationale.

"Maybe. Anyway, he might be one of my favorite people, but I know that in John Anderson's world, his allegiance is to his own moral code regardless of what we might read in our law books. It's a debate we've had many times." The sheriff then put his hand on the box. "Thanks for this."

She stepped back. "Sheriff, I don't mean to be rude, but I've got a thousand things I have to do this morning." The sheriff took her cue and stood as well.

"Please, take Simon's gun. And here . . ." She dumped her coffee in the sink, dropped the mug in a Ziploc, and handed it over. "For prints. Do whatever you need to do, but you've got it wrong if you think I shot anyone."

The sheriff thanked her and left. As soon as his car was out of the driveway, she got the Chardonnay out of the fridge.

Her hand was still shaking as she lifted the glass to her lips.

~ • ~

Brooklyn woke early to the chirping birds in the sugar maple, a sound so unlike the beeping trash truck that usually woke her in New York. She looked up at the poster of the Brooklyn Bridge and the New York skyline hanging above her bed—the wildest, busiest, loudest, oddest, and most exciting place she'd ever been—it felt so far away.

She cleaned the kitchen and vacuumed the first floor, determined to get this house ready for her dad's return, as if wishful thinking was all that was needed.

After a quick shower, she went to the hospital and texted Ginny, hoping to meet and finally get some answers. She'd tossed and turned all night, wondering what had happened around the year Ginny graduated high school that had derailed her life. Something had happened, she was sure. It was bad enough that Dad's comments suggested a secret between them, but Ginny's explanation of Sunday night wasn't adding up. Brooklyn had even shot off a blunt text before the sun rose asking what happened to their dad's gun. Ginny still hadn't answered.

When she arrived at her dad's room at the hospital, he was sitting taller and appeared better. He asked about New York and talked about getting out. He seemed okay and left moments later for physical therapy. Brooklyn stayed behind in his room imagining outlandish scenarios to explain Ginny's change from good girl to troubled mess, wondering if Dad would finally provide some answers now that he seemed more clearheaded. She then sought out the appropriate social worker to determine her dad's next steps. The woman was available to meet within the hour, and Brooklyn texted Ginny again—they should be handling this together—but she got no response.

The social worker offered a lot of information, and yet Brooklyn left her office without learning anything. She'd received a large folder filled with pamphlets—about hip breaks, dementia, making the decision between nursing home care and other options, how to care for an elderly patient, how to find in-home care, where to look for financial assistance. Lots of phone numbers and websites. Brooklyn wasn't sure which questions to ask, and she didn't have any answers when the social worker asked her own questions. She needed Ginny.

When she returned to her dad's room, he was asleep, but she pulled up a chair, determined to wait patiently and finally get some answers. After the nurse brought in some food and woke him, Brooklyn tried to make conversation, but he grumbled, scoffed at the soft food, and soon fell back asleep. After another hour, she finally asked Wanda if he seemed okay. Wanda just patted Brooklyn's shoulder. Therapy was exhausting, she explained, for the body and the brain. Sleep was the best thing for him.

At six o'clock, Brooklyn finally went home, determined to find answers with or without Ginny or her dad. She stood in the doorway of her parents' bedroom—the one room that felt like their private domain. The bed was made, and the nightstands on both sides of the bed were loaded with magazines, water glasses, readers, as if two people still shared the space.

She didn't know where to begin or what she was looking for. She got on the floor, lifted the bed ruffle, and spotted Dad's shotgun. He was like every other gun nut in town. He'd offered to take Brooklyn to the range every year since she was nine, but she never wanted to go. He said handling a gun was a survival skill, like swimming, pointing out that he'd even taught Bonnie to shoot back when they first married, and that Ginny knew all about guns too. She'd been able to take out a coyote since she was fourteen, he boasted. Brooklyn always refused.

She'd been at a friend's house once—she was six or seven at the time, she couldn't remember—but they were using chalk to draw flowers on the porch floorboards when the girl's dad suddenly came outside, rifle in hand, and told the girls not to move. Before they'd even had time to react, he'd pointed the gun toward the woods' edge. Brooklyn and her friend had followed the barrel of the gun to see a deer grazing in the distance as the shot exploded. The deer fell slowly, its front legs buckling, then its back, as it collapsed to the ground. The girl's dad had yelled triumphantly. Brooklyn was stunned to silence, but her friend screamed and began bawling as she ran into the house. He'd looked at Brooklyn and said, "They're a menace. Eatin' all my brambles." Brooklyn didn't know what that meant but didn't ask. She just knew it scared her to death and she never wanted to be around guns or people with guns and was grateful that her dad confined his firing habits to the range.

At one point, Dad had told Brooklyn she couldn't drive if she didn't learn to handle a gun. It was one of the few times his rules brought her to tears.

"You wouldn't do that," she said, eyes pleading.

"We keep a gun in the glove box of the truck and Mom's car—it's just good safety—you need to know."

"Just take it out of Mom's car. I'll never drive the truck."

"Seems a little unnecessary, John," Mom had said in her defense. "I've never needed it."

"I've got pepper spray," Brooklyn had added with a smile. "Picked it up at the store."

He'd huffed but let it go.

Now she got off the floor and sat on the bed, facing the open closet. Her dad had made no effort to clear out any of her mom's things. It had to be tough for him to face it every day, and besides, Mom had practically made a career of organizing clothing drives at the church. It was time.

After piling all the clothes on the bed, separating the few items that she'd keep, she stepped back into the closet. Shoeboxes lined the floor, and the first several she opened revealed shoes that had probably not been worn in thirty years. A few were so outdated, they might even be a good donation to the vintage shop down the street from her New York apartment. But the last box in the closet felt light. She opened it to find a mess of newspaper clippings.

Brooklyn sat on the closet floor and pulled out the first article. It was from the *Eden Journal*, dated May 13, 1999: LOCAL DOCTOR IN HOSPITAL AFTER SHOOTING. Another clipping, a *Washington Post* article, dated just a few days later, was headlined SHOOTING AT ILLINOIS WOMEN'S CLINIC SPARKS OUTRAGE. She read on. *Abortion-rights activists are concerned by the uptick in deadly attacks against abortion providers in the Midwest . . .* The photograph of the clinic included its address on Hummingbird Boulevard in the neighboring town. She knew that address, but it was the location of a Walmart and some outlet shops.

And then Brooklyn's breath caught as she read another clipped article from the local paper. An unnamed local teen had been extensively questioned but had been cleared as a suspect after several community leaders came forward in her defense. *Her.* The suspect was a girl. An eyewitness had described a car leaving the scene that matched the teen's car, she'd been absent from school on the morning in question, and the teen had been involved in several protests at the clinic since its opening a year earlier. According to the article, the leaders of the First Hope Baptist Church had provided an alibi, clearing the girl of all suspicion. No other "persons of interest" had been revealed by the FBI, which was running the investigation.

Brooklyn's church. She recalled a sermon her senior year, during which the pastor had outrageously compared abortion doctors to Hitler. But when she'd looked at her mom in that moment, her mom's eyes were closed, her head nodding at the pastor's words. She knew her mom was strongly pro-life—Brooklyn had spent her entire childhood playing among the six rosebushes planted in memory of her mom's unborn children in the backyard.

She'd asked her mom once if she'd ever tried fertility treatments, but her mom had scoffed. "Only God opens and closes the womb," she'd said, "and he certainly doesn't believe in monkeying around inside a woman's body." But Brooklyn knew how much her mom loved children, how much she'd longed for a house full of them. She'd volunteered in the NICU at Burns Memorial for as long as Brooklyn could remember, sitting for hours, cradling the tiny babies whose biggest need beyond the hospital's technology was for human touch. Her mom always said that everything happened for a reason, and if she'd had a house full of children, maybe she wouldn't have been able to go on mission trips for all those years, helping others; maybe she wouldn't have been able to adopt Brooklyn. "And you have been such a gift," she'd say with a broad smile. It was hard for Brooklyn to find fault in that. Her mother had a huge heart.

Abortion was a gray topic for Brooklyn, despite being adopted. She always felt like those decisions were personal and couldn't imagine getting mixed up in those debates, but Ginny had been the leader of that teen group. They were the young voices of the church's strong antiabortion beliefs. Even when Brooklyn was in high school, she knew those youth group kids got vocal about elections—whether local or national—promoting and protesting candidates and picketing businesses that offended the church's sensibilities.

Was it possible that Ginny had been involved in that shooting? May 1999. Ginny was a senior. What if the suspicion cast in her direction was enough to derail her college plans? Could she have actually shot a man?

It had to be her. Why else would their mom have these articles? Did that mean the church leaders lied to protect Ginny? Or, an even worse thought, what if the church leaders had put her up to it? It was so outlandish, so impossible to imagine that any church might condone such violence, that she shook off the thought as simply her flair for melodrama creeping forward again.

But something her dad had once said made her linger on the idea. It was summer, right after Brooklyn's junior year, and she'd remarked at dinner about the horrifying Orlando shooting that had happened the week before, marveling aloud about how anyone could commit a crime like murder without a second thought for the innocent victims. Her dad found none of it surprising. He'd said when someone's ideology was under attack, when that person believes in the righteousness of his actions, and his entire belief system supports it, it doesn't matter what the law says. To that person, it's a moral war, and every war has casualties.

"I just think that unless you're a psychopath, it would be impossible to live with what you'd done. It's probably why so many shooters kill themselves."

"Nonsense. They kill themselves to avoid prosecution. Simple. Not everyone suffers over the violence they've committed. Look at me. I received the highest military honor for blowing up an entire platoon."

It was a shocking admission, delivered so casually. Her dad never talked about Vietnam, and though she'd seen his Medal of Honor and she'd heard adults in town refer to him as a war hero, it was hard to think of him as being capable of killing someone. She looked at his permanently raised eyebrow, frozen from the nerve damage caused by shrapnel, wondering if she would be capable of killing without regret or torment, given the right circumstances. "Did you ever have nightmares? I've heard that a lot of vets have PTSD."

He shook his head and offered a reassuring smile. "First of all, it's been more than forty years. Besides, I am a man of God. I've never acted without justification, and I'm okay with what I've done. I sleep just fine."

"And thanks to men like your father, we can all sleep a little easier," her mother offered. Brooklyn thought that was a stretch. She didn't know much about Vietnam, but nothing about the world of 2016 made her feel safe.

Brooklyn leaned back against the doorjamb, still sitting on that closet floor, and thought again of the possibilities. Her church was extremely pro-life, that had always been clear. Ginny had led the youth group that staged multiple protests at this clinic, and the doctor had been shot by a teen.

Maybe that was why Ginny fell apart. She watched a man fall to the ground, realizing in that moment that she might have killed another person. What if she'd struggled with what she'd done . . . protected by her parents and her church from the consequences, but never able to live with herself? It could have led to drinking, to her failure to go off to school as planned.

Her dad's comments that first night in the hospital when he thought Brooklyn was Ginny replayed in her head. He'd said he forgave her. "And I always protect my family." Was that the secret? And if so, what was it about Sunday night that would have brought all that up?

CHAPTER FIFTEEN

ANOTHER DAY, ANOTHER FAILURE. GINNY had sat at the kitchen table after the sheriff left, drinking until the wine was swimming in her blood. He'd managed to derail her hopes of a better day with that one comment: ". . . feels a little familiar, doesn't it?" That May morning of twenty years before rushed forward like a speeding train, and suddenly every detail of that day—and all the days that followed—plowed over her in crushing detail. Sitting in that empty clinic parking lot five miles outside town, having slid down in the driver's seat so no one could see her, her plans and dreams suddenly suspended in midair. She'd wondered if everything was about to fall apart.

And of course, everything did.

By ten o'clock that night, Simon still wasn't home, so Ginny finally put the food she'd plated for him back in the fridge, turned off the lights, and headed upstairs with an empty glass and a near-empty bottle of wine, pausing every few feet to examine the photographs on the wall. The kids' beautiful freckled faces were everywhere, their smiles lighting her way. She and Simon were only featured above the first step—their wedding day. She never wanted to be in pictures. It was too difficult to look at herself.

She looked in on the kids, their blissfully unaware faces. Maybe Sheriff Wilson's test of Simon's gun would end his suspicions. Maybe if Darius survived, he'd give up on this movie project. Maybe this would all just go away.

"Mama," Lyla whispered, her eyes suddenly open and looking at Ginny in the doorway.

"Hey, baby," Ginny whispered, stepping closer. "Back to sleep. It's late."

"Where's Daddy?" she asked.

"He's not home yet. He'll kiss you when he gets here."

Lyla closed her eyes, satisfied. "Love you, Mama," she whispered.

"You too, baby," Ginny replied, leaning over and kissing her forehead. "Night, night."

She walked down the long hall lined with the kids' artwork—her favorite pieces from every year in school—and got undressed for bed.

Pouring the remaining wine in her glass, she put the empty bottle in her drawer, another attempt to hide evidence.

But the truth was coming, like a storm she couldn't outrun. Brooklyn was trying too hard to understand what happened. She'd even texted earlier about Dad's missing gun. Ginny's fingers had hovered over the phone screen, desperate to craft a reply that would end the inquiry, but she couldn't think of anything to say. John was muttering about forgiveness and protecting his family. Sheriff Wilson was already suspicious, and he was going to read that screenplay. What if Brooklyn said something to Sheriff Wilson about the gun? Ginny needed to put it back without Brooklyn hovering, watching every move. But she didn't trust Ginny, and why would she?

Tomorrow, she thought, *I'll have to make Brooklyn see that I'm not the enemy.*

Ginny crawled into bed and loaded Facebook on her phone. When Simon first learned that she'd signed up for the social site, he'd accused her of cheating. He didn't approve of social media, and the stories he heard backed up his concerns. The only way to end his sermons had been to pretend she quit. Instead, she just deleted the app after each use. The information never went anywhere—hovering in some abyss she never understood.

After the Facebook app had loaded, she found her password in the back of her notebook among the long list of passwords she could never keep straight, signed on, and saw a new message. It was from Darius. She couldn't breathe.

> Hey, I don't know if you heard, but I'm in the hospital. Burns Mem. I'm okay. Guess Eden isn't as safe as it used to be. Hoping you might come by and see me. I'm really curious about your reaction to the screenplay.

Her stomach churned painfully. Acid began to rise, but she swallowed hard. She didn't deserve to feel better.

Darius, though, was well enough to be on his phone, joking like his old self, downplaying his near-fatal shooting. Which meant he was probably well enough to talk to Sheriff Wilson.

He was going to survive. And he was going to make his movie. She scanned the trail of messages between them.

That first contact on Facebook, back in 2012, had been such a harmless reconnection. Just a simple hello. He said it looked like she had a beautiful family, and he was glad to see she'd become a nurse, as she'd always planned. She said nothing about quitting and instead replied that he, too, seemed to be following his dream and doing well. She wished him continued success, and neither followed up. She just watched from afar as his star rose from magazine covers to the Oscars.

But last week he wrote again. And the words on the screen wiped out thirteen sober years in a flash.

> I wrote a screenplay . . . Finally, I got the green light
> . . . I don't want to cause any trouble for you, but it's

kind of impossible to talk about my life there without talking about everything that happened. I've changed names. It's not going to be marketed as a "true story"—will only be "inspired by . . ." so please don't worry. It has been 20 years at this point, so . . . anyway, I've attached a copy. Thought you might want to read it. I'll be arriving in town on Saturday. If you'd like to see me and talk, I'd be glad to.

She'd read the script now too many times to count. Every mistake, secret, lie, and regret . . . it was all there. He had no idea that he'd written something with the power of a grenade that could destroy two homes.

She thought about her children, soundly asleep down the hall, oblivious to the lies that filled their home, secure and happy despite the secrets inside these walls. And it would all end.

Everyone would learn the truth. Simon would never forgive her. He'd abandon them. Then she really would have failed everyone she'd ever loved.

Her thoughts returned to a day thirteen years earlier when Simon told her to go to church and pray. She should have paid more attention to the darkening sky, the warning in the strong spring winds that whipped her hair into her eyes.

She'd just wanted to keep her husband. But she was going to lose him, that much had been obvious. He'd sought a young bride to fill his house with children. She'd wanted them too. Babies would fill her up with love and push out the dark things she'd done. But she couldn't hold on to a pregnancy—just like her mother. Three miscarriages in the first two and a half years of marriage. She was sure they were punishment for what she'd done at seventeen. Simon began pulling away. He probably felt his own biological clock ticking as he neared forty, impatient to get what he wanted.

He'd said God would make it happen if she was worthy. But something compelled a stop to that liquor store first, ending her four years of sobriety in an instant. Only after she'd numbed the pain did she follow Simon's instructions.

She'd been sitting in a pew, crying in the middle of the day, wondering if she should let him go. Maybe she was being selfish. She'd always been selfish—if she wasn't, she wouldn't have made the choices, told the lies, kept the secrets she had. Simon had no idea what kind of girl he'd married. She was silently begging for guidance when Pastor Gary appeared.

Seeing him walking toward her in church that day was almost like a dream. Or a nightmare. She wasn't in Eden. She'd moved to Harrisburg years before and avoided ever setting foot inside First Hope after high school. She'd never wanted to see him again. But he was standing at the end of her pew, smiling like an old friend.

"Ginny?"

She said nothing. He'd always stunned her to silence.

"I just transferred here a couple of weeks ago. What a small world." He sat on the pew, a few feet between them. She couldn't contain the tears.

"What is going on?" he asked, his voice low, his tone dripping with sincerity. She shook her head, unable to speak, and he slid closer along the smooth bench, putting his arm around her. "There, there," he said. A woman a few rows ahead turned back, a silent suggestion to keep it down. He stood, offering his hand. "Come with me. Let's talk in my office."

She scanned the room before moving. There were maybe five other parishioners, and they'd all stopped their own prayers to watch. She stood and followed.

It was as if all the years just melted away. Sitting on a couch in his office, wiping away tears, watching him bolt the door. He offered her a drink and sat beside her. "Talk to me," he said.

She took it but couldn't look at him. "My husband is going to leave me. I can't have a baby."

"Well, that's not true," he said, with that paternal, all-knowing confidence. "When couples struggle, there's a reason. God always has a reason."

"Simon says barrenness comes from a sinful heart."

He took a sip of scotch and leaned back. She instinctively sat forward. He talked for a long time, but she heard nothing. She downed her drink, holding out her glass for more. Soon after obliging, his hand was on her lower back—a slight rub. It would have been harmless, a comforting gesture if done by a friend. But he was no friend.

"The miracle of life is a mystery, Ginny, but you must never give up."

She took a sip, trying to take comfort in his words.

"Remember when we used to sit like this? All those hours working together?"

It was a ridiculous question. A girl never forgets something like that.

"Maybe it's a sign—you coming here. Me finding you. I always wanted to take care of you, Ginny. You haven't changed a bit," he said, brushing the hair off her shoulder. "I was always so sorry for the way things turned out. I've missed you."

She took another sip.

"I want to help," he added. His hand made clear what would happen next.

She didn't flinch this time, but her heart raced as it had when she was sixteen. She had run from all the reminders of him and the church and everything that had happened. It felt like every decision she'd made since high school had been the wrong one. "Maybe I'm just getting what I deserve," she whispered.

He took her hand, his thumb stroking her skin. "You deserve to be happy, Ginny. I've always wanted what was best for you."

He leaned toward her. Everything about his proximity made her stomach turn, but she didn't resist. In that moment, her alcohol-soaked brain believed that every bad decision, lie, and secret had led her right back to this man's couch. Maybe it was where she was supposed to be.

Ten minutes later someone knocked at the door. "Pastor Gary, they're waiting for you in the choral room," a woman said.

"Coming," he shouted.

He dressed quickly and returned to his desk. "It was so great to see you again, Ginny. Please come back and visit, okay?"

She was numb. "Sure," she said, slipping her spaghetti strap back on her shoulder without looking at him. She'd gone to church and betrayed her vows with a man she hated even more than her father.

"I'm here to help," he said, returning to the couch. He offered a hand, pulled her to standing, and brushed some of her hair away from her face. "You're so beautiful, Ginny." He led her to the door, unbolted the lock. "You're still my favorite girl."

She said nothing.

"I'm going to pray for you," he said. "If your marriage is meant to last, it will. And if you're meant to have a child, you will. Remember, the Lord works in mysterious ways."

She had walked through a downpour, sat in the car, dress soaked, gripping the steering wheel, her knuckles turning white, and cried. Thunder boomed, and she pounded her fist against her head, vowing she would never speak to Pastor Gary again.

But then, a miracle. She was soon pregnant again, and this time, it stuck. Simon stayed, and Mikey arrived—a son—what Simon had wanted most. It seemed like there would be a second chance to make her marriage work. It was impossible not to recall Pastor Gary telling her how the Lord worked mysteriously.

She never wanted it to happen again. Whenever she looked at the pastor at church during the next three years and their eyes met, she'd quickly look away. But God knew something she didn't, because even though she got pregnant four times over the next three years, they never lasted. One night, after attending a BBQ at a neighbor's house, the host announced the impending arrival of another child. Ginny watched Simon's face fall. He didn't touch his food and barely spoke all night.

After putting Mikey to bed, she found Simon, sulking in the dark.

"You have a beautiful boy sleeping in that room," she said, kneeling beside him. "Can't that be enough?" She needed him to take care of them and love them. She and Mikey had nothing else.

"I'm sorry. I'm forty-two years old. I thought this house would have been filled by now. I picked a young girl from a devout home. I thought . . ."

She didn't wait for him to finish. She slowly stood, went to the bedroom, and stood at the balcony door, looking up at the stars that held her secrets. Her plan—to avoid her own darkness by filling a home with light—was failing.

Simon followed and stood beside her, brushing the hair from her face. "I need more."

She looked away.

"You don't take care of yourself. You . . ."

She knew he felt trapped. He didn't believe in divorce, but he wasn't getting the bargain he'd hoped for.

"I'm sorry," she had whispered. She felt guilty for failing, for causing him pain. His needs came first. That was supposed to be her job, her greatest joy—she'd heard it since she was young. But she was angry. She hadn't gotten what she wanted either. She'd been trapped by rules and force-fed this life. She'd run to this house and into his arms to escape, but nothing had worked. And she'd tried to be what he wanted. She'd quit her job. "Maybe we should get tested."

"Nonsense," he said, raising his voice. "You know that's not the way He intended."

It didn't matter that Simon was a doctor. His faith ruled. It was the quality that made her parents happiest. Science was supposed to stay out of these affairs. But Ginny was a nurse. She knew that Simon might be the problem—probably a high yield of abnormal chromosomes in his sperm. After all, she'd only struggled to maintain a pregnancy when he was involved. But that would never be discussed. She knew what had to be done. "I'll try harder," she'd whispered.

And so she had returned to Pastor Gary's office—to that couch—until she found herself pregnant again. After a life of hearing that there was a reason for everything, that God had a plan, she convinced herself God was trying to help. In her heart, she knew it was a deal with the devil. But Simon would stay; Mikey would have a sibling. She was doing what had to be done.

Unfortunately, Mikey had Gary's dirty-blond hair, Lyla had his dimples, and they both had his freckles. When the tiny dots first started appearing on the kids' noses, it felt almost supernatural—the universe warning her that secrets don't stay buried forever. She'd searched Simon's old photo albums, looking for freckles on his parents or siblings, anyone she could point to if he ever began to wonder who they looked like. Darius's movie would end the deception. As soon as Simon learned of her history with the pastor, he'd see what was becoming more obvious with every passing year. The truth was hiding in plain sight.

She wondered what Darius would think of her now. Barely functioning. He thought he'd saved her from Pastor Gary all those years ago. He had no idea that she and Gary were forever connected, that her entire life had evolved into a house of cards, built upon lies and secrets.

She finally typed a quick reply to Darius's message:

I'm glad you're okay. I'll come see you tomorrow.

She tried to imagine walking into his hospital room, facing him after everything she'd done. Would he take one look at her smile and know that it was a facade? Darius was the actor, but she needed to give the performance of a lifetime.

CHAPTER SIXTEEN

DAY FOUR
Thursday, May 16

WHEN BROOKLYN PULLED INTO THE hospital parking lot the next morning, the news trucks were gone. Darius had probably been released. She hoped that was it, rather than the more cynical thought that followed—that some other celebrity tragedy had simply pulled focus. She wondered, too, if she'd ever see Martin again, if she'd ever get to meet Darius.

When she got to her dad's room, she heard him yelling before she even stepped inside. He was cursing at someone. Brooklyn recognized the voice of one of the nurses. She quickly went in, hoping to calm him, but was met with a furious stare as he spit venom in her direction. "Not another one. Get out, all of you. Where's my wife?"

Brooklyn stepped forward. "It's me, Dad, Brooklyn. I'm here."

"Dad?" he scoffed. "Don't play mind games with me. I don't care who you are. I told this one, I'm sick of all of you. Now get out of my room and tell my wife I'm ready to go."

Brooklyn stepped over to the nurse and spoke under her breath. "How long has he been this way?"

"Ever since he woke this morning."

"Maybe I should call my sister, Ginny."

"Ginny?" her dad yelled. "She's the reason I'm in here!"

The nurse put her arm around Brooklyn's shoulders. "Come on," she said, walking her toward the hall. "It's okay."

"What do I do?" Brooklyn asked. "Shouldn't I try to make him understand who I am, and that Mom is gone?"

"Let's just let him rest a bit. The stress of realizing you're confused can put a lot of strain on the body. I'm going to give him a sedative. Perhaps when he wakes again, he'll be doing better."

It felt like yesterday's progress had disappeared. She pulled out her phone and sent Ginny a text: Please come to the hospital. WE HAVE TO TALK! She wanted some answers—like why Ginny never showed up yesterday or even responded to her texts, why she hated their father, why he said he forgave her, what happened to his gun, why their mom had all those clippings from that clinic shooting . . . The questions felt endless. She'd searched the internet last night for information about the clinic shooting but learned nothing. The doctor had survived, the clinic had closed, a Walmart was built within the year.

And her dad had just said Ginny was the reason he was in the hospital. What did that even mean? Did she cause his fall?

Brooklyn's heart raced; her throat began to contract. Suddenly dizzy, she quickly found a seat along the wall and put her head between her legs. If Ginny'd shot a man all those years ago, there was no way to know what she was capable of. Dad was hurt, his gun was missing. What did it all mean?

She looked down at her phone, and three dots began dancing: a reply from Ginny. I'll be there in two hours. I'm sorry about yesterday. And yes to lunch. We need to talk.

~ • ~

It was after ten in the morning when Wilson finally went to the station. It had been a long twenty-four hours. He'd dropped Eddie at the treatment center in Fairfield before visiting Ginny's house yesterday, but twenty minutes after he left her, he'd received a call from the intake counselor. Eddie had disappeared. The man on the line was defensive when Wilson's anger flared. It wasn't a jail. It was voluntary treatment. They couldn't help someone who didn't want to be there. Wilson then spent the entire day trying to find him. All his calls and texts to Eddie were ignored until, finally, around ten that evening, Eddie had sent a text: I'm fine. Back off.

Around two o'clock in the morning, Wilson woke to pee—he never made it all the way through the night anymore—and looked into Eddie's room on his way back to bed. He still wasn't home, and Wilson couldn't do as Eddie asked. His son was in trouble. He could feel it. There was no way to turn off the worry switch. Didn't matter that Eddie was thirty-eight, at the age when he was supposed to do the worrying. He was an addict, and his life had long ago spiraled out of control.

Wilson had driven around town, stopping at the few bars he knew in the area that would be open at that hour, but he didn't find him. He even drove a couple of towns over to an abandoned apartment building known for addict squatters. He'd walked through those halls, stepping over desperate, strung-out bodies, and felt a tiny sense of relief when Eddie wasn't there. But he didn't know how much longer he could do this. He was seventy-two years old. He was starting to wonder if Eddie would die before he did.

Wilson didn't want to give up on his son, but it was obvious that he wasn't helping. He'd arrogantly thought that as a man of law and order, he could control the situation. But that boy had been waging a war in his mind for years that no one else seemed to understand. He'd been impossible to reach since the day his mom had died, maybe before that.

When Wilson returned home a little before four in the morning, Eddie was asleep in his bed. Wilson sat on the edge of the twin bed, brushing the hair from Eddie's face, just like he'd done when he was a little boy. That's when he saw the scrapes on his nose and cheek, his yellow sweatshirt dotted with blood. Probably another bar fight. He was a Jekyll and Hyde, a sweet, soft-spoken boy who cried during emotional movies and flew into bitter rages fueled by resentments and drugs. It was as if his mind were a teakettle sitting on a low flame, always just moments from the shriek.

Wilson went straight to the coffee station before finding Donny in his office. "So you all solve the Woods case yet?"

"Not yet," Donny said.

"Roger get Woods's yearbook from his dad?"

"He didn't have them. The boy took all his stuff when he moved away."

"What about our stalker in LA? She have an alibi?"

"Still working on it."

Wilson wondered if anything would get done after he retired. "Well, what about the screenplay—you read it yet?" he asked, exasperated.

"Never arrived," Donny said.

"What the heck?" He went back to his own desk, found his notes, and called the agent, something Donny should have done yesterday. It was two hours earlier in LA, and no one answered. "Please give me a call first thing," he said in a voice mail message. "We're still waiting for that screenplay. Maybe you wrote down my email wrong." He rattled off the address again before hanging up.

Collapsing into his swivel chair, he turned on the computer and checked his email. The screenplay had finally arrived after midnight. No apology for the delay. "Typical Hollywood," he muttered to Donny. He assumed all those types acted as if they were the center of the universe.

Wilson forwarded a copy to Donny and opened the document. Finally, maybe they'd catch a break. The phone rang, and as soon as Wilson answered, Martin Woods spoke without introduction. "What are you doing about my son's case?"

"Hello, Mr. Woods. We're working on it. How's your son doing this mornin'?"

"Better. He's finally awake. Which is why you need to protect him."

"Mr. Woods, I don't think you have anything to worry about. We've spoken to the hospital staff. No visitors other than you are allowed while we run down some leads."

"You have leads then?"

Wilson couldn't admit that they were no closer than they'd been two days ago. "Nothing I'm ready to share. But trust me, I wanna get this shooter as much as you do."

"I doubt that. And I'm here at the hospital. Nothing would prevent someone from showing up and trying to finish what he started. There should be a guard outside the room. Someone with a gun walked in the front door of the hospital last night."

"What? Rog!" he yelled out the door of his office. Roger was walking by and stopped. "You get a report of a gunman at Burns Memorial last night?"

Roger shook his head while Martin continued to speak in the sheriff's ear. "Security guard told me. I've made a point of getting friendly with the men by the front entrance. Some man walked in with a gun in his hand last night around two in the morning. The guard asked him to stop, man panicked and ran out of the building. They never caught up with him."

"I'll be right over there, Martin. Did the guard tell you anything about the man?"

"Just that he was middle-aged and white. For all I know, that man wanted to come finish off my son."

"I'm on my way. Now that Darius is awake, I can finally talk to him about what he might have seen or heard and anyone he thinks we should consider. I'll be there in thirty minutes."

Wilson hung up, then stood to leave. "Hey, Donny, I just forwarded the email from Woods's agent to you. I can't read on the computer anyway. Make me a printout, okay? How about you do some reading? You're the movie fan, after all. I'll be back in a couple of hours."

~ • ~

Brooklyn's dad was asleep, and she was watching TV with the sound turned low when Ginny arrived. She clicked off the television and stood, ready to battle. But Ginny came at her before she could say a word and wrapped her arms around Brooklyn. "I'm really sorry for how I've treated you," Ginny said, still holding on.

Brooklyn slowly patted her back, unsure how else to react to such uncharacteristic kindness. "It's okay." She wondered if alcohol were involved in this sudden shift, though she didn't smell it and Ginny didn't seem drunk. Just different.

"I'm a terrible sister," Ginny whispered before finally releasing Brooklyn from the embrace.

It felt monumental. Ginny never acted as if they were family at all. Brooklyn smiled and held her hand for a moment longer. "It's been hard on all of us. Mom. Now Dad. I really want to deal with this together, okay?"

Ginny smiled. "You're right."

Nurse Wanda came back in. "Physically, he's doing pretty well, girls," she said. Ginny and Brooklyn remained side by side as the nurse confirmed that Dad's hip was healing appropriately. "But it's time to begin thinking about next steps." She handed them a brochure—the rehab facility the hospital recommended. The doctor would be available for a sit-down later that afternoon to talk more about the details and his recommendations, "but I can tell you," Wanda said, "your dad will most likely be ready to move in another forty-eight hours."

Brooklyn looked over at Ginny for some silent acknowledgment that they'd figure this out together, but Ginny's gaze was fixed on the window.

Wanda glanced up at the clock. "It's almost lunchtime. Maybe you both should grab a bite. The doctor can meet you in his office at two o'clock."

Brooklyn said thanks and headed for the door. Ginny hesitated. "You coming?" Brooklyn asked.

"Yeah, of course," Ginny said.

They got in the elevator, and Ginny stopped the door from closing. "Shoot," she said, jumping out. "I forgot something."

"What?" Brooklyn said, looking quickly for the button that would stop the doors that were already closing.

"I just wanted to ask Wanda something. You go on. Get us a table. I'll be down in just a few minutes."

The doors closed before Brooklyn could argue.

~ • ~

Wilson went directly to the main entrance of the hospital to chat with the security officer on duty about the alleged gunman. The guard said he hadn't been on in the middle of the night, but he pulled out the notes the night guard had made. Wilson took the binder.

"And police weren't called?" he asked the guard.

"Doesn't sound like it. I mean, nothin' happened. You know how it is."

"Actually, I don't. It's illegal to open carry; it's illegal to bring a gun into a hospital. Help me understand why my office wasn't called."

The guard shrugged. "Hey, it wasn't me. But I can see from this log that there were other issues the guard faced last night. We got over four hundred beds."

"Did you talk to the guard about the incident when you got in?"

"Yep. He figured it coulda been a domestic violence situation, some attempt at payback from a fight—could have even been a beef against someone on staff. Or maybe just a random lunatic. What we really need are metal detectors. Just lucky that the moron had the gun out in plain sight."

Wilson nodded in agreement and read the notes from the night guard: *Be on the alert for the following: White male, yellow hooded sweatshirt, maybe 35-50 years old. Spotted at 2:30 a.m. in front of the directory and hospital map by entrance, gun in hand. Guard drew weapon, called out to the man, who turned at the sound, looked down at his own hand—like he'd forgotten he was holding the gun, and took off running. No shots fired. Man ran into the woods at far end of parking lot.*

A yellow sweatshirt. Wilson's pulse quickened. The woods. It would explain the scratches on Eddie's face. Eddie had probably been to the hospital looking for drugs. Wilson couldn't imagine such desperation. That boy was going to end up dead or in jail.

"You got something?" the guard asked.

"Huh? No, no."

"Just looked like you thought of something after you read the notes."

"No. You're right, there are lots of possibilities." He could not spend his last days in office going after his own son. And maybe it wasn't Eddie. It was just a sweatshirt. It could have been a domestic dispute, like the guard thought. Or maybe it was about Woods. Martin Woods was right. Wilson needed to either find Woods's shooter fast or he needed to get him some security.

When he got off the elevator on the fourth floor and walked toward Woods's room, he saw a flurry of activity—nurses running in and out of the room and a doctor rushing through the door. Martin Woods came into the hall then, a hand over his mouth, and leaned against the wall, closing his eyes. A man in pain, or shock. Wilson could feel his own heartbeat quickening, wondering if this case had just become a murder investigation.

"Mr. Woods?" Wilson asked as he neared. "Everything okay?"

Martin Woods looked over, grief-stricken. "Could you pray with me? Pray for my boy?"

"What's happening?"

"He was fine an hour ago. But he got a fever, and it keeps climbing. They think it's another infection."

"Try not to worry," Wilson said. "I'm sure they know what they're doing."

"A man can only take so much," Martin said. He walked the few feet toward a row of chairs against a wall and sat. Wilson followed and sat beside him.

"We was just in there talking a little bit ago. He really seemed better. And then it was like he got so confused. Fever was messin' with him, I guess."

"What did he say? Did you ask about the shooting?"

"Course not."

"Why not?"

"Because he said, 'What happened?' He obviously doesn't know nothin'. I was telling him he should probably just go back to LA. It don't seem like you all are any closer to figuring out who mighta done this, and I don't want him to stay here and be a target."

"Well, actually, we have learned that your son has a stalker back in LA."

"What? Why?"

"Who knows. But he had a restraining order issued against a woman about six months ago. We're finding out more about her now. See if we can confirm where she's been the last few days."

"And you said it was a woman spotted on the street. He asked me if I 'saw her' just now. Like I said, I thought he seemed a little confused. I said, 'Who?' He just smiled and said he'd show me pictures. I didn't know what he was talking about, but he started slurring and I hollered for the nurse."

The doctor came out of Woods's room, and Martin and Wilson turned for his update. "He's asleep now. We'll be watching him closely and keep you posted. Hopefully, we don't have to go back in."

The doctor walked off. Martin dropped his head into his hands.

"You think you done your job when the kid grows up. Like the worrying is over. Nothing left but smooth sailing and grandbabies. No one prepares you for the heartbreak waiting around the corner."

Wilson knew all too well Martin's pain. Agonizing over your kids was universal. He watched the doctor walk toward the nurses' station. Ginny was coming around the corner at the far end of the hall toward them. Toward Darius's room, even though she'd said she barely knew him.

Wilson turned back to Martin and nodded behind him. "Mr. Woods. That blonde woman at the far end of the hall, walking toward us, do you know who that is?"

Martin looked in the direction of Wilson's nod. "I don't see anyone."

Wilson turned back around. She was gone.

CHAPTER SEVENTEEN

BROOKLYN SAT AT A TABLE, a tray of food in front of her, and stared at the cafeteria entrance. It had been almost thirty minutes. The anger began to build again. Why did Ginny want to suddenly talk to the nurse without her? They were supposed to be handling things together.

When her phone pinged, she grabbed it, half expecting a text from Ginny with a lame excuse for disappearing. But it was just a notification of new emails that had arrived since yesterday. She scanned the list of mostly junk and bills, deleting or saving them for later. But the last on the list was from a name she didn't recognize, its subject line Escape from Paradise, Callback. She opened the email and held her breath, reading and rereading as the words on the screen blurred in the haze of her excitement. There were so many indie and student films she and her roommates went out for that she'd learned to forget about them soon after the audition. She could barely remember what this was about. But it was a callback, and the movie looked like it even had a budget. The final comments were about a shooting date in late summer. Filming would be in New York and the Dominican Republic.

Home, she thought. It felt like a sign, too amazing to be anything else.

The details of her audition a few weeks earlier began to return. After an hour in the hallway with the other actresses waiting to read, she'd felt a glimmer of hope when she overheard one of the production assistants whisper that Brooklyn looked the part. But her performance had gone horribly off the rails. She'd used a new monologue, one that was supposed to be an emotional reading, as a girl copes with a breakup, but every word she uttered reminded her of losing her mom, and she'd gone into a full-on ugly cry, way too much for the scene at hand. The director had not even uttered a response. It felt like a disaster.

The email for the callback said they wanted her to read for a character named Lucinda, and the producer had attached pages from key scenes as well as a link to the full script. The character had a name! She'd never been called back for a named character. The closest she'd gotten was a call for Friend No. 2. When she got to the end of the message, the balloon of excitement popped with the final crushing detail. The call was at nine o'clock tomorrow morning. There was no way she could go.

"Hey," Ginny said, suddenly joining her at the table.

Brooklyn put the phone down.

"What is it?" Ginny said. "You look like you've seen a ghost."

"Nothing," she said, shaking her head.

"Bull," Ginny said. "I can see it on your face. Something happened."

"It's just an audition. I got a callback for something, but it's tomorrow morning so I can't do it, that's all." Brooklyn was trying hard to act like this happened all the time, but of course it didn't. Her eyes became misty, so she quickly rubbed her eyes. She couldn't be a baby. Family came first.

Ginny reached out and put her hand on Brooklyn's. "You need to go," Ginny said. She sat taller, as if she had solutions, as if she was trustworthy enough to handle things here. "What are you going to do today, anyway? We were to meet with the doctor. I can do that without you."

"There's a lot to talk about."

"There's really not," Ginny quickly answered.

"Jeez, Ginny. We've barely had a conversation since I got here. Dad needs help. This morning he blurted out that you're the reason he's in here. The other day he said he forgave you for something. What is going on with you two?"

Ginny looked around the room before answering. "We don't get along, Brooklyn, you know that. And he's talking nonsense these days. Half the time he thinks I'm Mom."

That she believed. But there was more to it. "Ginny, I found blood in the hall on the floor."

"That was from his fall."

"But you said he fell in the study."

Ginny's brows furrowed, like she was trying to remember what she'd said. She pulled away and rubbed her eyes. She finally looked at Brooklyn. "Do you think I hurt him?"

"He said you're the reason he's in here."

"That's just because I brought him here." Ginny reached for her hand again. "Brooklyn, I swear to you, I did not do anything to John. He was unconscious on the floor when I got there."

"There you go again! You told Simon you made him dinner!"

"I lied, okay?"

"Why?"

"I don't know!" she screamed. Both of them looked around the cafeteria, and Ginny lowered her voice. "Things between me and Simon aren't good. I was gone from home a long time. I didn't want him . . ." Ginny shook her head and gripped Brooklyn's hand hard. "I didn't hurt John. I promise you. I was the one who called 911. Why would I have done that if I wanted to hurt him?"

She had a point. But there were a lot of questions.

Brooklyn sat back, suddenly unsure how to begin, how to ask why Ginny was such a mess. "I was looking through Dad's files, and I was kind of shocked when I found some things about you in high school." She paused, hoping Ginny would fill her in without more prodding, but Ginny leaned forward, her elbow on the table, resting her head in the palm of her hand, as if the conversation, or inquisition, was already exhausting.

Brooklyn pressed on. "You were an A student, a National Merit Scholar, and had an offer from Columbia. I had no idea you ever considered leaving the state after high school."

"I was a good girl," Ginny said sarcastically.

"It seems like something must have happened the year you finished high school that changed things."

Ginny stared into Brooklyn's eyes, as if she was trying to say something without speaking.

"Something happened, didn't it?" Brooklyn reached out to take Ginny's hand in hers. It was the closest she'd ever felt to her sister.

Ginny pulled her hand away, wiping at tears that began to fall. "I've made some life-altering mistakes, that's all."

Brooklyn had never seen this side of her sister. Suddenly, she didn't see her as cold. She was broken. Brooklyn wanted to ask about the shooting at the women's clinic but hesitated. It didn't matter that Ginny was older. She was fragile, almost like a child in some ways. "But look at you now," Brooklyn said. "You have a beautiful family, a nice house, a nursing degree, a great husband who loves you . . ."

Ginny scoffed and shook her head. "It's a mirage."

"What do you mean?"

"My marriage is a joke."

Brooklyn didn't know what to say. She barely knew her sister or Simon. And what did Brooklyn know about marriage? "This could just be a rough patch."

"Ha. For sixteen years? I never should have married him."

Brooklyn didn't know what to say. "You don't love him anymore?"

Ginny shook her head. "We never loved each other. We both needed something. I was broken. He was a doctor. I guess I just assumed he would fix me. It seemed like a good decision at the time. But . . ." She didn't finish, and her eyes remained on Brooklyn's tray.

Brooklyn waited for her to muster the courage to finish the thought. She was finally talking, revealing some truth.

But Ginny said nothing more. She crossed her arms and sat back, uncrossing them to wipe her tears, crossing them again, determined to be strong.

There was so much to ask, but looking at Ginny's red eyes, she didn't press. "Everything seems really bad right now, but it's going to be okay. How about finally letting me be a sister to you?"

Ginny smiled and sniffled. "I've been so terrible to you."

It was the admission she'd always wanted. "Hey, I'm still young. We've got time. Whatever has happened in the past, it can't be that bad. Dad said he forgives you. You need to forgive yourself."

Ginny's eyes glazed as she looked away, processing the comment. "You should go back to New York."

Brooklyn sat back. Ginny was pulling away again. "We need to help Dad."

Ginny leaned forward and put her hands on Brooklyn's again. "This callback is a big deal. I could see it in your face when I sat down. We both know how hard it is to get out of this place. To make something of yourself. You can't miss it. I shouldn't have even called you home."

"Of course you should have. He's my dad too."

"I just mean that I'm here. I can handle it. I know I've been a mess, but I swear, Brooklyn, I've had my last drink. I even went to an AA meeting yesterday. I'm pulling myself together, and I'm gonna take care of things."

Brooklyn searched her eyes, her promises lingering in the air. She wanted to believe.

"Really, Brooklyn, Mom would want you to pursue your dream. You have to do it. You can come right back. He's not going to be moved for at least forty-eight hours."

Brooklyn let the possibility seep back in. She did want to try.

"I got this. I promise. By the time you come back, things will be better." Ginny smiled and squeezed Brooklyn's hand.

Brooklyn looked down at their hands. It was the smallest gesture. One hand on another. A squeeze. But it meant everything. Ginny had never been kind or interested. Suddenly, she was being both. Brooklyn's smile slowly returned.

CHAPTER EIGHTEEN

AFTER BROOKLYN LEFT, GINNY GOT a cup of coffee and a plain bagel, amazed that she'd been given this reprieve, and sat at a long empty table by the window. At least now she had a little more time. She just had to put the gun back in the safe. And she had to talk to Darius.

She sipped her coffee, staring out the window at the cloud cover, trying to imagine what she'd say.

That gray August sky of '99 had been a lot like today's, except the air was filled with threats, and Darius's screams, and that shotgun. She'd done *nothing*. A gun to his face, and she'd done nothing. She should have done something, or said something, but she didn't. It was the last time she'd seen him before Sunday night. And after everything that he'd done, that he'd tried to do . . . Knowing her had brought him nothing but pain.

In the screenplay, Darius had written about all their early encounters junior year—the day he found her in the pastor's office, a subsequent day in the lunchroom, and then finding her in the gym during senior year. Reading those scenes was like stepping back in time.

He'd come up to her at school during lunch, a week after the incident in Pastor Gary's office, and found her sitting alone, pushing macaroni and cheese around her plate. He sat down across from her, trying to make small talk, but she couldn't look at him, not after what he'd seen.

"Must be really good," he joked.

She looked up, and he was pointing at her meal. She cracked just a half smile at those green eyes that seemed to be searching her face for answers.

"You okay?" he asked.

She returned her focus to the food before answering. "You must think I'm disgusting." It was barely audible.

"Not at all," he said. He put his hand over her tray so she'd finally look up.

She did.

He leaned forward. "Do you want to tell anyone?"

"No!"

"I'll back you up if you're worried about people believing you."

She shook her head and looked him square in the face. "You don't understand. It wasn't like that. It was a test . . . He's not a bad guy."

Darius didn't push. He barely knew her.

But when they saw each other again at the start of senior year, he was more insistent. She was crying in the gym when she heard the big metal door burst open, and he strode toward her, looking even bigger and more confident than she remembered.

"Ginny Anderson," he'd said with a broad smile on his face.

She'd wiped her tears and tried to pretend nothing was wrong, but he wouldn't play along anymore.

He crouched down in front of her. "This is about that pastor, isn't it?" When she didn't answer, he'd continued. "I don't like that guy."

His lack of deference was almost funny. "Everyone loves him. He's like a mentor to all of us. He's in charge of the youth group, and I'm the teen leader. You wouldn't understand."

"I understand that no matter what has happened, he's too old for you. He's crossed a line. And I'd like to kick his ass."

Darius Woods wasn't afraid of anyone.

Eddie Wilson walked into the gym then, she remembered. "You okay, Ginny? This boy bothering you?" He'd stepped up to them as if she needed protection from Darius, some big bad wolf.

Darius had straightened, towering above Eddie. "Who you calling boy, boy?"

"You," Eddie said, puffing out his bony chest.

"Eddie, stop," Ginny had countered, standing and wiping her face again. "Darius is a friend. Back off."

"If you say so, Gin," Eddie said. "But I'm watching you," he said to Darius, pointing at him as he walked away.

She and Darius looked at each other, rolled their eyes, and chuckled. "Family friend," she said. "He's an idiot."

"Obviously."

She grabbed her books, prepared to leave, and Darius stopped her. "You need to get away from that pastor," he'd said. Truer words had never been spoken.

She was staring at her bagel now, mindlessly ripping it into crumbs only a bird would enjoy, when someone came and sat right beside her at the table, sidling over until their shoulders touched. She turned, leaning away as the man said, "Ginny Anderson, I thought that was you. I'd know those long blonde locks anywhere."

He was scruffy, about her age, wearing a baseball cap. His straggly hair, desperate for a shampoo, spilled from beneath it. Despite the fresh wounds and bruises on his acne-scarred face, she instantly recognized him. It was as if her high school memory had conjured him to appear.

"Eddie, hi," she said. "My goodness, what happened to you?"

He touched his face, gently poking his bruises. "Oh, not much. Just a little scuffle. It looks worse than it feels."

She recalled Sheriff Wilson's comment about Eddie living with him and struggling a bit. The dark circles under his eyes, the raw picked-at wounds on his forearms, were typical of meth users. She was in no place to judge, though there was nothing about Eddie that invoked her empathy. "I haven't seen you in ages," she said, her tone sunny, as if they were long-lost friends. Her mother had always said that kindness was contagious and should be used even in the face of dark and mean-spirited souls. That was definitely Eddie Wilson.

It had been twenty years since that Sunday night in the Garden. A night that had started so typically, with the sheriff and Eddie at the house for dinner, just as they had been nearly every Sunday since Mrs. Wilson died a couple of months earlier. Eddie had been annoying Ginny for years, always disrupting class with offensive jokes, causing trouble in the halls, but given the circumstances, she'd tried hard to be kinder that night.

After dinner, he followed her to the garage as she was leaving, worming his way into her car. She'd told him she was meeting a friend. "What friend? You have a boyfriend?" he'd asked, getting in the passenger side before she could complain.

"No."

"Good. Then drive me to the ice cream shop, please."

She did, and when she parked, Eddie leaned in for a kiss.

"What are you doing?" she said, pulling back.

"Come on, Ginny. Just give me a kiss. Please, I'm so sad."

"Jeez, Eddie. I can't believe you'd use your mom's death to get me to kiss you."

Eddie pounded his head against the seatback, as if enraged. "Why you acting like such a prude? We both know your good-girl image is a farce. I know you're a closet wild child."

The accusation terrified her. He knew something.

He turned and raised his eyebrows, a hint that he knew more. "I'd bet money you wouldn't want your parents to know what I know."

She tried not to fall for the intimidation. "And what's that?"

"Maybe I've seen you sitting in someone's car last summer. Having a few drinks. Maybe more."

She felt sick. The only time she'd ever had alcohol was with Pastor Gary, and they had been alone in his car once last summer. The thought that Eddie might have seen what happened made her stomach flip.

"Maybe you should reconsider that kiss. Just a little one." He leaned in again.

"Get out," she'd said, pushing him back.

"Fine," he said, before climbing out and slamming the door. "And hey, thank your mom for the dinner. And dessert," he said, losing his balance as soon as he began walking away.

They hadn't had dessert. Had he stolen money from the house to buy ice cream? "What did you do?" she yelled after him.

He giggled before walking back toward the car, confessing. "Just enjoying a little after-dinner relaxer I found in the bathroom."

"Mom's pills? That's for her vertigo."

"Funny," he said. "Making me feel awfully dizzy!" He laughed as he ran off to join some of the other burnouts on the corner.

Maybe he's changed, she thought now. But then she looked again at his eyes, and the bruises, the signs of drug use. Probably not.

"What are you doing here?" she asked.

"I'm here for you," he said, leaning in again and nudging his shoulder against hers.

"What do you mean?" She leaned back, like this was some dance of revolt.

"Well, I heard your dad's in here. I know you lost your mom a few months back. Obviously, I know what that's like, and I just wanted to see how the Andersons are doing. I mean, I think of you and your parents like family. Remember how our moms used to always sign us up for activities together?"

"Of course," she said with a nod, feigning interest. That was back when Eddie was just a sweet, harmless kid.

"So what do you think about Darius Woods?" he continued. "He gonna make it?"

"I have no idea," she said, suddenly sitting taller, guarded. Eddie probably relished the idea of Darius fighting for his life.

"Well," he said, lowering his voice, "I guess if he bites the dust, your problems will be solved." He raised his brow and smirked, as if they shared a secret.

"What are you talking about?" Did he think she shot Darius? The sheriff would not be so unprofessional as to tell his idiot son that he suspected Ginny in the Darius Woods case. Would he?

"That is who you were talking about last Saturday night, right?"

Her mind raced back in time. Last Saturday. She'd rushed out of the house around five o'clock, telling Simon she needed to check on her father. She had to talk to Darius about what he'd written, and he'd said he was arriving in Eden that day. But she chickened out, hitting a bar just outside Eden instead, drowning her panic in vodka, wiping away those thirteen years of sobriety in an instant.

"I was at the meeting," he said with a wink. "Eight o'clock, First Hope. I don't think you saw me, but I saw you," he said, raising his eyebrows again.

The eyebrows, the winking—she hated Eddie Wilson. He was still an ass. But she had to know what he was talking about, so she just smiled.

"I've been trying to do thirty meetings in thirty days, so even though booze isn't my primary substance of choice, I do the AAs when I can't find an NA meeting. Sometimes I go after a bout. You know, better than nothing, right? I guess we got that in common. One hour at a time . . ." Another wink.

Suddenly, she remembered. She'd left the bar, disgusted with herself for falling off the wagon and terrified of what was going to happen and how she was going to handle things. She'd convinced herself to do the next right thing and find a meeting. A quick search on her phone led her back to her childhood church. But she'd still been drunk. And she'd shared with the group.

"Anyway, it didn't take much to know you were talking about Darius Woods. You said someone had written a screenplay that was going to destroy a lot of lives. I mean, who else we know coulda written a screenplay?"

She felt sick. An entire room of people—probably all from Eden—and she'd basically alerted them to the impending revelations in Darius's story.

"I never liked that guy," he added. "But, of course, you know that. Frankly, if he thinks he can come back here and exploit all our lives for his own financial gain, well, I say screw 'im."

Eddie was a master of inserting himself into her business. He had no idea what he was talking about. Though ignorant people were often the most dangerous.

"I'm sorry," she said, pressing her hands against the tabletop to stand. "It was good to see you, Eddie, but I've got to go visit my dad."

Eddie threw his hand across hers. "Hey," he said urgently.

She looked at his hand, pressing down on hers.

"I never meant to hurt you," he said.

Her mom would say the Christian thing would be to forgive, but she couldn't do it. Everything Eddie had done in high school was with intention. She pulled her hand out from under his.

"Anyway, we're both struggling, right?" he asked. "Maybe we can help each other. We could go to some meetings together."

"I'm sorry, Eddie," she said. "I've got to go." Eddie would never be anyone other than the person he'd been in high school, a drug-addicted burnout who spewed hate and tried to ruin her life.

CHAPTER NINETEEN

GINNY LEFT EDDIE AND WENT back to the fourth floor. Sheriff Wilson had to be gone by now, but she was sure her chest was turning blotchy and red as she stopped, leaning up against a wall before making that final turn to Darius's wing again.

When she got to the nurses' station and asked for his room, the nurse looked at the computer. "No visitors, hon. Sorry, it's in the system. He's not to be disturbed."

"He asked me to come."

"I can't help you."

"Is he doing okay? I'm a friend from high school."

"I'm sorry," the nurse said. "I can't share patient information."

Ginny didn't know what to do. She pulled out her phone. Maybe she could send him a message through Facebook and let him know she was here, trying to get in.

"Miss? Hello?"

She turned toward the voice. "I'm Martin Woods, Darius's dad," the man said. "Can I help you?"

"Oh, hello, Mr. Woods," she said, offering her hand. "I'm Ginny Smith. Darius and I went to high school together. He sent me a message on Facebook last night. He asked me to come by today."

"I'm sorry, sweetie, he's heavily sedated now. Unfortunately, he's fighting a new infection, but everyone's watching him closely. You can come back another time. I'll tell him you were here."

Martin Woods's eyes, red and swollen, exposed the fear behind that optimism. Darius might still die.

"I'm so sorry," she said. "I'll keep him in my prayers."

She walked back to her dad's room, dazed, as the implications of Darius's condition, of his potential death, hovered overhead like a new storm cloud. Secrets would stay buried forever, but the investigation would be for murder.

John was still asleep. She sat in the chair, watching him. It was the only time he looked harmless. And he'd said he forgave her? What a joke. She did not forgive him. She didn't know if she'd ever forgive him. The John Anderson she knew was nothing like the one Brooklyn knew.

He began to stir, and she stepped back to the wall, adding several feet of distance between them. She never wanted to be too close to him when he was conscious and capable of inflicting so much pain.

"Where have you been?" he asked. "You gonna get me outta here already?"

Before Ginny could answer, the doctor came in. "He's actually doing much better this afternoon. I think he's ready for a move."

"Works for me," John said. "I'm ready to go home."

Ginny ignored him and spoke to the doctor. "The rehab facility will have a bed next Tuesday. Can he stay a little longer?"

"Bad idea," John said.

"We can keep him here, though I can't guarantee his insurance will cover the time, since he's mobile. He's really recovering quite well."

"Get me outta here," John bellowed.

Ginny looked at him. "You can't do all those stairs."

"So put a bed in the living room."

The doctor shrugged. "It's your decision. The nurses' station has the number for a medical supplier."

"I need to keep moving," John said. "Isn't that what you all keep telling me? So I do that at home. I go to work, I tend to the garden. I'll be fine."

"You need help," Ginny said.

"So help me, goddammit! You owe me that, don't you?"

That was the man she knew. She hated him. Turning her attention back to the doctor, she said, "Let's go. I'll get that number."

When Ginny returned to the room after ordering the bed, John was confused again. "There she is," he said, his tone light and friendly. He hadn't been pleased to see her in years. It almost felt like a gift, his inability to remember. She couldn't forget anything despite trying for all these years.

"B," he continued. "You gonna get us outta here?"

"I'm working on it," she said. It didn't seem worth correcting him. Perhaps this would all be easier if he thought she were Bonnie.

"You look worried," he said.

"Little bit," she offered sarcastically. He'd be worried, too, if he remembered what had happened.

"Don't worry, B. Ginny's not going to say anything."

She stopped and looked at him, wondering where his mind was in their history. "Really?" she said, playing along.

"Stupid girl," he continued.

Ginny winced, squeezing her eyes shut, and said nothing. He'd always shut her down. Every time she tried to do the right thing, he shut her down.

"Remember when she was a little girl? She was such a delight."

Ginny turned away, holding back the tears. She remembered those days—when she idolized him. He would read to her and even sing songs at bedtime in that deep voice. He'd carry her on his shoulders.

"I really thought she could do no wrong, B," he continued. "I thought that because she was always hanging out with the other kids from youth group, she couldn't get into any trouble. I guess that was my mistake. No kids are immune from finding trouble."

Ginny thought again of that morning at the clinic all those years ago and the mere seconds that passed before the doctor hit the ground, holding his stomach, moaning, as blood seeped from his hands, her panic after that woman ran from the front door into the lot, screaming.

She'd heard nothing but her own heartbeat and those gunshots, the moaning, the woman's scream running like a loop in her head as she sped toward school through a blur of streetlights and passing cars, rushing, drenched in sweat, to her second-period class.

By later that afternoon, she was sitting in a windowless room being questioned. She and her dad never looked at each other the same way after that day.

John stirred now and groaned in the bed. The war hero who'd worked the counter of his general store for half a century, offering help to everyone in town. To Brooklyn, he was still a saint, a hero, a father she loved and respected, but he'd taken the most terrifying time of Ginny's life and made it worse. She closed her eyes, envisioning a pillow over his face, snuffing him out.

Sheriff Wilson had surely read the screenplay by now. She couldn't take any of this anymore. Damn the consequences. Tomorrow morning, she would not put her father's gun back in the safe. She'd take it to Sheriff Wilson. It was time to tell the truth.

~ • ~

When Wilson got back to his office, Donny was sitting at the sheriff's desk, reading the screenplay. "Suits you," he said to Donny.

"What's that?"

"This office. My desk."

"I'm sorry," Donny said, rising from his seat.

"Stop," Wilson said, his hand up, cutting him off. "I'm just trying to get used to this new reality."

Donny sat back down, and Wilson took the chair in front of the desk.

"How's Woods doing?" Donny asked.

"Not great, actually. This may still become a murder investigation."

"And what about the gunman at the hospital . . . You learn anything?"

Wilson shook his head. "Nah. Coulda been anyone." He looked back at the desks to see what other cops were in the station house. There was no reason to mention Eddie. If he'd been there, it was unfortunately about drugs. Wilson waved over a young officer from the far end of the room. "I think Martin Woods has a point," he said to Donny. "We better get a guard for his room. At least for the next forty-eight hours." He was not going to let something happen to that man while he was still in charge. He turned toward the officer he'd beckoned and sent him to take the first shift.

"You get to see your friend while you were there?" Donny asked.

"Actually, I did pop in on him for a minute." Wilson had gone to John's room after leaving Martin Woods, in part to ask Ginny why he'd seen her on Woods's floor, but she hadn't been there. "He's doin' much better."

"Oh, that's good news."

"It is," he said. There was just one thing about that visit with John that continued to gnaw at him. John still didn't remember how he fell. It made Wilson wonder if Ginny was right about John's memory issues.

"Well, thank goodness Ginny found you," Wilson had said, but John muttered, *"Right,"* as if he either wasn't glad Ginny found him or maybe he didn't believe that she found him. It was odd.

"Anyway," Wilson said, waving toward the script on the table. "You done with that yet?"

Donny leaned back. "No. Sorry, got sidetracked. Seems that stalker didn't show up for work last weekend."

Wilson crossed his arms, resting them on his belly, and leaned back on the chair's hind legs. "What do we know about her?"

"She's twenty-five, attractive, works in retail, a boutique in LA. She's a frequent poster on Instagram and Twitter. You might look at her profile and assume she's perfectly normal. But she broke into Woods's house, told him it was their destiny to be together, and when he asked her to leave, she fell apart, locked herself in his bathroom, and started screaming about him messing with the plan. Police got her out of there. Cuckoo crazy, if you ask me."

"And no word about where she was over the weekend?"

"Working on it. She's back at work. I'm in touch with LAPD. They went by, and she said she had the flu over the weekend. Said she never left her apartment."

"It's a little past flu season."

"Yep. I've already asked Roger to prep requests for warrants to get her credit card statements and bank records to see if we can determine her location on Sunday. LAPD's gonna do some digging, too— talk to neighbors, see if anyone can confirm her whereabouts during the weekend. She was radio silent on her social media during the weekend, so no clues there."

It would be nice if the shooter was from LA. Wilson much preferred the idea that Woods brought the trouble with him and it would leave with him too. And he really didn't want to see Ginny pulled into this mess.

"Guess what else?" Donny continued. "She's blonde. Didn't that neighbor say she saw a blonde outside his house when he was being carted off?"

"Yep. But those license plate registrations . . ."

"Actually, I looked at Roger's list. One of the registrations was owned by a rental-car company, so it's not out of the realm of possibilities. We're checkin' it out."

Wilson felt himself starting to relax. Maybe this case would be in good hands after all. "And how far are you with the screenplay?"

"Only a third in, but it's pretty good. I'm interested."

Wilson uncrossed his arms. "I don't want a review. Do you see any reason someone might get upset about what's in there?"

"I'm assuming yes. But I can't say yet. Starts with an interesting first-person narration during the opening camera pan across town . . . the main character is named Anthony, and it's about how he and his dad moved to Eden from Chicago when he was about twelve after his mom was killed. His father was determined to provide a safe environment for his son and was struck by the name of the town when he looked on a map. He took it as a sign." Donny flipped the pages back to the beginning and read directly from the text. "Then the narrator says, *My father didn't know that danger is everywhere, whether a big city or small town. Some people are hunters and some are prey, and when you're a black kid in a white town and you cross certain lines, you're bound to be hunted.*"

Wilson looked up at the ceiling tiles, at the water marks from last year's roof leak. "Go on . . ."

Donny began flipping ahead. "So this first part sort of establishes how Anthony didn't fit in, no interest in sports, even though he had the build. Made him a misfit. Some examples of racism in the classroom and cafeteria here and there, but nothing I'd consider motive. I'm just getting to the part where a sophomore English teacher has suggested he try out for a play. That's as far as I've gotten."

Wilson let his chair fall forward, returning the front legs to the ground with a thud. "Any word yet on the gun and coffee mug I dropped off yesterday?"

"Yep. No match."

"Was the gun wiped clean?"

"Nope. Prints all over it, but not the same as the mug."

"Good." Thank God.

"What was that all about?"

"Virginia Smith. That was one of the names on those vehicle registrations Roger gave me. Virginia Smith is the married name of my buddy John Anderson's oldest daughter, Ginny. That yearbook confirmed that she was in the theater group with Darius Woods. She got in some trouble back in high school. It's tricky. Didn't want to officially point a finger before chatting with her."

"What kind of trouble?"

"Could have been the worst kind. It was a case from the spring of 1999, the year they graduated, and given the similarities of these cases and the fact that Woods probably knew her, I wondered if he knew something about what happened back then—maybe something she wouldn't want him to write about."

"You've got my attention," Donny said, sitting back and crossing his arms.

CHAPTER TWENTY

WILSON SHUT THE DOOR TO his office and took a seat on the sofa by the window before continuing. "It was a shooting at a women's clinic—you know, one of those places that does abortions in addition to health care."

"I'm aware." Donny smirked.

"Anyway, the doctor survived, but the evidence required us to bring in Ginny. It didn't look good for her. It was a federal case, and the FBI swarmed almost instantly. She'd been a frequent protester, she'd lied about her whereabouts that morning, and there was a good ID of her car and of a blonde girl at the scene. And she said nothing to defend herself when we questioned her. She wouldn't speak at all." Lifting the plastic blinds, he turned his attention from Donny to the sky, just moments from full darkness. Everything about the spring of '99 was tough to think about.

"How old was she?"

"Seventeen. Feds would have tried her as an adult, for sure. That was a rough year. For all of us." Wilson sat back and finally looked at Donny. "My wife died about two months before that happened."

"I'm sorry."

"It's okay. The thing is, you learn who your friends are when bad stuff happens. Bonnie and John Anderson really helped me out. All spring, Bonnie insisted that me and Eddie come over for dinner at least once a week, and she sent casseroles over every week for two months. My other kids had already moved out, so it was just me and Eddie at that point. I didn't know how to do the whole parenting thing without my wife. Bonnie tried to help, though Eddie wasn't the easiest kid. And John—well, he took me and Eddie hunting, made sure the weekly poker games continued. They were both determined to keep us well fed and distracted."

"Nice."

"Yeah—which made it difficult when all that happened with Ginny. It was not fun being the one to bring their only child in for questioning." He could still remember Bonnie pulling him aside after they got to the station that day, begging him, with tears in her eyes, to do something. "You know this is a mistake," she'd said. "There's no way."

He'd tried to calm her, though his eyes may have betrayed him. The description of the girl was a compelling match for Ginny. She'd obviously lied about her whereabouts. And the subject of abortion had been raised at dinner just two weeks earlier. He'd said nothing about it to the feds, but it was too easy to imagine that Ginny had gotten the idea from the conversation they'd all shared.

Bonnie had brought it up while she dished a second helping of casserole onto his plate, saying he needed to get the place shut down. She'd said as much before. At least every couple of months since it had opened.

He'd laughed. "Not the way it works, Bonnie. They're breaking no laws."

"They're killing babies."

Wilson had looked to John for help, and John nodded to Ginny and Eddie. "You two can be excused."

"They're not little kids, John," Bonnie said.

"Thanks, Mrs. Anderson. I say that to my dad every day," Eddie said with a smile.

Ginny stood and began clearing the dishes.

"Ginny cares as much as I do, John. She's spent I don't know how many Saturdays over the last year picketing that place." She handed Ginny her plate. "I'm sure you've saved some lives, too, baby."

Eddie stood and began helping Ginny clear the dishes. "We should just blow it up."

Wilson had glared at his son.

"I'm jokin'," he replied.

"That's the thing," John added. "Those places attract violence. I don't want my daughter gettin' hurt. Maybe you could use some creative policing to figure it out, because with the news these days, that parking lot is essentially a health hazard."

"Come on, John. That's ridiculous," Wilson said.

"Pastor Gary and I had a meeting about this today," Bonnie said. "It was just last month that an abortion clinic was bombed in North Carolina."

"I heard," Wilson said. "But it didn't fully detonate, right? Minimal damage."

"But you remember that bomb that exploded in Alabama last year? Killed a security guard and blinded a nurse."

"And whoever did that is still on the loose," John added. "The smarter crime was the New York shooting last year."

"Did you just say *smart* and *crime* in the same sentence?" Wilson joked.

"I'm just saying—the doctor was killed—sniper style, while he stood at a kitchen window. No collateral damage. And I heard that several other doctors in the area quit after it happened. So I'd have to say the tactic worked."

"You sound like you approve," Wilson said, tossing his napkin onto the plate.

"Didn't say that. Just noting that it was effective."

"It was murder. And terrorism," Wilson said.

"I don't care what you wanna call it," John said, "but the kids aren't safe. They still haven't caught any of those people."

"Maybe what I should do is have a talk with this Pastor Gary—get him to stop sending those kids over there."

"That's no solution," Bonnie said.

"She's right, Dad," Eddie chimed in from the doorway. "Teenagers are the only ones who aren't afraid to make waves."

Ginny joined him. "It's true. I mean, teenagers were the first to stand up for desegregation."

"I thought we were talking about 'good activism,'" Eddie said sarcastically.

"Ass," Ginny muttered.

"Ginny!" Bonnie exclaimed.

Eddie laughed it off. "I know she loves me, Mrs. A. We're just jokin' around."

It had been a harmless conversation, or so Wilson had thought. Eddie and Ginny went out for ice cream afterward. Typical teenagers. But two weeks later, Ginny was being questioned for attempted murder, and Bonnie was hysterical.

"She couldn't have done this," Bonnie continued. "She's a good girl. You know it. She's got her whole life in front of her. And that place is awful! We've all been trying to shut it down since the minute it opened." Bonnie's fingers were digging into his forearm. She wouldn't let go. "She did not do this."

"Please, Bonnie," he'd said. "Don't get ahead of yourself. I've got to speak with her alone. I have to ask questions. The FBI is involved. We can't ignore the evidence."

Bonnie finally let go of him and ran over to John, who was walking in the front door of the station. "John! You have to do something." It was all Wilson heard, but John left the building moments later without talking to him, and forty-five minutes after that, a pastor from their church had arrived.

"So what happened?" Donny asked. "Was she the shooter?"

"I suppose we'll never know. That Pastor Gary came in—he worked with the youth group—said he could vouch for Ginny's whereabouts, which was odd, because she'd told her mother she was leaving early that morning to help at school. But I brought him into the room, left, and watched from outside."

"What did he say?"

"Something like he was so sorry about what happened and that he understood why she felt she couldn't say anything. She stared at him, just frozen. He said he'd already told me she'd come to church before school to help him and he had asked her to keep it a secret. He apologized for putting her in that position. He gave me a story about how they were working together to organize the teens' upcoming mission trip and that she'd worried her mother wouldn't allow her to miss a class to help him, so he'd told her to lie, and that it was wrong, but that's where she'd been."

"And you didn't buy it?"

"Of course not. I watched him telling her exactly what he'd told me, so she could back up the alibi. I mean, it was a conflict for me, obviously. I didn't want to go after the only child of a close friend, and I didn't believe the pastor, but when I went back in that room after I left them in there alone, she just looked at me and said nothing. It was hard to know if she was silently pleading for help or what, but we both knew that lies were being told. Within hours, other ministers from their church came in and backed up Pastor Gary's story, some even saying they'd seen Ginny at the church with him. We all knew that testimony from her church's leadership would be nearly impossible to overcome without something more concrete on Ginny, and we didn't have much more than a vague description from a hysterical woman."

"So that was the end of it?"

Wilson nodded. "FBI continued digging, but months later, they'd come up with nothin'. And I wondered if maybe the pastor had put

Ginny up to it. He was the organizer of all the teen protests. The kids worshipped him. I'd seen the way they looked at that guy. He was a man of God, but I'm telling you, there was something there that I didn't like about him. Those kids marched down Main Street a few times, up in arms about one thing or another, and when I would approach the pastor, telling them to disperse, those kids swarmed around him. I don't know. I mean, he was always spouting Scripture. I'm a churchgoing man, but that church—I mean, Bonnie and John are great people—but that church seems a little extreme, if you know what I mean.

"Anyway, it's one of only two unsolved cases dealing with abortion clinic violence in the last thirty years. The trail went cold. No one else saw anything. I'm telling you, being the law isn't always easy. Maybe it was easier in a big city where everyone's a stranger, but you get to know people real well in a small town. It's not always easy going after 'em. I mean, you should, you need to—don't think I'm saying otherwise, but that was a tough year, that's all. For all of us."

"Sure," Donny said. "I get it." He broke eye contact as he said that last bit. Wilson could feel his unspoken judgment.

"Anyway, we're gettin' off track," he continued. "What I wanted to tell you was that Pastor Gary got on my radar that day he saved Ginny's butt, and several years later a woman came in here and wanted to file a complaint against him. Said that he'd been inappropriate with her daughter."

Donny leaned forward. "Oh jeez, I fear I know where this is going."

"Yeah. She'd complained to the church, but they'd talked to the pastor, who denied the allegations. His story was that the girl had been inappropriate with him, and when he shut it down, she got angry. So I went to the church to question the pastor but learned that he'd been reassigned to a different ministry. Before I could find him, the woman returned, saying she didn't want to put her child through the ordeal of a criminal investigation, and the matter dissolved. She was satisfied that he was out of the church. But it always made me think of Ginny. She looked at Pastor Gary that morning with such fear, and soon after that shooting, it seemed like her life began to unravel. I had this sinking feeling that she'd been involved with that clinic business, but I didn't have the heart to continue digging. She was such a good kid, and I always wondered if she'd been another of Pastor Gary's victims."

"Man," Donny said.

"I sort of figured that whatever happened, even if she'd done it, the doctor survived, and Ginny was a naive kid who may have been under that pastor's thumb. She didn't go off to college as planned, and then a few months later, Bonnie said she'd been hospitalized for depression. Whatever happened that spring, it haunted her. I'm guessing that's punishment enough."

"So you're thinking that maybe Woods knows what happened back then. Maybe he wrote about it."

"Exactly, so let's finish that damn screenplay. You print me out a copy?" Wilson asked.

Donny handed it over. "Here, take this one. I'll read online. And please," he said, "take your desk back. I gotta grab a few things at the store before heading home." Both men stood, and Wilson returned to the proper side of his desk.

There was a weak knock at the door, and Wilson looked up. "Hey, Pops," Eddie said, standing in the doorway. Wilson took one look at his son—the glazed eyes, the Cardinals T-shirt that had been on the floor of Eddie's room all week, dirty jeans, greasy hair under that baseball cap—and he knew Eddie had never even showered. Just rolled out of bed and started the madness all over again.

"What are you doing here?"

Eddie stumbled past Donny without acknowledging him and plopped onto the couch before Wilson could reach him, throwing his head back and staring at the ceiling as if he had the worst news to share. "I don't know. I just don't understand why . . . ," he said, his voice beginning to crack, "nothing I do matters?"

Wilson glanced at Donny and shook his head before answering his son. This was not the time for Donny to ask questions. "Of course what you do matters," he said in a soft tone, sitting by his child. "You just feel like this because of whatever you've taken. You need to stop, Eddie. Please."

Eddie raised his head and scoffed. "That's bullshit!" he said, raising his voice. "The drugs didn't make me feel this way. I took the drugs because I feel this way. I mean, she hates me. No matter what I do. It's like she'll never forgive me."

Eddie had to be talking about his daughter. Eddie's wife had left him several years earlier, and his daughter had never forgiven him for the damage he'd caused their family. He was always texting her, trying to rebuild their relationship, but she didn't want anything to do with him. She was thirteen and stubborn.

Wilson sensed Donny looking at him in his peripheral vision, but he didn't return his gaze. He didn't want Donny's pity. "Come on, Eddie, you hungry?" It wasn't time to challenge or scold him. He had to tread lightly. "Maybe we can hit that McDonald's by the expressway before we go home. I'll drive."

Eddie fell over to a sleeping position. "I'm so tired."

Wilson looked at Donny, who was probably wondering if lockup or an ER was a more appropriate resting place. "Go on," he said. "I'll call you later."

"You sure?" Donny asked.

"It's fine!" Eddie yelled at Donny. "Can't a man visit his father? Who is this yahoo, anyway?" he asked his dad.

"My replacement," Wilson said. "So please, be nice."

"Fuck off," Eddie mumbled, his eyes already closed.

"Go on," Wilson finally said to Donny. "It's better this way." He looked back at Eddie after Donny walked out.

Eddie's eyes were closed, but he strained every facial muscle as if he couldn't block out the light, finally covering his face with his hand as the tears came, full despair pouring out. "I'm sorry," he said. "You don't deserve this. I'm such a disappointment."

Wilson took his son's hand in his, looked at his thirty-eight-year-old face, broken and fragile as a child's, and held back his own tears. "It's okay," Wilson said. "You're just having a bad day. Come on, let's go home. Tomorrow will be better."

He had no idea if tomorrow would be better. He'd already tried to help his son every way he knew how. He'd refinanced his house to pay for that Fairfield treatment center, twice; he'd reminded Eddie and cajoled him into attending meetings nearly every day; he'd set up job interviews, hoping that with some focus and purpose, he could finally recover. But Eddie lost every job he managed to get, and Wilson was powerless to cure his son of his addictions or his darkness. He didn't understand where it came from, but deep down, he felt responsible. He'd done something wrong as a parent—either too lax or too strict, too busy, or maybe too consumed by grief after his wife died to see what was happening . . . he didn't know.

But Eddie was a grown man, and there was only so much a father could do. He could not turn his son out on the street, but sometimes he wondered if Eddie would only find peace with that final breath.

Eddie finally sat up. "Big Mac sounds good."

Wilson grabbed his jacket and the screenplay, hitting the lights on the way out.

CHAPTER TWENTY-ONE

DAY SEVEN
9:15 p.m.
BOLINE COUNTY JAIL

THE DOOR AT THE END of the hall opened, and Brooklyn assumed the guard was returning her cell neighbor, who'd requested another bathroom visit after dinner. But instead, another officer appeared and told her she needed to come with him. Maybe Ginny had finally arrived. Maybe the nightmare was finally over.

Brooklyn was put in a small room with a table and chairs and told to wait. As if she had a choice.

Sheriff Goodwin came in and sat at the table across from her. She immediately looked at his ears again, that feature she'd first noticed when they met last Monday, the one that made her like him. Seven days ago. He'd been investigating Darius's shooting, and now they were here because of her dad. He probably didn't even understand that everything was connected.

The sheriff reminded her that she didn't need to talk. She had a right to silence, but he wanted to help and the more she talked the easier things would be. "Brooklyn, Ginny was here," he finally said.

It felt like her heart stopped beating as soon as he said the words. Ginny was supposed to get her out of this. But she'd come and gone? Brooklyn wiped the tears as soon as they hit her cheek. This time she stared at the badge on his shirt while he spoke.

"Listen," he said. "She told us everything, and I want you to know that I understand you received a shock earlier today. Frankly, it's easy to see why you might have snapped. So maybe you better tell me exactly what happened."

She couldn't talk. Not to him. The rock in her stomach was rising to her throat. They really thought she'd killed her dad.

"Brooklyn, why did you have your dad's gun in your hand when Sheriff Wilson arrived?"

She shook her head. "I didn't shoot him." It was barely a whisper.

"We know. But the gun was fired. We found the bullet in the ceiling. It's pretty clear there was a struggle. How did the lamp break?"

"I don't know," she said.

"Brooklyn, we really need you to talk. If someone else was there, if you saw anything, now's the time to say so."

"No one was there."

"Did you hit your father?"

"No!"

"He had a pretty good-size gash in his head and a mark on his face. And we found that bat in the kitchen."

She looked at him, thinking of all the assumptions that could end lives. She didn't know what to say.

"His blood was on your hands. I need to understand exactly what happened. Maybe it was just an accident. Did he say something that made you angry?"

"It wasn't like that."

"Well, you need to start talking if you don't want this all going south."

She stared at the sheriff, remembering what she'd read earlier that day in Darius's screenplay. "I think I should speak to a lawyer."

Sheriff Goodwin sat back and looked at his watch. "Okay then," he said, standing. "Come on."

"Where are we going?"

"Back to your cell. It's Sunday. We can't get a court-appointed rep until the morning."

CHAPTER TWENTY-TWO

BROOKLYN READ THE SCRIPT FOR the audition on the train from Carbondale, eyes wide as she recognized similarities between herself and the character. By the time she'd reached Lambert Airport in Saint Louis and parked herself in front of the gate, she had less than an hour until boarding. Everything was falling into place.

The story was about an eighteen-year-old girl, Lucinda—the lead role, a fashion model of all things, ironic since a full ten years of Brooklyn's childhood had been spent wanting to look like Ginny— the fair-skinned petite blonde. It was a rags-to-riches orphan tale. The orphanage was set in the Dominican Republic; the man who saves Lucinda from certain poverty, a human trafficker posing as a modeling scout. Lucinda escapes him, navigating New York City and creating a career on her own while overcoming painful childhood memories. It was a powerful, inspiring role.

She'd researched the production company and director online. They were legitimate players in the industry. One of the guys had been connected to an indie movie she'd seen audition notices for six months earlier, and they all had IMDb profiles and lists of past projects on their websites. This role could be the start of an actual career.

She decided to mention her heritage to the director. Maybe it would seal the deal. She was sure she knew more about the Dominican Republic than anyone else being called back. She'd spent hours over the years looking at YouTube videos of the island, reading Wikipedia listings, trying to understand everything about where she came from. She knew that seventy-three percent of the population was mixed-race, that it was a country of ten million people—the most-visited destination and largest economy in the Caribbean. There were tons of orphanages, most of the kids coming from child pregnancies, HIV-infected mothers, and mothers with disabilities. Abortion was illegal, even in cases of rape, incest, or danger to a mother's health, and a fifth of the country lived in shacks, most without running water.

It had proven strange information to have last year when those girls in her dorm returned from spring break with stories about their beautiful adventure to the island paradise with swim-up bars, great bargains, and gorgeous beaches. She'd been so envious of their trip. When Brooklyn's mom first shared that picture of Eimy, she'd asked if they could go there. She wanted to see where she was from. Mom had smiled and said, "Maybe." Brooklyn asked several times over the years. The answer was always the same, and she finally realized that "maybe" was just the long road to "no."

She reviewed Lucinda's lines during the flight, and by the time she landed, her roommate Cindy had texted celebration GIFs and lots of smiling faces, champagne bottles, and balloon emojis. All the room-mates were going to try to swap out their Friday restaurant shifts so they could hang out and hear all about it.

It would be after midnight by the time she got to the apartment, and she just hoped she'd be able to sleep. She needed to perform a scene from the day her character meets the man who promises a modeling career in New York. Her character has doubts about the man, but she wants to believe in miracles and wants an easy way out of her life. Brooklyn closed her eyes, envisioning herself doing the scene and nailing it. It wasn't difficult to relate. She was counting on Ginny in the same way. Nothing about the last twenty years suggested Ginny would step up, but Brooklyn needed to believe. She'd finally gotten out of that town. She knew it was selfish and she loved her dad, but she didn't want to spend the next five or ten years stuck in Eden.

Today's conversation had been a start. When Ginny swore she hadn't hurt their dad, Brooklyn believed her. But still, so much had not been said. As her mind rewound their conversation, it was amazing how much she hadn't learned. And she hadn't even asked Ginny about Dad's missing gun. Between the callback email and Ginny's sudden showing of emotion and regret, Brooklyn's steely resolve had collapsed. And now she was almost a thousand miles from home. Had she been manipulated? Was Ginny so insistent that Brooklyn leave town not because she wanted to support her dream but because she wanted Brooklyn and all her questions to just go away?

Brooklyn jumped in a cab for home and renewed her resolve. First, she'd nail that audition, and then she'd get back to Eden and finally get some answers. If she wanted to be treated like an adult and help make decisions about her dad's care, she couldn't back down so easily.

~ • ~

After Ginny left the hospital, she drove home, her only game plan being to do the next right thing. If her life was going to blow up, maybe she could control the damage by coming clean. She wanted to get home to her kids, make her family dinner, brew some coffee, and maybe even find a meeting. She'd go to one tonight if Simon was home. If not, first thing tomorrow. She'd gone thirteen years without a drink, but after falling last Saturday night, every sunrise since had brought unbearable pain, stress, and anxiety, leaving her powerless to fight that demon. There had now been five days of failures. She was not going to let there be a sixth. No matter what came next, she couldn't escape it in a bottle. Her kids needed her.

She made a meat loaf with hash browns and a chopped salad with ranch, the kids' favorite, and when Simon still hadn't appeared or called by seven, she fed them and sipped her coffee while they entertained her with stories from their school day. Miraculously, they seemed oblivious to her struggle and absenteeism of the last week. They were gloriously self-absorbed, exactly what she'd needed. They knew their grandpa was in the hospital and that their mom needed to visit him a lot, so neither had complained about the after-school playdates she'd arranged every day. She gazed at their sunny, freckled faces, amazed that out of such horror could come so much light.

Simon finally got home at nine thirty. The kids had already gone to bed, and she watched from the doorway as he roused each child with a good-night kiss. Mikey and Lyla both responded with closed-eye smiles and whispered hellos before returning to their blissful sleep.

"You hungry?" Ginny asked as he came out of Lyla's room. "I made meat loaf. I can heat you a piece."

"Sure," he said. "That would be great. It's been a long day."

She prepared his food and placed the plate in front of him, wondering, as she took a seat across from him at the table, if now was the time. It was late, and he was tired, but it felt like the next right thing. Maybe, once she'd confessed, he would understand why she'd done what she did. If he could forgive her, they could get through it and maybe even have a fresh start.

She opened her mouth—pulling the pin from a grenade—and froze, willing the words to come that would cause the blast.

"Ginny," he said, beating her to the punch, "I want a divorce."

It was like a slap, stinging her cheek, shocking her entire body. It was a word he'd never used without disdain. In that way he was like her father, who spoke of those who considered divorce as lesser than, godless souls. Marriage was a sacred endeavor, and even though she'd known Simon only three months when he proposed, he'd made clear

160

that his beliefs dictated a lifelong commitment. She'd jumped at the chance. Just twenty-one at the time, she'd felt old and tired, white-knuckling sobriety with constant church attendance, AA meetings, and diligent focus on getting an LPN license after her first attempt at college and normalcy had crashed and burned. She was desperate for some sort of salvation and she'd looked at Simon—thirty-five at the time, a successful doctor, devout—as a sign from God.

"I didn't think you believed in divorce," she said.

"I've made peace with my decision. I've tried to make it work for a long time. I can't do it anymore."

She didn't know how to respond. It had been sixteen years. The only good that had come from them were the kids. It would break their hearts. "Do you really want to do this? You hardly see the kids as it is."

"Actually, I'm going to seek custody."

Ginny's mouth fell open. He could have punched her in the gut and it would have hurt less. It was absurd. He worked ten- and twelve-hour days; he never spent more than thirty minutes a day with them. She quit her job because he wanted her focus at home. She kept up with this big house; she did everything. He had no idea what he was saying. The children were a mother's domain—those were his words.

And then she understood.

"Who is she?" Ginny asked.

Simon's eyes turned away while he put down his fork, took a sip from his water glass, and wiped his mouth, slowly and carefully. Finally, he resumed eye contact, his face absent of emotion, regret, confession, anything. "You're unfit. I've found someone who can give us what we need."

She felt physically sick. "Are you kidding me?"

Simon stood and tossed the napkin onto the table. "Ginny, let it go."

She wanted to scream.

"This was a partnership that simply didn't work. You have a lot of problems to sort through. You aren't capable of giving any of us what we need. And I'm sorry, but you can't be trusted with those kids. I'm going to seek custody, and I'm going to get it. I had you followed the other day."

She held her breath, terrified of whatever else he knew.

"You went to Good Samaritan after leaving the hospital on Tuesday. You walked into the church with Pastor Gary, and forty-five minutes later you drove to a liquor store, went to the forest, got drunk, and then drove thirty minutes home. I found you passed out in Lyla's bed that night and had to carry you out. You couldn't even be roused the next morning. That is not a fit parent."

She opened her mouth but hardly knew what to say.

"I'm sleeping in the guest room. Please, don't fight me. I don't want to argue. It's been a long day."

He walked upstairs, leaving his half-eaten plate for her to clean.

~ • ~

It was after ten when Wilson finally sat down with his tea to read Woods's screenplay. He was mentally exhausted from babysitting Eddie, but he'd managed to get him to eat and go to sleep, telling him stories while sitting on the edge of his bed, just as he'd done when Eddie was a child. He was getting too old for all of it—the job, Eddie, everything.

In that moment, it was hard not to envy his friend John Anderson. The idea of lying in a hospital bed while staff brought in food almost sounded like a vacation. Though he was ready for John to heal up. In two days Wilson would finally be retired, and he was practically pining for one of their card games or a fishing trip.

Wilson sipped his tea and leaned back in his La-Z-Boy before beginning page one of the script. He hadn't thought he'd get through it before morning, but once he got through the first twenty pages, he had to push his calves against the leg rest, return to an upright position, and focus. He couldn't put it down.

It was just before midnight when he turned the last page. He pushed back against the seat to fully recline again and stared at his ceiling as the people he knew and the narrative he'd read merged into a painful epiphany.

"Oh, Ginny," he muttered.

CHAPTER TWENTY-THREE

WILSON CALLED DONNY AS SOON as he woke at eight. "You done reading?" he asked.

"The screenplay? Yep. Pretty compelling, right?"

Wilson grunted his agreement. Donny had no idea what this story meant. He was too new to Eden and didn't know who it was about.

"It wasn't what I expected," Donny said.

"Me either."

"I guess we can't be certain about any of it without talking to Woods, though. I mean, it's inspired by a true story, but he may have taken some artistic license, right?"

"True," Wilson said. But the truth was in there, even if Woods didn't know it.

"I'm guessing the sheriff referenced in the story was you, huh?"

"Mm-hmm." Eddie was obviously one of the characters as well, though Donny was sensitive enough to leave that nugget alone.

"And the girl . . . do you think that's the woman you told me about yesterday? Ginny Smith?"

"I'm afraid so," Wilson said. This story was going to rip his friend's family apart. If they were all lucky, Woods would reconsider doing that stupid movie.

"Well, then I guess it's pretty clear that this screenplay could be the motive for shooting Woods—assuming we can establish that anyone around here has read it."

"Yeah. Meet me at the station at ten, okay? I gotta do something first."

Wilson hung up the phone and drove to Burns Memorial to visit his friend. He owed him that.

When he got to the room, John was sitting up, eating breakfast.

"Two visits in two days," John said. "Now that's a good friend." John's color was good—he was sitting taller in the bed, getting stronger.

Wilson smiled and sat in the chair beside John's bed. "Hey, bud, I need to talk to you about somethin'."

"Sounds serious," John said, putting his fork down. He pushed the tray away. "Awful stuff."

"There's something I need to tell you," Wilson began. "Do you remember Darius Woods?"

John's face seemed to tighten as if he were fighting against any reaction. "Should I?"

"Black kid in class with Eddie and Ginny back in high school. He's become a famous movie star . . ."

"Oh yeah," John said, nodding slowly. "I think I heard something about that."

"He's written a screenplay about his life in Eden."

"And?"

"I guess that means you haven't heard about it?"

John crossed his arms. "Wilson, I don't have the foggiest idea where you're going with this. Get on with it."

"I've read the screenplay. I hate to be the one to tell you this, but it may mess with your family."

John turned to the window and said nothing. He didn't press for more. Did he already know what Wilson was talking about?

There was so much in there that could hurt, Wilson suddenly didn't know how to proceed. "There are some scenes between a couple of characters—one of whom I believe is Ginny, and the other . . . well . . ."

"Come on, Wilson," John barked, finally meeting his gaze. "What are you trying to say?"

"Do you remember that pastor from First Hope that led the youth group?"

John looked genuinely perplexed. "Pastor Gary, of course. He was a good friend to this family. Still is."

"You're still in touch with him? Even since he left First Hope?"

John tilted his head, that one eyebrow going up a little higher. He was searching Wilson's eyes, trying to pull it out, like a mind reader. Wilson didn't have the heart to say any more. "Maybe you better read the screenplay."

"O-kay."

"John, someone tried to kill Darius Woods the other day."

John held his gaze, waiting for more.

"Last Sunday evening. Same night you fell. Same night Ginny came to Eden and found you on the floor."

John turned toward the window as if trying to remember last Sunday. Wilson let the silence fill the air between them.

Finally, John looked at him. "We've been through enough. I've already lost Bonnie. Please . . . don't let that boy destroy my family."

The two men looked each other in the eyes.

"You wanna tell me what happened last Sunday night?" Wilson asked. "Off the record?"

"Nope."

"Do you remember last Sunday night?"

"I'm not an idiot."

"No, I'm not suggesting. Ginny just told me you've had some memory issues."

He scowled. "Yeah, she'd like that, wouldn't she?"

"What do you mean?"

John just tilted his chin down. "Come on, let's not do this. Is Woods gonna make it?"

"Not sure yet. I think so."

John looked out the window. He didn't seem happy about it.

"It'll be okay," Wilson said. "I'll do what I can." He stood and patted his friend's shoulder. His envy of John had vanished. Suddenly his problems with Eddie seemed far less daunting than John's problems.

Wilson left the hospital, wondering how he could help. Donny was taking over as sheriff tomorrow. Wilson needed him to move on or at least keep his eyes off John's family. They needed to focus on the one man in that screenplay who deserved the trouble it would bring.

He grabbed Donny from the station and arrived at First Hope around ten fifteen in the morning. Being a Friday, it was pretty quiet. Wilson removed his hat as they walked into the main nave. A minister was up at the altar, practicing a sermon to an empty room, but he stopped and waved at the men standing in back.

"Sorry for interrupting," Wilson said. "But could you answer a couple of questions for us?"

"Of course," the man said, stepping down and walking up the aisle to join them. "How can I assist you gentlemen?"

"We're looking for information on a Pastor Gary Nichols."

"I'm not familiar with that name."

"He was working here from at least 1999 to 2006."

"I've only been here five years. But given those dates, I'm sure Reverend Thomas could help. He's been here since the early nineties."

"Great," Wilson said. "And where do we find him?"

"California, right now. His youngest just graduated from school out there."

"What about some records?" Donny asked. "We'd like to find out where Pastor Gary is working now."

"Just head on over to the office. The secretary should probably be there by now. She comes in around ten. I'm sure she can help you out."

They left the church and walked the grounds toward the adjacent building, where a woman was unlocking the office door. Wilson and Donny jogged over. "Ma'am?" Wilson shouted.

"Just the woman we wanted to see," Donny added.

The woman turned and froze. Perhaps two officers coming at her first thing in the morning was a bigger jolt than coffee.

"We need help with some church records. We heard you'd be the one to talk to about a former pastor of the church," Wilson said.

"O-kay," the woman said slowly. The corners of her mouth turned up, and her eyes widened, as if a crime-related mystery would add great interest to the day ahead. "What's going on?"

"We just want to find out where he is now. He might be able to help with something we're working on," Wilson said.

"Well, that's easy enough," she replied. "Can I ask what you're working on?"

"You can," Wilson said with a smile, "but I can't tell you."

"Figures." The woman's smile faded, and she unlocked the door. She hit the light switch, hung up her coat, and plopped down in her chair behind the desk. "Gonna take just a minute to get the computer going."

The men both sat in the chairs in front of her desk. "No problem," Wilson said.

"Have you been with the church a long time?" Donny asked.

"Oh, sure. I grew up in this church. Married here. Raised my kids here. My daughter even brings her kids here."

"That's great," Wilson said. "So you must remember Pastor Gary Nichols."

She smiled. "He was darlin'. Sorry to see him go. He was so great with the kids. Pastor Neil, he's a nice man, of course, but between you and me, the kids don't really connect with him the same way."

"Mm-hmm, and do you know where Pastor Gary was reassigned when he left?"

The woman looked at the screen. "Okay, here we go," she said, scrolling the mouse across the screen. "Let's go to staff . . . Oh. He's not too far. He went to Good Samaritan over in Harrisburg. Just about thirty minutes from here."

Ginny lived in Harrisburg. There had to be several Baptist churches there, but Wilson's dread returned. He did not want to find out she was still connected to that man.

~ • ~

After Ginny got the kids off to school, she went to the nine o'clock AA meeting at her local public library. She didn't share with the group, other than expressing gratitude for one day of sobriety and the will to finally do something she'd needed to do for a long time. She walked out with a little more strength than she'd walked in with and drove directly to Good Samaritan.

Pastor Gary was in his office, wearing jeans and a sweatshirt. It felt like one sign in her favor. At least she didn't have to speak to him while he was in his collar. Something about that ring around his neck was like a superhero force field. It had intimidated her from the time she was a little girl.

"Isn't this a nice surprise," he said, rising from his desk. "It's a bit early for one of your visits, but I'm always happy to see my favorite girl." He shut the door behind her.

She sat on the edge of the couch, and he sat beside her, draping an arm around her shoulders. "You look like you've got a lot on your mind," he said, moving that arm down, stroking her hair.

She took a deep breath before beginning. She was done letting him touch her. She was done letting him do whatever he wanted in order to repay the never-ending debt for the gift of giving her children. She'd prepared this speech all night long. "Gary," she said, turning to look him in the eyes, and dropping the "Pastor," "I'm going to tell Simon the truth about the kids."

Pastor Gary blinked slowly, his eyes widening as the rest of his body froze. His cheeks flushed as he stood and walked away, returning to the chair behind his desk. "Ginny," he finally said, tone firm, "you can't possibly do that. You'll destroy your family."

"My family is already destroyed. He's going to find out anyway."

"You don't know that. You don't even know if Darius will survive. I saw a mention of it on the news last night. It sounds like he's still critical." His tone lifted, as if Darius's death would be a welcome turn of events.

"Do you hear yourself? You're supposed to be a man of God. Besides, he's going to be okay. He texted me again early this morning. They're releasing him on Sunday."

Gary said nothing. He stood and paced the room in silence. Finally, he stopped in front of her and looked down, as if determined to wield his power. "Ginny, you can't let Darius make that movie. You need to talk to him."

"As if he's going to do me any favors after everything I've done. It doesn't matter anymore. I need to come clean with Simon. There's no other way."

"There has to be."

"Listen to me," Ginny said, finally raising her voice to him. "I've thought about this all night. Simon wants a divorce, and he's going to try and take my kids. He says I'm unfit." The tears came. Just the thought of losing those kids felt like her limbs were being pulled away, tearing muscle, popping tendons. She would never survive. "I'm not unfit! I've done some terrible things, but those kids are the only good thing I've done in the last twenty years. I can't lose them."

Gary turned away. He went back to his desk and sat, staring at the papers in front of him. "You can't do that, Ginny," he said, his tone flat, unsympathetic. "You'll ruin me. I'll lose my job. I may never be able to minister again. I thought you understood. I was trying to help you. I never did anything you didn't want . . ."

"What?" she said incredulously. She finally had the courage to say it. "I was sixteen."

"Stop!" he yelled. "It wasn't like that. You were attracted to me, Ginny. Come on!" he pleaded.

The tears fell from her eyes as she recalled every encounter between them back in high school, including the last time they'd been alone together. He'd played that Prince song "I Would Die 4 U," explaining how the song was about Jesus, how sexuality was linked to worshipping God, how his desire of her was holy and that he wanted to help her express her faith.

She couldn't say any more.

He slammed his hand against the desk. "You're not a victim, Ginny. You were an adult when I got to this church. I helped you! I thought this was our special bond."

She couldn't deny her culpability. She couldn't defend her actions, even though she'd been broken and drunk that first time before Mikey. But she was done living under his unspoken repayment plan. She'd never again lie on this couch or drink his alcohol or let him touch her. She'd made a mess of countless lives, but she loved Mikey and Lyla and she couldn't let Simon take them. They would suffer. They needed her.

Telling Simon the truth was her only hope. His notions of family never included raising someone else's kids. His outrage over Bonnie's request that Brooklyn be a flower girl in their wedding all those years ago made that clear enough. He'd said the role was intended for family and Brooklyn didn't look like anyone's family. He'd left the room, angry, and Ginny had looked at her mom, terrified. She didn't know him at all. "I can't marry that man," she'd pleaded.

But Bonnie had taken her hands and said, "You must, he's a good man. Brooklyn doesn't need to be in the service. She's only three. She probably wouldn't want all the pressure anyway." Bonnie had held her by the shoulders, shaking her, warning her that she was not to blow it.

Ginny took a breath and stood from the couch. There was nothing left to say. She walked to the office door.

"Ginny, stop, please."

She paused, her hand on the doorknob.

"We have to protect each other," Gary pleaded.

She opened the door and turned back to look at him one last time. "I can't do this anymore," she said.

"Do what?" a voice said from behind her.

Every hair on her head turned to needles as she turned around.

Sheriff Wilson was standing in the doorway.

CHAPTER TWENTY-FOUR

GINNY WAS THE LAST PERSON Wilson wanted to see in Pastor Gary's office. It meant she'd never gotten away from this scumbag. Her face lost all color when she saw him in the doorway. Donny probably noticed it too.

"Well, isn't this a coincidence," Wilson said.

"Hi, Sheriff." Ginny's voice was barely audible. "Are you looking for me?"

"Not right now," Wilson said. "Actually, we're here to talk to the pastor." He watched Ginny look back at Pastor Gary before returning her gaze to him.

"Well, I'm in a rush then. I'll see you later," she said.

"Sounds good," Wilson said as she left. He didn't want Ginny to hear what he was about to say to this guy, and he'd rather talk to her again without Donny around. If she was tied up in this mess, he couldn't help her if Donny knew too much.

Wilson stepped inside, and Donny followed. Pastor Gary remained seated at his desk, offering only a determined look of nonchalance.

"Sorry to bother you, Pastor," Wilson said. "We need a few minutes of your time."

Pastor Gary leaned back and smiled. "Sure, gentlemen. Come on in. How can I help you?"

Wilson sat in one of the chairs in front of the desk. Donny did the same. "Pastor, do you remember me?" Wilson asked.

The man smiled, squinting, as if this were a game.

"It's been twenty years, so I was probably twenty pounds lighter, my hair wasn't quite this white, and of course, no beard," Wilson said.

The pastor tilted his head to the side, carefully examining his face.

"Remember that shooting at the women's clinic a few miles outside Eden back in '99?"

Pastor Gary sat forward, his expression serious. "Oh, yes. Okay. Right," he said nodding. "That was an unfortunate misunderstanding."

"Misunderstanding?"

"You—thinking that sweet girl could have had anything to do with that shooting. It's absurd, really."

"Absurd," Wilson repeated. "You said she'd been with you the morning in question, remember?"

"That's right."

"And what brought you to this church?"

"I go where I'm needed. It's the nature of the work."

"And you were needed here?"

"I suppose I was."

"Small world that Ginny Anderson, now Ginny Smith, is a congregant here as well."

"True. I believe I said the same thing the first time I saw her at a service."

"And obviously you two are still close."

"She's a wonderful girl. She's really helpful to me, still. As a volunteer."

Wilson looked over at Donny, who seemed content as spectator, before leaning forward and lowering his voice. "I find it interesting that you refer to Ginny as a girl. She's almost forty years old."

Pastor Gary smirked and nodded, relaxing into his chair back. "You're right. Well, I guess since I'm fifty, I think of everyone younger than me as a kid. I'm sure you understand."

Wilson sat back and crossed his arms. "Actually, I think you need to understand that Illinois recently wiped out the statute of limitations on sexual assault of a child. We're treating it just like murder these days."

Pastor Gary sat upright. "Excuse me, are you implying something?"

"Actually, I am."

The pastor's focus left the men suddenly, and he looked at the door behind them. Wilson turned. There was no one there, though he imagined the pastor wished someone would arrive to interrupt.

"I don't know what you've heard, Sheriff, but I assure you, I've never behaved inappropriately with a child. I'm horrified that—"

The feigned indignation lit a fire under Wilson. He was out of his chair quicker than he'd have believed possible, leaning over the desk, his face now spitting distance from the pastor's. "I've known Ginny Anderson since she was a baby." He put his finger in the pastor's face. "You mighta been able to keep her mouth shut when she was a teen, but I'm betting all that might change now."

The pastor leaned back, away from Wilson, and stood, walking toward the door. "Sheriff, I don't know what you think you know . . ."

"Oh, I know all about you," Wilson said.

The pastor pushed the door shut and turned around.

"In fact," Wilson continued, leaning against the desk, "a woman came to my office back in, what was that, 2006? A complaint about you. About your behavior with her daughter."

"That's absurd. I know what you're implying, and—"

"And that's just about the time you left First Hope."

"I left First Hope because I was needed elsewhere. You can check my records. I didn't run from anything."

Wilson nodded. "Uh-huh. Remember Darius Woods?"

The pastor looked at Donny as if he needed help placing the name.

"Big movie star now," Donny offered.

"From Eden," Wilson finished. "Someone took a shot at him last Sunday. It was national news. You tellin' me you don't know about that?"

"It sounds vaguely familiar . . ."

"You knew Darius back when he and Ginny were in high school."

"Did I? I don't think he was a member of the congregation."

"Nope. But you asked him to be in a play at the church, and he came to your office to turn you down."

The pastor raised a helpless hand. "You're talking about something that was at least twenty years ago. I'm sure I don't remember all the teens I met over the years."

"Aren't you curious as to why I know about that particular encounter?"

"I suppose," Pastor Gary said. "It hardly sounds earth-shattering."

"He wrote about it. Darius Woods wrote a screenplay about his days in Eden, and there's one character in that story who sounds a lot like you."

The pastor shook his head. "Well, I can't imagine that's true. I don't remember that boy at all. And like I said, he wasn't in the congregation."

Donny finally stood and sat on the edge of the desk beside Wilson. "You have any guns, Gary?"

Pastor Gary scoffed and went to the couch. "Well, who doesn't?" He dropped down onto a cushion like this was nothing more than a humorous conversation. "I hunt. Sacrilegious not to, right?" He smiled, as if trying to make light.

"What about pistols?" Donny added.

"No. I don't have any. The church has one, of course. For protection."

"Mm-hmm. And the make on that?" Wilson asked.

"No idea."

"Well, how about you let us take a look at it. Where's it kept?"

"In Pastor James's office. You'll have to see him about that."

"Is he here? I'd like to do that now."

"He's not."

Wilson paused and looked around the room, hoping the silence would unnerve this degenerate. "And where were you last Sunday?"

"Well, I'm sure I was here, of course."

Wilson stood and moved toward the couch. "I'm wondering where you were in the early evening—say between five and seven o'clock."

"I don't recall."

Wilson gestured to Donny that it was time to go. "I'm gonna need you to remember. You think on that, Pastor, and I'll be in touch."

Outside, Donny trailed Wilson to the squad car.

"Hey, slow down," Donny said. "Can you catch me up? What are you doing?"

Wilson opened the driver's door and paused to look at Donny on the other side of the car. "Rattling the cage, that's all."

"I take it he's Pastor Ed in the screenplay?"

"Exactly. And everyone who lived in Eden twenty years ago, everyone who had a teen at First Hope Baptist when he was there, is going to realize that too."

"Well, that's . . ."

"That's motive," Wilson said before climbing in the car. "So let's find out the make on the church gun."

Donny got in and shut his door. "Of course, we're talking about the pastor of a church. And if he didn't know Woods was in town, if he didn't know about the screenplay, this goes nowhere. I mean, I get that he's unsavory, but . . ."

"There is no *but*," Wilson said. He put the key in the ignition and turned. "Justice is more than following evidence, Donny. It's doing the right thing."

"The right thing according to whom? Sounds a little too subjective if you ask me."

Wilson shook his head. "Come on. Only one person can tell us who's read the screenplay. Let's just hope he's doing better. If any good comes from that script, it's the possibility of getting that piece of garbage away from kids."

~ • ~

Ginny was sitting at the kitchen table drinking coffee at ten that night, her eyes fixed on the wall clock, watching the dial slowly tick past each minute. The kids were asleep, but she was determined to stay awake. She might lose her nerve to tell Simon everything if she waited even one more day, so she'd called his hospital. He had come out of a surgery an hour ago. He had to be home soon.

When she'd left Pastor Gary's office after the sheriff arrived, the urge to drown in a bottle was overwhelming. But she'd gripped the steering wheel, closed her eyes, and inhaled deeply, pushing the air out slowly, promising that alcohol would never again be her escape. She also promised herself that she'd never walk into that church again. Her life was about to change forever, and maybe she'd even need to move somewhere new with the kids, but she was not going to do anything that could hurt them ever again. She was going to turn her life around and make those kids proud.

A car door slammed shut outside. Her heart began to pound in her chest. It was time. It felt like all blood stopped pumping, her whole system frozen, while she waited for the front door to unlock. Instead, there was a light knock on the door.

She looked through the peephole, seeing only the top of someone's head resting against the door. She opened it and watched as Gary stumbled and stepped back to an upright position.

"What are you doing here?"

"Did you do it?" he asked. His eyes were bloodshot, his lids a little puffy, as if he'd been crying.

"He hasn't come home yet. Gary, you really need to go. I don't think you want to be here when he gets home."

Gary stepped inside, uninvited, and she immediately smelled the alcohol on his breath. "Ginny, I've prayed on this all day. I think your plan is a mistake."

"I'm sure you do."

"It's not just about me. I know you think I'm only worried about myself, but your kids love their dad." He looked past her to their pictures on the wall behind her. "Do you really want them exposed to a scandal?"

She looked at the pictures too.

"Simon's the only dad they've known. And despite what's happened between you and me, there are people in that church who need me, who come to me for counseling. You'd be causing a ripple of pain and trouble for more people than you're thinking about. I know you're worried that Simon's going to figure it all out because of the movie, but maybe not. People see what they want to see. He doesn't want to think those kids aren't his."

She was done listening to this man. He'd been spinning rationales and justifications for his behavior since she was a girl. "Just leave. Please."

The phone rang from the kitchen, startling them both.

She turned to get it, but Gary grabbed her arm hard. "Ginny, I don't think you want me to tell Simon or the sheriff that you shot

Darius Woods on Sunday, do you? Or maybe I'll tell him that you were the shooter at the clinic all those years ago. If I were to lose my position with the church, what would stop me? And you'd certainly lose those kids."

The phone rang again. She was paralyzed. "You can't do that."

It rang again, and Gary let go, stumbling toward the living room. "I can do anything. And I'm not leaving until I talk some sense into you," he said, collapsing into a chair.

She wanted to scream. She ran to the kitchen to get the phone, afraid it was Simon with some lame excuse for not coming home.

"Hello?"

"Is this Ginny Smith?" It was a man's voice.

"It is."

"I'm sorry to call so late. Actually, I assumed I'd get voice mail. I'm just catching up on my calls."

"I'm sorry, now's not—"

"Again, my apologies for the timing, but I represent your husband, Simon, and he asked that I call and set up a meeting with you so the three of us can discuss the divorce and custody arrangements. Obviously, if you'd like to retain an attorney, it's your right. I am representing him, but he suggested we talk about mediation to keep things out of the courts."

"I can't do this . . . ," she began to say. The front door opened and closed again. She hoped Gary had come to his senses and left. "I need to go," she said before hanging up.

She returned to the front hall. Simon was in the living room, shaking Gary's hand.

Hearing Ginny walk into the room, Simon turned around and said hello. "Sorry I'm late, honey. Another long day."

He was obviously going to pretend theirs was a happy home as long as there was a visitor present.

"Pastor Gary said you asked him to come by," he continued. "Are you okay?"

"I'm fine. And the pastor was actually just leaving. Thanks for coming so late," she said to Gary.

"Of course," he said. "Just remember what I said, and everything will be fine."

Ginny looked over at Simon, but he'd already lost interest in the conversation. "Good to see you, Pastor," he said, walking back into the hall.

Ginny walked to the front door and held it for Gary. "Take care," she said. She was about to shut it behind him when she became distracted by Simon, who was rifling through the hall closet. "What are you doing?"

Simon was looking up at the shelf. "Where's my gun?"

CHAPTER TWENTY-FIVE

At ten thirty, Brooklyn was on the train, starting her long journey back to Eden. She'd need to ride sixty minutes and transfer twice before arriving at Kennedy airport for her one o'clock red-eye back to Saint Louis. It was going to be a long night, but she didn't care. She was sleepy from all the tequila, but still giddy about her day.

She'd practically skipped the eight blocks home from the call-back, grinning as she sprinted up the six flights of stairs to her apartment. The director, his assistant, and the producer had asked her to speak some Spanish after her reading. She'd overstated her abilities on her résumé—calling herself "near fluent" under "special skills"—but hadn't thought to prep for that. She laughed as she often did when terrified, then, as if her life depended on it, she frantically spit out a Spanish poem she'd once memorized for class in high school. They all laughed. The director said he had no idea what she'd said, but her accent was great.

No one made any promises, but his assistant asked if she had a passport. "No," she said, sitting taller, trying to appear serious, "but—"

"Get one," the director said before dropping his pen, like the matter was resolved. "Just in case," he added after she flashed a wide grin. "They can take a couple of months."

It was hard to focus after that comment. She was going to get the role. She could feel it. They talked about the shooting schedule, she guaranteed her availability, and they said there were a couple of other contenders and they'd be in touch within the week.

She'd returned to an empty apartment and turned on some music, pushing away concerns about her dad, lingering on the hope that she still had a chance to live her dream. She sent Ginny a text, thanking her for insisting she do the callback and sharing her excitement about how it went. Everything okay there? she finally asked.

Ginny's answer was immediate. Fine. Congrats.

Brooklyn didn't follow up, desperate to stay in her good mood.

Her phone pinged moments later, but the next text was from Tony: Thinking of you. When you coming back?

There was no time to see him now. He might be a serious mismatch, but it was nice to think he was still out there somewhere, thinking about her, that her life in New York wasn't slipping away. Soon, she wrote. I'll be in touch asap.

When her roommates returned home, the celebrating began. They'd all had little bit parts and gigs here and there, but this job, if Brooklyn got it, would be the biggest thing that had happened to any of them. She didn't even want to consider that the role might not be hers. It felt like destiny.

It wasn't until she was waiting at the gate for her plane that her thoughts returned to her family again. She pulled out her phone. The weight of what she faced back in Eden began pressing toward the front of her mind. She spotted a penny on the carpet near the trash bin and stepped over to it, silently asking if everything was okay at home. She needed to see a heads up.

Tails.

~ • ~

Wilson sat at the kitchen table at midnight, drinking coffee. There was no way he'd sleep anyway. When he'd gotten out of bed that morning, he never would have imagined that the day would end as it had. He hoped his wife, looking down on him, understood why he'd done what he did.

He picked through the shoebox full of old photos in front of him, searching for that little boy he'd loved so much. The youngest child, the sweet, shy kid who used to sit on his lap and beg to go fishing and say that he wanted to grow up to be a policeman like his dad. It felt like that boy had died. Or at least been kidnapped. Wilson didn't know the man Eddie had become, and he still couldn't believe that loving him and helping him had never been enough.

He and Donny had left Pastor Gary and driven to Burns to finally interview Woods. But when they got there, Eddie was on the floor in the hall outside Woods's room, shouting, and one of Wilson's officers had him pinned, a knee on his back, putting Eddie's wrists in cuffs.

"Hey, hey! What's happening?" Wilson had asked, rushing to his son. "Eddie, what's going on?"

"This creep jumped me," Eddie said. "I wasn't doing anything." He was bucking under the man's weight, writhing around as if he could escape.

"Stop moving, Eddie. You're gonna end up with a broken arm."

"Sir, I'm sorry," the officer said to Wilson, still holding Eddie down. "He was trying to get into Woods's room. I'd stepped over to the nurse for just a second. I spotted him at the door and asked him to stop. That's when I saw the gun in his hand."

"He's got it all wrong," Eddie said.

Wilson could see that Eddie was high on something. "Don't say another word," Wilson said.

The other officer stood, leaving Eddie cuffed and lying on the ground.

"I'll take him." Wilson pulled Eddie by the arm until he was standing.

Donny looked at him, one eyebrow raised. Wilson knew what Donny had to be thinking . . . that Eddie might have been Woods's shooter and that Wilson wanted to sweep it under the rug.

"I'll get to the bottom of this, Donny. You get in there and talk to Woods. If there's a reason Eddie wanted to hurt him, Woods'll know. He might even be able to tell us more about what he saw or heard the day he was shot.

"Come on," he said to his son, pulling him by the elbow down the hall. Neither spoke until they got in the elevator.

"What in God's name is going on?" he finally asked.

"Nothin'," Eddie slurred, as if the whole conversation were too exhausting. "I just wanted to talk to him."

"With a gun in your hand? Where'd you get that, anyway?"

"It's yours. Found it in the garage."

"Great."

"I wasn't gonna do nothin'. He's causin' trouble round here, Dad. I was gonna encourage him to get the hell outta town."

"Eddie, please don't tell me you shot Darius Woods."

He looked at his dad and smiled. "I did not shoot Darius Woods."

"I read Woods's screenplay," Wilson said.

"Yeah, me too."

"What?"

"You left it on the coffee table this morning. Couldn't help myself."

Wilson felt the air catch in his throat. "You can't still be upset about what happened between you two back in high school. You can't be so petty as to go after him all these years later."

"I'm not. Jeez, Dad. I just came here for some pills. Security was too tight. I thought I'd pop in on the local celebrity, that's all."

Wilson didn't know what to believe. He thought back to Sunday, when he got the call about the shooting. Eddie, gone all day, had walked in moments after the phone rang. Soaking wet, his clothes dripping onto the kitchen floor, that story of fishing in the rain. "Best time to catch 'em," he'd said, even though he'd come home empty-handed.

Wilson had left, passing Eddie's muddied sneakers at the front door, not giving it another thought. His son was safe. But Woods's shooter would have been soaked and his shoes muddy.

Wilson said nothing more until he pulled into the station parking lot.

"What are we doing here?" Eddie asked.

Wilson pulled the keys from the ignition and turned to his son. "You realize that as of tomorrow, I'm officially no longer the sheriff? I can't continue to get you out of trouble. I can't be sure that you don't get a DUI, like I did last year. I can't continue to smooth over your chaos."

Eddie let his head fall back against the seat rest and closed his eyes. "I promise, Dad, I'll do better. Just drop me at a meeting. You can pick me up later. It's all I need. Really. I promise."

Wilson got out of the car, went around, and pulled Eddie out of the squad car. "I know you're gonna do better. I'm gonna be sure of it." He began pulling him toward the building.

"What do you mean? Seriously, Dad! I'm your son. Stop!"

Wilson said nothing more until they were inside. When he spotted an officer, he waved him over. "Put him in lockup."

"Goddammit, Dad! Stop. Seriously! You can't do this!" Wilson ignored his son while the officer walked Eddie down the hall. Eddie needed to get out of his own way. And maybe jail was the only thing that would let sobriety take hold—at least for a few days.

After Eddie was gone, Wilson pulled the gun from his jacket and gave it to another officer nearby. "Send it to the lab. I need this checked against the bullets pulled outta Woods."

"Where'd it come from?" the officer asked.

"Don't worry about it. Let's just find out. And tell them it's a rush. Actually, I got this," he said, picking up the phone. "I better cash in a favor, because I gotta know by tomorrow." The gun was a .38. He couldn't believe that his son could have shot Woods, but he had to know. It had been twenty years since Eddie had gone after Woods, but he would be a defense attorney's nightmare. And juries didn't care what addicts had to say.

CHAPTER TWENTY-SIX

GINNY BARELY SLEPT, AND WHEN she finally got up on Saturday, the dread of what was to come weighed on her shoulders like thirty-pound barbells.

When Simon had asked about the gun, she froze, her first thought being that if he knew Sheriff Wilson had it, having questioned her about an attempted murder, he'd use that information against her. Gary, seizing the opportunity to rescue her again, and maybe bargain for her silence, stepped back inside the front door with a quick apology, saying he'd asked Ginny if he could borrow it. He rattled off some story about a robbery at Good Samaritan, saying the church's firearm was among the taken items. He'd just wanted to have something until the paperwork on a replacement went through. Simon didn't seem to care, and Gary quickly left.

When Ginny finally asked if that was what Simon had been searching for in the closet, he'd said no, but he wanted to take the kids fishing tomorrow after church and couldn't find the rods in the garage. He was suddenly going to show himself as the better parent. She couldn't admit not remembering where they were. Everything was now a test of her fitness. And in that moment, she lost her nerve.

She needed a lawyer. And telling Sheriff Wilson the truth about Sunday night was no longer an option. It didn't matter that he might try to help—Simon was going to use every mistake she'd ever made against her.

After getting the kids up, dressed, and fed, they headed over to her dad's house in Eden. The kids chatted in the back seat about what they'd do first.

"Will the horses be out?" Lyla asked.

"I don't know," Ginny said.

"We gotta check that first," Lyla instructed Mikey.

"What about the frogs?" Mikey asked.

"We'll do that second," Lyla said. Despite being four years younger, she was the boss, and it made both Mikey and Ginny laugh.

Her kids only went to their grandparents' house on rare occasions and always looked forward to the open landscape, wildlife, the nearby pond that was full of frogs, and the neighbors' horses that lingered near the south-line fence. The simple farmhouse with its weather-beaten front steps and a few rotting patches on the south side paled in comparison to Ginny's house, one of Harrisburg's few grand leftovers from the early 1900s, with antebellum-style columns and detailed moldings, but to the kids, their grandparents' house was "the coolest."

As soon as she pulled into the gravel drive, Lyla and Mikey took off running.

Ginny grabbed her purse and walked up the front steps, stopping to sit on the porch swing and take in the scenery. It was a beautiful piece of land, with wild grasses and flowers covering most of the closest acreage. Even the air felt cleaner here. At least for her first sixteen years, she had loved growing up in this house and living in this town. When she was a little girl, she thought she'd be in Eden forever. Her mom and she even daydreamed about the day that Ginny would find true love and her dad would divide the property, allowing Ginny to build a house of her own while staying close. That way, they figured, the grandkids would run back and forth between them. She had never wanted to be too far from either of her parents or from her hometown back then, back before First Hope and Eden and this house began to feel like a prison.

She'd often wondered what might have happened, what her life would look like now, if she hadn't done the things she'd done, if she'd never seen the dark side of the men in her life, if she'd never known what they were capable of.

She spotted a delivery truck down the road and watched as it neared and finally pulled into the drive behind her car. The hospital bed. She directed the driver and his helper to bring it into the living room.

After the screen door slammed behind them on their way back out, she went upstairs to grab sheets and the quilt from her parents' bed. For so many years, she'd sworn she'd never look at John as a father again, and everything about his most recent behavior had only solidified her feelings, but she was her mother's daughter, and a nurse. The least she could do was get the bed ready for his arrival.

When she got to the bedroom, the bed was covered with her mom's clothes. Brooklyn had obviously been clearing out the closet. She peered into the bathroom, seeing the bucket of cleaning supplies by the shower and the open medicine-cabinet door.

Both shelves of the cabinet were filled with prescriptions. She pulled each one out, reading the labels, the drugs, and the dates, and placed them on the counter. She may have left nursing years ago, but she hadn't forgotten her training, and she recognized the drug names and what they were for: cholesterol, antianxiety, insomnia, bladder control, pain, memory issues, vertigo. Some in her mom's name, but most in her dad's. Some dated within the year, but several were older. Different physician names on each bottle. It was too much. She had no idea if he still took them all. She wondered if he always advised the doctors of other meds he was taking, if he even remembered whether he'd taken them. Combining some of them could lead to serious side effects.

She ran downstairs, grabbed her purse, and went back up the stairs, dumping the pill bottles into her bag. None of these excused his behavior, but they might explain the dementia-like symptoms.

The front screen door whacked against the doorframe, and the kids' little feet pounded up the steps as they called out her name.

"I'm in Grandpa's room," she yelled.

Lyla and Mikey barreled into the room to report on their adventure. Ginny came out of the bathroom and sat on the bed, smiling. They were both flushed, as if they'd done nothing but run for thirty minutes. Lyla handed over a fistful of wildflowers she wanted her mom to put in a vase.

"Why don't we come here more?" Mikey finally asked. "It's so cool."

"Maybe we will," she finally said.

"Is Grandpa gonna die?" Lyla asked.

"Well, at some point. No one lives forever, but I think he's got some time yet."

Lyla didn't smile.

"What is it?" Ginny asked. "You look disappointed!"

"He scares me."

Ginny felt the same way.

"It's that look he's always got," Mikey said. "One eyebrow taller than the other."

"He looks mean. And his voice is so deep," Lyla said.

"Well, he's harmless," Ginny said. He had never been harmless. "Come on, I've got to make up that bed, and then we need to go to the hospital, okay?"

"Okay," they said, running off. "We gotta see the frogs first!"

When Ginny finished getting the bed ready, she hit the lights and called the kids to meet her at the car. Glancing into her dad's study as she grabbed the front door handle, she suddenly remembered what she'd forgotten. And Brooklyn would be back soon. She stepped inside the room and carefully shut the little metal door of the gun safe without turning the combination lock.

She wanted to do the right thing, finally, but everything felt like a road to losing those kids. She didn't know what to do.

~ • ~

It was a few minutes before noon when Brooklyn finally pulled into the driveway, sleep-deprived but slightly wired from the intermittent coffees throughout her journey home.

When she got inside the house, the hospital bed, covered in one of her mom's best quilts, was set up near the window in the living room, a little antique side table beside it, and on it, a mason jar full of fresh-cut wildflowers. She stepped over, smoothing her hand over the patterns Mom had so carefully pieced together. Had Ginny finally realized that being home would be better for their dad? Was it possible that he and Ginny had already mended their fences? The bed was even topped with one of Mom's favorite needlepoint pillows, its bright flower design surrounding the proverb she'd carefully stitched: *Whoever walks in integrity walks securely, but whoever takes crooked paths will be found out.*

If felt like a sign, the greatest homecoming gift. Her family was healing.

She sent a quick text to Ginny telling her she was home and glad to see the bed. Her sister's response was immediate. I'm at hospital with the kids. Call you tomorrow. Dad gets out in the afternoon. Ginny called him *Dad*. It felt like a miracle.

He was coming home. Life was going to return to normal. She was going to get this movie role and go back to New York, and her family here was going to be just fine. She changed, brushed her teeth, and went to the hospital.

Dad was out of bed, walking the halls with the help of Nurse Wanda. She wondered if he had even noticed she'd been gone. It had only been forty-eight hours.

"Hi!" Brooklyn said, as she approached from the end of the hall. "You look great, Dad. How do you feel?"

He stopped for a second, looked at the nurse, and then back at Brooklyn. She got closer, holding her breath. Didn't he recognize her? Suddenly his expression changed. "Oh, hey, Brooklyn. I didn't see that was you. My distance vision isn't great these days."

Brooklyn sighed with relief. "I hear you're getting out tomorrow?"

"Can't be soon enough. And don't you see? I'm gonna be fine."

"He needs to avoid stairs for a while, but he is doing much better," Wanda confirmed.

Brooklyn followed as Wanda led her father back into the room. "Well, I just came from the house. Ginny's already set up a bed on the main floor, so I think we're ready. There are several steps up the front porch, though. Is that okay?"

"Sure," Wanda said, helping him into bed. "It's only for a couple of days. You'll just need to help him."

"What do you mean, a couple of days?" Brooklyn asked.

"The rehab facility won't have a bed for a couple of days. I believe the setup at home is temporary, right?"

Brooklyn looked at her dad, who shook his head but said nothing. She wondered if he was acting agreeable so he could get out, like a prisoner plotting the best escape route. Wanda left, and Brooklyn sat beside the bed and leaned forward. "I'll talk to Ginny about the plan. Don't worry."

Nothing was resolved. She'd been kidding herself, suffering from a severe case of wishful thinking spurred by her brief return to normal life. Ginny still wanted their dad sent off to a rehab facility and probably a nursing home too. She'd gotten Brooklyn out of town and set the wheels in motion. She'd probably already taken steps to sell the store and the house, and Brooklyn didn't know how to stop it.

No matter what was going on with him, Brooklyn had to bring him home. Regardless of whether Ginny would help, she would make it happen. It was the right thing to do. She wiped at the tears preparing to fall. This wasn't about her. It was about her dad.

Maybe she could stay for the summer, and if she got the movie role, Ginny could take over while she was gone. The dread was back. Suddenly, New York felt a million miles away again.

"Dad, I have good news," Brooklyn said, determined to rid her mind of spiraling into panic. She reached for his hand, sitting taller. "I got a callback for a movie. It's the lead. I think I might get the part."

Her dad nodded. His expression didn't change. He was always so stoic. Just once, she wanted to see him get as excited about her life as he did about catching a big fish.

"The best part," she continued. "It's about a girl from the Dominican Republic. Isn't that crazy? I'd get to go. Finally! Can you believe it?"

Her dad leaned forward, pointing toward the pillows behind his back. She adjusted them, and he sat back slowly. "Be sure it's legit, Brooklyn. You see that movie *Taken*? Came on cable recently. You can't trust people. You're too trusting to be in that horrible city."

Brooklyn rolled her eyes and smiled. He was starting to sound more like his old self. "It's legit, Dad, and yes, I've seen *Taken*. I'm not going to get kidnapped. I just need to get a passport. Where should I look for my paperwork? I already checked your files."

"Don't go rifling through my things!" he said, his volume rising. "Your mom's in charge of that stuff."

"Well, I can't ask Mom," she said, sharply. She regretted it as soon as the words came out. Her exhaustion had trumped patience.

"Why not?" he barked.

Was it possible that he didn't remember Mom was gone? She took a breath, wishing she could start the conversation over. "Dad, I've been wanting to ask you more about last Sunday. If you tripped on something, I want to be sure it doesn't happen again. It looks like you fell in the hall, right?"

"My gun," he muttered.

"What about it?"

His eyes burrowed into hers.

"Dad," she said, leaning forward. "What are you saying? You tripped on your gun?"

His face hardened. "Stop. That's stupid."

"Well, how'd you fall?"

"I'm old, okay? Enough with the questions!"

"Dad, when I got to the house on Monday, your gun safe was open, but I can't find your gun. Did you do something with it?"

He closed his eyes.

Brooklyn waited for a moment. "Dad, do you remember last Sunday?"

"Of course. It was Mother's Day," he said, his eyes still shut. "I went to church, worked the store, it rained, I went home."

His memory was fine. "Was Ginny there?"

"Ginny . . ." He opened his eyes and searched Brooklyn's face. She wondered if he was confused again. "She hates me," he whispered.

"No, she doesn't."

"You don't understand . . ." He closed his eyes again. "I'm tired." He put the heels of his hands to his eyes, rubbing them hard. "Too many pills," he said, eyes closed.

"Pain pills? Did you just get some pain pills?" she asked. "Because if you're having some side effects, I'll call the nurse—"

"Enough. Just go. Let me sleep."

Brooklyn stood. "Okay, big day tomorrow. I guess Ginny and the kids wore you out."

"I haven't seen those kids in ages," he said. "Now please, I need to sleep."

Brooklyn walked out of the room and stopped at the nurses' station. "I'm sorry. My dad seems a bit off from whatever pills you just gave him. I'm wondering if there might be side effects we should worry about?"

"I didn't give him anything," Nurse Wanda said. "He gets something for the pain in an hour, but he's doing well."

"Did you see my sister earlier?"

"The skinny little blonde thing?"

"Exactly," Brooklyn said.

"No, she hasn't been here. I've been here for hours."

Brooklyn was back to square one. Dad was confused; Ginny was lying. And he was getting out tomorrow. She didn't know how, but she was not going to go one more day without finding out what had happened between them.

CHAPTER TWENTY-SEVEN

DAY SEVEN
9:35 p.m.
BOLINE COUNTY JAIL

THE GUARD WALKED BROOKLYN BACK down the long hall to her cell. Her neighbor was standing at the bars, staring at her. He said nothing until the guard had locked her inside and walked away.

"Holy hell. You're John Anderson's girl, aren't you?" And he was Sheriff Wilson's son Eddie. She'd never met him, but as soon as he'd said his shoulder still hurt from a fight with Darius, she knew who he was. The truth about everyone had come out in the pages of Darius's screenplay.

"I've seen your picture up at the general store," Eddie said. "Wait a minute. You said your dad died. Did you kill your dad?" His voice rose, incredulous, and she could hear the unspoken judgment.

"No."

"He was a good man."

Eddie obviously didn't know her dad. Though maybe someone like Eddie wouldn't care.

"I heard about his fall last Sunday. Damn. I thought he'd be okay."

Brooklyn had no response.

"You hear about Woods's screenplay?" Eddie asked.

She looked at the cinder block between them, wondering what he knew.

"Well, you're sitting in here, so I'm guessing whatever happened to your dad didn't look like no accident," he said.

She had no response.

"Yeah, you must've read it. Me too."

How? She walked toward the wall between them.

"Prick," he said. "Made me look like some hillbilly. It's not true. I didn't give a crap what color that asshat was. I was just an angry kid. Maybe I used some words that offended people, but my mom frickin' died, okay?" he said, raising his voice defiantly. "Just left for groceries one day and never came back." He was still angry, twenty years later, about a senseless car accident.

Everything she read in that screenplay made her dislike and distrust Eddie Wilson, but she knew the pain of losing a parent. Twice now.

And today she'd learned the power of rage, its blinding force. The memories of the day rushed at her again, the assault of violence begging to be replayed in her mind. She couldn't stop the tape, and the pain of seeing her dad, dead on the floor, knocked her back. She'd been a coward. And now he was gone.

There was no justice in the world.

CHAPTER TWENTY-EIGHT

WILSON DRESSED IN HIS UNIFORM for the last time. When he had first thought about retiring a year ago, he'd envisioned fishing, relaxing, poker games. He'd never have guessed it would lead to this day, being forced to walk away in the middle of an investigation that was pointing not only toward his closest friend's family but even his own son. He wanted to fire Donny, stop this whole mess, and close the case.

He stopped at the station to pick up his box of things before heading to Donny's swearing in. There was a note on the desk. *Call Frank. ASAP.*

Frank had run the test on Wilson's gun. He dropped into the chair and picked up the phone. For the first time in his career, he was nervous about where an investigation was going. Could he really stand by and allow his own son to be prosecuted for attempted murder? Could he even stop it? If Eddie had taken a shot at Woods, it wasn't gonna be a short detox in that jail. It would be years in prison. Given the history between them—if Eddie had really used the words Woods wrote in his screenplay, he could just imagine the prosecution's narrative, painting Eddie as the drug-addicted racist.

It wasn't right. Eddie made jokes and called names, but he wasn't a racist. He was just so angry. He'd gotten so angry after his mom died.

Please, please, please, he silently begged. *Don't be true.* His boy's demon wasn't hatred. It was those frickin' drugs. They brought out such ugliness. He didn't know who Eddie had become.

Phone to his ear, he continued to silently pray until Frank picked up. "Hey, Frank, Sheriff Wilson here. Thanks so much for the quick turnaround."

"Well, I thought you'd want to know right away," Frank said. "Those bullets that hit Woods definitely did not come from the gun we tested."

"Did not. Did not?" He took a deep breath and pushed it out. "Oh, that's fantastic. Thanks, Frank. I owe you a million."

Wilson disconnected and leaned back in his chair. He would not watch his son get put away for attempted murder. No parent needed to live through watching their child go to jail. The thought brought him back to John's implicit request and the promise Wilson had made when he'd visited him yesterday morning. Donny didn't have much to go on yet, and there was still a chance the shooter was Woods's LA stalker, but John's comment haunted him. It wasn't exactly what he said; it was how he said it. Like John knew Ginny was involved somehow. "Don't let that boy destroy my family," he'd said. It was hard to imagine, after everything Wilson had read, that Ginny would do something like that, but then again, she was still connected to that pastor. She'd lied about knowing Darius. Wilson didn't know what to believe.

He pulled out the Woods case file and reviewed the interview notes from Woods's neighbor—the one who'd seen a blonde woman and had rattled off several digits from the car's license plate. He wrote down her name and address. He could at least pay her a visit, see if her ID could even hold up in a courtroom. It had been raining and dark. Perhaps she wore glasses, or maybe she'd been drinking that night or was overtired. It wasn't much, but he wanted to do something for his friend.

He went to Centennial Park after leaving the station, where the department had set up for Donny's official swearing-in ceremony. Many in the town had arrived for the event, and Wilson smiled, shook hands, and posed for photos with Donny, now in a uniform, too, standing tall and proud—the new, young, progressive face of justice in Eden. At least that's what the press would say.

~ • ~

Brooklyn lay in her bedroom that night, head dangling over the foot of the bed, just like she used to do as a kid, watching the upside-down sunset out the window. Nothing was resolved; her dad was returning tomorrow, and she had no idea what would happen. She'd swung from the high of that audition and the surprise of finding a bed set up at home to seeing him confused, saying he'd never even seen Ginny and the kids today, saying Ginny hated him. And Ginny had lied. Again. She said she'd gone to the hospital when she obviously hadn't. Was this it? Was it time for Brooklyn to finally give up on her dream and return to the town she'd run from?

With blood rushing to her head, she finally sat up, propped up on her elbows, and gazed at the poster of the New York skyline that had hung over her bed since she was a child. The sunrise view had inspired her dreams for years, with the Brooklyn Bridge—a massive architectural wonder of cables and stone—front and center, sailboats on the East River below, and a distant pink-and-orange horizon behind the skyline.

As soon as she and her friends had decided to drop out of college and stay in the city, they'd trekked south from their newly acquired East Village apartment until they reached the bridge. She'd spent her entire life looking at that poster and as a kid had even assumed that it was the only way to get to New York City, a sort of yellow brick road to Oz. It was a spectacular and enormous suspension bridge, more than a mile long. The girls had walked across the bridge to view the city from the same perspective she'd had on her bedroom wall. Those neogothic-style arches above the passageways reminded Brooklyn of something in a church. The only difference between the poster and the actual view on that day, of course, was that when she stood, looking back at Lower Manhattan, the twin towers were gone.

Brooklyn had been looking up at that poster the first time she asked her mom how she got the name Brooklyn. She was in second grade at the time, and earlier that day, a classmate had pointed out that her own middle name was Lynn. She assumed Brooklyn's name was two names, Brook and Lynn, and had told her she needed to add another *n* because *Lyn* was not the right spelling. Brooklyn was a terrible speller, but she was sure the girl was mistaken; it was how her mom spelled it too. The teacher finally got involved and said that no, *Brooklyn* was one word, that it was a unique name for a person, but it was also the name of a borough in New York City, and there was even a big bridge named after that borough. The kids had all asked what a borough was, leading the discussion in a whole new direction.

As Mom had tucked her into bed that night, Brooklyn gazed up at the bridge, realizing the connection. It had never been more than a background fixture to her—something that was just part of her room.

"Was I born on a bridge?" she asked.

Her mom had laughed. "What in the world—"

Brooklyn pointed up at the poster. "The Brooklyn Bridge. I learned about it in school today. Am I named after that? Or the *borrow*?"

"No!" She laughed again.

"But Ginny's named after Virginia, right? Because you were at that famous cemetery in Arlington, Virginia, when you went into labor?"

"That's right," her mom had said with a smile.

Brooklyn had turned the conversation back to herself, looking up at the poster again. "So that's not why you hung this poster here?"

"Nope."

"Have you ever been to New York?"

"Lord, no. I'm not exactly a big-city girl," she joked. "It is a beautiful view, though," she said, gazing at the poster.

"Where did you get it?"

Her mom stared at the poster, trying to remember. "I think I saw it at the Walmart a few years ago."

"How did you come up with my name?"

Mom smoothed a hand over Brooklyn's hair and said, "I heard the name in a movie and I thought it sounded pretty. It's not an exciting story, but I do love your name."

By the time Brooklyn had turned sixteen and fallen in love with acting, she decided that Ginny's name was inspired by the past, and her own name foretold the future.

Brooklyn checked her phone again for any new emails from the producers of the movie. She couldn't let go of the dream. But there was no news. And tomorrow was Sunday. She probably wouldn't hear anything before Monday.

She had to focus on Dad. And Ginny. And fixing this broken family.

CHAPTER TWENTY-NINE

DAY SEVEN
Sunday, May 19

ON SUNDAY MORNING, BROOKLYN WAS up before six. She spent a couple of hours organizing Mom's clothes for charity and walked around the house, restless. It was too early to get Dad. And she couldn't confront Ginny yet. It was church time.

Brooklyn got dressed and went to the family store. It would make Dad happy to know she'd opened for the postchurch crowd. She made the coffee and stood behind the counter, surrounded by all the familiar sundries of her childhood. The bells chimed as the front door opened and several little boys, all wearing loose ties with their untucked shirts and sneakers with their slacks, rushed toward the candy shelves beside the register. Church was out, obviously. If her dad had to sell this place, she hoped the buyer would keep it going. It had become an institution.

She'd just rung up the last of a gang of ten kids when the door chimed and Martin Woods appeared.

"This is a surprise!" she said. "I noticed the media trucks were gone on Thursday and I figured Darius had probably been released. I didn't know if we'd ever cross paths again."

Martin held the door for the departing children and stepped to the counter. "Actually, he's not out yet, but looks like I'm gonna get to bring him home later today."

"My dad too!" she said.

"What in the world are you doing here?" he asked.

"Just wanted to open for a few hours. My dad never missed a Sunday."

He looked taken aback. "Your dad is John Anderson?"

"You know him?"

He nodded. "So John is in the hospital? He broke his hip?"

"He did."

"I'm sorry, Brooklyn . . . I'm just so surprised by all this."

She smiled at him. "I'm surprised too. How do you know my dad?"

"He's a customer. I been selling him plumbing parts for a couple a years." His gaze dropped to the counter, searching. "Huh."

"What?"

Martin looked at Brooklyn, reconsidering her. "I thought something about you looked familiar. From the very moment we met. I guess perhaps I saw you in here before. Just never put it together."

"Could be. I spent most of my childhood helping out here. At least until I went off to college a couple years ago."

"Well, this is a little awkward, Brooklyn, but you mentioned that your dad might be suffering from some memory issues, so perhaps that explains what happened."

"What do you mean?"

"I'm here today to see if I could finally get your dad to pay his bill."

"Oh." She flushed. "I'm sorry. Was there a problem?"

"Well, I came in last Sunday, and things between us didn't go very well." He seemed to be choosing his words carefully. "I'm only now able to think about work again. I mean, I been consumed with Darius all week, of course."

"Sure. What happened between you two?"

"I come in 'bout once a month, usually on a Sunday or Monday. John seemed to be in good spirits. We chatted as we usually did, but then his mood took a swift turn. I know all too well about personality changes with dementia. My sister," he said, nodding the implied finish. "Anyway, he suddenly told me to get out and refused to pay his bill."

"That's strange." She'd never seen her dad act unprofessionally with vendors, even the ones Brooklyn found creepy. Her heart sank. It was hard not to take it as further evidence that something was happening with his mental state. "Do you have a business card? I'll go look up your account in back and see if I can't fix this."

Martin fished one out of his wallet.

"Be right back."

She quickly found the records at her dad's desk. Despite the mess she'd discovered on Tuesday, he'd continued to keep good records. Martin had delivered a supply thirty days earlier. Her dad still owed several hundred dollars. There were no notes about defective parts or returns. It didn't make sense that he'd refuse to pay. She pulled out the checkbook and wrote a check to Martin for the amount owed before returning to the front of the store.

"Here you go," she offered.

"Thanks, sweetie."

"So, Martin, do you remember what you and my dad were talking about when his mood turned?"

"Nothing really," Martin said. "Seemed like small talk. Of course, I mentioned that my son, the movie star, had just come home. Gotta let a parent brag a little, right?"

Brooklyn smiled. "Of course."

"Then John was dealing with a young man who was walking the aisles, acting kind of suspicious."

"Suspicious, how?"

"Oh, one of these guys who look a little drugged up, if you know what I mean. But John didn't seem overly concerned. In fact, he told him to come in the back and get some danish and coffee. I believe he knew him. John turned back to me then, like he'd figured something out, and asked if Darius Woods was my boy. I guess most folks in town have heard of Darius at this point. Of course, I said yes, and John asked what brought him home. I think I mentioned that he'd planned to film a movie about Eden, that he'd written a story about his life here. I guess that's it, really. Next thing I know, John's telling me that I'd been overcharging. It was like he suddenly didn't trust me because my son was a celebrity."

It was entirely baffling. With his lack of interest in pop culture, why would her father care who Martin's son was? "Weird. I'm sorry about that. He really hasn't been acting like himself lately."

Martin nodded. "I remember you telling me that at the hospital. Makes sense. Anyway, I ain't gonna hold a grudge. Life too short for all that. Well, thanks, Brooklyn. All the best to your family," he said, taking a few steps toward the door.

"Hey, Martin. I meant to ask you, do you know my sister?"

Martin turned and came back toward the counter. "The sister you have trouble with?"

She smiled. "Yeah. Actually, I've been trying to take your advice, hoping we can work out our issues. She went to high school with Darius. Turns out, she was even on the stage crew."

"Huh. Small world. Though Darius didn't really bring kids over to the house. What's her name?"

"Ginny. Now it's Ginny Smith, but she was Ginny Anderson back then."

His eyes widened. "Well, that's a coincidence."

"What?"

"She came by Darius's room at the hospital on Thursday after-noon. Said he'd asked her to come. He wasn't doing well at the time, so I had to send her away, but . . . that's a small world, isn't it?"

"It is," Brooklyn said. Ginny had acted as if she barely knew Darius. But they were in touch? And he'd asked her to come see him Thursday? Ginny had disappeared for thirty minutes on Thursday before she met Brooklyn in the cafeteria. Was that so she could see Darius? And if she knew him well enough to visit, how could she not mention it when she knew Brooklyn was such a fan? Instead, she'd practically pushed Brooklyn out the hospital door Thursday, convincing her to get out of town. She was up to something. This couldn't all be Brooklyn's wild imagination.

"Anyway, I gotta run," Martin said. "Going back to Burns now to get him. Hey, maybe you two can meet before he heads back to California. Being an actress and all."

Brooklyn's smile grew wide. "I'd love it."

Watching Martin leave, she tried to envision the exchange between him and her dad. She couldn't imagine why mention of Darius Woods would have set off her dad, changing his mood so suddenly.

The pieces were all there, like a puzzle on the table. Darius was shot last Sunday night. And Dad fell. Ginny was in Eden. Ginny may have been involved in a shooting back in high school. Darius knew her. He wrote a screenplay about Eden, and she tried to see him in the hospital. If Darius knew about whatever Ginny did in high school, if he wrote about it, it could ruin Ginny's life when the movie came out. Maybe Dad would have been worried about that too? Brooklyn's breathing nearly stopped, but she tapped her chest as that familiar flush of heat hinted at a possible panic attack. She thought about Dad's gun safe, open and empty.

Her mind was zooming toward a dark conclusion. But it was too outlandish to be true. It couldn't be . . . Could Ginny have taken Dad's gun and shot Darius Woods?

~ • ~

Brooklyn closed up the shop as soon as the postchurch rush had ended and drove to Ginny's house in Harrisburg. She called the hospital on the way. Nurse Wanda said the doctor wouldn't be getting to her dad for checkout until around five o'clock. She had plenty of time. She'd only been to Ginny's a few times over the years, but it was easy to remember the route—just a long and flat, four-lane country highway between them, nothing remarkable but that nine-hundred-acre bike club.

She wasn't sure what she'd say—but she was done with all the secrets. She had to finally understand what happened on Sunday night.

Ginny's house was on Walnut in the oldest part of town, on one of those rare blocks still paved in brick, with stately looking homes built in the early 1900s. She spotted the idyllic white house on the knoll with that huge porch on both the main and second stories. Simon was just pulling into the driveway.

Lowering his window, he yelled a friendly greeting from the car and as soon as he parked, got out, and pulled her in for a big hug. "Good to see you, Brooklyn. How's your dad doing?"

She'd noticed some gray coming through his dark-brown hair when she'd seen him at the funeral, but it was even more apparent now. Maybe that was life in your fifties, or maybe it was living with Ginny. "He's got a ways to go," Brooklyn answered, "but I think he's going to be okay. He's just going to need some help."

"Well, if there's anything I can do, or if you need me to find you any doctors, please, just ask. Ginny doesn't tell me much, but I'm happy to help."

"Thanks," Brooklyn said. She recalled Ginny's earlier comments—dismissing Simon's concerns about her drinking, telling Brooklyn their marriage was a mess. Was that a lie? It was hard to know if she should trust anything Ginny said.

Brooklyn hadn't seen the kids since they made a brief appearance at Mom's funeral back in December, but they both got out of the car and offered barely audible hellos. No big hugs or excited reunions. They both seemed to have inherited their mom's inability to hold eye contact, an insecurity or discomfort with all polite conversation. Brooklyn was just someone they associated with their grandparents—not a stranger, but not exactly a relative either. Mikey was getting so tall, and his hair had darkened from Ginny's lighter color to a dirtier blond, though Lyla still shared the same white-blond hair, delicate features, and petite frame. She was beautiful. Brooklyn just hoped that she survived adolescence and the rough waters of life better than her mother had.

"Where's Ginny?" Brooklyn asked as the kids rambled toward the house.

"She wouldn't go to church with us," Simon said. "She said she was done with that place and wanted to go to an AA meeting."

"Well, going to a meeting is good. Right?"

"Maybe," he said, shaking his head as if he were done trying to understand her. "Come on in."

The kids disappeared inside, and Simon led Brooklyn into the kitchen for coffee.

"Brooklyn, I suppose I should tell you," he said, lowering his voice. "I finally told Ginny that I want a divorce—"

Brooklyn sat at the table. "Oh, Simon, I'm so sorry."

He waved off the concern. "She's not taking it well, even called Pastor Gary over here Friday night, but it had to happen."

"Pastor Gary?" Brooklyn asked.

"He runs the youth group at the church, and he's been great counsel for Ginny. You know him, right?"

"I don't think so. Should I? I've never been to your church."

"Oh, right, but he actually used to be at your church in Eden. He's known Ginny since she was a little girl."

That pastor. The one Bonnie said Ginny loved. "Sure," she said.

"He's been here for more than a dozen years, so maybe you wouldn't even remember him, but he seems to be the only one who's ever helped her."

Brooklyn recalled the newspaper clipping—the church pastor who'd provided the teen an alibi for the time of the shooting at the abortion clinic. She nodded while Simon poured the coffee.

"Have you and Ginny been able to agree on a game plan for your dad?"

"I don't know, actually. I was hopeful when we last spoke on Thursday, but there's a lot we need to talk about. She set up a bed for him at the house, but yesterday I learned that she's lined up a rehab facility, probably found him a nursing home too."

"Well, the rehab facility is the best place for him right now. But there aren't great options for nursing-home care around here. There's just not enough help to go around."

"Exactly." It was Brooklyn's biggest fear.

"Well, please feel free to wait for her. I'm guessing she won't be too long, but I've got to do some work in the study, if you don't mind, and then I'm taking the kids fishing in a little bit."

"Of course. Don't let me keep you. I've got a bunch of emails to get through anyway," she said, raising her phone.

Simon left her in the kitchen, passing the kids, who'd planted themselves in front of the television in the adjoining room, and went down the hall to his office.

Brooklyn sipped her coffee and stared at the mess on the nearby desk. She'd raced over here, convinced Ginny might have shot Darius Woods, but as she looked around the kitchen, and at those two kids in the next room, it felt impossible. She didn't know her sister, and the chaos of the kitchen sink alone suggested someone depressed or overwhelmed or unorganized, but . . . this house was filled with love. The evidence was all over the room—the painted handprint pictures on the fridge, the little handmade pottery on the table adorned with Lyla's and Mikey's signatures, the piles of crafts on the counter. Ginny was a good mother. Brooklyn couldn't believe that a good mother would shoot someone. It seemed absurd. She might have done something awful as a teen, and maybe Darius wrote about it, but Brooklyn had to believe that Ginny went to his hospital room to talk to him. That had to be all.

Of course, if Ginny *had* shot that doctor back in high school and the screenplay would expose that secret . . . she'd feel desperate. She'd drink too much. She'd lie. And Brooklyn still felt like she hadn't gotten the whole story about how Dad fell.

What if Ginny shot Darius? What if Dad tried to stop her and she pushed him . . . What if she really was the reason Dad was in the hospital? What if she had hit him in the head? That cast iron doorstop. He could have fallen on it. He could have been hit with it. She didn't know Ginny at all.

Brooklyn took another breath and a sip of coffee. Was this her melodramatic mind at work? Or was Ginny struggling to hold her life together, with a marriage falling apart, a substance problem, and a secret she was desperate to stop from getting out?

She looked around the kitchen. If Dad's gun was in this house . . .

She walked to Simon's study and stood in the doorway. "Sorry to interrupt. Ginny said she had one of Mom's sweaters that I wanted to get. Would it be okay if I went up and checked her closet?" She couldn't imagine where in this big house Ginny might have hidden Dad's gun, but the bedroom seemed like a good place to start.

"Knock yourself out," Simon said.

Brooklyn walked up the steps, passing all the pictures of the kids on the wall. In the master bedroom, she found a large closet that must have been a small bedroom at some point in the home's history.

Both Ginny's and Simon's things filled the space, and the entire back wall was covered in shelves. She opened a few shoeboxes and pushed around some of the clothes on the shelf. Nothing. She couldn't tear the whole closet apart. It could take an hour. But as she walked back toward the bedroom, she spotted some big hardback books stacked on a shelf. Eden High yearbooks. The design hadn't changed in the two decades between their graduating classes.

Ginny had gone to school with Darius. Had they known each other well enough to write in each other's books? If they were friends, she couldn't have . . . Brooklyn had to look. She pulled the first one. Ginny's freshman year. She leafed through the pages until she found Ginny's picture. A waif of a girl with a self-conscious smile. No one had written any notes, but a few of the other kids' photos were framed with marker—her friends, Brooklyn guessed. She leafed from the As to the Ws and spotted a young Darius. If he hadn't been the only black kid on the page, she might not have recognized him. He looked so small as a freshman, like he still belonged in middle school. There was no marker around his face. Brooklyn grabbed the next year's book and checked again. No marker, but Darius had transformed, his shoulders now broad and his smile wide. She closed the book. She was getting sidetracked.

But as she turned the book on its side to put it back, a large photo slipped out from between its pages. It was a shot of the church youth group, on a mission trip, dated 1997. Brooklyn found her parents in the photo, the chaperones, no doubt, alongside about fifteen kids.

Ginny was standing at the end of the row, a big grin on her face, the pastor behind her, his hands resting on her shoulders. Brooklyn had never seen her sister look so happy. But those hands on her shoulders reminded Brooklyn of that creepy Pastor Neil from First Hope, always massaging Brooklyn when he came up to talk to her and her parents. She'd never been able to articulate why she found him creepy and even felt a little guilty for her discomfort, but after *Spotlight* came out, and then *The Keepers*, Brooklyn realized that no men were above suspicion. Something had told her to be wary.

She put the picture back in the book. She was supposed to be looking for a gun. She went to Ginny's dresser in the bedroom and felt around inside the drawers. She felt something hard and grabbed it. A half-empty wine bottle. More lies. When she'd talked to Ginny on Thursday at the hospital, Ginny had sworn she'd had her last drink. She'd told Simon she was going to AA this morning.

Brooklyn looked at the bed and the tables beside it. One table housed a medical journal and reading glasses, so she went to the other side of the bed, quickly pulling open each drawer of the table. No gun. She grabbed a notepad from the drawer, scanning the empty pages until she was left with the inside of the back cover. On it was a handwritten list of usernames and passwords.

Brooklyn sat on the bed and scanned down the list . . . email, bank, PayPal, Facebook. She grabbed her phone, took a snapshot of the list, and then, after only a brief hesitation, signed in to Ginny's email. She didn't even know what she was looking for.

Lots of unopened junk mail.

She closed out of the email and opened her own Facebook app, signing in with Ginny's information. She searched Ginny's friend contacts. Darius was there. Checking Messenger, she found his name again. Ginny had been in touch with Darius just before he arrived in town. And there was an attachment.

The screenplay.

Brooklyn could finally see for herself what happened all those years ago and whether this script had anything to do with his shooting. She downloaded it to her phone.

"What are you doing?" a voice said from the doorway.

Brooklyn jumped and looked up. Lyla was standing there, head cocked. "Daddy said you needed a sweater."

Brooklyn smiled. "That's right. Just checking something on my phone." She dropped the phone and went to the walk-in closet. Lyla trailed behind her.

"What does it look like?" Lyla asked.

"Uh. Pink. Stripes," Brooklyn said. She went to the back of the closet, facing a wall of shelves and began lifting the stacks while Lyla, crouched on the ground, looked on a shelf by the door.

"I don't see it," Lyla said. "Mom hates pink."

"I guess it's not here," Brooklyn said, her hand deep under a pile of sweaters on the bottom. But then she felt the corner of something. A plastic bag.

Brooklyn let the sweaters fall back down and turned to Lyla. "Shall we go back downstairs?"

She waited until the little girl had left the closet, then she lifted the stack of sweaters, peering beneath.

There was a Ziploc bag. And in it, Dad's gun.

CHAPTER THIRTY

GINNY PULLED INTO THE DRIVEWAY and looked at the huge house. When Simon had shown it to her all those years ago, it had almost felt like a dream, like he was going to save her from despair. But now, the only thing she knew was that it was over, and she and the kids had to get away from here.

It had only been three days of sobriety, but she was feeling stronger. Clear. She knew what she had to do.

The law would be on Simon's side, she'd learned after a few Google searches, because he'd always believed the kids to be his, had signed their birth certificates, and she supposed that was how it should be. She hoped that once Simon learned the truth, it wouldn't affect his love for them. She didn't want them to lose the only dad they'd ever known.

When she walked inside, both kids left the TV and ran to her with hugs and hellos. She kissed them both and asked how church had been. "Boring," they said in unison.

"You just missed Brooklyn," Mikey said.

"I did?"

"Yeah, she wanted one of Grandma's sweaters. But she couldn't find it."

"She was in my closet?" She began running up the stairs before Lyla answered.

If Brooklyn had found Dad's gun, she might go to the sheriff. Ginny had never given Brooklyn a reason to trust her or care about what happened to her. She'd lose the kids for sure.

Ginny ran into the closet and shut the door behind her. She went to the pile of clothes that sat atop the gun. It was gone.

When she opened the door, Lyla was standing there, her arms on the doorframes like a barricade.

Ginny grinned, attempting a calm she couldn't even remember. "You scared me!" she said.

Lyla laughed. "I scared Brooklyn too."

Ginny looked around the room. The bedside drawer was open. Her notepad was on the bed. "Were you up here with her?"

"Yeah. I helped her look in the closet." Lyla stepped inside the space. "I looked through these stacks," she said proudly, her hand brushing up and down the shelves, "and Brooklyn looked at all of those." She was waving toward the area where the gun had been.

"And what was she doing when you scared her?"

"She was just sitting on your bed, looking at her phone. You ready to play with me now?"

Ginny patted the top of Lyla's head and smiled. "Soon, baby," she said, looking around the room.

"What's the matter?"

Ginny crouched down to eye level with Lyla. "Grandpa gets out of the hospital today, and I gotta get him situated at his house. Daddy's taking you and Mikey fishing, okay?"

"But I want you to come," Lyla said.

"Me too. But we'll do something special after school tomorrow, okay."

"Like what?"

"It's a surprise. It'll be an adventure, though. Okay? But I gotta go."

~ • ~

Wilson had brunch with his daughter and her family at Mary's Diner after the ten o'clock service. At least some things would never change. He'd thought of Eddie all morning, sitting in a jail cell, but it hadn't even been forty-eight hours. Eddie needed all the mandatory sobriety he could get.

Wilson walked to the counter to pay the check. Donny was there, paying his own bill.

"Hey, there," Donny said. "I kind of liked your Sunday ritual. Figured we'd give it a try." He nodded toward the table where Rosa, sitting with two young kids, was finishing her coffee. "Anyway, you got a minute?"

"I got endless minutes," Wilson said.

"Step outside?"

Wilson followed Donny out the door.

"I wanted to talk to you about the case, and about Eddie."

"Yeah, about that. It was my house gun on Eddie at the hospital on Friday, but I've already had it checked. It was not the gun used against Woods."

"I heard."

"But I'm hoping you'll keep him locked up for another day or two. Maybe we can scare him straight. I'm running out of ideas."

"Actually, we're gonna have to let him out today. It's the law."

Wilson smiled. "So a favor then. I'll get him in the morning, Donny. Sunday's supposed to be a day of rest, right?"

Donny's face hardened. "Sheriff, please don't take offense, but I'm just gettin' started, as you know. I'd really like to avoid letting personal connections influence justice. So just do me a favor and get him today."

"Wow," Wilson said. "Kinda thought we'd become friends this week."

"It's not personal. We are friends. I'm just trying to do my job. I don't need to start my time in office with a lawsuit for civil rights violations."

"Eddie's not gonna sue anyone, but sure, okay," Wilson said. Thirty-five years running this town and suddenly, it meant nothing.

"Anyway, I thought you'd be interested in this. I finally talked to Woods after you left the hospital," Donny said.

"Did he see anything?"

"No. He did have a few run-ins with Eddie back in high school, though. Pretty racially charged. And that scene in the screenplay at the Garden of the Gods—the kid who got roughed up on those rocks—that was Eddie."

Wilson stopped him. "Yeah, I know." He'd remembered taking Eddie to the hospital for that dislocated shoulder. Eddie had told him a story about fighting off some black kid who was messing with a girl. The sheriff had asked for a name, but Eddie had refused. He'd figured his kid had been doing something chivalrous and let it go. He'd always had a blind spot when it came to Eddie.

But he still didn't think that confrontation would make Eddie want to hurt Woods now. "I really think that yesterday's nonsense was about drugs, unfortunately."

Donny nodded. "There's something else, though. Woods sent a copy of the script to your friend's kid, Ginny Smith, before he arrived in town. Far as I know, she's the only one who saw it before he got shot. I'm gonna have to pull her in today and ask some questions."

Wilson kicked at the dirt under his shoe. "You've read the screenplay. Do you think Ginny would shoot Woods?"

Donny shrugged. "Maybe. I'm not ruling it out. She can't want all this to come out—maybe she never even told her husband about what happened in high school."

Donny still didn't understand exactly what that screenplay revealed, and Wilson wasn't about to enlighten him. "I just don't believe it coulda been Ginny," Wilson said. "What about the stalker?"

"I heard from LAPD late yesterday. They can confirm her being in Los Angeles all weekend."

Wilson didn't like it. "Well, Woods is okay. His dad tells me he's getting out today. Maybe you should just move on."

"Are you suggesting I drop this investigation?"

"I'm just saying, if I were you, I wouldn't want my first case in Eden to be another racially charged, high-profile case. No one's gonna notice if that shooting doesn't get solved. I'm sure Woods is leaving town soon, anyway."

Donny tilted his head. "Sheriff, I get that the Andersons are friends of yours, but I need to follow the law and let the chips fall where they may. You must see that given the racial tension these days, getting justice for the Woods family is more important than ever. I checked the ambulance records. Woods's father called an ambulance at 8:44 p.m. last Sunday. Mrs. Smith called an ambulance for her father, just four miles away on the other side of town, at 8:58. She could have shot Woods, watched from her car down the road—maybe trying to see if he was dead—and still got home in time to make that call for her dad."

Wilson's thoughts were on John. He'd sarcastically agreed when Wilson said John had been lucky that Ginny found him. Maybe because he knew what Ginny had done? Maybe because she'd hurt him too? Now that Wilson had read the screenplay, he finally understood why she might have hated her father. But regardless of their strained relationship, John loved his daughter and wanted to protect her. If something happened to her, he'd suffer.

"Well, Ginny's in touch with the pastor," Wilson offered, hoping to move the focus from his friend's daughter. "If he knew what was in that screenplay . . ."

"I'm gonna pull him in today too."

"Good. I gotta get home," Wilson said, walking away. "I'll get over there for Eddie in a little bit."

It was the first time he'd lied to a fellow officer of the law. Wilson had lost his power, but he couldn't sit idly by and watch Donny, so eager to prove himself in Eden, destroy the Andersons.

~ • ~

After Brooklyn rushed out of Ginny's house with the gun, she was tempted to call Sheriff Wilson. But there was so much she didn't know. She felt certain the screenplay held the answers. She went back to the house.

Dropping into a chair in the kitchen, she set the gun in its plastic bag on the table and pulled Darius's screenplay up on her phone.

It was called *Surviving Eden*. A narrator introduced the story as the camera panned across a rural landscape before following the path of an old Buick as it drove into the quiet town of Eden.

I remember the day Dad and I came to Eden. It was summer of 1993, I was twelve years old, and I sat with my back turned toward the road behind us as Dad headed south down the expressway and I watched the Chicago skyline fade into the distance. I'd never been outside the city limits before. I was terrified. But excited too. I would never again worry about gangs, drug lords, violence, or gunfire. He went on to describe the fresh start he hoped for after his mother's death.

The Chicago streets had killed her, but here in Eden, we'd be safe. That twelve-year-old kid could never have guessed that six years later, he'd be staring down the barrel of a gun and the only way to be safe would be to leave and never look back.

The story then jumped forward a few years while the scenes showed Darius's character, Anthony, as a boy who hadn't yet had a growth spurt and didn't fit in at the high school. The scenes showed how Anthony rarely opened his mouth, making him a target for bullies who chose verbal abuse. He never had the one-line quips or other ability to fight with words, and he was not going to throw a punch and get kicked out of school. Brooklyn was immediately drawn to the character, an outsider in this small town, just like her.

I tried to stay outta trouble, the narrator added. *But sometimes trouble finds you.*

The next scene jumped forward to the boy's sophomore year, showing that he'd grown several inches, his voice had lowered, and his build had broadened. He looked like an athlete. His English teacher, impressed by his reading in class, suggested that he look into the drama department. He had no interest in sports and nothing else to do, so he went to drama club and fell in love. The words, the scenes, the freedom . . . a chance to be more than he'd been pegged to be. Brooklyn was beaming. It felt like her story.

The next scene jumped forward a year. Anthony was at rehearsal when the director announced that the youth group from a local church was there to talk to the cast, hoping to collaborate on a community service project. But the story took a dark turn when Anthony went to the pastor's office a few days later and walked in without knocking, finding the pastor on top of a petite blonde named Margaret Carr.

Brooklyn had just finished reading the scene—horrified—about how Anthony rescued Margaret from the office of the pastor—Pastor Ed, he was called—when the crunch of gravel under tires wafted into the house through the open living room window. Brooklyn darted to the kitchen's side door. It was Ginny.

"Brooklyn!" Ginny said as she barreled through the front door.

Brooklyn quietly moved through the kitchen as her heart raced. She wasn't afraid, exactly, but she didn't know or understand Ginny at all. She'd lied about so much. It was impossible to know what this woman was capable of. She watched from the kitchen doorway as Ginny frantically checked the living room and yelled up the stairs.

She disappeared around the corner, entering the study. Brooklyn followed.

Ginny was standing at the bookshelves, peering into the empty gun safe.

"Are you looking for this?" Brooklyn asked.

Ginny spun around. Brooklyn held Dad's gun in her hand.

CHAPTER THIRTY-ONE

"What the heck is going on?" Brooklyn said, holding up the gun, still inside the Ziploc bag. "Why were you hiding it?"

Ginny looked out the window before returning her gaze to Brooklyn. She took a slow, cleansing breath and stepped toward her.

"Stop," Brooklyn shouted.

Ginny froze. "Why are you looking at me like that?"

"You did it, didn't you?"

"What?"

"You shot Darius Woods."

"No! Is that what Sheriff Wilson told you? Why would I do that?"

"Because of this!" Brooklyn said, raising the phone in her other hand. "His screenplay."

She held her ground, prepared to run if Ginny rushed her, but Ginny simply looked at the small screen and deflated into the chair in the corner. Brooklyn stepped into the room, keeping her distance. She leaned against the wall.

Ginny didn't look at her. She was staring straight ahead, her gaze at the window. "Have you read it?"

"Not all of it, but it's obvious you don't want the world to know what's in here. Darius knew about the shooting at the clinic, didn't he?"

Ginny looked at her then, as if processing just how much Brooklyn had figured out. "It's not what you think."

"You lied. You said you barely knew him. But he sent you the script. He asked you to come by and talk about it. His dad told me you went to his hospital room on Thursday. Same day you shooed me out of town."

"I didn't shoot Darius! You have it all wrong. He wrote about that shooting at the clinic, but he knew I didn't do it. I saw who did it."

Finally, she was getting some answers. Brooklyn's tone softened. "You were there?"

Ginny nodded. She stared at her hands in her lap.

"Were you an accomplice?"

Ginny shook her head.

"Then what? I know you were a protester, Ginny. You and all those youth group kids."

She shook her head again, but she wouldn't look at Brooklyn. "I couldn't risk having anyone see me go in or come out, so I'd gone early before it opened and was waiting in the car. I wanted to be the first in and get to school before anyone would know." Finally, Ginny lifted her chin, looking at Brooklyn, but as soon as their eyes met, she shifted focus and looked out the window.

"What are you saying?"

Ginny took a deep breath and slowly exhaled, one long, measured flow of air. "I was pregnant."

Brooklyn felt her breath catch in her throat.

"It didn't seem real. I just had this stomachache that wouldn't go away. I drove all the way to the Walmart in Marion to get a test. I took it in a filthy gas station bathroom on the way back. Just buying the test felt like a failure of everything I'd ever learned. I can still remember the smell of urine in that bathroom. It felt like my legs were going to buckle."

"But you were in that group. I heard about the chastity pledges . . ."

"Yeah, what a joke, right?"

Brooklyn didn't know what to say.

"I had to know how far along. I'd never had regular periods. I never paid attention. It only happened a couple of times, and we'd been careful. I couldn't tell anyone. I certainly couldn't talk to Mom and Dad. They would have lost their minds."

Brooklyn thought of the scene she'd just read, the pastor and the girl. And that mission picture she'd found at Ginny's house—the pastor's hands on Ginny's shoulders. He was the one Mom said Ginny loved.

"The screenplay . . . are you Margaret? The girl Darius found in the pastor's office?"

Ginny nodded. Streams of tears riddled her cheeks. Sitting in that big chair in the corner, she looked like a young girl, a frail, broken shell. "You have no idea what a mess I've made of everyone's life."

Brooklyn dropped the gun on the desk and went to the chair. She knelt in front of her sister, taking Ginny's hands in her own. She couldn't imagine anything so awful. "You're not to blame for whatever happened with him, Ginny."

Ginny stared at their hands twined together. Brooklyn looked at them too.

"You don't understand. He started hitting on me during junior year. I had such a crush on him back then. We all thought he was—he was everything. He knew it." There was an eerie calm in her voice, as though she were resigned to telling the story. She sounded almost as though she was in a trance.

"It's not your fault, Ginny. You were a kid."

Ginny took a deep breath. "After the shooting at the clinic, they thought it was me, and Dad got Pastor Gary to provide an alibi for me. Mom and Dad both thought he was a saint. I wasn't showing. I felt fine. I figured I'd leave town before anyone found out about the pregnancy. I'd be at Columbia in New York and deal with it there."

"What were you going to do?"

"Give it up." She shook her head, punctuating the point. "They passed a Baby Moses law in Texas that year. It was big news, and lots of states were following. Girls could just drop the babies at hospitals or fire stations, no questions asked. No one would ever have to know."

"But you didn't go to school."

"Mom and Dad went to the Dominican Republic for a mission trip. I was supposed to go, but I couldn't be in the same room as Pastor Gary by then. I'd avoided him for months. I convinced Mom and Dad that I needed to start packing up for school. They figured I could stay back and tend to the store."

"Did the pastor know about the pregnancy?"

"You don't understand—I put the pregnancy entirely out of my mind. I couldn't think about it. I just had to hold on a couple of months. Just get through summer and get out of here. All I knew was that I was about to move to New York and start a new life."

Brooklyn didn't get it. Ginny was pregnant. And someone shot that doctor.

"I got really sick. It was the day of Mom and Dad's return. I was alone at the store. I went to the bathroom and had these terrible cramps. I . . . God, Brooklyn. You don't understand. I didn't know what was happening. I was so scared."

"A miscarriage?" Brooklyn asked.

Ginny shook her head. She began sobbing, pulled her hands from Brooklyn's, and cupped them together. "It was so tiny. Too tiny. It didn't even make a sound at first. It didn't look right. Its eyes never opened—it couldn't have been more than a few pounds. I cut the cord with some scissors and wrapped it in a towel. I didn't even know if it was breathing. I didn't know what to do."

Brooklyn covered her mouth.

"I drove to the hospital," Ginny continued. "I walked into the ER, handed the bundle to the nurse behind the counter, and ran out the door. She called out to me, begging me to stop, but I couldn't even look back."

Brooklyn let out the air she'd been holding, suspended in her throat.

"I went home. The rest is such a blur. I guess I passed out."

"Where?"

"Here. I woke up in the hospital. Mom and Dad had returned home and found me unconscious on the living room floor. There was blood all over my jeans." Ginny pressed her fingers against her eyes, as if she could dam the flood of tears.

Brooklyn got off her knees and scooched beside her on the chair, putting her arm around Ginny's shoulders.

Ginny couldn't stop crying. She'd obviously been tormented all these years.

"You were just a teenager. You did nothing wrong. Did you ever tell Mom and Dad?"

Ginny shook her head, wiped her tears, and got up from the chair, like she wanted to get away from Brooklyn, and went to the window. "You don't get it," she said, raising her voice, keeping her focus outside. "As soon as the doctor examined me, he knew I'd just given birth. It wasn't long before they found the abandoned baby in the maternity wing."

"So that's what this was all about? What Dad forgave you for? The chastity stuff? For getting pregnant? Having a baby and giving it up?"

"Listen to me!" Ginny shouted, finally turning back to face her. "They wouldn't let me give it up."

"What do you mean?"

"Turned out, Illinois had not passed a Baby Moses law at that point. They said I could be charged with child endangerment, that I had to take responsibility."

"Was that true?"

"I didn't know," she said. "But it's what they said. I was in the hospital bed, and John came at me, enraged, his face in mine, screaming, 'Who did this to you?' He was terrifying. Pastor Gary was standing there, in the room. He'd been with them when they found me and drove them to the hospital. He stepped forward, getting between Dad and the bed, like he would rescue me. He said it wasn't important how it happened. It was like an unspoken signal. So I didn't speak. Mom acted as if the question was irrelevant. Nothing mattered except that little baby that was fighting for its life."

Brooklyn marveled at Pastor Gary's ability to remain blameless as he stood in that room.

Ginny continued. "It would be in the NICU for weeks, but Mom said as soon as the doctors made sure it was okay, we'd bring it home. It was only like twenty-nine weeks. It had pneumonia. No one was sure it would survive. But Mom said she'd help me, that we'd raise the baby together. I'd go to school locally. She said it was God's plan and that perhaps the unexpected gift was the reason she'd never had more kids."

"It didn't make it . . . ," Brooklyn said, trying to understand.

Ginny rushed back to the chair, kneeling on the floor in front of her. "Don't you get it? Think about it. Twenty years ago, Mom and Dad brought home a baby. You weren't adopted from the Dominican Republic." She put her hand on Brooklyn's.

The words burned Brooklyn's skin, like acid eating away at everything she'd ever known about herself. She held her breath, finally understanding what Ginny would say next, but she couldn't move.

"You're not my sister."

Brooklyn shook her head and closed her eyes. It couldn't be. It wasn't possible. She looked down at their hands, at Ginny's fair skin against Brooklyn's. "That's crazy. Look at you. I'm . . ."

"I'm so sorry. I wanted to tell you. I did. I tried once years ago, but John wouldn't let me. He said it would ruin everything."

Brooklyn stood and paced the room. It didn't make sense. She knew where she came from. She'd looked into Eimy's eyes in that photo for as long as she could remember. They had a connection, even beyond the grave. She had never belonged in Eden. "Why are you doing this? You're not my mother! You want me to believe my father is some pastor who assaulted you?" Every fantasy she'd entertained about her birth parents was being shattered in an instant. She was from the Caribbean. "This is crazy." She could barely get out the words.

"No, Brooklyn, you don't understand. That's not what happened. This is not about the pastor!"

Brooklyn stopped and turned back to Ginny.

"I'm so sorry, Brooklyn. I fell apart. I wasn't ready to be a mother. I lost everything. I knew the future I'd planned was over. I barely ate for a month. I didn't pick you up. I was in shock. I never had anything to do with you, because it was all too difficult. Looking at you just reminded me of what I'd done."

Brooklyn walked to the door. She had to get away from this nonsense. But she looked down at the phone still in her hand. She had proof. She searched the pictures and finally turned back, holding up the screen to Ginny. "This is my mom! Eimy! Look at me. You're acting crazy."

Ginny shook her head. "It was all a lie. She's not your mother. Eimy was the daughter of the woman that ran the orphanage. We'd known her for years. She was just another pregnant teen. She didn't die either."

Brooklyn lowered the phone.

"Brooklyn, please. Just listen. Mom got worried about me. She finally said that no one needed to know. That she'd be happy to raise you as her daughter. That she'd always wanted more children. She loved you so much. Instantly. Brooklyn, I was a pathetic mother, but our mom—she was incredible. She came up with the story about the mission trip and the teen mother who'd died to explain the new baby in the house, and Dad went along. He'd do anything Mom asked of him. She told me to go off to Columbia as planned. She and John told everyone at church about Eimy. It was just a story."

Brooklyn leaned against the wall. She wanted to be as far as possible but couldn't leave until something made sense. "But you didn't go."

"I couldn't. They didn't understand. No one spoke of your father after that day in the hospital. No one asked. They acted as if someone had violated me. But it wasn't like that, Brooklyn. We were in love. And when Mom said I had to bring the baby home, I knew it would all be over with him."

"Who?"

"None of this was his doing," she said, standing, stepping forward as the tears continued. "And he'd already left town by then. No one knew we were going to be together. No one, except a couple kids at school, even knew we were dating. He knew I was pregnant. We planned to give you up for adoption." She wiped her face, smearing mascara across her puffy face. "I'm so sorry. I was young, Brooklyn. I wasn't ready for any of it. All I knew was that I was going to go to New York with my boyfriend, where we'd be accepted."

"What do you mean?" But then Brooklyn understood. A reality beyond her wildest imagination.

"He was the love of my life, Brooklyn. It started as friendship. He saved me from Pastor Gary—at least, he thought he did."

Brooklyn's heart began racing, the heat rising, Ginny's face blurred in front of her. She could hardly imagine that it was real. "Darius Woods." She slid down the wall to the floor. The world was spinning. She put her head between her knees.

Ginny joined her on the floor. "I had joined crew and started hanging out with all the theater kids. He was so talented. He dreamed of New York, and after a while, it became my dream too. We wanted to be together. I applied to school there. No one would have ever known. It's not like Mom and Dad would ever go to visit me in that city."

Brooklyn thought of the poster in her bedroom—formerly Ginny's bedroom—of the New York skyline. "The Brooklyn Bridge," she said.

Ginny smiled. "Darius gave me that poster."

Brooklyn couldn't speak.

"He got it before graduation. He found us an apartment in Brooklyn."

She looked at Ginny, barely able to get air past the lump in her throat.

"I sat on my bed, staring at that poster, trying to come to terms with what happened, what I thought was my future. And I'd never get there. You changed everything."

"So you named me Brooklyn. As what, a reminder of what you lost?"

"No. I don't know. It sounds awful. I was trying to cope and embrace the future, and you, but . . . I failed."

Suddenly, it all made sense, but it meant everyone was a liar.

And Darius Woods was her father.

Ginny tried to smile as she wiped away tears. "So now you know where you got that acting bug."

It was a terrifying brew of emotions, too many, too much information to process. She began to hyperventilate. Her dad, John Anderson, was her grandfather. Her mom was her grandmother. Her sister was her mother. Her idol was her father. Martin Woods—he was her grandfather too. It was like a Jerry Springer show. She stood to leave, to storm out, but her vision filled with black fuzzy dots and she lost her balance.

Ginny jumped up and grabbed her. "Sit," she said, pulling her back down to the floor. "Just breathe. It's a lot. I know. Focus on the breathing."

Brooklyn closed her eyes. She couldn't look at her.

"Does he know?" she whispered. "Darius?"

"No." Ginny began to cry. "After you were born, I had to break it off. I told him the baby was gone."

Brooklyn collapsed onto the floor, her eyes closed.

"He started calling the house. He was heartbroken. But I never answered the phone. Mom and Dad answered and brushed him off. By then they realized it wasn't some assault, that he was the father. I heard Dad on the phone telling him to stay away, that he'd done enough to their girl."

"So he has no idea about me?"

Ginny shook her head. "He sent me some letters after the breakup, but I never answered. He came back from New York in August and tried to talk to me at the house. You were still in the NICU. Dad answered the door. When Darius asked for me, Dad left him on the porch and returned with a gun. He told Darius if he ever saw him at his house again, he'd have him arrested."

"You didn't say anything?"

Ginny shook her head as the tears continued to fall. "I know I should have done more. I have replayed that day so many times. But Dad was crazed. I was standing at the top of the stairs, listening. Darius told him we were in love, and it only made Dad angrier. He began asking how long Darius had known me and then said he'd get him on statutory rape—my consent was irrelevant. Said he'd better walk away and never look back or he'd make sure Darius ended up in prison. I knew what he was capable of. And his best friend was the sheriff. I went to my bedroom window and watched Darius leave. He looked up and saw me in the window. It was the last time we saw each other."

"So that was the gun Darius referred to in his story. This was the racism he meant, the threat to his life, the reason he left Eden all those years ago."

Ginny nodded. "I fell apart. I couldn't forgive myself for what I'd done to Darius, for the secrets, for letting Mom and Dad just take over and determine everyone's future. It took years before I started getting myself out of that darkness. But I finally got through nursing school and tried to see that everything worked out for the best. Mom was so happy. You were her baby. I met Simon and tried to start over."

"Why couldn't you all just tell me the truth?"

"I wanted to," Ginny said. "Just before Simon and I were going to be married, I came to Mom and begged her to let me tell the truth. I knew it was wrong to start a life with Simon that way. She fell apart, saying I'd destroy everything. She said Simon wouldn't want me. She said I'd be making her a liar."

"Simon doesn't know?"

Ginny shook her head. "After a while, it felt like the truth would only be about easing my own guilt. You were happy. Mom was happy."

"But Darius—"

"I've never forgiven myself for what I did to him, to either of you. And then he reached out through Facebook to reconnect. You were eleven. He was acting—making a living, it looked like—and living his dream. He was in New York. I didn't know what he'd do if he knew. Mom would have died if Darius came back and suddenly insisted on some sort of parental rights.

"And then he got in touch again last weekend about that screenplay. He'd written our story. But he didn't even know the truth. And I knew if that movie was made, it was all going to come out."

"Oh my God," Brooklyn interrupted. "You did it, didn't you? You shot him?"

"No! I swear, Brooklyn. I read the script and I knew the truth would come out. I was going to tell Darius about you, but I chickened out. I got drunk. First time since before Mikey. And then Sunday was Mother's Day, and I couldn't take it anymore. Everything the kids did for me, everything they said, their notes about me being a good mother, it was all a lie. I'd abandoned you. I'd lied to Darius. I'd lived a whole life built on lies.

"I told Simon I was going to check on Dad to see how he was handling the day. But the truth was that I came to tell him that I was going to come clean and tell you the truth. But when I got to the house, his muddy shoes were at the front door and he was sitting in the living room ranting about 'that boy' destroying his family with his story. I couldn't imagine how he knew, but I could tell he was talking about Darius."

Martin, Brooklyn realized. He'd come to the store that day. That's why her dad had turned on him.

"John was talking to me as if I were Mom. He told me he was sorry. He said it would be over soon. And then I looked into the study and noticed the gun safe was open. The gun was on the desk and when I turned back and looked at him, he said nothing. I ran out the door, terrified of what he might have done. When I got to Darius's house, he was being put in the ambulance."

"Dad shot Darius Woods?" It seemed incomprehensible. "He could never do that."

"You don't know him like I do. He's done it before."

"What?"

"Senior year. At the women's clinic. It was Dad."

She was lying. She had to be lying. John Anderson was not some outlaw who went around shooting people.

"It's not like I could tell Sheriff Wilson and the FBI that it was John Anderson, the local war hero and the sheriff's poker buddy, driving off in his truck after shooting that doctor. It would have destroyed our family whether the sheriff believed me or not—and I figured there was a good chance he wouldn't believe me anyway. And then Pastor Gary came in with that alibi for me. It was an impossible situation."

"This is beyond crazy," Brooklyn said. "You're making Dad sound evil. He's not like that. Why would he shoot that doctor?"

"Come on. You know our parents. Dad's never had an issue with killing for a cause."

Brooklyn winced. He was righteous and judgmental, but he was a man of . . . She stopped herself, recalling those dinner conversations of years ago, and his cavalier attitude about certain crimes. "You're saying that Dad shot Darius because the screenplay would expose him as the shooter at the clinic?"

"No. The screenplay doesn't spell out who did it. But people would realize you were mine and Darius's. That you're not adopted. That I, all of us, lied for all these years."

Brooklyn thought back to her dad's comment in the hospital, about how he would always protect his family.

"He was ashamed?" Brooklyn whispered. He'd proudly been her father and protector. "Brooklyn's my girl," he'd said to Tommy Waters all those years ago. It didn't make sense.

"I think he was afraid of losing you."

Brooklyn didn't know what to feel. She recalled her dad's final warning to Tommy that day on the playground. He'd said people who messed with his family tended to regret it. And then she thought of his constant reminders to lock up the house, his insistence at having armed weapons on both floors. "Gotta protect what's ours," he'd say. She didn't know him at all.

"How could you hold on to all this? Why didn't you tell anyone?"

"I didn't know what to do. You just lost the only mother you'd ever known. Was I supposed to tell you the story of your life? That your dad, the man you loved and admired, may have just killed your real father? What if Darius died and John went to prison? You would lose everything, everyone."

Brooklyn's mind was racing. She looked at Ginny. "Oh my God, did you?"

"What?"

"Did you hurt Dad? Is that why he said he forgave you? Did you come back and attack him?"

"No, no! I've barely spoken to Dad since that summer twenty years ago. I found him on the floor when I got back to the house. His head was bleeding, and he was unconscious. I swear. I think he hit his head on that stupid doorstop."

"Why'd you say he was in the study? And the living room? Why all the lies? Why did you even call me home if you were just going to keep this from me all week?"

Ginny wiped at her face one last time, as if she was done falling apart. "I was such a wreck, Brooklyn. The doctors at the hospital were concerned about his head—they weren't even sure they could operate. Then I heard that Darius was probably not going to survive. I left the hospital and practically drowned myself in vodka. I barely even remember sending you that text, but I was sure Darius was going to die and I didn't know what would happen to Dad. I had to tell you something. We'd just lost Mom, and you were so angry that no one had told you she was sick. I didn't know what the right thing was anymore."

"Do you really think he has dementia? Was that another lie?"

"I wasn't lying . . . but I found a bunch of his medications yesterday. There were some dangerous combinations. It might explain some of his issues. I don't know for sure. I brought them to the hospital yesterday and showed the doctor. He agreed that we have to carefully monitor and reevaluate all of it. It's been a week, and now with anesthesia wearing off, we'll finally see what's really happening with him."

Brooklyn didn't know what to believe. "Dad said you weren't there yesterday."

"I was there. But I didn't see him. I only talked to the doctor. The kids were with me, and I didn't want them to see him confused. It would have scared them."

Brooklyn let her head fall back against the wall and closed her eyes. She couldn't take anymore.

"I swear to you, I didn't hurt Dad. I took the gun and called an ambulance. All I knew in that moment was that I couldn't say anything. Not until I knew if he'd survive. And if Darius would survive."

Brooklyn had nothing to say.

"I know I don't deserve your forgiveness. I've done a lot of terrible things. I'm so sorry."

Brooklyn remained still, eyes closed, as tears pushed their way out, trailing down her cheeks.

Ginny got off the floor and walked out.

"Where are you going?" Brooklyn finally called after her.

"I need to see Darius."

CHAPTER THIRTY-TWO

BROOKLYN SAT ON THE FLOOR for what felt like hours after Ginny left. But when she looked at her watch, it was four thirty. Her dad would be released from the hospital soon. *Her dad.* But Darius Woods was her father. In one day, in one conversation with Ginny, her entire life had become unmoored. A lifetime of feeling like an outsider, someone who belonged somewhere else. But there was nowhere else.

Ginny was probably with Darius right now. Brooklyn had known his name for years, followed his career, stared at his photo—he was her father.

The edge of a smile rose and fell an instant later as she imagined his reaction. What if he rejected her? If anger over Ginny's betrayal and her dad's threats superseded every other emotion? What if he went straight to the police and told them her dad was the one who'd shot him? What if her dad went to prison?

John Anderson was the only dad she'd ever known. He had been good to her. He loved her. Even in the hospital, when he recognized her, his face relaxed, a smile emerged. He was sick. He had to be. She couldn't believe he would shoot Darius. And even if he had, could she watch him go to prison?

She couldn't place her allegiance. She'd never even met Darius. Every emotion was coming with such speed it was like an assault. Pain began behind her eyes, overtaking everything else. She searched the kitchen for some ibuprofen and went to the hospital.

~ • ~

The nurse at the station said the doctor hadn't been by yet. It might be another thirty minutes. Brooklyn looked into the room. Her dad was lying in the bed, eyes closed, looking peaceful—innocent and needy as a child—but he was a stranger. She couldn't go in.

She sat in a chair in the hall and pulled up the screenplay on her phone. She had to know the rest—to at least understand Darius's perspective. She'd left off reading about Darius's character, Anthony, finding Margaret with the pastor and getting her out of there. The scene ended with the narrator's voice: *I had no idea at the time how much my life would change after that day.*

Anthony saw Margaret at lunch the next week. He sat with her and struck up a conversation. Margaret barely looked at him. When he asked if she wanted to tell anyone, she said, "It was a test. I failed. It was my fault."

Brooklyn's heart broke a little for Ginny, imagining the young, shy, straight-A student she'd once been. Was this how it really happened?

She skimmed the pages looking for the name Margaret, for hints of what had happened between Ginny and Darius, her dad and the pastor. She got to a scene of a new school year—a homecoming poster in the background, a **WELCOME BACK SENIORS** sign hanging on the wall above the bank of lockers, when Anthony found Margaret sitting alone, crying.

"This is about that man at your church," he said. She didn't respond. "Is he . . . ?" Margaret looked at Anthony with a mixture of guilt and fear.

"It's not right, Margaret. He's, like, old, and he's a minister. I don't know what's happening, but it's not right."

"Everyone loves him. And he's like a mentor. He's in charge of youth group and I'm the teen leader. I have to spend time with him." Tears fell to her cheeks. "You don't understand. There's no getting away."

"You can't tell your parents?" Anthony asked.

"No!" the girl shouted. "I'd be in so much trouble."

"You haven't done anything wrong."

"That's not how they'd see it."

Anthony finally sat down, leaning against the wall beside Margaret. "What's so great about that teen group, anyway?" Anthony asked.

"You don't know my family. That church is practically our second home."

"Well, I'm not suggesting you give up your religion or anything. But you need to get away from that group. Do something fun. It's our senior year."

"What am I gonna do?"

"What about theater?"

"I could never do what you do. I can't even stand singing in the chorus at church. My chest gets all blotchy red when the congregation focuses on us. I just mouth the words."

"Then do stage crew. We all hang out together. Come on. You'll love it. And we rehearse every night, so you won't have time for much else."

"I don't think my parents would approve."

"So don't tell them."

"But Pastor Ed . . . He'd tell . . ."

"Let me handle it."

Margaret smiled, and the scene ended. Ginny had joined stage crew to escape a predator.

In the following scene, Anthony went to the pastor's office and opened the door without knocking again.

"Yes?" the pastor asked. He stood as Anthony walked inside. "You're that boy from last spring. The actor?"

"Margaret's not going to be in the teen group anymore, and you're not going to say anything about it."

"Excuse me, Anthony, right? You need to adjust your tone. I think you're making some grave miscalculations."

"I think you're sick."

"Anthony. Margaret's a troubled girl. She lies. This doesn't concern you."

"Why don't I just talk to your boss and see if he agrees."

"You're talking out of turn, son. Girls like Margaret must admit what they've done to the congregation. I've forgiven her for her behavior, and I wouldn't want to put her through that kind of shame. Would you?"

"She's not coming back. The law is on my side," Anthony said.

"Don't be so sure about that," the pastor said.

Nurse Wanda came up to Brooklyn, apologizing for the delay. "Doctors," she said with a smile.

"It's fine. Is my dad awake yet?"

"Nope." Wanda walked away, and Brooklyn kept reading. A montage began after the confrontation with the pastor, showing the two teens discover shared interests, authors, and bands, and laughing, mostly in the company of the entire drama department, but always having private moments, or glances across a room. The montage ended with Anthony offering Margaret a ride home after a long rehearsal. When he neared her house, she had him stop several hundred feet away. "Right here is fine," she said. "My dad's a little overprotective. I wouldn't want him coming out here and giving you the third degree."

Anthony pulled over and the girl grabbed the door handle, stopped, turned back, and leaned over. She kissed him. "Thanks," she said.

Anthony said, "Anytime," with a huge grin on his face. The narrator added, *I didn't even remember driving home.*

In the next scene, another friend from the drama group pulled Anthony aside. "I see what's going on between you two." Anthony acted as if the friend was mistaken. "Seriously, you need to keep that on the down low," the friend said before walking away.

Anthony ran after him. "What do you mean?"

"You don't want to mess with her father."

"Who's her father?"

"My dad and he are good friends. They play poker together. We all go to the same church."

"And?"

"Let's just say I've overheard the jokes and conversations between our dads over the years. I can tell you that you and Margaret—there are some people in this town that still think that's a big deal, some sort of unnatural thing. Hey, I ain't one of 'em, but her dad—oh yeah, he is. Whatever you got going there, it would be over."

Brooklyn scanned through several pages quickly. She couldn't read fast enough. The fall play had wrapped, and the theater kids planned a "friendsgiving" for the holiday weekend.

Afterward, Anthony drove several kids home. He saved Margaret's stop for last. "I don't want to go home," she said. They parked the car a few miles out of town in a field. She pulled a CD from her bag and grinned.

"Shania Twain," Anthony joked, scanning the cover. "You're determined to get me to like country."

"I am," she said. "But I really love the words of this song. I wanted you to hear it." She put the CD in the player and played "From This

Moment On." They listened in silence, holding hands, and as it ended, Anthony looked at Margaret. "I'm in love with you."

Margaret smiled. "Me too."

They began to kiss, softly at first and then with more passion as the scene faded to black.

The narrator's voice would play over more scenes of the two together. *Within a month, it seemed like every conversation was about the future and leaving Eden for our own paradise, where we could walk down the street, hand in hand. Suddenly, it felt impossible to graduate and move away without her.*

~ • ~

Ginny stood on the porch of Darius's house and knocked on the door, holding her breath.

A moment later, his father opened the door just a few inches.

"Hi, Mr. Woods," she said meekly. "We met on Thursday afternoon at the hospital, remember? I'm Ginny."

"Oh, sure, sweetie," he said, opening the door wider. "I just saw Brooklyn at your dad's store yesterday. I had no idea you were sisters."

She nodded, unable to come up with a response.

"Guess you heard the good news about my boy getting out."

"I did. He home?" she asked, noticing the binder in his hand.

Mr. Woods smiled and raised it. "You know about this? Darius's screenplay. I finally get to read it."

Her face flushed. This man would soon hate her too.

"Just a sec," he said, waving and leaving her at the door.

Ginny's heart rate picked up as she heard the slow footfalls on the wood floor getting louder, closer. The door opened wide. Darius suddenly stood before her. It was hard to believe twenty years had passed since they'd stood this close. Everything about him still felt familiar—his emerald-green eyes, his easy smile, like nothing could take him down. Not even gunshots. There was no stress on his face, no furrowed brow, no residual . . . anything, as if he'd forgiven her for breaking his heart, for failing to stand up to her dad, for being a coward when he needed her to be brave. She never thought she'd get to feel the warmth of that smile again.

All the years instantly melted away, and she recalled their farewell that summer, their long embrace, the way he'd lifted her during that hug, making her laugh and lightening the mood, whispering in her ear that the weeks apart would pass quickly. He'd promised to call every week at the pay phone in town until she joined him. "We'll be together soon," he'd said.

"I'd give you a hug," he said now, "but everything is still pretty sore. I'm moving slower than my pops right now."

"You look . . . good," she said. The words caught in her throat. She had to knock her chest to get it all out. "I'm so sorry about what happened to you."

"No big deal," he said, waving it off sarcastically. "I been shot dozens of times."

"Ha-ha. Listen, Darius, I really need to talk to you."

He stepped out to join her on the front porch. "Sure. I've been wanting to catch up with you, Ginny. Wanna sit?"

She looked over at the chairs, suddenly terrified of what was to come, what might be said.

"Maybe I can take you out for coffee?" Neutral territory, a way to escape quickly.

He looked down at his sweatpants and T-shirt. "I'm in need of a shower," he said.

"You look great," she said. "Please." If she waited, she might lose her nerve.

"Okay," he said. "Let me just tell my dad. He's a worried mess these days." He went back into the house before she could say more.

She walked down the porch steps, keys in hand, and stepped over to the driver's side of her car.

Darius came outside. Twenty years had passed, but the pain of lying to him and watching him walk out of her life came back like a wind that might knock her over.

"Should we take my dad's car?" he asked. "Convertible would feel great today."

A silver BMW convertible, as unlikely in this town as a movie star.

She looked down at her hand, tightly gripped around her door handle. "Actually, let's take two cars. I've gotta get to the hospital as soon as I leave you." Riding together after she shared her news felt impossible.

He nodded. "Mary's Diner. See you there in a sec." Darius slowly eased his way into the driver's seat. She watched him grimace in pain. She was at the root of it all.

~ • ~

The waitress poured them coffees and removed the menus they'd rejected. Ginny gripped the mug with both hands and stared at the table, unable to break the silence. She couldn't look him in the eyes.

"You look good," Darius said. "The same."

She smiled. It wasn't true, but he was being kind.

Twenty years melted away. She wanted to reach out and hold his hand and take back everything she'd ever done. She took a deep breath, trying to stir up the strength to come clean.

Darius filled the void before she had the chance. "So I know I've been busy fighting for my life and all, but before that happened, I was really just excited to see you and hear what you thought of the script. You okay with it? I mean, no one will guess it's about you and me, don't you think?"

She let go of her mug and, with elbows on the table, rubbed at her temples. She didn't know how to start.

"You read it, right?"

"I read it," she said, nodding. She took another deep breath and blew it out, pushing past her fears. "Here's the thing," she said, removing her hands from her face, sitting back. "Everyone will know it's about you and me."

The creases between his brows deepened, his soft expression suddenly hard. It was hard to tell if he didn't understand how, or if he was just hurt that she wanted to hide their relationship after all these years.

"There are a lot of things that you don't know," she continued. "Things I've kept from you and other things that happened—and your movie is going to bring everything to light."

Darius pulled back and tilted his head, searching her face.

"I've never had your courage. You were always so brave. It's part of what made me love you."

"O-kay."

"Before I tell you, I just need to say how sorry I am. I know you'll probably never forgive me for what I've done, but I've struggled my whole life to live with this."

"Ginny, what is going on?"

"First, I gotta tell you—" She pushed out one final breath to summon the courage. "I believe my father shot you last Sunday night."

His fingers tensed around the mug in his hands. "What? How do you know . . . Why?"

"He's not well. He's not thinking clearly. I thought it was dementia. It might be some drug interactions." She shook her head. "Anyway, it's not the point. I found him last Sunday night. He was rambling about you coming back here, ruining lives with that screenplay. I don't know how he knew about it. He said he couldn't live if you destroyed his family. It was almost like he was in shock. There was a gun on the table. I ran out of the house, afraid of what he might have done. By the time I reached your house, you were being put in an ambulance. And Sheriff Wilson confirmed—you were shot with a .38. My dad has a .38."

Darius sat back and took it in. "But I don't understand. You read the script. I thought it might be great if something happened to that pastor, if he were exposed for the man he is, but I didn't use names, and I didn't make it clear that your dad was the shooter at the clinic. No one could arrest him based on any of this. I really thought—"

"It's not that," she interrupted.

He reached over, putting his hand on hers.

She pulled her hand away. "When I broke it off with you, I told you I had a miscarriage. It wasn't true."

She looked into his green eyes, wide and watering, his expression frozen, waiting for her to finish.

"I didn't know how far along I was when you left after graduation. I assumed it was early. I didn't show at all. I didn't feel sick. But I obviously got pregnant that first time we were together. After Thanksgiving. Darius, I didn't know what was happening, but I had a baby that summer. A tiny, premature baby, clinging to life, and my parents found out, swooped in, and took over." She couldn't go on. She couldn't get any sounds out as the reality of that summer came crashing forward.

She couldn't look at his face but watched his fingers wrapped tightly around his mug.

"I know it's unforgivable," she continued. "I should have told you. I was in shock. I wanted to run away and go to New York and start our life together, but they wouldn't let me give it up. No one would let me go."

"What are you saying?"

"My mom said they'd bring the baby home and that I needed to take responsibility. They acted like I'd been attacked. They didn't even ask about the father. It was the day they came home from the mission trip. Pastor Gary was with them when they found me. The three of them got me to a hospital. He stood in the corner of the room, advising Bonnie, consoling her, saying he wished he'd known, agreeing with her that of course I needed to stay in Eden, that even from tragedy comes miracles. They stood there, whispering, plotting my future, and I knew I couldn't tell them about you. I knew it wouldn't even matter."

Darius's gaze dropped to the table. Tears began to fall.

He was the one man who'd never hurt her, who showed her what real love looked and felt like. "I couldn't tell you. We had this plan. You had a dream. I didn't want to hijack all of it. I didn't want you to feel guilty or obligated. I knew our plans would never happen. I—"

"So when I came to your house, when I called out to you, begging for you to come to the door, and you just ignored me, you were hiding our baby?"

"She was in the hospital," Ginny said, shaking her head. "I didn't even know at that point if she was going to survive."

"But she did?"

Ginny nodded. "And I heard my dad threaten you. We both knew what he was capable of after he shot that doctor. I didn't want anything to happen to you. I thought he'd try to ruin your life. I just thought you'd be better off forgetting all about me."

"So you've raised our child all these years without me? Without even telling me that I was a father?"

"No," she said, the guilt overtaking her ability to speak at all. She finally shook her head and wiped at her face. "You don't understand. I fell apart. My mom even put me in a hospital because I shut down so completely after it happened. She said no one would ever know. They told the whole town that they'd adopted a baby from their mission trip."

Darius sat back in his chair, stunned. "Our child has been raised by your parents and never knew about us? You either?"

"I just told her. Literally, just before coming to see you."

He shook his head. He wasn't looking at her anymore. Ginny felt the wall rising between them. She'd never again see him look at her with love or compassion.

"I have barely been in her life all these years," Ginny said. "I felt so guilty, I avoided her. Looking at her reminded me of you, and I hated my father for what he said to you that day at the house, what he wouldn't let me do. I tried to come clean after she was a few years old. It seemed so wrong to have this secret and get married. But my mom was terrified of the scandal and of losing her. She loved her."

Darius shook his head. He said nothing.

Ginny couldn't stop the tears. "She's beautiful," she added, sniffling. "She turned out great. She's an actress. She's nothing like me—"

"I have a daughter," he uttered, his voice barely audible.

"Her name's Brooklyn. Every time I heard my mom call her name, I thought of you, of the life we planned, the apartment you'd found, how being with you—it was the happiest time in my life. Everything got so dark after she was born, after I watched you walk away. That girl you loved—it was like she was the one who died that summer. I was a coward."

Darius was staring out the window. She needed him to look at her, so he would see her regret.

"I've made one disastrous decision after another, and that screenplay," she said, "it will bring it all to light. And I know you don't worry about exposing Pastor Gary. But he's not the only villain. I've kind of built my life around denying reality."

Darius finally looked at her. She could feel the pain, the anger seeping from his silent glare. His eyes filled with tears again, but he pushed his way out of the booth, wincing as he stood.

"I gotta go," he said.

She didn't try to stop him.

CHAPTER THIRTY-THREE

ANOTHER NURSE APPROACHED BROOKLYN. "SORRY the doctor is taking so long, but your dad is awake now if you want to see him."

She didn't. She couldn't face him until she got through the rest of the story.

She thanked the nurse, looked back down at her phone, and kept reading.

It was just days after that moment when everything began to go horribly wrong.

The next scene was to take place at the Garden of the Gods in the Shawnee Forest. Anthony and Margaret would be sitting on one of the high rocks, watching the sunset over the vast treetops that were just beginning to bud. "You gonna miss this view?" Anthony asked.

"I've been coming here my whole life," Margaret said. "My mom always said church was for communicating with God, but this is where you see his best work."

Brooklyn smiled, recalling all the times Mom had said the same to her.

"But I'm ready for a view of skyscrapers," Margaret continued, resting her head on his shoulder. "Should we stay for the stars?" she asked. Before he could answer, she lay back, cradled her head in her folded arms, and crossed her ankles, ready for viewing.

"I don't know. It'll be tough to see when it gets dark. Don't want anything happening to my girl. Aren't there copperheads in here?"

"A few," she teased. "Come on. A couple more minutes. These stars are the only thing I'm going to miss. I hear you can't really see stars when you're in the city."

Anthony lay back beside her and looked at the cloudless abyss. She was right. Anthony had never seen a sky like Eden's when he lived in Chicago.

"When I was ten, I started crawling out my bedroom window to sit on the porch roof after I was sent to bed," Margaret said. "I'd look up at the millions of dots in the dark sky. I'd talk about my day." She turned her head to Anthony and smiled, embarrassed. "Didn't have a lot of friends as a kid."

"Me either," he said.

Brooklyn had sat on the same roof outside her bedroom window, staring at those same stars. She'd felt the same loneliness.

"Anyway, I'd whisper all my secrets—a crush I had or an insecurity. Anything I couldn't share with people. I'd cast them out into the sky. I told myself that all those millions of stars were other people's secrets. Made me feel better."

Anthony looked up at the darkening sky, imagining the blanket of dots that would soon arrive. "Have you whispered our secret to the sky?"

"Many times," she said, smiling.

"Then I guess it's safe." Anthony propped himself onto his elbow and leaned in for a kiss.

Until today, Brooklyn had spent years imagining her parents. She'd looked at that photo of Eimy, wondering if she'd been in love, hoping that even if the pregnancy had been unwanted at such a young age, that something good was behind it. She'd always feared the possibility of an assault, a criminal's genes swimming around in her veins. But suddenly, she was reading her parents' love story. It was the strangest gift.

The stage direction on the next line of the script simply read: *The sky darkens. A bunch of burnouts from high school show up. Margaret and Anthony recognize one.*

"What in the world is going on here?" a voice behind them said.

Margaret and Anthony sat up and turned.

"Margaret, you can't be serious," one of them said.

"Shut up, Evan," she answered. "You remember Anthony?"

She and Anthony stood. Anthony offered a nod and his hand to the guy, but Evan ignored it, staring at him. "Margaret, I knew you liked chocolate, but come on now."

The other burnouts laughed. "Go to hell," she said. Anthony looked at the seven guys behind Evan. None were big, but they looked drunk and excited, wild dogs ready for anything.

"He's on drugs," Margaret whispered to Anthony.

"We don't want any trouble," Anthony said to the guys. The sun had disappeared behind the horizon, and it was quickly getting dark. In another few minutes, it would be tough to see and difficult to climb down to the path. Anthony took Margaret's hand to help her down from the rock, but Evan climbed up to where they stood, blocking the path.

"I don't think this is gonna work," he said. "Margaret, what would your dad say?"

"Get out of my face," Anthony said in a measured tone.

"Or what?" Evan asked. "You gonna take on all of us?" He looked back at his friends. "I think we better show Anthony the way outta here."

"How 'bout the shortcut?" one of them yelled.

"Margaret, you better be careful. I think your friend might be in danger," another of them said before laughing.

Anthony dropped her hand from his grip just as Evan took a wild swing. Anthony ducked and grabbed him by the shirt collar, whipped him around like a rag doll and took him down. It only took a second and Evan was on his back, his upper body hanging over the edge of the rock, Anthony's full body weight holding him in place. Evan began a panicked scream. Anthony looked back at Evan's friends. "Don't move."

"Hey man, we was only playin'," one of them said.

"He never touched you," another of them shouted.

"Get off me!" Evan yelled. Anthony got up and pulled Evan back to standing. "You'll regret this," Evan said. Anthony let go as Evan continued the rant. "Picked a real winner, Margaret. Fuckin' animal."

"Let's go," Anthony said to Margaret. But then Evan stumbled and tripped, losing his balance. Margaret and Anthony looked back to see Evan's eyes widen as he took another step toward the edge, unable to stop himself, like an invisible force was pushing him back. Margaret screamed. He was going to fall off the cliff. The other guys gasped, coming closer, but Anthony stepped forward, grabbed Evan's arm, and yanked him back from the edge. They both tumbled to the ground and Evan fell hard against a rock. "Aaaa!" Evan cried out. "My shoulder!"

His friends rushed to get him, and Anthony took Margaret's hand, helping her climb down. He put his arm around her and neither said a word as they carefully began walking the path back to the car. "We're not done here," Evan yelled. He followed up with a few more words for Anthony, the kind that showed how dark Evan's soul really was.

Anthony knew his luck in that town was running out.

Brooklyn continued reading. She'd heard this part from Ginny—that it was May of their senior year when she took a pregnancy test. Anthony held Margaret close after she told him, and she said she felt nothing—no morning sickness, no weight gain. He said maybe the test was wrong. Margaret grabbed onto that hope and said she'd go to the clinic in the next town the following morning to find out for sure—early, before anyone might see her. He offered to go, but she said no.

The story continued, from Anthony's point of view, when Margaret found him in school the next morning and told him what happened in the parking lot. They agreed that speaking up would only compound their problems. But then Margaret was accused, then cleared, thanks to Pastor Ed, who naturally wanted something in return. He wanted her back in the teen group again. He wanted her to go on the mission trip.

And then Brooklyn got to the part she hadn't heard from Ginny. Anthony went to the pastor's office and confronted him. He said if the pastor ever laid another hand on Margaret, he'd go to the police. He'd tell them what he saw last year.

The pastor's reply made Brooklyn's skin crawl.

"We both know she was at the clinic that morning. Maybe the two of you have your own secrets. I'd think twice about those threats if I were you. I know Margaret's dad. Who do you think he's going to believe?"

Anthony swung hard, his fist meeting the pastor's jaw first, then his nose. He fell back against his desk, bleeding. "Grave mistake," the pastor said.

Anthony panicked. A black kid assaulting a white pastor the whole town revered. His dad's words flooded his mind: "We always gotta work harder, be kinder, be more careful. A black man who gets in trouble with the law will always lose. No assumptions of innocence, no excuses. It's a stacked deck."

And Anthony had just hit the man without physical provocation. He'd never be able to explain—not without complete honesty, which Margaret wasn't ready for. The pastor wiped his nose. "I better not see you in here again."

Anthony ran.

The story followed Anthony to New York, where he found an apartment and a job in a restaurant. They'd planned for him to call Margaret every week. He couldn't call her house, so he was to call a pay phone in downtown Eden each Sunday at noon. But the third Sunday after he left town, the phone rang, and no one answered. The fourth Sunday, Margaret answered.

Brooklyn cried as she read of Ginny and Darius's breakup. Margaret said the baby was gone and she'd changed her mind. She wasn't coming to New York. Anthony was heartbroken.

And then Brooklyn got to the scene when Anthony returned to Eden. He sat in his car, parked down the road from Margaret's house, trying to work up the nerve to see her. A car pulled into the drive. Margaret. He let his tires roll forward, watching her go inside the house. He sprinted after her and rang the bell. Her father answered the door.

"Sir, you don't know me, but I'm Anthony Forrester," he said, holding out his hand.

The man looked at Anthony's hand and crossed his arms. "So you're the one who violated my child. I'm guessing you're the one who assaulted the sheriff's son too."

"Sir, no, it's not—"

"You know that someone punched a pastor at our church?" he asked sarcastically. "Black kid," he added, shaking his head. And then he stepped closer, his breath on Anthony's face. "You come near my daughter, I'll have you arrested or shot."

Anthony stepped back. "Sir, I love your daughter. And she loves me."

Mr. Carr left him on the porch. Anthony thought he went to get Margaret, but the man came back with his gun and cocked the trigger, raising it to Anthony's face. "I don't want to hear another word. I should put a bullet in your head right now."

Anthony backed up. "Sir, please. Margaret!" he called out. "I know you hear me. Please!"

"How old are you, boy?"

"Nineteen."

"Since when?"

"Last week."

"And how long you known my daughter?"

"We met junior year, sir," he said.

"Tell you what," Mr. Carr said. "Round here, any adult who's been with a minor has committed statutory rape. You wanna go to prison? I got friends who'll make it happen. You best walk away and never look back if you know what's good for you."

In that moment, all Anthony saw was a white man, a war hero, the sheriff's best friend, beloved by the community, pointing a gun at his face. Mr. Carr could kill him and get away with it. Anthony was just a young, poor black kid who got a white girl pregnant. He could just imagine Evan making up lies about him, and that pastor too. He'd crossed the wrong people.

Anthony walked to his car. He didn't know what else to do. He didn't know if he'd committed statutory rape. He was barely a year older than Margaret. But Margaret never came to the door. Her parents had obviously found out about the pregnancy. He didn't know what she'd told them. As he pulled out of the drive, he glanced up and saw her looking, her hand on the bedroom window. He knew then it was over.

Brooklyn was now reading the part of Darius's story that she'd known nothing about. It was a scene after Anthony returned to New York, to the apartment he'd found for them in Brooklyn. The stage direction indicated that Anthony was sitting on the couch as the camera panned through the near-empty space, across the few bits of furniture, moving into the bedroom, across the poster of the Brooklyn Bridge over the bed, and then into the closet. It was to be one continuous shot, ending in the back of the closet where the camera would focus on the large box: a crib.

Brooklyn smiled. He'd wanted her.

She skimmed through the final pages, covering his life in New York over a ten-year span, until the final scene.

Anthony was starring in a Broadway play. A woman came to the dressing room after the show, and he turned to the door. It was Margaret, wiping tears, smiling but unable to speak. He recognized her immediately.

"You let me leave," he said.

She said nothing.

"Did you tell your parents you were raped?"

"No. Mom found me in the bathroom after the miscarriage." Brooklyn had to stop and remind herself that Darius would have never guessed that Ginny had the baby. He'd seen her get out of the car and go in the house when he came back in August, and she had probably looked no different than when he left in June. She'd never even showed.

Margaret said her mom refused to believe that she could have intentionally broken her chastity vows. She didn't even have a boyfriend. Her mother said God took care of the pregnancy because it wasn't meant to be. "But then you started calling and you showed up at the house," Margaret said. "They knew."

"How could you not say anything?" Anthony asked.

Margaret began to cry, and the story flashed back to her, standing in her bedroom the day Anthony came to the house, listening to her father shouting at him at the front door. Her mother was standing in the doorway, listening with her. "I have to go down there," she'd said. But her mother said no. "Let him go, Margaret. The world will never accept you with that man. And neither will your father."

"My dad might have killed you," Margaret said. "We both know what he was capable of. And I knew that you were better off. You had dreams and plans, and I didn't want to ruin that. If I'd gone with you . . . I don't know. I just couldn't do it."

"So why are you here now?" Anthony asked.

Margaret looked around the room and smiled nervously.

Anthony didn't say anything. He wasn't going to make it easier.

"I just wanted to tell you I'm sorry and to tell you . . ." She hesitated and shook her head. "This is stupid. It's been ten years. I'm sure you've moved on and you're probably in love with some beautiful actress . . . Maybe you're married."

"I'm not. What did you want to say?"

Margaret met his eyes then, and it was as though the years between them dissolved. "Can I buy you a drink?"

Anthony smiled.

She smiled.

Fade to black.

Brooklyn lowered her phone, letting her emotions overwhelm her. In that moment, she couldn't hate Ginny for what she'd done.

But she did hate John Anderson.

CHAPTER THIRTY-FOUR

DAY SEVEN
10:00 p.m.
BOLINE COUNTY JAIL

BROOKLYN WAS CURLED UP ON her side, her hands sandwiched between her legs, trying to turn off her brain. It was impossible. This morning she'd still been planning to bring her dad home; she'd been excited about her audition, assuming that things might actually work out. And less than twelve hours later, everything she'd ever known had fallen apart. Darius Woods was her father, and twenty years ago John Anderson had put a gun to his face, threatening his life and freedom, ridding his family of Darius like a virus.

Her stomach turned with every memory twisted under the new lens. Her dad had once guilted Brooklyn into chores while sharing stories of how difficult her life might have been in that orphanage. He'd watched her dress like a beach bum in high school, her desperation to understand her history so clear in every request for more stories about Eimy. He'd seen the pain of feeling like an outsider; he'd seen the way kids treated her.

He'd hurt so many people. Even the way he died was hurting people.

CHAPTER THIRTY-FIVE

AFTER BROOKLYN FINISHED THE SCRIPT, she stood outside her dad's hospital door, shaking, willing herself to go inside and confront him.

When she finally stepped inside, he looked at her blankly. "Yes?"

Just one word, and she knew what it meant. He wasn't really there. There was nothing to say.

The doctor came in and reminded his patient to take it easy, accept help, stand slowly, and use the cane they were providing. Brooklyn played the role of concerned daughter, despite the new brew of emotions bubbling under the surface. Her dad said nothing, offering only impatient groans.

Neither of them spoke during the ride, but once she pulled into the driveway, he opened the door and used the cane to pull himself up and out of the passenger seat before she could help. "Get my bag, Brooklyn." He was back.

She ignored his request and ran over to help him up the front steps. He pushed her hand away and braced the banister carefully, easing himself back into his home.

"What is this?" he barked, waving the cane toward the bed in the living room. He was lucid again, fully aware of who she was and what was happening, and he was just acting like the stubborn man who refused to be babied. He'd walk upstairs to his own bed, he yelled. No one was going to tell him how to live his life.

She stood inside the front door, watching him inspect the room, bellowing his demands, seeing him with new eyes. The air felt toxic. She couldn't breathe. "You're a monster," she exploded before turning and throwing open the screen door. It smacked against the frame behind her.

That old wood floor in the hall creaked, and the screen door squeaked behind her as he pushed it open. "What's gotten into you?" His voice had softened, as if he had no idea what he'd done.

She turned. He stood there, looking so harmless with that cane, both his brows raised. He was dumbfounded.

"You're a liar," she said.

"Watch your mouth, young lady. I'm your father."

She leaned against the porch railing and held it tight. "But you're not."

His brows came down, and he pressed his lips together. He understood that she knew the truth. But instead of responding, he ignored the comment, focusing on her stance. "Don't lean on that. It makes me nervous."

"Seriously? You're going to act concerned for my welfare? You've lied to me my whole life!"

He swatted the air dismissively and shuffled to the bench under the living room window. "You wouldn't understand," he uttered, as he lowered himself to sit.

"I'm your *granddaughter*," she yelled. "I've been a misfit in this town my entire life. The little brown-skinned orphan with this fictional backstory. You'd rather I be from a foreign country, just so you—what?—didn't have to admit that Ginny had gotten pregnant? Or was the worse sin that my father was black?"

The weight of her accusation hung in the air between them. She wanted to be wrong, but there was no other explanation.

"I knew you wouldn't get it," he said, exhaling hard, as if exasperated by her nonsense. "This is why I never wanted you to know."

He actually thought he'd done the right thing. She hardly knew what to say.

"I can't make you understand what we were thinking back then," he said. "We couldn't let her give you up. Who knows what might have happened to you."

"But why the lies? You could have just told the world you were helping Ginny. You were raising your grandchild. You could have at least acknowledged that I'm your blood, that I belong in this godforsaken town just as much as any of these people."

"No, we couldn't."

It stung to hear him admit it.

"We could have lost you," he continued. "That boy could have claimed a right. We didn't know what might have happened."

"That boy was my father."

"Stop! You don't understand," he shouted, a vein bulging along his temple. It was that anger she'd seen in the hospital, a rage she'd never known inside the walls of this house.

"I don't even know who you are. Don't you see how much you messed up Ginny? Forcing her to live with that secret? Threatening the man she loved?"

"Is that what she said? That girl made a mess, and we cleaned it up."

Brooklyn couldn't stop the tears, but she wiped them aside, refusing to fall apart. "You put a gun to Darius's face. I'd say she had good reason to fear you. And she saw you at that clinic."

Her father stared out into the horizon, pushing his hand over the top of his head, as he considered this. He looked confused. Brooklyn remained motionless, waiting for a response.

He said nothing.

"Are you going to finally admit it? You do whatever you want. Your Bible-thumping nonsense, all to cover your violence. You shot that doctor as if it was hunting season or something, as if he was not even human. You're like a terrorist."

He finally looked at her, his brow raised. "You don't know what you're talking about, Brooklyn."

"Ginny was at the clinic that morning. She saw you."

"No, she didn't," he said quickly.

"She told me! She saw you speed off in your truck. We all know you keep a pistol in the glove box."

"That's not what happened."

"Jesus. I'm not wearing a wire! Just tell the truth!"

"You watch that mouth."

The anger was sapping every ounce of her. It was hard to do more than whisper. "Enough with all the secrets."

He leaned against the house siding, crossing his arms. "It doesn't matter."

She raised her voice one last time. "It matters to me."

The air stilled between them, the silence broken only by the birds in the trees, blissfully unaware of his crimes. Finally, he uncrossed his arms, placing a hand on each thigh, ready to leave. "I wasn't driving the truck. I wasn't even there."

Her heart began to pound; heat flushed her cheeks as the words and the implication finally came together in her mind. There was only one other person who drove the truck. "You're lying," Brooklyn said.

He looked at her. "If I'd shot that doctor, he'd be dead."

"How? Why?"

"It wasn't planned. It just happened."

"How did she—"

"She had to stop Ginny."

"Jesus. She knew about the pregnancy."

"Please don't talk like that."

"You've got to be kidding me right now. We're talking about my mother trying to murder a man and you're angry that I said 'Jesus'? JESUS F-ING CHRIST."

"Stop!" He leaned forward, wincing, holding his head.

Maybe it hurt to have someone finally talk back. He couldn't control her anymore. She was glad to see him suffer.

"Eddie came to see me at the store about a week before it happened," he continued, his head still in his hands, his eyes on the porch floorboards. "Sheriff Wilson's boy. He had a black eye. His face was all scraped up. He wouldn't say what happened, but he looked like he'd been hit. He said I needed to keep an eye on Ginny, that he didn't wanna snitch, but he thought I should know that she was spending time with someone I wouldn't approve of."

Brooklyn said nothing. Her dad was a racist.

He sat up slowly, lifting his head, returning his focus to Brooklyn. "You don't understand. Eddie's arm was in a sling. I said, 'Is this someone the reason you look like you do?' He wouldn't answer. I got in his face and grabbed his good arm, insisting that he spit it out, but he just said, 'Mr. Anderson, look at who she's hanging out with.' We were worried. As far as we knew, she spent all her time at the church with the youth group. I went to Pastor Gary. He didn't know anything. He said he was worried about her, too, that she'd stopped coming to youth group months before."

The thought of that pastor taking the opportunity to make Ginny look like the troubled one turned Brooklyn's stomach. "Did you talk to her? Does anyone in this family actually talk about things that matter?"

"Don't condescend to me, young lady. I asked her if there was something she wanted to tell me, and she said no. I asked if she had a boyfriend. She said no. But I'm no fool. Talking to teenagers isn't always the way to find answers."

Brooklyn had no reply. Of course, teenagers didn't always share. She'd certainly never shared every instance of being bullied over the years, even when her parents could tell she'd been crying. She'd never seen the point.

"We started watching. A few days later, when Ginny said she was going to school early for a project, Bonnie searched her room."

Brooklyn shook her head.

"You're not a parent. You don't know what it's like. Brooklyn, we had one child. One. We begged and prayed for more, but she was all we had, and we were not going to let her throw her life away. Anyway, Bonnie found a receipt in the trash can—from the Walmart in Marion—a pregnancy test. She took the truck without saying a word, and when she didn't see Ginny's car in the school lot, she kept driving until she got to the clinic, fearing the worst. It was pure intuition."

"But why—"

"You weren't there, Brooklyn. You don't know. You can't judge. She said it happened very quickly. Her child was in danger. A murderer was going to ruin Ginny's future and kill her baby. B pulled into the used-car lot across the street. She needed to figure out how to approach Ginny, what to say. We couldn't lock her in a closet."

Brooklyn rolled her eyes. "Sounds like you spent some time justifying this to each other."

"Don't you judge me in my own house. This is my house," he repeated, pointing down, raising his voice, that master intimidator still alive in the broken shell. "Anyway, it wasn't planned, that's what you need to understand. Another car pulled into the lot and parked right by the entrance before B could think. As soon as the man's door opened, she saw Ginny's car door open. Your mom was moving on instinct. Her daughter was in danger."

Brooklyn said nothing. It was like she'd been transported to some 1800s Wild West set. Her family solved problems with bullets and cover-ups while spouting from the Bible.

"She thought she was protecting her child. In that moment, she saw a man who was going to ruin her daughter's life and kill her grandchild. She just wanted to stop it. You can't say she had choices. Ginny might have ignored B's pleas. She might have returned another day. Parents needed notice, but the law didn't require consent. B had to end it. She came home, shaking, and handed me the car keys. She didn't even say what had happened."

"She tried to kill a man."

"She was defending a life."

"And she left Ginny at the crime scene."

He shook his head, as if that were the only negative outcome. "She nearly lost her mind when the police pulled Ginny in for questioning. She hadn't thought any of it through, but Brooklyn, it's ancient history. None of this matters. We took care of it."

"Yeah, by having that horrible pastor rescue her with his lies."

"You don't know what you're talking about. That pastor has helped this family for years."

"That pastor assaulted your daughter. My dad—Darius Woods is the only reason she got away from him."

"Assault . . . that's nonsense. Ginny adored Gary."

"You only see what you want to see."

He leaned back against the house again, closing his eyes. "We need to stop all this. You're making my head hurt."

Brooklyn's heart rate quickened, and she braced the railing, catching her breath.

He slowly stood, shuffled to the front door, and stopped in the doorway. He kept his back to her. "Ginny was in the lot that morning because of you."

He actually thought she should be grateful. "What is wrong with you?" she said, straightening. "Do you think you're God or something?"

He swatted the comment behind his back and slowly walked to his study.

She followed him in and watched him pick up a picture of Bonnie perched on the desk in a little silver frame. His gun, still in its Ziploc, sat beside it.

"So you both knew Ginny was pregnant and said nothing."

His eyes stayed on the photo. "We intended to. It was just two weeks before graduation. We wanted to give her time to come to terms with the situation. We planned to discuss it as soon as we returned from the mission trip."

It was no wonder Ginny never considered telling either of them. She was a girl in crisis twice, first with Pastor Gary and then with a pregnancy. This house, with all its rules, took on new color as she imagined it through Ginny's lens.

Suddenly, her parents' introversion, mission trips, charity drives—all felt like some ridiculous masquerade. The air in that house was thick with hypocrisy. Was this why Brooklyn found it so difficult to breathe sometimes? Her thoughts rolled back, cataloging her panic attacks, the recent one in the kitchen, the ones throughout childhood, the first one she ever remembered. They only happened here. In this house, this town. She hadn't had a single attack since moving away from Eden.

Her dad lowered himself into the chair.

"You watched me struggle. I was treated like garbage, like I didn't belong. You didn't care."

"Of course I did," he shouted, slamming his hand on the desk. "I just didn't think it would matter. It might have made things worse."

"You were ashamed."

"I wasn't. I just couldn't . . ."

Brooklyn turned to leave. There was nothing left to say.

"I was afraid," her dad said quietly.

She turned back. His head was still down. He wouldn't look her in the eyes. "What happened to the fearless war hero? I thought you were supposed to be brave."

"I know." Raising his head, looking at her. Tears. She'd never seen tears. Not even at her mom's funeral. "I'm sorry. I thought it was the right thing."

There was nothing else to say. She turned to the steps, then stopped. She had to get it out—his most recent crime. "You tried to kill my father," she uttered, almost under her breath.

He said nothing. She looked back, determined to get a final admission. His eyes were closed; he was holding his head in his hands, wincing in pain. The truth hurt.

She went upstairs to her room and slammed the door behind her. She sat at the window, looking out at the view she'd known her whole life, suddenly clouded by all the secrets and lies. She looked down at her hands, balled into fists. It wasn't fair. It wasn't right. She'd had no feelings for Ginny a week ago. She'd worshipped her parents. She'd been lucky to have John and Bonnie Anderson, just like those church ladies had whispered all those years ago. Now, she just felt rage.

~ • ~

Ginny drank one more coffee at Mary's. Brooklyn had sent a text. I picked up John. *John.* She didn't say "Dad." Ginny had taken that from her. She looked at the time. They'd be home by now, but it might be days before Brooklyn was ready to see her.

It was about fifteen minutes later when she finally paid the bill and mustered the courage to do the next right thing. She had to talk to Simon. He had a right to know that the kids weren't his. It was as if the lies and secrets had been eating away at her insides like an infection. Truth was the only medicine.

Dark clouds had gathered on the horizon. A blue sky still hovered above, but she could feel it in the air. A storm was coming. She was at a stop sign, gripping the wheel, terrified by the forward motion and the inability to go back.

She carefully looked left and right and left again before hitting the accelerator, suddenly desperate to get home.

She noticed a light-colored convertible in the distance, making a right turn. It was probably Darius in that BMW, probably heading for her dad's house. It was hard to imagine the storm of emotions Darius had to be feeling. John had stolen his child, taken away his chance at fatherhood, put a gun to his face all those years ago, and then gone on and shot him on Sunday. Darius had the right to confront him. He had a right to meet his daughter. At least John couldn't hurt him anymore.

As she watched his car disappear from view, her phone rang. She didn't recognize the number on the screen.

"Is this Ginny Smith?" a man said.

"Yes."

"It's Sheriff Goodwin over here at the Boline County station. I'm hoping you can come over here. I've gotta ask you some questions."

"What about?"

"Darius Woods, ma'am. Are you free?"

She swallowed before answering. "Of course. When would you like me?"

"Right now."

CHAPTER THIRTY-SIX

GINNY SAT IN A CHAIR along the wall at the station. An officer who looked barely older than Brooklyn said it wouldn't be a long wait. She pulled out her phone and texted Simon. She didn't know when she'd be home. His response was immediate, as if he'd been holding the phone. Where have you been? Great mothering. She had no defense. I'm sorry, she wrote. Things just taking a long time with John.

A few minutes later, a conference door opened and Pastor Gary walked out, followed by the man who'd appeared with Sheriff Wilson at Gary's office on Friday morning. Her heart pounded. She instantly felt her cheeks get hot, imagining what terrible things Gary might have said about her. He'd made it clear that he'd say anything to protect himself. He was as desperate as she had been that their secrets not get out. She looked at him, but he looked away, suddenly pretending not to see her.

Her gaze followed him out until the uniformed man appeared in front of her. "Hi, Ginny. We didn't meet properly on Friday when I saw you at Pastor Gary's office in Harrisburg, but I'm Sheriff Goodwin."

"Sheriff?" she questioned.

"That's right. Sworn in yesterday. Sheriff Wilson is officially retired."

Ginny felt her insides collapse. She'd hidden evidence about Darius's shooting and kept information from the police all week. And now the one person who might have looked the other way was gone.

"Thanks for coming so quickly. Let's go in here." He led her into the room, and a young officer followed them inside.

As soon as she sat down, Sheriff Goodwin and the young officer sat across from her.

The new sheriff had a pad in front of him, a pen in hand, ready for answers. "Ginny, you knew Darius Woods in high school, correct?"

"Yes."

"And you knew he'd written a screenplay about those years, right?"

"I did."

"And have you read it?"

"Yes."

"So have I," Sheriff Goodwin said.

So he knew all about her history with Darius. About what Pastor Gary did back in high school. And Sheriff Wilson had already shared that someone had seen her and her car near Darius's house around the time of the shooting.

"I was there," she blurted. "At Darius's house last Sunday night. I saw him being put in the ambulance." She'd already told the truth to Brooklyn and Darius. There was no point in any more lies.

"Why were you there?"

She wondered again if the right thing was to share what her dad had done or to say nothing. Darius was alive. Brooklyn knew the truth. John was still her father and the only father Brooklyn had ever known. Sharing the truth could send him to jail. If Darius wanted to tell the police what she'd told him, he had a right. But she couldn't do it.

"I wanted to see Darius," she said. "He had reached out on Facebook about coming home. He wanted to see me and talk about the screenplay." It was the truth. Just not all of it.

"And were you upset by what you read?"

"Yes."

"Why?" the young one asked. She could see from his blank stare that he hadn't read it. "Because no one knew about me and Darius— no one knew I got pregnant in high school. And I knew that as soon as people realized that, they'd know . . . well, they'd know that Brooklyn was our child. Everyone would know my parents didn't adopt a baby on a mission trip that summer like they'd claimed. It wouldn't take much imagination to know we were all liars."

"Dang," the young one said. "That's a heck of a secret."

And that was only half of it.

"Anyway, I got there as he was being put in an ambulance. I went to my dad's and found him on the floor."

"And earlier in the day, last Sunday, were you with Pastor Gary?" the sheriff asked.

"Yes. I went to church with my family for Mother's Day. He asked me to stay afterward to talk."

"And did you discuss Darius Woods?"

"Yes."

The sheriff took several notes.

"Pastor Gary told us that you were pretty upset last Sunday," the younger officer said.

She looked at the table and said nothing. It wasn't a question.

"He also said after you left, he realized the church's handgun was missing."

She looked up at the sheriff. "What?" Gary was setting her up. Just like he'd threatened. He was going to make sure she said nothing to Simon.

"Ginny, did you shoot Darius Woods?" the sheriff asked.

"No." She couldn't stop the tears from coming. "I could never do that. I've loved Darius for as long as I can remember."

The young officer rolled his eyes and sat back, crossing his arms. "Are you having an affair with your pastor?"

"Is that what he said?"

"He said a lot of things." The officer smirked. "And—"

Sheriff Goodwin put his hand on the man's arm to stop the young officer from continuing. "Ginny, just tell us your side," the sheriff said.

"Pastor Gary assaulted me in high school," she whispered. "Darius wrote about it in his story."

"So you're denying the affair?" the young officer asked.

She didn't know what to say. She couldn't call what had happened over the last decade an affair, but what happened between them at Good Samaritan wasn't assault either. She didn't know what it was, other than a twisted and desperate arrangement.

"Mrs. Smith," the young officer continued, "Pastor Gary says you have a history of substance abuse—that he found you drinking alcohol in his office several times over the years, even back in high school. He also said you'd been intimate on a few occasions, that, against his better judgment, he'd succumbed to your advances many years ago. According to him, he's simply tried to be a spiritual adviser to you."

"It wasn't like that."

"You never drank in his office?"

"He gave me my first drink . . ." She wiped her eyes. "Darius knows the truth."

"So after the pastor allegedly attacked you in high school, did you tell anyone?" Sheriff Goodwin asked.

"No."

"Why?"

"Because at the time, I felt responsible. I had a crush on him. He made me feel special. And I didn't say anything to stop him when he touched me. I was stunned."

"So maybe you encouraged his advances?" the young officer suggested.

"No," she whispered.

"Was it just the one time?" the young officer asked.

"No. He had other tactics after that. He left me alone for a few weeks, acted like nothing happened. He was very good at manipulation. Still is."

"Did you ever sleep with him in high school?" he pressed.

Even the question suggested something consensual, harmless. "I never *slept* with him. He assaulted me on three different occasions. His office first, that was the time Darius wrote about. Then he drove me home from a youth group meeting a few weeks later. Of course, this was after he'd given several of us alcohol in his office—it made everyone think he was so cool. But when he was driving me home, he turned left when he should have turned right, saying he wanted to show me something. Pulled over on a dirt road. I asked what we were doing; he pulled out the flask, saying he wanted us to finish it together."

"And did you?" the officer asked.

"I did. But then he began kissing my neck and unbuckling his belt. I was afraid. I felt sick. He told me to relax. I threw up in the car. That put an end to it.

"The third time he was more determined. When I resisted, he got angry, told me that he didn't think my parents would approve of my drinking. I only got away because my mom had unexpectedly shown up at church to offer me a ride home. Someone knocked on his door looking for me, and I ran out. That was the start of senior year, when Darius finally convinced me to get away from the youth group and join the theater crew."

The young officer sat forward. His tone was skeptical. "If he attacked you back in high school, why did Sheriff Wilson and Sheriff

Goodwin find you coming from the pastor's office on Friday? Why are you still friends?"

Her gaze returned to the table. "Desperate people do desperate things," she said.

"Like shooting Darius Woods in his kitchen," he said.

He wasn't wrong. Her dad had been desperate too.

CHAPTER THIRTY-SEVEN

DONNY IS GOING TO RUIN *that family with this Woods investigation,* Wilson thought. John had already lost his wife, his oldest child hated him, and that screenplay would make Brooklyn hate him too.

Wilson had now visited the Woodses' neighbor who'd identified the blonde. He was relieved when she shared more. The driver hadn't been sitting in the shadows watching to see if her victim had died. She'd sat with her headlights on, even opening the door for a second, like she was gonna get out, causing the interior light to go on. It made the description of the driver more credible but made her far less likely to have been the shooter. The ambulance had shut its doors and pulled away, and that's when the woman in the car took off.

Wilson thought about Woods's story—about John putting a gun in Woods's face, threatening to have him arrested for rape. It was easy to believe that happened. John didn't walk around shouting racist comments, but his views were clear. There was *us* and there was *them*. And John had never been slow to pull a trigger. Only ten years earlier, John had taken a shot at a couple of kids as they ran out of the store after shoplifting. Luckily, no one was hurt, and Wilson convinced him that a security system might be the better way to go.

But John knew something. He wanted Wilson to protect his family. And if Ginny hadn't shot Darius . . . Wilson didn't want to believe John was capable. But if John knew about that screenplay, if Ginny'd told him about it, he mighta done something stupid. Back when Brooklyn was still a baby, Wilson remembered John joking during one of their fishing outings that Bonnie was crazy to want to raise one of those little orphans in Eden. "But that baby," he'd said, "not even two years old, and she's stolen my heart for good."

Darius had been shot sniper-style. Two shots from the woods *through the kitchen window*. It sounded familiar, like that conversation all those years ago at John's dinner table about the violence against clinics. John had spoken about how effective that sniper-style shooting of the clinic doctor had been.

Ginny was trying to convince everyone that John was losing it. If she'd been on Darius's street and then went to John's, maybe she suspected John as the shooter.

Wilson felt helpless. Donny was probably questioning Ginny right now. A lifetime of being the man in charge, and now everything was beyond his control. He had to talk to John. He had to find out exactly what happened that night. It was the only way he could help any of them.

It was nearly dinnertime. John was getting out of the hospital today. Wilson grabbed his keys and headed for the door.

~ • ~

Ginny sat on the rocks with the sun barely peeking through the distant horizon and looked up at the clearing sky, the moon already visible. She'd intended to go straight home after leaving the station, but when she thought of Simon, of what lay ahead, she had needed a moment, or a couple of hours, and the storm had come and gone while she'd been inside the station.

Sunset viewing was a popular attraction in the Garden but, fortunately, the rain had thinned the crowd. The only people she'd passed on the trail were headed toward the parking lot.

The sky was now a smear of gray clouds encased in pink. She tried to remember that she was small, her problems a mere speck of dust in the grand scheme. But the way that young officer raised his brow as she confessed secrets and lies, the way he minimized what happened between her and the pastor, it felt like a prelude to what lay ahead.

She leaned back on her arms and let her head fall back. She looked up at the dim flecks of light, all those stars, those secrets, getting ready to come out.

It was past dinnertime, she suddenly realized. She grabbed her phone. Simon had called twenty minutes ago. How had she not heard the phone ring? And here she was, not with a bottle this time, she realized, but still avoiding reality.

She hit the buttons on the screen to call home, to let him know she was on the way, but of course, there was no signal. There was never a signal deep in these woods. She had to go.

"Hi," she suddenly heard someone say. She turned. Gary was walking toward her.

"What are you doing here?" she asked. Her thoughts returned to where she'd last seen him, coming out of that interrogation room at the station, avoiding her eyes.

"We have to talk." He was getting closer, blocking the path between the rocks and safe ground.

She scrambled to her feet, as if he were a wild animal, capable of anything. She was just a few feet from a hundred-foot drop, and he'd obviously followed her here from the police station in Eden. There was no other way he could have known where she'd be.

"Don't," he said, throwing his hand up in silent protest as she tried to move away from the edge. That's when she noticed the small bottle. "What did you tell the sheriff?" he demanded, stepping closer.

She froze.

"Please . . . don't tell me you talked about us." Drunkenness and desperation dripped from each word.

"I told them the truth," she said quietly. "I'm done running from the truth, Gary."

"Did you tell Simon yet?"

"That's next."

"Don't do it, Ginny." He was shaking his head emphatically. "It's a mistake."

She took another step toward him, the only way to distance herself from the edge.

"Stop!" he yelled. The panic in his plea startled her. "You don't get to ruin me after everything I've done for you. I'll tell them you confessed to shooting Darius. I'll tell them that you love your family and you were afraid of losing them because of our affair. You'll go to prison, Ginny. Attempted murder. You'll lose those kids."

There was no real evidence connecting her to Darius's shooting, and she'd already explained why someone saw her at his house. And she'd told the police about Gary. He couldn't be credible after everything he'd done. Could he? That young officer seemed to find nothing about her story all that shocking or disturbing, but before she left, the sheriff told her he had evidence of other misconduct. He'd asked her if she'd consider testifying against Gary. Another loaded suggestion. She'd be putting their entire history on trial. Simon deserved the truth, but all those salacious details in public . . . "I don't know if I can," she'd finally said.

She took another step toward Gary. "No one will believe you. I loved Darius. I've already told Brooklyn and Darius what happened last Sunday."

He took another step toward her, blocking her way out. "Did you tell the police your theory about John?"

She didn't answer. She finally pushed against his body, knocking him off balance. "Just leave me alone," she said, passing him and stepping away from the edge. She was done listening to him.

He said nothing as she distanced herself farther and got to safety. The silence was unnerving as darkness descended. She turned back. He was facing the canopy of treetops.

"Your dad didn't do it, Ginny," he pronounced theatrically, raising his voice above the chorus of crickets rising from the forest floor below.

He turned back, looking at her now. "I was with your dad on Mother's Day."

"That's a lie. I saw you at church."

"Later. He called me. He asked me to come to the house."

"Why would he call you?"

"Because he needed to talk. It's what I do. I counsel people when they need help." His tone had softened, like she just needed a gentle reminder of his goodness. "And I was the only one who knew the truth. I was there the day you gave birth. He was despondent, Ginny. It was Mother's Day, his first one without Bonnie in more than forty years. And he'd heard about Darius's screenplay at the store. When I got there, he was soaking wet, sitting at the table, his gun in front of him."

None of this changed what John did. Ginny didn't care why he did it.

"But he didn't go to Darius's house. He'd been standing outside in the garden in the downpour. He was crying. He was suicidal, Ginny. Missing his wife, now terrified that the only daughter he had left would find out the truth and hate him for it if Darius wrote about you in that script.

"I told him not to worry. I said that Bonnie was still with him in spirit, and that the movie hadn't even been made yet, that maybe it never would be. He needed to take one day at a time and face the future when it came. I took the gun. I didn't want him to hurt himself. I sat with him for an hour, cleaned up the floor, and finally convinced him to change out of those wet clothes. He had some tea and felt better. I left."

Ginny didn't know what to think. She searched the endless landscape, considering his story. After everything her dad did, after the horrible things he said to Darius twenty years earlier, it was easy to imagine him raising his gun and trying to finally be rid of him and the truth he'd brought with him. But suicidal? And why wouldn't Gary have told her about this last Tuesday when she came to see him and shared all that had happened?

She could believe that her father was a mess over Bonnie's death, even months later, and that Mother's Day would have been particularly hard. And she could believe that he would have panicked over the thought of Brooklyn learning the truth. He loved her.

But if John didn't shoot Darius, then . . . She returned her gaze to Gary.

He raised his brows, as if he'd been waiting for her to realize the truth. "I left John and started back to Harrisburg," he said, "and then I glanced over at his gun on the passenger seat. It occurred to me that I could help. I pulled off, found the address on my phone, and parked around the corner on the other side of the woods that butted up to the house. It was still raining and getting dark. I stood there, watching, and he came into view. Darius had the power to ruin too many lives, Ginny. Yours, John's, Brooklyn's, Simon's, your kids."

"Yours," Ginny said.

"Yes, mine too. He had to be stopped."

Ginny was dizzy with rage, her fingers curling into fists, as she imagined Gary in the woods, in the rain, shooting at Darius like a hunter.

"I went back to John's afterward. He was sitting in his living room chair, staring out into the dark night. I told him I was just checking on him. I said everything would be okay and I wiped off the prints and put the gun on his desk and left. It was just moments later that you arrived."

Ginny opened and closed her hands, hardly able to process what she was hearing, and yet, it made sense. Her dad had been sitting in the living room chair. The gun had been on his desk in the study. How else did Gary know? Regret and guilt rippled through her body. This horror of a man had tried to kill Darius. Because of her. It was her fault. She'd never stood up to him. She'd even allowed Gary to console her after she found out what happened to Darius, after she found her dad and jumped to the wrong conclusion. And no one knew the truth.

She'd told Brooklyn and Darius that John did it.

She lunged at him. It was a blinding rage. He was going to get away with it. He'd deny this conversation. John didn't even remember the evening.

Gary stumbled as she came at him, pounding her fists against his chest, but he threw both arms around her as the liquor bottle he'd been holding dropped from his hands and tumbled over the edge.

"No!" she cried, thrashing against his hold. "Please!" Gary tried to killed Darius and he would get away with it. He could just toss her over this ledge, along with her accusations against him. He'd get away with everything. The wild animals below would probably ravage her remains before anyone discovered her. No one even knew where she was.

~ • ~

Brooklyn took a long shower until the hot water ran cold. The air felt heavy with the residue of her fight with Dad. They had never argued like that in her entire life. She felt ripped open.

When she came out of the bathroom, her bedroom had darkened, the sun now moving toward the horizon. She'd called him a monster. He'd held her close for so many years, squeezed her hard, loved her. The affection was always brief, his stoicism never far from the surface. But he'd tucked her into bed, read her stories, taught her to drive. He did love her.

Her phone pinged as she got dressed. The only word she saw when she opened the new email was the only one that mattered. Congratulations.

She got the role. She'd landed the lead in a movie. For just a moment, everything else faded into the background, and she was swept up in the idea that her dream was actually coming true. She looked at that poster of New York, her city of dreams. She had to tell someone. She had to tell her dad. She looked at the closed door between them. He was the only dad she'd ever known.

She threw on a shirt and some sweats and headed for the stairs. But when she descended the first step, someone was shouting from inside his study. "I oughta kill you right now!" She froze.

She knew that voice. The door was ajar. The anger from inside that room wafted into the hall, rising up the steps, wrapping itself around her body like a chokehold. That's when she heard the crash.

CHAPTER THIRTY-EIGHT

BROOKLYN STOPPED ON THE SECOND stair when she heard the crash, terrified. She now knew of her father's violent streak. "Get out of my house!" he yelled.

"You're not going to get away with this." It was Martin Woods, another victim of Dad's violence, yelling about all that her dad had taken from him. She wanted to run down there, but she couldn't imagine bursting into that room, standing between the two men.

Suddenly, Martin was in the doorway, his back to the stairs, a baseball bat in one hand. "Sheriff Wilson can't protect you anymore," he shouted. "No one shoots my boy and gets away with it."

"Get out!" John yelled.

Martin threw the bat to the floor as he barreled out the front door and down the porch stairs. The screen door smacked against the frame behind him. Brooklyn took another step toward the suddenly silent room. A faint click, then a second click wafted into the hall. She knew those sounds. His gun. He'd checked the chamber, cocked the trigger. *Dad!* She raced down a few more steps.

"Whoa! Put that down." She froze again. Someone else was in that room. Her dad wasn't about to kill himself. It was Darius. A voice she'd only heard in the movies and interviews. He was in her house. He'd been standing in the study, silently, as his father unloaded his rage on hers. But now . . . "What, you gonna shoot me again?" Darius scoffed.

"This is all your fault," her dad said. "You made a mess of my girl's life and now you wanna take Brooklyn too? I don't think so."

She started creeping down the stairs, inexplicably terrified of being heard but knowing she had to stop him. "Get back!" her dad yelled. And then a grunt, bodies colliding—they were fighting for the gun.

A shot blasted through the air. She instinctively ducked when the gun fired. Her hand was like a vise grip on the stair rail. Breath held, she remained still for a second, waiting to hear their voices again. Instead, she was pummeled by silence. She slowly rose, but her knees began to buckle. She wasn't sure she could bear to see what had happened in that room.

Darius Woods suddenly walked out, head down, shaking it slightly, back and forth, as if he couldn't believe what just happened. She couldn't move or speak. He went straight for the front door, never noticing her on those steps. The screen door smacked behind him, and she watched him descend the porch stairs, stretching his fingers, shaking out his hand.

A familiar feeling rose inside her, the flash of heat, her heart exploding, chest walls contracting. She couldn't breathe. And then she heard the thud.

Her feet wouldn't move. The panic was coiling around her neck, choking her airway. Her vision blurred. Then nausea. *I'm going to pass out,* she thought as she stumbled down the final steps, reaching the floor and collapsing to her knees, gasping, desperate for air. *Breathe, goddammit,* she silently yelled at herself. There was no time for one of these attacks. "Dad!" she yelled.

No response.

She had to calm down. *Stop, stop!* she silently begged. She let her elbows collapse; her forehead touched the floor. She tapped on her chest. *It's okay. He's okay. It's going to be okay.* She lifted her head, finally stood, woozy, and stumbled into the room.

He was on the rug in front of his desk, facedown. "Dad!" He didn't respond. She fell to her knees, grabbed his arm with one hand, his torso with the other, struggled to roll him over, then finally put her ear to his chest. Nothing. His eyes were closed. His face was red, and there was a small scrape on his cheek. A gash on his forehead, blood oozing. She grabbed his hand, pressing her finger across the inside of his wrist. "Come on! Are you there?" He looked like he was sleeping, just as he had in the hospital. "Dad!" she yelled, finally slapping his face. Nothing happened.

She scanned his head, his torso. She didn't understand. Had he been shot? The gash didn't look too deep. He must have hit the corner of the desk as he fell. Where was the bullet wound? She looked at the gun on the desk, the broken lamp shattered on the floor. The bat in the corner. Martin probably swung at the lamp, enraged by her father's insults.

She finally looked up and saw a small hole in the ceiling. The bullet hadn't struck him.

She wiped the blood from his face as tears filled her eyes, clouding her vision. She needed to call for help. She put her fingers on his neck, searching for a pulse. Nothing. She pounded his chest. "Come on," she shouted. "Wake up!" She tried CPR, what little she remembered from high school health class, but nothing mattered. He was gone.

Collapsing beside him, replaying the last moments, she thought about Martin, that bat, the gun, Darius shaking out his hand as he walked out the door. Had he struck her dad? It was so senseless. If she'd just run into the room. If she'd been there. None of it would have happened.

She'd been a coward, crouching on those steps, listening, unwilling to stop the argument. She'd had another ridiculous panic attack. And now her father was dead.

She ran up to her room and grabbed her cell. When the 911 operator came on the line, she spit out the facts, panicked. She gave her address. The woman on the line was too calm, asking too many questions. "Just get here!" she screamed before hanging up. She paced the room and called Ginny. It rang and rang.

She put on the speaker function and ran back down the stairs with the phone in her hand. Finally, Ginny's voice mail picked up. Brooklyn disconnected and threw the phone to the floor. She looked at her father, lifeless. It wasn't Darius's fault. He had a right to be angry. Her dad had pulled a gun on him. Her dad had said vile things. If Darius hit him, she understood why. John Anderson was an old man, but he was not harmless.

Her mind raced through the questions the sheriff would ask. What she heard, what she saw. What if the sheriff didn't believe her? What if someone decided that in that moment Darius had wanted to kill him? That he and his father came over here to hurt her dad? She looked at Martin's bat.

She could imagine the assumptions of those white officers, framing the scene as an elderly, sick white man trying to defend himself against the young, strong black man who struck a fatal blow. They might not care why it happened. They might not listen. She was biased, they'd think, as a girl who'd want to protect her idol, a man she'd just learned was her birth father.

She couldn't tell anyone.

Darius and Martin were never here, she suddenly decided. Her dad simply collapsed again. She grabbed the bat and ran to the kitchen, quickly rubbing it down with paper towels. She dropped it, running back to the study. The gun. Darius's prints might be on it. She felt the tingling of an impending panic attack, walls closing in. Fuzzy edges and black spots clouded her vision as she held the gun, using her shirt to clean the handle.

Suddenly the screen door slammed closed. She jumped and turned toward the doorway. Sheriff Wilson was standing there, his eyes moving from her father, dead on the floor, to her, standing there with a gun.

CHAPTER THIRTY-NINE

DAY SEVEN
10:45 p.m.
BOLINE COUNTY JAIL

EDDIE WAS SNORING LOUDLY. *It had to be after ten,* Brooklyn thought. She didn't understand how Ginny could have come to the station and not asked to see her. Would they have refused to let them talk? Was that even legal? *Maybe she'd come to the station earlier in the day,* she thought, *before Brooklyn's arrest.* It's not like there hadn't been time. She'd left to tell Darius the truth. That couldn't have gone well. She wondered if Ginny was off somewhere drinking, maybe drowning out the pain of that conversation.

The door hinges at the end of the hall squeaked. And then the familiar lock, the footfalls on concrete. Only two feet this time, she realized. It was probably just the guard.

He stopped before reaching her. "Hey, Eddie," a man said. "Eddie, wake up!" Eddie grumbled. "Eddie," the man shouted. "Sheriff Goodwin wanted me to let you know that you're free to go. Lab came back on that gun you were carrying. We know it wasn't used in the shooting."

She could have told them that.

"Where's my dad?" Eddie asked, still groggy.

"Can't get ahold of him."

Eddie mumbled something she didn't hear, and then, "You gonna drive me home?"

"I can't leave right now. I'm the only one on duty. Sheriff Goodwin just took off for an emergency at the Garden of the Gods. But listen, you're free to leave. Okay? You're not being held any longer."

"Yeah, yeah," he said. "I'm not gonna sue." The bedsprings squeaked under his weight. She imagined him rolling over. "Bed's no worse than the twin at home. Just have my dad here in the morning."

Brooklyn quickly went to the bars, looking down the dimly lit hall as the guard walked away. "Hey, what happened at the Garden?" Darius had written about going there with Ginny, about how she often went there when stressed. There was no reason to think this emergency had anything to do with Ginny—it could have just been Brooklyn's imagination running wild again—but she had tried to call Ginny after what happened at the house. Ginny never answered.

The guard stopped and walked back to her cell.

"I couldn't help but overhear," she continued. "You said there was an emergency."

"Someone died," the guard answered. "Can't imagine there will be any real answers before morning."

CHAPTER FORTY

WILSON'S BEST FRIEND WAS DEAD. He would have thought nothing could be darker than the moment he saw John lying there, but watching Brooklyn get put in that squad car was worse. He had sat with her on the front steps of John's house, his arm around her, comforting her until Donny and the others arrived. She'd refused to speak, saying only that it was an accident. She was in shock, but it was clear she was holding back. The room indicated a struggle. She was wiping down a gun. His blood was on her hands. But there was zero chance that girl was glad for what had happened. He'd known her for twenty years. She loved John.

"I'm so sorry," Wilson had said. "I loved your dad. And I know he loved you."

"Did you know?" she asked, her focus remaining on the dusty gravel driveway.

She'd obviously learned the truth about her parents and all the secrets and lies. "No," he answered, squeezing her closer.

"He lied and he—"

"Shhh." He stopped her. He didn't want her saying anything to incriminate herself. He didn't want to see another child of his dear friend in trouble. This was all a terrible accident.

"He tried to kill Darius last week. Ginny told me today."

Wilson nodded silently, his worst fear confirmed. It made sense, though *sense* was probably the wrong word. "Was Ginny here?"

"Earlier. Before I picked up Dad at the hospital. She left to see Darius. She was finally coming clean with everyone."

Wilson couldn't imagine how difficult it would be for Ginny to tell Woods the truth, how difficult it would be for him to hear it. In all his years on the force, the worst pain, sometimes the worst violence, came after the secrets spilled. Today had been no different.

"I still loved him," she'd cried. "He was my dad." She could barely get the words out.

When Donny and the other officers arrived, Brooklyn said no one else had been there. She told Donny that John must have collapsed, but his body wasn't even close to the broken lamp. She had no explanation for the gun or the bullet hole in the ceiling or the bat they found in the kitchen.

Wilson pulled Donny aside and said he didn't believe that Brooklyn did anything, but Donny just smiled and raised one brow. He said he'd just gotten a lot of information from Ginny at the station. "That girl," he said, nodding in Brooklyn's direction, "had plenty of reason to be angry. And she's obviously hiding something." He was too hung up on the marks on John's face. "There was clearly a struggle," Donny said, "and she's not talking. Swears she was the only one here."

Donny didn't get it. He didn't know Brooklyn. Wilson had looked up at the sugar maple then, all those crows still squawking in its limbs, oblivious to trouble on the ground. "He was my closest friend, Donny. If there was someone to blame for his death, I'd be first in line. I promise. But Brooklyn's his baby. She didn't do this. Look at her."

Both men turned their attention to Brooklyn, sitting on those porch steps, staring vacantly at the gravel on the driveway.

"Hard to say," Donny said. "But you told me she's an amazing actress. Takin' New York by storm. Isn't that what you said?"

Wilson wanted to scream. Donny didn't know these people. "He coulda just fallen," Wilson said. "Heck, he fell a week ago and knocked himself a concussion. He would not want her to go down for this, no matter what happened."

"And maybe she won't. But you and I know the law, and there were marks on his face. If you strike someone and he dies, well, that's at least involuntary manslaughter. I mean, it could even be murder. We got a gun and a bat. That looks like intent to harm. I can't just let this go without an investigation."

"She didn't take a swing at her dad. Look at her! She'd just brought him home from the hospital. She's here because she cares, because despite everything, she loved him."

"Let's just let the evidence shake out. If the coroner backs up the accident theory, great. But she's not a resident, and there's too much incentive to run. And I'm sorry that these are your friends, but I'm not gonna be influenced by personal connections. That may be how you liked to run things, but those days are over. No offense."

Wilson had to step away before he took a swing of his own. Donny was too determined to follow the letter of the law. That wasn't justice. He thought about sharing what Brooklyn had said—that John shot Darius—but it might just bolster a case against her, and he didn't even know if it was true.

Wilson watched as the team processed the scene, powerless to stop them. The only thing he could do was find Ginny.

CHAPTER FORTY-ONE

GINNY WAS STARING AT HER house, her spine rod straight, gripping the steering wheel with white knuckles. When she finally released her fingers, her hands shook. She couldn't make them stop. She might lose everything after all.

Gary had finally released her from his hold at the ledge, and she'd stumbled back on the rocks. She was no match for him. He'd proven that he could do anything. He could try to rape her as a girl, he could shoot Darius, he could toss her over the edge of a cliff like a rag doll. He could probably set her up for attempted murder, and he would get away with all of it. "Why did you even tell me that you did it?" she had shouted.

He stood before her, arms down, suddenly calm, and said, "Because, Ginny, the truth sets us free." He took a step back. And then another. He was staggering, but he wasn't off balance. He knew what he was doing. She screamed as he disappeared into the darkness while branches cracked against his falling body. She heard a faint thud as he hit the ground.

It felt like everything had stopped. She heard nothing. She could barely even see past the ledge anymore. The world had turned to darkness. But then a swell of crickets resumed singing. The wilderness below had swallowed him. He was gone.

Her whole body convulsed. First shock, then fear engulfed her. There was nothing to do. Nothing to see. Would she be believed? Would Sheriff Goodwin hear of this and assume something even worse? Would he think she pushed him?

When she got back to the parking lot, Gary's car was parked next to hers. The rest of the lot was empty. No one had seen what happened. She could drive away and hope that by the time anyone reported him missing, by the time his car was found and his body discovered, the assumption would simply be that he'd killed himself or fallen accidentally. She drove slowly through those woods, her high beams lighting the way, wondering if Gary had planned to die after confessing the truth, if he'd hoped to convince her to keep their secrets, or if he'd planned to kill her and suddenly changed course.

Now, she stared at her hands, willing them to stop trembling. She looked up at her children's darkened bedroom windows. She couldn't live with another secret for the rest of her life, and she needed to tell everyone what Gary had said. Her father had not shot Darius.

She pulled out her phone. The signal was back. The forest was considered part of the neighboring county, but Sheriff Goodwin would know what to do and whom to call. There was probably very little that could be done before sunrise, anyway. It was too treacherous.

After she calmly shared the sequence of events, Sheriff Goodwin asked her where she was now, and she told him. She couldn't run anymore.

When she walked in the front door, Simon was sitting at the kitchen table drinking coffee. "Where have you been? I've been trying to call." He stood, ready for battle.

"Sorry. No signal. I was in the forest. I haven't been drinking. I promise. You better sit." He did as she asked, and she sat in the chair across from him, exhausted. "The kids asleep?" she asked.

"Of course."

She squeezed her hands together, willing herself to blurt it out before she lost her nerve. "Pastor Gary killed himself tonight. Right in front of me."

"What?"

She had no response.

"Why?" Anger seeped from the question, his tone a silent accusation. She knew what he was thinking. No one would do something like that in front of someone else . . . not unless they had some sort of intimate connection.

She propped her elbows on the table, resting her head in her hands, and closed her eyes. Tears began streaming down her cheeks. "There's a lot you don't know," she said without looking up.

"So tell me," he said gruffly. "And look at me."

She sat back and met his eyes. "We were both called into the Boline County Sheriff's station today about Darius Woods's shooting. I'm sure you heard about that. He's a famous actor now and wrote a movie about his life in Eden."

"I heard. But what does that have to do with you?"

"He was shot last Sunday in Eden, the same night I took my dad to the hospital."

Simon opened his mouth but said nothing. He probably had no idea what to say.

"Darius knew things about Pastor Gary. And me, back in high school. He wrote a screenplay. Gary and I knew it would expose some secrets that we've both tried hard to keep. Pastor Gary was a terrible person, Simon. And he shot Darius."

"That's insane." He crossed his arms. "What are you not telling me? That man has been a friend to you since you were a girl. You've sought his counsel for more than a decade."

"It wasn't like that," she said, still choosing her words carefully. "Darius and I were . . . we were close in high school. He knew about what Pastor Gary did to me back then. Darius helped get me away from him."

"What are you saying? Wait. I don't think I want to hear this. I . . ." He pushed back in his chair, got up from the table, and paced the room.

"The sheriff told me that I wasn't the only one. There were probably dozens of girls over the years. He asked if I'd testify."

"But if all that is true—"

"Don't," she pleaded. She knew what was coming next—the same disbelief she'd seen at the sheriff's station on that young officer's face. It was the same judgment she'd feel from everyone: If he was such a predator, why turn to him years later? No one would understand or believe her, or care.

Simon stopped pacing and leaned against the counter, his arms crossed, waiting.

"After I left the station today, I went to the Garden. I needed to think about everything that's happened—to my family, to us." She stopped for a moment to gauge his reaction. "Gary followed me. When he got there, he was drunk and upset."

"Why?" He spit the word out, like he already had the answer in his mind.

"He wanted me to keep my mouth shut about what happened back in high school." And then she finally said the hardest part. "And what happened between us since he joined our church thirteen years ago. He knew that if I finally told you the truth, if I told the sheriff, he could lose everything."

Simon's arms fell open, as if she'd just taken all his strength. He closed his eyes and tilted his head toward the ceiling, taking deep breaths—seeking strength from God, she guessed.

"But I wouldn't agree to keep quiet. And suddenly, he admitted shooting Darius last Sunday. Then he stepped off the cliff."

Finally, his focus returned to her face, and he stepped forward. "What did you do?"

The tears fell faster than she could get the words out. "I'll never be able to make you understand what's happened. I know that. It's hard for me to understand. But please don't ever think that what I did was based on desire or love or anything more than it was. It was desperation."

Nothing changed on his face. He didn't understand.

"I was desperate to give you children," she whispered.

Shock and confusion passed through his eyes. He moved to the table quickly, like he needed to sit before he fell. "My kids. They're his?" he whispered, his eyes filling with tears.

She shook her head quickly. "They're still yours, Simon. You've been their dad from the moment they entered this world. Please don't stop loving them. Divorce me, start a new life with someone else, but don't stop being their father. Don't punish them for things they had nothing to do with."

He didn't speak, so she didn't either. The silence was deafening.

Finally, he got up from the table and walked away. He stopped in the doorway, though he didn't turn around. "Go kiss them good night. I promised you would."

~ • ~

When Ginny came back downstairs, Simon was in the living room without the lights on, staring vacantly at the empty fireplace. She prayed she'd finally done the right thing. It was too soon to tell.

A car's headlights suddenly flashed through the window. Ginny stepped to the glass, assuming it was Sheriff Goodwin, coming to bring her in and question her more about Gary.

But Sheriff Wilson got out of his car.

"What are you doing here?" Ginny said, standing at the open door as he walked up the path. Simon was at her side.

"I've been trying to reach you."

"I was at the sheriff's office. Then I went to the forest."

"So you know?" he asked.

"About Pastor Gary?"

"What? No. I'm sorry, Ginny. John is dead. And Brooklyn's in custody."

"What?"

Sheriff Wilson explained what he'd seen when he got to the house. He shared his belief that Brooklyn would be cleared, his feeling that she couldn't have hurt John.

Ginny wasn't as sure. Not after everything Brooklyn had learned today. But it didn't matter. No one could convince Ginny that Brooklyn belonged in a jail. Ginny didn't care what happened. She'd told Brooklyn that John shot Darius, that he'd forbidden Ginny from telling Brooklyn the truth for years. Even if Brooklyn had struck him with a frickin' bat, Ginny didn't care.

She had to do something. Finally, she had to be there for that girl.

She rushed back to Eden. Driving along Main Street, the turn to Darius's house came into view. He needed to know.

She pounded on the door. No one came. It was nearly eleven o'clock. It didn't make sense. Where was his father, Martin?

She looked in the driveway. Neither car was there.

She thought back to Mary's Diner, sitting there while Darius got up and left the booth. She was certain he'd never want to see her again. She'd been at that intersection when she got the call from the sheriff and noticed Darius's BMW in the distance. She'd assumed he was headed to her dad's.

She pulled out her phone and sent him a message through Facebook, the only way she knew to reach him. He hated her, she was sure, but he would want to help Brooklyn.

She sped to the sheriff's station. The officer at the door wouldn't let her in. He said it was too late for visitors.

CHAPTER FORTY-TWO

Monday, May 20

WILSON ROSE EARLY FROM A restless sleep. His closest friend was dead, Brooklyn was in trouble, and he'd lost all power to control the situation. It didn't matter that he found her wiping prints off that gun or that there'd obviously been a fight in the room. John would not want that girl being punished.

It was still hard to believe John had kept this secret for twenty years, why he felt it necessary for the world to believe his grandchild was adopted. *No one woulda judged,* Wilson thought. But even as he tried to persuade himself, he knew that honesty would have required a reckoning of sorts. Like why, upon learning that Ginny had a baby and that she was in love with Darius, no one pressured the teens to marry. Wilson had known plenty of shotgun weddings in his day. Though none of them looked quite like that. Eden did have lines people never crossed; he'd just never thought about it. He supposed that was the thing about lines. They were easier to see from the outside.

Wilson never considered himself a racist. He'd been offended by those reporters who smeared his former deputy, Tom Delaney. Calling out Tom was calling out the whole force; it was calling out all of Eden, maybe all of Little Egypt. But they were good people, Wilson knew. Good, kind, churchgoing folks.

He thought back to Tom's trial and his own willingness to accept without question that Tom was in the right when he shot Jaden White on the side of the road. Wilson hadn't even pressed Tom about it. He'd refused to listen to protesters, to consider whether the outcome would have been different had the man been white. He'd automatically understood why Tom had panicked. But why? What did that really say about him? The man had a gun in the glove box. So did almost every man Wilson knew. The man warned Tom he needed to open the box to get his registration. And that had ended his life.

Wilson never said an offensive word to anyone's face, but he'd certainly laughed at jokes and even told a few of his own. It seemed harmless because he never did it in mixed company.

He thought back to his wife's death, his explosion of grief and anger, his desire to blame the other driver, even though the witness said his wife had run the red light. He'd used hate-filled slurs. And then he thought about Eddie, the way he'd treated Woods back in high school—the things he'd said that night in the Garden, and the way Wilson hadn't even pressed Eddie about that shoulder injury or the fight—just assuming that Eddie was in the right, the black kid was in the wrong. But Eddie had been the villain that night.

Kids never start a life with hate. That stuff was taught. Suddenly it felt like John's choice, his actions, his lies—they indicted more than himself. They indicted all of them.

And now, Wilson was supposed to sit back and do nothing? Donny's only parting comment last night was that Wilson still needed to get Eddie out of jail.

Wilson needed to do more. Though when it came to Eddie, maybe less was more. If John had taught him anything, maybe it was that parents, even with the best intentions, could really screw up their kids when they held on too tight, when they tried too hard to protect them and stopped them from living their own lives. Wilson's attempt at protecting Eddie from consequences had done nothing to help him.

Eddie needed to move out. Wilson would encourage inpatient treatment, he'd even pay for it, but it was Eddie's decision to make. Live or die. Rise or fall. Wilson was done trying to control that boy's destiny.

He drove toward the station, letting his thoughts return to Brooklyn. Donny was too preoccupied by the bat, that it could mean intent to harm. Brooklyn wouldn't swing a bat at John. In fact, he couldn't imagine where she'd found it. No boys had been raised in that house. No athletes. No sports were played.

As he got closer to town, he noticed an abandoned car on the side of the road. Wilson slowed. It was impossible to turn off his investigative instincts. A black Cadillac SUV. Pretty swanky. He called the station. Roger picked up after two rings. "Hey, Rog—"

"Sheriff! How's it going?"

It was just what Wilson wanted to hear. He needed those boys to think of him as the sheriff for just a bit longer. "Can you run a plate for me?"

"Shoot," Roger said.

"Illinois JV9 16T."

"Got it. Should I call your cell?"

"Please. Did Donny hear back from the coroner yet about John?"

"I don't think so. He's been busy dealing with the other thing."

"What other thing?"

"Didn't you hear? Ginny called him last night a few hours after we questioned her. Said that Pastor Gary jumped off the rocks at the Garden. *After* confessing to the Woods shooting."

"What?"

"Crazy, right? I think they're still over there trying to get the body, or what's left of it. I can't even imagine. Glad it's in another county. Anyway, so far, her story is checking out. She said he was drunk yesterday, and we've confirmed a stop at the liquor store after we called him in for questioning. She said he used her dad's gun and that he found Woods's address with his phone. Gun's with forensics. We'll get the records on the phone. Just a matter of time."

"Wow. Well, keep me posted, and let me know about that plate."

Wilson quickly turned the car around and drove to Martin Woods's house. It wasn't Wilson's case anymore, but he'd promised to keep Martin posted on developments, and Roger's news would provide some comfort.

There were no cars in the drive at Martin's house. No one answered the door. Woods had been released from the hospital the day before. Wilson walked around the property, peering into the windows. As he cupped his hands against the glass slider on the back of the house, he saw Woods's screenplay on the kitchen table.

That damn screenplay. That story had nearly gotten Woods killed. It had cracked open two decades of his friend's family secrets; his friend was dead, and Brooklyn was in jail. His anger bubbled up and focused on Woods. He wanted to blame him. To create a villain.

But Woods was a victim too.

Wilson headed back toward the car, passing a shed on the way back to the driveway. Its doors were open. A bin of sports equipment had been overturned, its contents now all over the grass.

~ • ~

Wilson was pulling into the hospital parking lot when he got the call from Roger. "Hey, I got that plate run for you. It's a rental, Avis."

"And who rented it?"

"Darius Woods."

Wilson hung up the phone and immediately recalled something Brooklyn had said last night—Ginny had left to tell Darius the truth.

And at the time, Wilson realized, Ginny believed her father shot Darius.

Woods had gone to John's house. Wilson was sure of it. He didn't understand why he'd then abandon his car on the side of the road, but there was no doubt in his mind. Suddenly, it all made sense—Woods racing over there, a baseball bat in his hand, having learned about Brooklyn and believing at the time that John had gunned him down a week before.

The only one who might have seen Woods at John's house last night was Brooklyn. There was no chance she'd say anything. Not after everything John had done.

But Wilson could not let her go down for this.

Walking into the morgue, he found his buddy Bennington sitting at his desk, drinking coffee and writing up some notes.

"Hey, Sheriff," Bennington said. "I take it we got one of yours in here?"

Bennington obviously assumed Wilson was there in an official capacity, despite the street clothes. He was not about to correct him. "Yeah, but he's a friend too. John Anderson."

"John Anderson, as in the General Store?"

"Exactly."

"What a shame. I'm so sorry, Sheriff. I just got on, but let me pull the chart, see what Dr. Anton wrote."

Wilson sat in the chair next to the doctor's desk, waiting, while his friend read through the notes.

"So?" Wilson finally asked.

"Gash on head. Mark on his face. Unresponsive at the scene."

"Right. But he was just released from the hospital yesterday, hours before it happened. I need to know if he simply collapsed or if he was struck. He broke his hip a week ago and hit his head pretty bad then too. But the girl at the scene, she said she heard him fall, and he was dead by the time she got to him."

"Mm-hmm," Bennington said. "Yeah. Well, I don't think this was an aneurysm. See here," he said, pointing to a photo of one dissection. "Looks like we've got a subdural hemorrhage . . ."

"And that means . . ."

"Blunt-force trauma."

"Can you say what from? We found a bat at the scene."

"No. No. That would have been a very different kind of injury. The gash is from something sharp."

"Like maybe the corner of a desk? That's what the girl thought happened."

"Maybe. But the scrape on his face," he said, pointing to another picture, "that looks like the kind of mark we sometimes see after a punch."

Wilson considered it. There'd been a struggle in that room. The gun had been fired into the ceiling. And John's face . . . if he'd been punched and then he fell . . .

Darius might have killed him.

"That would be pretty cruel, wouldn't it?" Bennington added. "If someone actually punched an old man with a broken hip in the face? I mean, you hit someone that fragile, you gotta intend some serious harm."

"Right." Wilson could just imagine how a prosecutor might frame the narrative. A break-in, fueled by rage. A fatal blow . . .

"But here's the thing," Bennington continued. "These are tricky cases. It's hard to get too definitive. The CT from last week looked clean, but he might have developed a bleed while he was in the hospital. It happens, especially with older patients."

"So you're saying he might have simply collapsed from a brain bleed caused by the fall last week? "

"It's possible. But I think a case could be made . . . if you can show violence at the scene, then it's plausible that someone is responsible."

He could not let Donny move forward with this case. It wouldn't be right. The Anderson girls had been through too much. The Woodses too. John's actions had started it all. "Benny," Wilson said, cutting him off, "I need a favor. It's a big one."

"Well, I do still owe you several hundred from that last card game," Bennington said. "Shoot."

~ • ~

Wilson hustled to his car. He was pulling out of the parking spot when he spotted Darius Woods coming out of the main hospital doors, wincing, a phone to his ear, and holding the free hand against his rib cage as he moved, walking too quickly for a man who'd been shot the week before. He was obviously in a hurry to get somewhere.

Wilson moved down the lot slowly, following Woods until he got to a BMW convertible. Wilson pulled up, blocking him in.

"Darius Woods," Wilson shouted through his open window, "I need you to come with me."

"Who are you?"

"Sheriff Wilson, Boline County. It's about Brooklyn."

Woods still had a phone to his ear. "Ginny, I'm getting in a car with that sheriff. Yeah. I'll meet you at the station."

Woods ended the call and walked around to the passenger side, lowering himself into the seat. "Ginny just told me what happened," he said.

Wilson looked at Woods. "I know you were there."

~ • ~

Ginny pulled into the sheriff's station, thirty minutes later, and ran inside. There was someone behind a front counter, ready to stop her.

"I need to see Brooklyn Anderson. She was brought in last night."

"Okay, just a minute," the man said. He walked away, and she stepped around the corner, watching. He went inside the sheriff's office. The wall was glass. Sheriff Wilson was in there, and the new sheriff too. And Darius. She couldn't wait. She started toward the room, ignoring the clerk's request for her to stay put. Sheriff Wilson stepped out of the room to greet her.

"Why are you both talking to Darius? And where's Brooklyn? I need to see her!"

"Calm down," Wilson said. "It's okay. Come on."

CHAPTER FORTY-THREE

WHEN BROOKLYN WOKE UP, THERE was that nanosecond of peace until her mind caught up to the new reality. The only parents she'd ever known, John and Bonnie Anderson, were dead. She was in jail, and everyone had lied.

The door down the hall opened, and she sat up and waited, listening to the footfalls on the concrete, the jangle of keys on the guard's belt. It sounded like an army was heading her way. She braced herself for the worst.

When she looked up, Darius Woods was standing there. And the new sheriff. And Sheriff Wilson. And Ginny. "Hi," Darius said, waving at her. She couldn't speak. She slowly stood.

Sheriff Goodwin stepped inside first. "Brooklyn, I'm sorry we had to keep you in here all night. It's been quite a long one, but Wilson just came back from the coroner's office."

She looked at her dad's oldest friend. "It was an accident," Sheriff Wilson said. He glanced at Darius as he said it. She wondered if he knew Darius had been there. "Autopsy confirmed it," he continued. "The marks on his head and face didn't come from a bat. Coroner said the gash on his head was consistent with what you'd see from hitting the corner of a desk. He figured that John probably scraped his face during the fall. Fact is, your dad had an internal hemorrhage. Probably died instantly. According to the chart, he suffered a

TBI during last week's fall. Doctor said it can take days or weeks for the bleed to show up. It wasn't anyone's fault. He was a ticking time bomb."

Brooklyn didn't know what to say. It seemed like she was supposed to smile or react, but it was as if she'd survived an explosion—standing there, intact, but covered in soot, still trying to understand what it all meant. She gazed at Darius.

"We know Darius was there," Sheriff Goodwin said. "He told us about the struggle for the gun. But after speaking with the coroner, it's clear he's not responsible either."

"I'm so sorry, Brooklyn," Darius said. "My dad found out what John did and took off with a bat, so I followed him to your house."

She didn't know what to say.

"The point is, " Sheriff Goodwin added, "there won't be any charges. It was a terrible accident, and I'm really sorry for your loss. I hope you understand why I had to take you into custody."

She scanned the faces of Ginny and Darius. And then it hit her. She was looking at her parents. And the dad she'd known all her life was gone. Nothing would ever be the same.

"Hello?" Eddie shouted, breaking the awkward silence from the cell next door. "Dad! Come on! These asshats held me all night!"

Sheriff Wilson smirked and waved. "I'll see you later," he said.

"Just meet me out at the desk to sign some papers," Sheriff Goodwin added before leaving. "Take your time."

Brooklyn looked at Ginny, then Darius.

"I'm gonna be outside," Ginny said, walking away.

"Wanna sit for a sec?" Darius asked, waving toward the cot.

Brooklyn nodded and sat at the edge of the mattress, staring at the cinder blocks in front of her as he sat beside her. "You and I have both been given an extraordinary amount of new information in the last twenty-four hours," he said.

Brooklyn nodded, unable to figure out the best response.

"I'm sorry I didn't get here sooner. I didn't know. They told me you wouldn't speak and that you were wiping down the gun when Sheriff Wilson arrived."

She opened her mouth to answer, but the sounds came out in a whisper. "I was in the hall. I heard you."

Darius nodded. "I shouldn't have hit him."

"He said some awful things to you. He had a gun. I didn't blame you."

Darius nodded. "I'm guessing you feared I was responsible?"

She looked at him finally. "I feared it didn't matter. You said it in that screenplay. It's a stacked deck when a black man is in trouble with the law. And it didn't look good. Who'd believe me, anyway?"

Darius took her hand. "Thank you for trying to protect me, a stranger."

"You're my dad," she said, shocked by the words as they spilled out. The rush of emotion came at her with the same speed as one of her panic attacks, but this time she felt overwhelmed by the moment, this reality, of something good coming out of this nightmare. "And Martin's my grandfather."

Neither of them spoke as their new connections hung in the stagnant air.

"It's been the strangest twenty-four hours of my entire life," she finally said.

Darius smiled. "You should come see him with me. It would make him feel so much better."

"Martin? Is he okay?"

"Yes, but he's in the hospital. That's where I've been. It's why I never heard what happened to you until this morning."

Her eyes widened, but he put his hand on her knee.

"He's okay, he's just not supposed to get that worked up. He's got a bad heart."

Brooklyn remembered Martin's lighthearted comment about his "bad ticker" and how stress will "kill ya." She'd heard his pain, his anger at her dad for robbing him of the chance to know his own blood.

"I found him on the side of the road a few miles down from your house. He was having a heart attack. I left my car, jumped in, and got him to the hospital."

Her eyes widened as the panic washed over her face.

"Really, I think he'll be okay," Darius said, patting her knee. "Gave me a good scare, but he's got a great reason to live. He just found out he's got a grandchild."

Brooklyn smiled.

"Come on," Darius said. "Let's get out of here."

CHAPTER FORTY-FOUR

BROOKLYN WAS HOLDING A BOUQUET of flowers when she walked into Martin's hospital room.

"Well, hello, there." Martin smiled. "Child, I hardly know what to say."

She smiled. "Me either."

"I guess that's why you looked familiar."

She walked a little closer to the bed.

"Yes, come in. Sit with me. I just can't believe any of it."

Brooklyn sat in the chair beside the bed. "You doing okay?"

"Never better," he said with a smile. "I couldn't quite put my finger on it, but there was something about you."

Brooklyn sat a little taller.

"You have your grandmother's eyes."

"Really? I'd love to see a picture of her sometime."

"She was a knockout. Just like you."

Brooklyn couldn't stop smiling, but she didn't know what to say.

"How you dealin' with all this? I can't really imagine what you're feeling. Part of me is so angry."

Brooklyn broke eye contact, suddenly ashamed.

"Hey, none of this is on you. Of course not. And I am sorry he's gone, Brooklyn."

"What he did . . ." She shook her head. There were no words.

"He was your dad and I know you loved him. It's a lot to process. Losing someone you love is hard, no matter how complicated those feelings. Don't forget, I knew John Anderson. I knew the good side too."

"He was a good father. That's what's so hard. But I spent so much of my life feeling like an outsider and trying to learn about where I was from. My mom gave me a picture of this girl from the Dominican Republic. She said the girl was my mom and that she died. I spent so much time thinking about her. But all this time, my mom was walking in and out of my life like a ghost."

"Wish I'd known. I would have loved having a granddaughter all these years."

"Me too. A grandfather, I mean." Brooklyn leaned forward. "I'd like to have a grandfather."

Martin smiled and extended his hand, palm up. "You got it."

Brooklyn leaned forward and took his hand.

CHAPTER FORTY-FIVE

Wednesday, November 27

BROOKLYN PULLED UP TO HER childhood home at sunset. The sugar maple had just dropped its leaves, creating a spectacular red carpet on the gravel drive. It was still strange to think of someone else living there, but when Ginny and the kids came out the front door to greet her, it felt right.

Lyla and Mikey took off to catch frogs after a brief hello.

Ginny looked better. Those dark circles were gone. She was smiling. "Good flight?" she asked.

"Holidays, so crazy. Just glad to be home."

They walked up and sat on the front porch swing.

"So how about you? Things okay? Kids seem happy."

Ginny smiled. "Yeah, they love this place. Sometimes I'm amazed by what kids can handle."

Brooklyn nodded, turning her focus from Ginny to the yard. The comment felt loaded. They'd all been through so much. "I'm really glad you changed your mind about selling."

"Yeah. You were right. I didn't think I could live here after everything that happened, but the kids love it. It's gotten easier. Surprisingly, I think being here has helped. I don't know what'll happen when the divorce goes through, but at least we have this."

"And you have me," Brooklyn added. Ginny began to tear up again. She was still struggling with the guilt. Brooklyn slapped Ginny's knee and smiled. Time to change topics. "Nervous about tomorrow?"

"Terrified. You?"

Brooklyn shook her head. "It'll be good." Simon was taking the kids for Thanksgiving, and she and Ginny were going to Martin's for the holiday meal, along with Darius, who was arriving in the morning.

"I made pie," Ginny said. "Three, actually."

Brooklyn took her hand. "It's gonna be fine. I think he's glad you're coming."

Brooklyn and Darius had been communicating for months online, but she hadn't seen him since they had gone to breakfast last May. It had been a surreal first meal, looking at this man she'd watched from afar, noticing for the first time that his ears were slightly asymmetrical and his otherwise green eyes had some hazel flecks, just like hers.

The waitress had showered him with compliments, excited to have a celebrity at her table. They'd both giggled nervously from the strangeness of the situation. At the end of the meal, he'd put his hand on hers. She'd looked down at the connection she never thought she'd know.

"This has been the greatest gift," he said. "I came home to make a movie, and I got a daughter."

They'd texted constantly, ever since.

"Well, come on inside," Ginny finally said, grabbing Brooklyn's suitcase.

Brooklyn followed her in, marveling at all the changes. Every room had been painted. Most of the old furniture was gone. Her dad's study walls were now a moss green. The floor was covered with toys. It looked alive again.

~ • ~

The next morning Brooklyn took the car three miles out of town and up a hill to finally have the conversations she'd spent weeks having in her mind.

After pointing her toward a bluff, the caretaker reminded her to look for the large oak tree. She passed several grave markers and headstones and little fake flowers perched in front of them before finally spotting Bonnie and John Anderson. Mom and Dad. The only names she'd ever called them. Their markers were just a foot apart, much like the couple had been in life.

Brooklyn knelt in front of her mom's marker first. She'd been unable to look at it when they buried her dad back in May, still trying to grasp the revelations about the clinic shooting. But it had now been almost a year since her mother's death. She'd mourned her mom through the previous winter and spring, missing that voice and constant support, and then stewed in the lies and secrets for most of the summer. There had been too many days to count of crying and railing against her mother for what seemed selfish, cruel, and criminal. But her mind always circled back to the love.

The anger was exhausting. Finally, Brooklyn decided that maybe Mom had just been afraid, like Dad. And, maybe, the pain of her own loss, year after year after year, had built a villain to hate, a group for her to blame. Maybe she just didn't want Brooklyn to feel abandoned. Maybe every misguided decision was about protecting others. Or maybe she was just desperate not to lose another baby.

"Things are happening," Brooklyn said to the marker. "I've now done a movie and a small part in a commercial. And I didn't even have to use my new celebrity connections," she added, grinning.

Brooklyn liked to think that her mom could hear her, that she knew the secrets were out and even knew Brooklyn was going to spend the afternoon with Ginny, Darius, and Martin. She liked to think her mom would be glad to know her girls weren't alone, that after all these years, they were finding their way back to each other.

Brooklyn turned her knees and focused on her dad's grave.

"Hi," she said. The last conversation they'd had had been a fight. She couldn't let it be the last time they spoke.

"Did you hear?" she asked. "Ginny's running the store. I don't know if it's forever, but it's working out for now, and the kids love sitting on the counter helping out and greeting customers, just like I used to do."

Brooklyn sat in silence, as if to allow his response.

"She was pretty worried for a few weeks last summer that the sheriff wouldn't believe her story about how that pastor died and what he did to Darius, but they ruled his death in the Garden an accident. Ginny said the church really didn't want it to be labeled a suicide, but stories of his abuse multiplied after he died, so I'm guessing everyone was glad to resolve it quickly. And his cell phone records confirmed your call to him on Mother's Day and his search of Darius's address.

"We all know you didn't do it." She paused and added, "I don't understand you. Either of you. But I still miss you." She paused again. "I don't believe what you believe, and I don't think you made good decisions." She let out a small chuckle at the absurdity of that statement. It was something they'd always said when she was a child: "Make good decisions."

Ginny's life might have looked very different had her parents not taken over. She would have moved to New York. Maybe they would have given Brooklyn up. Maybe not. Ginny would never have married Simon, though, never have turned to alcohol or Pastor Gary. But her kids were the product of all those desperate paths. Ginny loved Lyla and Mikey, no matter what train wreck they came from. She was done looking back.

Darius had told Brooklyn that the best audition of his early career, the one for *Unbound*, was when he'd performed a monologue he'd written about losing Ginny. What if he'd never lost her? What would his life look like now? It was impossible to know.

Brooklyn had finally realized she couldn't look back anymore either. Her life would have turned out entirely different if Ginny had been in control of her own destiny. It might have been better. It might have been worse. Right now, on this day, Brooklyn was about to celebrate Thanksgiving with family. She'd gotten the role of her life because she'd walked into that callback convinced that, as an orphan from the Dominican Republic, it was meant to be.

"Anyway, I just wanted to say happy Thanksgiving." She smiled. "You always said we needed to say what we're grateful for on Thanksgiving. Well, I lost both my parents this year. It's been a tough one," she said, choking back tears. "But I'm not alone. And I know the truth about who I am and where I'm from. For that, I'm grateful."

She slowly stood, wiped the tears away, and looked down the hill at Eden. Everyone had been damaged; everyone lost something. In some ways, all the revelations of the previous spring had felt as destructive as a bomb. But as she watched the fallen leaves on the grass, dancing in the breeze, getting swept down the hill while the sun rose higher in the sky, she remembered something Mom had said as they sat on the rocks in the Garden of the Gods, looking out at the forest that had once been a sea and the majestic rock formations that had once been sand.

"All that erosion," she said, "but look what it left behind. Extraordinary."

ACKNOWLEDGMENTS

With every finished book there have been people to thank, but never have I felt more indebted to my editors and readers than I do this time around. To the readers of my first chapters and that rough, stream-of-consciousness outline—my trusty Oak Park Novelists— fourteen years together, and it's hard to imagine writing anything without having your feedback. Cynthia, Martha, Julia—your humor, support, and insights stay with me long after our meetings end and there's nothing more fun than pondering potential twists, turns, and murders with you. To David Hale Smith, agent extraordinaire, and to my family, thank you again for all your notes, insights, and unwavering support. To my editors, Jessica Tribble and Caitlin Alexander—you were both as invested in this story as I was, you saw its potential, you challenged me and helped in countless ways. I'm excited by the finished product and so grateful for all that you both did to help me get here. And of course, to the whole team at Thomas & Mercer—Grace, Sara, Liz, Sarah, Bill, and everyone else who had a hand in this, thank you for your guidance, support, and enthusiasm. Writing a draft is a solitary endeavor, but getting it ready for publication is truly a team sport, and I feel lucky to be a part of such a talented team.

To Jimmy and Caroline, thank you for joining me on my research trip—wandering through the Shawnee Forest in ninety-degree heat, climbing rocks at the Garden of the Gods, and exploring the long and winding country roads of southern Illinois. To Jim, my biggest cheerleader, thank you for reading, supporting, encouraging, and counseling throughout the process.

And to my readers, as always, I thank you for being such an enthusiastic audience. You are the fuel that powers me through.

BOOK CLUB DISCUSSION IDEAS

1. Ginny had a relationship as a teen that seemed scandalous to some residents of Eden in the late 1990s. Do you think that would be true in 2019 where you live? What about in other parts of the country? Why or why not?

2. Do you view Ginny's adult interactions with Pastor Gary as happening between equals or as a continuation of the power dynamic established when she was a teenager? Did the pastor's actions toward Ginny as a teenager groom her toward later behavior and choices?

3. Ginny worries that secrets from her past will be exposed by Darius's screenplay. What obligations should novels, movies, and TV shows have to the real people and events their stories are based on? Should Darius have obtained Ginny's permission, for example? Does it make a difference that he's also telling the story of his own life? Does it make a difference that he's changed names and plans to market the movie as "inspired by" rather than "based on" a real story?

4. Both Bonnie and Ginny suffered multiple miscarriages. Discuss the choices Ginny made before Mikey and Lyla

were born. Did the ends justify the means? What about Bonnie's choices?

5. Do you think Ginny does "the next right thing" by finally telling Simon the truth? Why or why not? Do you think Ginny was obligated to tell him no matter what, or should her choice have depended on what she felt was best for her children?

6. Bonnie Anderson concealed her cancer diagnosis from Brooklyn until she was on her deathbed. Why do you think Bonnie made that choice? Do you agree with it? Brooklyn ultimately forgives her mom for that and other, bigger, lies. Would you be able to forgive a loved one after learning they'd committed similar acts?

7. John Anderson explains some of his actions by saying, "I was afraid." What do you think he and Bonnie were afraid of? Do you agree that fear, their beliefs, or any other reasons justified their actions?

8. Were the Andersons good parents? To Ginny? To Brooklyn?

9. By the end of the novel, Brooklyn and Ginny's relationship has fundamentally changed. How would you describe their new relationship? What do you think the future holds for them?

10. Sheriff Wilson observes that "justice is more than following evidence . . . it's doing the right thing." Once Donny takes over as sheriff, Wilson realizes that Donny has a stricter law-and-order view. Whose position do you agree with, and why? Do you think Wilson did the right thing, convincing the coroner to manipulate his report? Did he ensure that justice prevailed, or did he thwart justice?

11. Sheriff Wilson comes to realize some truths about himself, Eddie, and Eden that he seemed blind to before the events of the novel. Did his acknowledgment of these flaws change your feelings about the characters and the town? Do you believe ingrained prejudices can truly change? Under what circumstances, if any, should bad past behavior be forgiven?

12. Multiple characters in this novel struggle with addiction. Discuss the roles their addictions play in their actions and choices. Should their family members have offered more help? Less? Do you agree with Sheriff Wilson's radical treatment plan for Eddie after he's discovered at the hospital?

13. Brooklyn's habit of asking her birth mom questions through found pennies was inspired by a story Diskin heard about a woman who kept finding dimes around her house after her father, a March of Dimes supporter, passed away. Have you ever communicated with deceased loved ones or felt their presence in similar ways?

14. Do you have any family secrets—either recent or generations old (that you can share)? Did the truth ever come out? If so, what were the repercussions?

If you'd like to see additional questions submitted by readers, add your own discussion idea, or share anything from a book club discussion, visit www.ecdiskin.com.